# *Her* HUSBAND'S SECRET

BOOKS BY ANN O'LOUGHLIN

*My Only Daughter*
*The Irish House*

# *Her* HUSBAND'S SECRET

## Ann O'Loughlin

**bookouture**

Published by Bookouture in 2023

An imprint of Storyfire Ltd.
Carmelite House
50 Victoria Embankment
London EC4Y oDZ

www.bookouture.com

*To John, Roshan and Zia.*

# PROLOGUE

Lily Walpole pulled on her cardigan and buttoned up the small, gold-coloured buttons at the front. She made her way slowly down the stairs to the hall.

This was her favourite part of the day.

In the hall, she stopped at the ornate mahogany table. Pulling out the drawer she scrabbled inside for her powder compact and lipstick. Angling herself to best use the sunshine flashing in through the fan light, she dabbed a little powder over her face, before carefully applying some peony pink lipstick.

Gently, she pulled back the heavy front door, and lingered for a moment on the steps to breathe in the chilly morning air. The city was still, and so was De Courcy Square. Lily glanced next door. Sometimes if Amelia or Jack were working inside the window, they waved, but this morning there was nobody.

Lily stopped to deadhead the pink Cosmos and Michaelmas daisies in pots to one side of the front door. She threw the withered and spent flowers behind the pots and out of public view, before descending the granite steps to cross the road to the park. The city streets were, for now, silent.

A blackbird balancing on the park railings let out a throaty call. Lily slowed her pace. The blackbird, its eyes darting, fluffed its feathers before suddenly whooshing away into the thickness of the trees.

Taking her key out of her pocket, Lily pushed it in to the old iron gate lock and twisted until the bolt released with a click. The gate creaked as she shoved it open, the sound tearing through the tranquillity of this early morning in Dublin city.

All her life she had lived on De Courcy Square, but this did not lessen her sense of anticipation as she wandered down the narrow path around the park.

This is when the park was hers only.

Running her fingers lightly across a small bank of rosemary, she breathed in the perfume. The patch of elegant lupins was next. There was a certain comfort in the upright lupin, returning year after year, a steady beauty that she admired. Sweet peas climbed up an old piece of fencing, cascading in a mass of colour from the top. A wagtail dropped down on the grass to one side of her, warily pecking at the remains of a sweet wrapper which had blown in from the street. Lily waited until the bird flitted off before picking up the shiny packaging and scrunching it into her pocket.

Best she came across it, she thought, rather than Gladys, who would probably blame the office staff who worked on the square and trooped into the park at lunchtime.

The park was for the sole use of the property owners on De Courcy Square. There was a time every house was occupied by families, but these days many of the old four storey brick houses had been converted into offices. Lily liked the young workers; they brought a sense of fun and vibrancy to this city square. They reminded her, too, of her own youth. Back then, she liked to walk barefoot on the grass early on a summer morning, the dew curling between her toes, her face full of excitement as she stole out to meet Eamon.

Lily turned to her favourite seat under the lilac tree and sat down. If she closed her eyes, she could peel back the decades, feel the rising sun on her face as she waited for the sound of his footfall behind her. If she closed her eyes, she could forget all the life that had happened between then and now, and for a few moments she would feel happy, wrapped in Eamon's love. This garden was her sanctuary, a retreat from the everyday, a place where she felt young again and full of hope.

Lily was so preoccupied with the past that she didn't see Gladys come across the grass until she plonked down beside her, making the seat shake.

'I am so glad to have caught you, Lily. And just in the right place. What do you think of a makeover of sorts for the garden?'

Lily opened her eyes. When she saw Gladys she turned slightly away, so she didn't have to look directly at her. 'What do you mean, "makeover"?'

'The Association has a bit of spare cash – maybe we could upgrade the garden furniture?'

'Upgrade? You mean replace it, right?'

'We in the De Courcy Square Association think...'

'What *you* think, Gladys. You *are* the association.'

'Now that is a little unfair, Lily. I know you love our little park and—'

Lily stood up. 'Gladys, we've known each other a long time.'

'Oh, this sounds serious,' Gladys said, not making any attempt to hide her relish for a friendly spat.

'I don't want the benches changed; I like this park just the way it is.'

'I think you are in the minority, Lily.'

Lily shook her head in exasperation. 'I have lived on De Courcy Square all my life; there are a lot of memories here.'

'And many more to make, I hope.'

Lily stared sternly at Gladys. 'Why change what isn't broken?'

Gladys guffawed loudly as she flicked off the white paint

peeling from the bench armrest. 'Broken, maybe not, but certainly run down.'

Lily sighed heavily and turned to walk away.

'Why don't you think about it and we can talk another time?' Gladys called after her.

Lily whipped down the path. She was cross at Gladys, but more cross at herself. She loved this park, she never wanted it to change.

She shook herself fiercely as she felt tears rising up inside her. The park was the one place where she felt completely at home. It was so important to her that she was about to blubber about it now, and that made her even more agitated.

She didn't stop to admire the roses or the patch of wild-flowers full of scraggly growth, but hurried to the gate and across to her house. Rushing up the steps, she didn't even glance at Jack and Amelia's window.

Lily knew she was being a little bit silly, but she didn't care. The park at De Courcy Square meant the world to her and she would not let anybody, not even busybody Gladys and her silly notions, do anything to change it.

De Courcy Square was just right the way it was.

# ONE

'You and Jack, I'm jealous. Hell, we're all jealous.'

Donna slapped the steering wheel of her old station wagon and looked at her friend. 'Everybody wants a Jack.'

Cora giggled, tilting her head so she could get the rush of cool air spewing from the dashboard vent.

'Jack's a bit special all right. He's back home next week, you and Chuck must come over.'

'Chuck can watch and learn.'

Donna swung into Cora's driveway.

'Ooh, you have a flower delivery, honey. No need to guess who from.'

'Stop it, Donna, now you're sounding jealous for real,' Cora said as she got out of the car.

She picked up the bouquet of roses propped in the shade of the front porch. Donna, who was unloading framed paintings from the trunk to the garage, stopped what she was doing.

'Girl, you're so lucky. My Chuck wouldn't even think of picking a bunch of weeds from our backyard. His idea of a good time is sharing a plate of ribs and a few beers at Smokin' Al's.'

'Nothing wrong with that, I wish Jack was home more, it's just me and my paint brushes most of the time.'

'You keep painting. Some day we will all be even more jealous when you land a big exhibition downtown.'

Cora guffawed loudly. 'That's never going to happen.'

'Keep doing what you do, sweetheart, your time will come.' Donna reached over to smell the bouquet.

'Ugh, how did that get there?' she said, jumping back quickly.

Cora pulled a rose from the bunch and flicked off a spider.

'It's only a spider. Chill.'

'You should complain. Are you sure he even ordered yellow roses?' Donna asked.

Cora unlocked the door and left the bouquet on the hall table.

'I know, something about yellow roses standing for a range of unlikeable qualities such as infidelity and jealousy. That's old hat; these days, they say *remember me*.'

'I wouldn't care what colour the flowers were if Chuck bothered his ass.'

Tearing off some of the cellophane, Cora carefully selected five roses.

'Here, take these home, add some green foliage and you'll have your own unique bouquet.'

Donna gathered the five stems together.

'Are you sure, honey?'

Cora nodded.

'You can route your flower delivery to me anytime,' Donna laughed.

'Come in, we'll have coffee.'

Donna shook her head. 'Chuck is going to the ball game and I have to pick up Jess from her play date. Don't forget to lock up the garage, you don't want anybody stealing your work.'

Cora stood at the front door and waved as her friend reversed her car and drove down the street.

Carrying the bunch of roses in one hand, she made her way to the kitchen.

Placing the bouquet on the draining board, she snipped away the remainder of the cellophane before spreading the stems out. Reaching for the mallet she normally used to tenderise Jack's steak before putting it on the grill, she bashed the stem ends until they cracked open. Jack liked to send flowers, so many flowers. Soon, they would celebrate ten years together; what would he do then, finally ask her to marry him? She didn't much care either way, it had worked all these years, there was no need to change a thing. Carefully she arranged the blooms in the cut-glass vase. She read the card. 'Thanks for all the wonderful years. Love, Jack.'

Taking out her phone she snapped a photograph of the arrangement. 'Just perfect. What a surprise. Thank you, see you soon. All my love, C. Xx' she texted. Balancing the card between the stems of the half-open roses, she thought she should be more grateful, but she didn't like roses. Jack didn't know, because he never bothered to ask.

The buzz of the doorbell pierced through the house. Thinking Donna must have forgotten something, she called out, 'Come around back.' When there was no answer, she picked up the vase and strolled to the hall. Swinging open the front door, she stepped back when she saw Jack's boss, Mike Underwood.

'Mike, what are you doing here?' Cora asked as she placed the vase on the glass table inside the door. His hands clasped in front of him, Mike Underwood hesitated. Nervous, Cora blabbed on.

'Jack sent flowers to remember the first day we met all those years ago.'

She suddenly stopped, rubbing the palms of her hands on the back of her jeans. Slowly, she took in Underwood's face, his pallor highlighted even more by the dark jacket he was wearing, the strange look, a mix of fear and sadness in his eyes.

'Why are you here? Is there something wrong?'

Fear snaked through her, tightening across her chest. 'Is it Jack? Tell me. What's happened?'

Clearing his throat, Mike put his hands out to Cora.

'Can I come in, Cora? I'm afraid I have bad news.' Panic rose up through her. She felt the comfort of her world fade away.

'Something has happened to Jack, hasn't it?'

Slumping against the door jamb, she felt Mike grab her by the shoulders and attempt to steer her back inside. His touch made her flinch. She pulled away, stumbling against the glass table, making the vase wobble.

'Mike, please tell me.' She bent over like she was going to throw up, but nothing came.

He reached out to help her up, but she jerked her arm away. 'Tell me now.'

Mike moved closer, she could smell the tobacco on his breath from when he had dragged on a cigarette before walking up the drive to the house. 'Jack has been in a car accident, Cora.'

The washing machine in the basement pinged loudly to signal the end of the cycle; the cat on the inside sill of the front window stretched and yawned.

'He's dead, isn't he?'

A woman passing on the sidewalk watched as Mike gently shut the front door, Cora beside him, her face crumpled in pain.

'I'm afraid he is, Cora.'

'I don't believe it.'

She pulled out her cell phone from her pocket and called up Jack's number.

Mike reached over, gently taking the phone from her hands, before guiding her slowly towards the velvet stool to one side of the stairs. 'Jack was in a car which crashed on a rural road outside Dublin city, Ireland. I'm sorry, he has been confirmed dead.'

She could see through into the living room, to his leather wingback chair, where he liked to sit and read on a Sunday evening. His to-be-read pile was too high, she counted ten books up and ten down.

'Let's move out of the hallway,' Mike suggested, steering her slowly towards the wingback chair. The smell of Jack enveloped her. She breathed in deeply. Running her hands across the armrests, she reached out and picked up his notebook from the side table. He kept it by his chair to jot down notes and reminders. His last entry, the time and date of his flight out of JFK to Dublin, his return date seven days later underlined in red.

'What happened?'

Her voice was peculiarly flat, her head thumping. Mike sat down on the couch opposite. 'They're not exactly sure, only that his car hit a wall.'

'What car? He never said he was hiring a car.'

Mike jumped to his feet. 'Cora, do you have brandy, anything like that in the house?'

She pointed to the mahogany cabinet in the corner. 'Jack keeps...'

Her voice trailed off. Why did it have to be Underwood breaking the news? Jack loathed him and now she did too. Mike turned the key of the cabinet, taking out a bottle of brandy and a crystal glass. Pouring a generous measure, he handed it to Cora. Wrapping her fingers around the glass, she smiled.

'Jack bought this crystal the last time he was in Ireland. It was to be a crystal table lamp on this trip. I thought it might be nice in the hall.'

'Is there anyone we can call? Family, friends?'

She gulped more brandy. 'Not yet.'

Mike paced the room. Once he stopped in front of Cora,

but said nothing. When he got to the window, he swung around. 'Do you know what Jack was doing in Ireland, Cora?'

'Why do you ask? He was working, I don't understand.' Her voice was impatient.

'We sent Jack to Amsterdam; he wasn't supposed to be going to Ireland this trip.'

Cora pulled herself out of the chair. 'What exactly are you implying?'

'We didn't send Jack to Ireland.'

'What does it matter?'

'It matters to the company. Jack was meant to be inspecting premises and taking meetings in Holland as part of our plan to push into Europe. Sites in Ireland had already been examined and rejected.'

'Why should any of this matter now?'

Mike sighed loudly.

'I know this is an incredibly difficult time, Cora, but if Jack was in Ireland on business, I need to know about it and I need to know why.'

Cora stared at Mike as he stood, his hands in his trouser pockets, jiggling his keys.

'Jack's dead, but you don't care. He always said you only ever cared about the bottom line and everybody, including him, the man who helped drag your stupid components company into countries all over the world, was only a number.'

'Cora, that's unfair and you know it.'

'I know I never want to see you again... *Get out*,' she shouted so loudly her throat felt like something had ripped up through it.

'You shouldn't be on your own. Do you want me to contact anybody who could come over?' he asked quietly.

Tears streaming down her face, Cora pointed to the door.

'OK, Cora, Jack's immediate supervisor, Richard Jones, will

call by in a while. By then we may have more information. I'm sorry if I upset you.'

He hesitated at the living room door before hastily moving away.

When she heard the click of the front door closing, Cora curled up in Jack's chair and shut her eyes. She saw him standing laughing at her, telling her not to be silly and to stop worrying so much. Jack never worried; he said there was no point, that she did enough for the both of them. Maybe, just maybe, somebody somewhere had made a stupid mistake.

Cold crawled through her, making her shiver. Loneliness folded around her. She walked through the rooms searching for her phone, finding it on the hall table, where Mike Underwood had left it. She rang Donna's number, feeling a sense of comfort in her friend's sunny greeting.

'Hi doll, what's up?'

'Can you come over?'

'You don't sound so good. What's wrong?'

'It's Jack, he's dead.'

'*What?*'

'Jack, I've just been told he's dead.'

She heard the sharp intake of breath at the other end of the phone.

'I'll be there in ten.' Cora slipped to the floor, too numb to cry, too exhausted to think.

# TWO

Cora was concentrating, intently, tracking a small ant creeping up the leg of the hall table as Donna pulled her station wagon into the drive. She couldn't help smiling when she heard her friend bang her car door and scurry up the front steps before cursing loudly and sprinting back to grab her purse from the front seat.

Cora couldn't move; she continued to follow the ant on a determined course to the yellow roses. Donna tried the door, but it was locked.

'Shit, honey. Let me in.'

Unable to respond, Cora remained slumped on the tiles.

'Cora, just open the door,' Donna said, tapping lightly on the glass.

Cora didn't budge. Outside, Donna threw her hands in the air, before disappearing down the side of the house. Cora heard her pull open the side door.

'I'm coming through. OK honey?'

Cora didn't answer, but when she saw Donna rush into the hallway, tears streamed down her face. Donna, letting her purse drop to the ground, skidded across the tiles until she was beside Cora, cradling her in her arms.

'I'm so sorry, honey.'

'What am I going to do without Jack?' she sobbed, burying her head against Donna's spangly T-shirt, letting the beads scratch her skin.

'I don't know, honey. I don't know.'

Gently, Donna pulled Cora to her feet, leading her to the kitchen. She sat Cora at the counter. 'We need a drink.'

'Top cupboard,' Cora said quietly.

Donna took down a bottle of Jameson whiskey and two crystal glasses.

'Jack got it in the duty free the last time...' Cora stopped and gulped the whiskey, spluttering so Donna wasn't sure what she said next.

'What happened?' she asked gently.

'Car smash.'

'Oh my God.'

'I just don't understand, what was he doing in a car?'

'Darling, maybe you should lie down.'

'To sleep? What's the point? Jack's dead. We can't make that better.'

'Honey, I'm only trying to help. Hell, I don't know what to do.'

Cora reached over and took her friend's hand.

'Just being here is enough.'

'I'm not going anywhere,' Donna said, downing her whiskey in one.

'Jack always said you drank too much.'

'If he wasn't dead, I might have something to say about that.'

Cora winced, making Donna immediately regret what she had said. 'Hell, I'm being insensitive, Chuck always says I talk too much when I'm nervous.'

Cora picked up Jack's mail from the bowl on the counter. 'Should I open these?'

'They can wait until later. Have you told anybody else? Family...?'

Cora snorted.

'Jack said I was his family and he was mine. Neither of his parents are around, though he has a sister; lost touch with her a long time ago.'

'I could get the word out.'

'I couldn't face the sympathy of others, not yet.'

'But...'

'Richard Jones is being sent over to tell me more. Maybe after.'

'Rich from my street?'

'He works with Jack and is liaising with the US embassy in Ireland.'

Rooting through the laundry basket, she picked out Jack's old cardigan.

'Lucky I didn't wash it,' she said, burying her head in the blue cashmere. It smelled of his tobacco and aftershave, the heavy, spicy scent that conjured up who he was, that reminded her of his broad shoulders, his curly black hair. In the aroma, she felt him, his arms wrapping around her.

Pulling on the cardigan, she dragged it tight around her. 'Donna, tell me what do I do now? What the hell do I do?'

'You have me and Chuck...' Her voice trailed off and Cora smiled nervously.

'At least Chuck in his own way is helping, by making us smile,' Donna said.

The sound of the doorbell twirling through the house made them both jump.

'Shall I answer it?' Donna asked.

Cora shook her head.

'I can't deal with this, Donna. Tell whoever it is to go away.'

'It might be Rich.'

Cora shrugged. 'OK.'

Stepping out into the backyard, Cora gulped some fresh air. She wanted to run away, to forget that Jack was dead, to go back and live a normal life. She wanted to climb up to her studio in the loft and finish the clouds on her sky, to inhabit that scene of a carefree, sunny day. She wanted to paint, to forget she had been told the news.

She listened to mutterings at the doorway, before Donna showed Richard Jones in to the living room.

Donna came out onto the deck, placing her arm around Cora's shoulders.

'Rich is waiting,' she whispered.

'Can you talk to him? I don't think I'm up to it.'

'Doll, you have to do this. He's pretty insistent he talks to you. We can do it together,' she said, taking Cora by the hand.

Too exhausted to resist, Cora followed her friend. She wanted to withdraw, live in the limbo of believing he wasn't dead. Details would only shatter that illusion.

When they reached the living room, Richard was standing at the bay window, his back to them, his hands in his pockets. Cora pulled Donna back, hoping to delay the encounter.

'I'm here, right beside you,' her friend said.

Richard walked towards them, extending his hand.

'I wish we were meeting under happier circumstances, Cora. I can't tell you how sorry I am. Everybody is gutted by what has happened. Jack was special to all of us.'

She grimaced at the tightness of his grip.

'What can you tell me, Richard? Is it true?'

She felt stupid for asking, but she was not going to believe he was dead unless she heard the words again.

'You need to sit down, Cora.

'Please tell me everything. I don't need to sit down.'

A grey colour washed across his face, making her tremble.

'There's something else, isn't there?'

Discomfort flashed across his eyes as he blurted out what he knew. 'Police say the other person in the car was Jack's wife.'

He paused, not sure if he should continue, but knowing he had to. 'She has been positively identified, they both have.'

Pain took over like somebody was punching holes through her. She expected to fall wounded, but Donna's arms came around her and dragged her to the couch.

'What do you mean, his wife?' Cora enunciated each word slowly and carefully.

'They are pretty sure that's who she was, Cora.'

'The only person in Jack's life was Cora. They've been together so long… It can't be right. How could Jack have a wife on the other side of the world?' Donna asked.

Richard, his head bowed, didn't answer.

'What the hell do you mean, his wife?' Cora asked again, louder this time.

'Police there are definite. There have been positive identifications of Jack and his…'

Pain coursed through her again. Feeling faint, she curled up on the couch. She heard Jack's laugh, his huff of indignation; she felt small for believing this news. 'When did he marry her?'

She tried to make the enquiry sound casual, as if it had come up in normal chat, but when the words came out, they were too loud, booming across the room.

'I don't know, Cora.'

Richard looked defeated. He took a handkerchief from his trouser pocket and mopped his brow.

'Did you know?' She stared intently at him. 'Did any of you know?'

'I swear I didn't,' he said, shaking his head. Cora laughed out loud, a peculiar sound that hacked through her body.

Donna marched to the cabinet and poured a glass of brandy and handed it to Cora.

Her fingers touched the glass, the curved smoothness of the shape somehow bringing home to her the reality of what had just happened. Gripping the glass tight, she turned and aimed at the far corner of the room. The glass spun through the air, flying under the chandelier and thudding against the wall, chipping off a chunk, the brandy spilling across and down the striped wallpaper. 'Jesus Christ, honey,' Donna said.

Cora heard Mrs Winters next door fuss about her garden, talking to her dog; the mailman stuffed letters and advertising pamphlets in the mail box.

'Somebody must have known,' she said, dipping her head into her hands.

Nothing had changed and everything had changed.

# THREE

## DE COURCY SQUARE, DUBLIN

Lily Walpole switched on the kettle and waited, tapping a sound like a drum roll on the worktop because she was agitated. When she heard the news of the crash on the radio, she never thought she could know the victims. It said the names weren't being released but Gladys Spencer knew, of course she did. She had made a beeline for Lily as she pruned the pot of Michaelmas daisies on her front step.

'Have you heard the terrible news?'

Lily continued to dead-head the spent daisies with her small scissors.

'It really is the most dreadful news.'

Gladys walked up the steps and tugged at Lily's arm. 'It's about Amelia and Jack.'

Lily straightened up.

'What about Amelia and Jack?'

'I've only just heard. My brother-in-law the fireman was there, the accident on the news... the car crash, it's Jack and Amelia.'

'What?'

Gladys put an arm around Lily.

'I wanted to tell you myself, I know you and Amelia were tight.'

'Jesus Christ, how can it be? I was only talking to her yesterday evening, they were going out for dinner to some fancy restaurant in Wicklow.'

'They must have been on their way back, it happened after midnight.'

Tears ran down Lily's face. She pulled her blouse cuff out from under her cardigan sleeve and used it to dab them away.

'It can't be, not Amelia.'

'Shocking,' Gladys said.

'That girl was so lovely, way too young to die. You must have it wrong.'

'I only wish I had,' Gladys said quietly. Conscious that people passing by had begun to stop and stare at the two of them, she suggested they go inside and have a cup of tea.

Lily pulled away. 'Do you mind, Gladys, I think I need to be on my own.'

Gladys let Lily go, calling out as she shut her front door, 'I'm here if you need me, I'll flash out an email in a while, I am sure everybody in the association will want to know.'

Lily got inside as quickly as possible, letting the door thud closed behind her. She stood unable to move, but her mind was racing, the impact of the news making involuntary tremors shudder through her. Scrabbling in her pocket for her phone, she called her daughter Hannah, but there was no answer. Going through to the kitchen, she thought she should keep busy, because if she didn't, she might just slip to the floor and not get up again.

She heard the roar of the kettle now, but she didn't remember switching it on.

Moving to the kitchen window, she gripped the edge of the old ceramic sink for support as she surveyed her back garden. It offered little comfort today. It was wild and unkempt at the far end where the lilac tree and the cherry blossom vied for space, brambles licking up the trunks, strangling the lower branches. Up near the house, there was more order, because she had managed to get out, prune and dead-head as well as dig out with a small shovel. Her daughter Hannah refused to allow anybody in to tend the garden, saying a vulnerable woman living on her own might be fooled into handing over her valuables and cash. Hannah dropped by after work most days, but Lily needed her to come sooner today.

Hannah might never understand why her mother, as she approached her sixty-ninth year, would not leave the big draughty house at No. 22 De Courcy Square, but on everything else, they mostly agreed.

Lily made a small pot of Earl Grey tea and sat in to the kitchen table. She was going to miss Amelia and their chats. Amelia never gave out or passed a remark on the old-fashioned lino, which was cracking at the corners, or the rickety wooden dresser crammed with crockery. Amelia knew too that she loved flowers and often came by with a pot or two, saying she saw Lily's name on them and had to buy them for her. Glancing out at the calla lilies, tears for Amelia rose up inside her again. Two days before she died, Amelia had arrived at the front door balancing two pots of lilies and laughing. Bowing her head, Lily let the tears wash down her face and soak into the creases around her mouth. She must plant those lilies somewhere nice, but right now she could hardly bear to look at them. She was already missing Amelia so much.

Leaving her tea untouched, she rang Hannah's number again.

'Mum, I'm just about to go in to a meeting, what's up?'

'I needed to hear your voice, I have bad news. Amelia next door is dead.'

'What?'

'And Jack, in a car accident,' Lily said, trying to stop her voice quivering.

'Jesus Christ. I'm coming over straight away.'

'What about your meeting?'

'Let me worry about that, it's time the new guy stepped up to the plate and started working like a real solicitor anyway. I'll be there as soon as I can.'

Lily was relieved Hannah was rushing over, but she was worried, too. The news from next door and the awful tragedy that had befallen Jack and Amelia was not going to help her case for staying in the square. Lily felt a stab of guilt that she should reduce the dreadful fact of their deaths to how it would affect her plans to stay put in her home.

She smiled when she saw a robin drop onto the window sill and peck at the breadcrumbs she left out the night before. She talked to this robin most mornings. Sometimes, the little bird cocked its head from side to side and Lily thought it might be desperately trying to understand her. In an effort to distract herself, she switched on the radio, turning the dial several times until she tuned in to classical music. Not bothering if her tea was cold, she added a little sugar, before hiding the sugar bowl behind a packet of cornflakes in the cupboard. Hannah was forever going on about the dangers of sugar and to silence her, Lily pretended she had given it up. She was sipping her tea when she heard her daughter turn her key in the front door lock.

'Who put the pots of flowers at the front of the house?' Hannah called out as she walked through the hall.

'Amelia gave me the daisies a few weeks ago, but I had them in the back garden until yesterday. The pink cosmos I bought from the florist on Baggot Street. He doesn't usually deliver, but nicely of him, he did for me, and he lifted them into place.'

'You know you're only advertising the house as a private residence. It's an open invitation to be robbed, especially at the weekend, when there are so few occupied properties on the square.'

Lily clattered a cup and saucer onto the table. 'Nonsense dear, that's just ludicrous.'

Hannah sat down at the table and poured herself tea from the pot.

'Mum, I'm so sorry to hear about Amelia.'

'I can hardly believe it.' Lily reached across to the worktop without getting up from her seat and pulled over the biscuit tin. 'Have a brandy snap with that.'

'When did you do the shopping?'

Lily bit into her biscuit. 'The strangest thing, the delivery came this morning, the usual time. Amelia must have done it before they went out to dinner.'

'That's a little bit creepy.'

'I was only telling her last week, brandy snaps are my favourite and I used to bake them one time. She must have added them in, she was such a sweet girl. I'm going to miss her so much.'

'And now next door will be sold for nearly two million euros and turned into offices, like most of the houses around here.'

'It's a bit early to be talking like that. Have some respect, Han.'

'Mum, we have to talk about it. You know this house is too big for you anyway. You should have sold it when Dad died.'

Lily got up, concentrating on folding the tea towel along its pre-set creases, because she was afraid how she would answer her daughter. Hannah stirred her tea, the click of the spoon sounding loud in the quiet of the old kitchen.

'This is my home, Hannah, and yours too. Anyway, where would I be going at my age?'

Lily didn't expect an answer. She reached out and lightly touched a bunch of puce, pink and purple Sweet William in a jug in the centre of the table.

'Will you carry it upstairs for me? I thought it would be nice by the window.'

'Why don't you put a sign up? Feel free to break in.'

Lily laughed as she followed Hannah to the hall. 'Contrary to what you might think, they're not queuing up to break in here. Anyone who knows me is aware I never carry any cash on me. The only things of value are my memories. Nobody can take those from me.'

'You know I'm only worried about you, especially with next door empty.'

Lily patted Hannah on the back. 'When I'm dead and gone, sweetheart, you can do what you like with the old place. But until then, it's my home.'

'But—'

'No buts, dear. Now let's talk about something else, before we have a humdinger of a row and we both say something we later regret.'

Hannah quickened her pace on the stairs, marching ahead of her mother. She plonked down the jug of flowers and stood at the window overlooking the park, as she waited for Lily to negotiate the last few steps.

'I can see Gladys on patrol. Does she ever give up?'

'It's what keeps her alive and kicking. Unfortunately, these days she has her eyes set on the homeless, trying to put them out of the park altogether.'

Lily sank into her armchair beside the window. From here she could see across to the central grassed area of the park with the inset flower beds, where the dahlias were bursting forth along with the deep blue delphinium spikes and lupins, almost at their full height. The trees rustled in the wind, children played hide and seek and a woman leaned over the spent oriental poppies, tapping the seed heads, letting the seeds flow into an envelope. Lily smiled: if Gladys, the guardian of all things in the garden, only knew. 'Gladys has no clue what it's like to be scraping the pennies together,' she said.

'She's an interfering busybody, stay away from her.'

'She can be fun, in small doses.'

'Surprising, with so few private residences on the square, that she has anything to gossip about these days.'

'Let's not go down that road, dear, let's just be thankful we can sit together. Let's not forget what has happened to our neighbours.'

Hannah deliberately angled herself so she couldn't view the park.

'Mum, I need to discuss something with you.'

'My head is not in the right place. I was so fond of Amelia.'

'OK, it can wait,' Hannah said, stretching out her long legs and sighing deeply.

'You need to get back to work, don't you?'

'I can stay a while longer.'

'Sweetheart, is it Derry? You know you're always welcome to stay here. This is your home, too. It will always be.'

Hannah jumped up, fidgeting with the strap of her handbag. 'Forget I said anything, Mum. I have to go.'

She leaned over and kissed Lily on the cheek. 'Don't mind me, we'll have that talk another time. I haven't got the energy for it today.'

'I'll have to go to the funeral, once we know the arrangements.'

'I'll take you, no problem.'

Lily heard her rush down the stairs, the front door swinging shut, sending vibrations shuddering through the walls. Lily leaned forward, so she could see Hannah cross to her car. Tall, with her long hair tied in a neat ponytail and wearing a charcoal-grey suit, Lily thought her daughter looked every bit the successful solicitor she was. Lily never did know why Hannah had taken to Derry, he seemed such a sullen individual. Maybe she wanted so badly to get away from De Courcy Square; she'd never seemed to settle here after her father's death. Lily turned to look at the silver frame on the coffee table. Hannah liked to see the photograph on display, so she always made sure to have it out when she came over.

Shaking her head, Lily regretted she ever had been persuaded to marry Reg Walpole. Lifting up the heavy old-fashioned frame, she studied her younger self. She detested that blue silk dress her mother had bought in Brown Thomas. She wore a single flower in her hair. She smiled, remembering she had insisted on a light pink carnation, her small act of rebellion, to send a message to the man she truly loved that she would not forget him. Her smile in the photograph was barely there; an insipid effort after the photographer had told her her children would want to know why she wasn't happy on her wedding day. Quickly she opened the drawer and shoved the frame in with such ferocity, the table shook.

She angled herself better so she could see the other houses peeping through the trees across the square. She liked the blur of colour from the flower beds and the small grove of lilac and cherry trees near the entrance gate directly across from the house. As spring took hold the white and purple flowers peeped through, reminding her of the happy times when Eamon tended to the garden. How many times had she sat watching Eamon, inventing excuses to go outside to stroll in the gardens, walking among the high canes propping up sweet peas at the height of summer. She was eighteen and her mother had told her to stop throwing eyes at the caretaker's son from next door; they had better things planned for their only daughter.

'You have to marry a banker like your father. It's what is expected of you. Look at this gardener chap, but know you can never have a life with him, it's not meant to be.'

Eamon had laughed it off when she told him, but the very

next day, he'd arrived at the door to surprise Lily's mother with a bunch of puce pink foxgloves tied with a white ribbon.

Flattered, she'd fussed about, arranging the flowers in her best vase and placing it on the marble-topped hall table. 'You are such a kind boy. I'll tell the park superintendent how good you are to the residents. Where on earth did you get these? They're not a city flower.'

He didn't answer, but smiled at Mrs Mooney, who was already calling her neighbour on the right to come throw her eyes over her bouquet. It wasn't until the next day that Eamon had told Lily the truth. 'There's a patch of wasteland out near the dump in North Dublin. It's boggy wet land; I picked them there.'

'She loves them; she told her florist he should stock them.'

Eamon looked anxious. 'Did Kenny tell her anything about the foxgloves?'

'He told her she deserved to get such prized blooms.'

Eamon had laughed so much, his cheeks went bright red and his eyes watered. 'I think we can take it Mr Kenny isn't a huge fan of your mother.'

'How can you say that?'

'He's surely a man who knows the language of flowers. Foxgloves stand for insincerity and selfish ambition; a perfect fit, don't you think?'

Lily remembered she had been a little annoyed at Eamon, but now she smiled to think how accurate the young gardener had been. If her mother had ever realised the intention behind the flowers, she would have gone next door and banged the door down, shouting about the 'young pup's insolence'. Lily was jolted out of her reminiscing by the loud ringing of her mobile phone.

Hannah sounded upset. 'Mum, I'm sorry, myself and Derry had a huge fight this morning. I wanted to ask your advice. We just seem to be at each other's throats all the time.'

'Maybe when you get home later, things will be different.'

'I'm not so sure about that.'

'Marriage is never easy, sweetheart.'

'You and Dad seemed to work it well.'

'Lily didn't answer, but Hannah barely noticed, saying she had to rush off. There was such a lonely tone to her daughter's voice, Lily worried. So strong in so many areas of her life, when it came to Derry Fitzgerald Hannah was completely the opposite. Maybe she had raised her that way: after all, her own marriage had hardly been a shining example of a happy relationship.

To divert herself from overthinking the past, Lily took out her phone and checked her email.

From: **GladysSpencer@gmail.com**
To: **all De Courcy Square Association members**

Dear residents and tenants,

We are sorry to announce today the untimely deaths of Jack and Amelia Gartland, who lived at No. 23 De Courcy Square.

The Gartlands were valued and active members of the De Courcy Square Association. We offer our sincere sympathy to their respective families. The Gartlands restored No. 23 to its former glory and it is the hope of everyone in the Association that this fine residence will remain in private hands.

In other business, I have been asked to point out that the railings of No. 10 are being used daily by employees of certain companies as a parking bay for their bicycles. On any given day, there are many as four attached to the railings and one locked to the streetlamp post. The occupants of No. 10 have even put up signs asking cyclists to please move their bicycles to No. 29, which remains empty. We would ask those who are defacing the square and the fine iron railings to please desist.

Keep your eyes open, people, and please report any antisocial behaviour to us.

Gladys Spencer,
Chairperson

Lily sighed and put her phone away.

# FOUR

## LONG ISLAND, NEW YORK

Cora and Donna sat side by side on the living room sofa, both silent. The hours passed into evening. Cora closed her eyes tight. The grey light of dusk seeped through the rooms, but nobody switched on a light. 'Why did Jack do it, why didn't he just leave me? Why in the hell did he keep sending the flowers?' She spoke her words into the half-light, knowing that they would dissipate into the darker corners. 'Do you think this wife knew about me?'

Donna, who was slouching at one corner of the sofa, straightened up. 'Don't torture yourself, Cora, please.'

'Torture is finding out all these years later. Do you think he meant anything by the flowers?' She fiddled with the leather buttons on the armrest. 'Did any of his bouquets mean anything other than empty gestures to mask his guilt?'

Donna got up and flicked on the standard lamp, the diffused light pooling across the wooden floor.

Cora watched as Donna walked the ground floor, switching on the lights. 'What am I going to do without him, Donna?'

Her friend stopped in the middle of the floor.

'Hell, darling, I don't know. I can't say anything that will make this better.'

Cora didn't register she had heard but continued speaking as if to herself. 'I wish it had been me, at least then I wouldn't have to suffer like this.' She stopped and stared at Donna.

'Have I been a fool? Jack never wanted to get married, he said not being tied together by a foolish outdated ceremony kept it fresh, kept us together. I guess he got that wrong, or maybe I did, by believing him.'

Donna dipped her head.

Cora took a tissue from the box on the coffee table and blew her nose. 'I thought I was so lucky to have met him. It was like we found each other in our mid-thirties. I really believed he loved me.'

'Hun, none of this makes sense and nobody is saying Jack didn't love you. Hell, he made such an effort to show us all how much he adored you.'

'I forgot to ask Richard what happens next. When is his body being flown back to the States?'

'He said you should contact your attorney.'

'Our attorney?'

'He said there was a note in Jack's personnel file saying his attorney will have specific instructions.'

Cora shoved her fists in her eyes, trying desperately to stop the flow of tears. 'I loved him; I thought I knew him and what made him tick. How can it be that I end up merely an extra in his life story?'

Suddenly Cora jumped up and bolted towards the stairs. Running up them, she quickly let herself into the master bedroom, locking the door behind her to prevent Donna from bursting in. Flinging the doors of the closet open, she fiercely pulled at the neat rows of freshly ironed shirts and pressed trousers. Pushing past them to the drawers, she wasn't sure what she was looking for. Scrabbling at his cufflinks and tiepins, she flicked some onto the floor. She hesitated at the safe, but the old code worked. It must hold some clue to Jack's secret life... but there was nothing of interest in there, only a few share certificates and the business card of attorney Brad Kading in downtown Manhattan.

As she walked back downstairs with the card, the light from the outside sensor light streamed into the hall through a narrow glass panel in the door, filtering between the stems of the yellow roses. Marching over to the table, Cora kicked it hard. The glass vase toppled over smashing to the ground, flowers and water spilling onto the floor. Picking up a rose, she viciously plucked the petals before scattering them into the air.

Donna dropped to her knees and began to gather up the roses.

'Throw them in the garbage along with anything else you see belonging to the bastard.'

Donna didn't reply, but she carefully picked the flowers up from between the shattered pieces of glass.

Cora stepped on the glass, crunching and grinding it into the floor, the sound giving her some satisfaction.

'Leave it, please, Donna. You should get home to your family,' she said, pulling the front door open.

'Don't expect me to walk out and leave you on your own at a time like this. Think again, girl, I'm sticking around. Anyway, I arranged a sitter.'

Cora let the door swing shut. Shrugging her shoulders, she went back to sit and tuck her legs up on Jack's leather chair. Donna cleared the glass and flowers and mopped the floor without saying a word. When she was finished, Cora heard her in the kitchen.

Fifteen minutes later, she carried in a tray containing a bowl of soup and some soft white rolls. 'You have to eat something, Cora. You have to keep your wits about you.'

Cora took the tray, but didn't touch the food. 'Who knew?

Who do you think knew he had this other life?' She looked directly at Donna as if she must have the answer.

'Maybe at work, somebody surely suspected something. They're the ones you should be cross-examining.

Cora got up again to pace around the room. 'The worst thing is I still love him. My heart wants there to have been a mistake, but my head is stating firmly that I've been a fool and Jack Gartland was a fraudster, a very good one.'

She felt Donna's arms enfold her and allowed herself to slump against her friend, who held her gently before leading her to the spare bedroom downstairs and helping her get into bed. When Donna handed her a sleeping pill; she took it and drank down a glass of water.

The light of dawn filtering though decorative spots on the window blind woke Cora up more than eight hours later. Her head was heavy and for a moment, she did not know where she was or that her life had changed so utterly. She heard the thud of the newspaper delivery, but couldn't face walking out front to pick it off the lawn. She got out of bed and went to the kitchen where she checked the messages on the house phone. Richard, in a late-night call, had asked her to ring him. Other work colleagues of Jack's had left awkward messages of condolence. She was feeling woozy and not paying much attention, when she heard the unmistakable lilt of Jack's voice.

*Message left Wednesday at 2.29 p.m.*

'Hi darling, I've bought the crystal table lamp. It'll be perfect in the hall, make such a statement. The weather is really bad here, raining a lot of the time.'

He made squeaky kissing noises before ringing off. She

replayed the message, taking in the happy tone of his voice, as jealousy and anger combined ripped through her.

When Donna walked into the room, wearing a pair of Cora's old sweatpants and looking a little crumpled from the night, Cora was sitting, the telephone on her lap. 'He left a message, probably a few hours before he died. He sounded so happy, happier than he ever was with me.'

Gently, Donna took the receiver from her and placed it back on a small table by the window. 'You shouldn't have listened to it.'

'I don't know why he didn't call my cell phone; he knows when I'm painting upstairs I don't hear the house phone.'

'Maybe he didn't want to talk, but guilt made him make some contact.'

'Maybe.'

'You look like shit, where did you sleep?'

'The couch. I wanted to be near, in case you needed me.'

The phone rang and they both jumped.

Donna, answering it, was relieved to find it was Richard.

'Why didn't he want to talk to me?' Cora asked, her voice tense.

'He wanted to be able to explain properly. He says the company is giving you one month's notice to vacate this property and while it's very sympathetic, the house is needed for the person who's going to fill Jack's shoes.'

'One month is nothing. I don't know if I can go to our other place; I presume there are tenants still there. Jack took care of all that. What am I going to do?'

'He said he and a few others are willing to help you find a new place. He was very apologetic about it, said Underwood is very angry that Jack was in Ireland and is insisting on this timeframe.'

'I'm to be punished for what Jack has done. I guess it doesn't matter to them that I have already lost my life partner along with our shared and past memories.'

'These guys are sharks, Cora. You surely know that by now.'

'I always knew it, I just thought Jack was different,' Cora said.

Donna placed a mug of coffee in Cora's hands. 'Maybe you should start thinking of the funeral or memorial service. I'm sure there are a lot of friends who would like to support you right now.'

Cora gulped some of the coffee, grimacing because it was too sweet. 'I'm going in to Manhattan to see the attorney.'

'You should go to your own attorney first, before approaching this one you don't know.'

Cora laughed.

'I rang Jeffrey, our man, when I woke up. Jack moved all his business to a downtown attorney three years ago.'

'And he never told you?'

'He must have had his reasons.'

'Yeah, he was leading a double life. Get ready, I'll drive you.

Cora went upstairs to the master bedroom. Donna had bundled away Jack's clothes when she was sleeping, the closet doors were shut. She could smell him here, his Tom Ford after-shave lingering in the corners of the room; she reached for her Chanel No. 5 perfume and sprayed it into the air in a vague attempt to obliterate the memory. Sitting on the bed, she looked at his PJs peeping from under the pillow, the crime thriller on his bed which would never be finished now.

Pulling her cell phone from her dressing-gown pocket, she called his number. She was surprised when it rang out, her heart skipping when it went to voicemail. He sounded happy. He was smiling, almost laughing, she knew by the intonation. She knew, too, he was stretched out on his office chair in his home study, looking at the ceiling. She left a message. 'Jack, I don't understand, I want to know why.' Her voice shaking, she ended the call.

Some people might have shouted and screamed, but she couldn't, she felt flat and listless, her head hurting, her heart empty. Deliberately, she ignored his shoes neatly tucked under the chair by the window, his dressing gown hanging on the back of the door, the chest of drawers on top of which lay his brushes; one for his hair, another for his beard, and his clothes brush, all neatly in a row. She picked the navy trouser suit she wore when she was asked to do a private viewing of her paintings for a valued client. She didn't want to have to meet this attorney, but then nothing was as it should be. She had no choice, Jack had made sure of that. Even in death, it was as if he had control over her life.

# FIVE

'Let me get this straight, Jack wants to be buried in Ireland with this other woman and the funeral is in three days' time.'

The attorney pulled off his reading glasses and stared at Cora. 'He is very clear in his instructions. Do you plan to attend the service?'

Cora didn't answer. The attorney sat with his back to the skyscraper view. Cora peeped over his shoulder to the river, the sunshine sheeting across the Hudson flashing on the chrome of the tall buildings opposite and to the side. 'I want his body brought back here; I'm here, his friends are here...' Her voice trailed off.

'Ms... what should I call you?'

'Cora, Cora Gartland. I changed my name to Gartland. Jack thought it was a good idea.'

'But you never married?'

Cora shifted uncomfortably in her chair. 'Jack didn't think that was such a good idea. Obviously, he changed his mind at some stage and got married, but just not to me.'

Her voice was low as if she felt somehow she had done something wrong.

'Ms Gartland, it is my duty to make sure that my client's requests are followed through. I realise this is an exceptionally difficult time for you and I want to reach out and offer you my support.'

Cora looked at the man in front of her, sitting with his back to the pulsing city. He was young, but appeared old-fashioned in the way he had his shirtsleeves rolled up and his hair slicked back.

'Jack has provided for you in his will,' he said.

'Is that supposed to make me feel better?'

The attorney shook his head in exasperation. 'Ms Gartland, Jack left crystal-clear instructions as to what was to happen to him once he died. He was very specific that while he remained married to Amelia, he wanted to be interred in a grave, purchased for the two of them in Ireland.'

'He bought a grave over there?'

'Yes.'

'What sort of man marries a woman and buys her grave at the same time?'

'Just as well he did, considering the circumstances.'

She and Jack had never even discussed the future, never mind death. 'He must have loved her a lot.'

The attorney moved his cell phone out of sight under the desk and checked it.

'Do you know why he didn't tell me, why he didn't just leave me?'

'I was not his counsellor, Ms Gartland, but I think you will find he has made good provision for you,' he said, slipping his phone into his breast pocket.

'Provision? We were together over nine years. I loved him, I thought he loved me. He has scrubbed out our life together and now I'm supposed to be glad he has made provision?' Cora jumped up so quickly, her chair wobbled before crashing to the ground.

'Please, Ms Gartland, sit down. Shall I call in your friend? Maybe this is too much for you on your own.' Without asking further, he buzzed his secretary to tell Donna to come through.

When Donna came in the door, she guided Cora to sit back down and held her hand while the attorney began reading the last will and testament of Jack Gartland. Cora heard a jumble of legal words and the name of a house and property she did not recognise. When he had finished reading out loud, she stared across the desk at him.

'What about the house off New Hyde Park in Long Island? It doesn't mention that. What has he done with it?'

'The three-bed at Laurel Drive?'

'Yes, it was our first home, we had it rented out for the last few years.'

The attorney shook his head. 'It's not mentioned in the will because Jack sold it about three years ago.'

'Sold it? When exactly?'

'I thought you knew. It was a few months before he got married in Ireland; he said he needed cash to purchase the property in Dublin.'

'And you think I would have known about that?' Her voice sounded strong, but inside, her stomach was churning. She looked past his shoulder to the river, now shrouded in a sludge of grey mist. 'Where am I going to live?' she said, her voice loud as if she was addressing a crowd.

'The property in Dublin is substantial, you can lease it or sell it. Either will bring in big bucks.'

Cora leapt to her feet once more. 'You think it's that easy, just a matter of money. I hardly know where Dublin is. What am I supposed to be, grateful for a goddamn house in Ireland?' she shouted. Donna approached Cora, her hands out to try and calm her down, but she pulled away.

'Hush, Cora, there's no need to shoot the messenger,' Donna said firmly.

Cora wrenched open the door and marched out of the office. Donna turned to the attorney.

'What do we do now?'

'I suspect it's the shock talking. Why don't I tidy up the paperwork and courier the details of the bequest, that house in Ireland along with the keys to her current address. It should be with her before close of business. I see no harm in her having the keys while all the legal stuff on the will completes.'

Cora was already at the elevator when Donna caught her up.

'You weren't fair on that man, he's only doing his job.'

'The job Jack asked him to do.'

As they entered the lift, she took Donna's hand. 'You've done enough, I need to sort this out on my own, I need time on my own.'

'You're not going over there for the funeral, are you?'

'I hardly think I would be very welcome.'

'We could have some sort of memorial service here, just to remember Jack.'

'And have everybody come and feel sorry for me.'

'No, Cora, sympathise with you.'

'I can't do it, Donna. I can't face anybody, particularly those who knew Jack. I have to get away.'

'At least let me drive you home.'

Cora kissed her friend lightly on the cheek.

'I can look after myself.'

Donna reluctantly agreed, saying she had to run some errands anyway and making Cora promise to ring her later that evening. Cora hailed a cab, telling the driver to bring her to Brooklyn Bridge.

'You want to walk the boards, lady?'

'Yes, the nearest access point.'

When she got out, she pushed up the collar of her coat as she crossed the road to get on the path to the bridge. Digging her hands deep into her pockets, she tramped along the wooden pedestrian walkway, the cars driving out of the city whizzing along the road below her in a steady stream. She didn't look at the river or the Manhattan skyline, but kept her head down, letting the rush of air whip past her as she tracked around groups posing for photographs. The damp rising up from the Hudson helped clear her head as she traipsed along.

She was halfway across when she stopped suddenly. The memory of a happier time flooded back. It was here, nine years ago, he had placed a ring on her left index finger. An emerald surrounded by diamonds in an old gold setting, it had belonged to his late mother. She closed her eyes, blocking out the low hum of the city on all sides, wind rushing past her, the traffic underneath making its own sweet rhythm, the river flowing silently below. It had been such a happy, exciting memory.

She hadn't expected anything that day as they set off to walk the bridge. When he pulled her to him as he fumbled in his pocket for the small, navy jewellers' box, she had giggled in delight. Gently he took her hand, placing the box on it and cupping her fingers over it. She heard his voice again. 'I love you more every day; please can we be together. This is my declaration of love for you. The only change you need to expect is that our love will grow even greater.' She was so shocked, she could not open the box, so he had taken out the ring and pushed it over her knuckle onto her finger. He had been clear, he was not going to marry. She was so sure of their love, she didn't question his thinking.

'You and me, we don't need to stand in front of anyone else to know we love each other and want to be together. That's never going to change, this ring is my pledge to you.'

All these years later, he was dead and their love was only a series of memories, recollections that now had the taint of untruth. She tugged the gold and diamond band, easing it over the knuckle and rolling it around the palm of her hand. She didn't want to wear it and yet, she felt strange without it. Unsure, she gripped the ring as she turned back to walk the way she had come, going against the tide of visitors trooping across the bridge. The diamonds in their tight settings pinched the palm of her hand as she grasped it tightly. Her stride was strong, the anxiety rising in her to get off the bridge.

On the sidewalk, she walked past a young couple, their arms locked around each other. When she saw them join a line at a coffee stand, she followed, standing so close that the man looked at her oddly. While the young woman was preoccupied placing their order, she gently slipped the ring into the large patch pocket of her jacket.

'Are you ready to order, ma'am?'

Startled, Cora shook her head and veered off. Pulling at her left index finger, it felt strange, naked. She had released herself from this symbol of his love, cut that tie with Jack. However, there was no sense of relief, only uncertainty. What the hell was she going to do? She had nowhere to live. If she wasn't going to move in with Donna or any of her other friends, all of whom were guaranteed to get fed up of her within a week; she was going to have to come up with a plan and fast. She hailed a cab to Penn Station to get the Long Island Railroad home.

As she stepped in the front door, she thought she heard Jack shifting in his leather chair. She stopped, waiting to find out if he would call out. Briefly, relief rushed through her that maybe life had readjusted, that Jack was home, but as quickly, grief made her falter.

She threw her keys on the kitchen island, the sound of them thudding against the marble bringing her sharply back to the present. Grabbing the bottle of Jameson from the counter, she climbed the stairs to her studio in the back bedroom. Slugging whiskey from the bottle, she sat in front of the half-finished painting. A watercolour full of roses and sunshine, a reflection of that perfect day when they had strolled around Southampton hand in hand. Jack had asked the garden owner could Cora sketch and she had spent a quiet hour or two on an old-fashioned wooden bench, Jack dozing beside her as she traced the shape of the blush-pink roses with her pencil. She had included Jack at the far end of the garden, snoozing on a recliner, his Panama hat covering his face.

She had been in a hurry to finish it, but now what was the point? Gulping from the bottle, she wandered around the room. So many paintings, what was she going to do with them all? Jack said because she was so drawn to painting the life around her, she should have a 'Long Island' exhibition. This painting she'd hoped would be the centrepiece. All the others were newly framed and in the garage. How could she have an exhibition now, with her main cheerleader gone forever?

How could she paint again? What magic and happy memories could she weave into her work, when her past with Jack was so blighted, her future forever tainted? She took the painting from the easel and placed it with other unfinished works propped against a side wall. She felt nothing but the pain of betrayal; it numbed her brain. She couldn't consider picking up a pencil, never mind a brush.

Was she going to feel like this forever? If she accepted things as they were, she would remain permanently paralysed by Jack's deceit. Knowing what she had to do, she took out her phone and called Donna.

'Donna, will you do me a favour?'

'Anything, honey, you know that.'

'I need to go away. Will you take the cat, pack up at the house for me?'

'What do you mean, where are you going?'

'Far away.'

'Cora, I know what's happened is so gross, but running

away is not the answer. What will you do on your own? Where the hell are you going?'

'I need to get away. I can't stay here.'

'You're not thinking of going to Dublin, are you?

Cora didn't answer.

'Jesus, Cora, this can come to no good.'

'I have to know more. What am I supposed to do, go quietly and accept this has happened and just get on with things?'

Donna said nothing for a few seconds, but when she did, her voice sounded strange. 'Please don't go.'

'Donna, stop. I have to go.'

'Wait until the fall when I have a week's vacation; we could go together.'

Cora laughed. 'Don't you realise I have to go there, visit his house when the smell of him is still there. I have to go. It is the only way I will get peace. I have to see the home they had together, I need to...' she stuttered over her words, 'I need to know about his wife.'

'Take some time; a friend has a lovely house in Vermont, you could take it for a while.'

'I'll leave the key with Mrs Rathborne next door. I know I'm asking a lot of you. I'm so grateful.'

'No problem, hun, but I'm going to be worrying so much about you.'

'I have to go, Donna. If I ever can put this behind me, I have to have all the information first. I want and need to see inside his life there.'

'It's nuts, but I'm with you, doll.'

Cora said goodbye before hitting the red button. She walked to the bureau in the small office, to the right of the front door. Opening the top drawer, she took out her passport. Gathering up the package from the attorney, she booked an Uber ride to JFK. Grabbing a change of underwear and her toothbrush, she stuffed them in her purse, before walking out of the house to stand on the sidewalk, waiting for her cab.

She had no intention of gatecrashing Jack's funeral, but she wanted to step inside his house, this life he had built with another woman. She had been a fool to think two weeks away every month was normal, just for work. He was married to this woman for three years, but were there others? In the Uber car, she said nothing, busy on her iPad booking a last-minute seat to Dublin. The flight cost her more than it should but she didn't care. After check-in at JFK she went to the bar and ordered a Jameson whiskey, one cube of ice. She sat watching all the other travellers, couples, people on their own. She was going on an adventure, but she felt only sadness. There would be nobody waiting for her in Dublin, no welcome. There was nothing for her here either, she had no choice but to follow in Jack's footsteps. One year after he gave her that ring, he had started this routine of two weeks working away and two at home. He was in LA mostly, but in recent years, Jack had travelled to Europe. She had been a stupid fool to ever believe him. She slugged down the whiskey and ordered another.

# SIX

## DE COURCY SQUARE, DUBLIN

'Mum, are you ready?' Hannah called out as she unlocked the front door and walked through to the kitchen. She stopped when she saw Lily standing by the fridge. 'Why aren't you dressed? I want to hit the road early, get out of the city, before the traffic gets bad.'

'Surely you have time for a cup of tea?'

'Mother, you're not even dressed yet.'

Lily pulled off her dressing gown to show a neat black suit with a pink blouse underneath. 'It's chilly this morning but I didn't want to switch on the heating, so I opted for an extra layer instead.'

Hannah sighed heavily. 'Let's get a move on. I've arranged a meeting for after lunch and I want to make it back in time.'

She stood on the top step as Lily slipped on a light raincoat. 'Mother, come on.'

'Patience, dear,' Lily said as she closed her front door, pushing against it to check it was shut properly. Hannah was already in the car and had it running by the time Lily made it down the granite steps at the front of the house. They didn't talk as Hannah negotiated the city traffic and onto the N11 to County Wicklow.

The church was packed out and a loudspeaker was rigged up in the small forecourt so everybody could hear the service. Local farmers had opened up their fields as overflow car parks. Hannah swung in to the field nearest the cemetery.

'They are all here for Amelia, such a lovely young woman,' one man said to Lily as they queued up to pay their respects to her brother, who was standing at the front pew of the church beside the two coffins. Many whispered that not one relative or friend had managed to make it from the States to give Jack Gartland a send-off, so far away from home. Lily joined a long line of those wanting to file past the coffins, say a prayer and gently touch the caskets. When she reached Amelia's coffin, she quietly whispered her goodbyes as the man from the undertakers gently took her home-arranged bouquet and placed it with the other more formal wreaths. A woman stopped to smell the sweet peas in deep pink colours, the heavy aroma of rosemary making people linger for longer at Amelia's coffin, the pale pink peonies tumbling over the top obscuring the nameplate. After the service, Hannah and Lily were making their way back to their car, when a man's voice called out after them: 'I am Amelia's brother, Tom. Do you mind if I have a word?'

'I lived beside Amelia at De Courcy Square,' Lily said to him.

'I know, Amelia spoke about you.'

'We were good friends,' Lily said sadly.

'I wondered if by any chance you have a key to the house. I just want to get in and get Amelia's stuff but I haven't a key.'

Lily hesitated.

'There are some things, family keepsakes and photographs, they're only of sentimental value. It's just I would like a chance to go through her stuff. There is just me left and my wife and children; Amelia is, I mean was, very special to us. Everything is up in the air, nobody has made contact from the States about a will or anything like that, so we don't know what's happening about the house. The last thing we want is for Amelia's possessions to be thrown in a skip, if the place is sold.'

'Strange that nobody came from the States.'

'There was mention of a sister, but nobody knows where in the US she is. I'm not sure Amelia even knew where in the US she lived.

'Did Jack own the house? I was never sure if they were just renting.'

'He owned it. I told Amelia she should have it put in her name too, but she never got around to it. I guess she thought she had plenty of time...' His voice wavered, making him look away in an an effort to compose himself.

'You're the detective, aren't you?' asked Lily.

'Detective Garda Tom Hooper.'

'Amelia spoke very highly of you. I suppose the house will be put up for sale.'

'No doubt somebody will make a lot of money from it. With Amelia gone, I'm not sure we'll have any say in that; she wasn't after all the legal owner. Can I give you my number in case you hear anything or if somebody comes to the house? Maybe I can ask them.'

Scribbling his mobile number on his card, he handed it to Lily.

'I'm very sorry about what happened, I was very fond of Amelia,' she said as she pushed the card into the zip section of her handbag.

They drove straight back to Dublin, because Hannah was in a rush and they didn't have time for tea. 'I have to get back to work, Mum, I can't swan off for the whole day.'

Lily, sensing an agitation in Hannah, stayed quiet until they turned off the motorway for the city. 'Amelia was very good to me. My bouquet was pink peonies with sweet peas and rosemary intertwined, though I suspect there aren't many these days who know the language of flowers.'

'Peonies are a funny choice.'

'Not really, traditionally they mean devotion and while Jack was not my favourite person, there was no doubt that Amelia was devoted to him.'

'And the sweet peas and rosemary?'

'Sweet peas a parting gift to my friends, the rosemary is there to highlight remembrance, so let's think of the happier times of this couple, who were only beginning a life together.'

'Honestly, Mum, you are too much sometimes. I don't know what she saw in Jack Gartland. He must have been a good bit older than her,' Hannah said, swinging into a parking space a few doors down from No. 22.

'You do sound old-fashioned, Hannah. What has love got to do with age?'

Hannah didn't answer but got out of the car to help her mother.

'Darling, you should find time to stop and stare, look at the flowers, lie in the grass, follow the clouds, otherwise you'll wake up one day and you'll regret this busy life you've had and it will be too late,' Lily said.

'Don't be silly, Mother, there's nothing wrong with being busy. You do enough staring at the flowers for the both of us.'

Lily smiled to herself; she knew Hannah only ever called her Mother when she was frustrated.

Lily waved her daughter off and waited until she had turned the corner out of the square, before she crossed the road to the park. Looking all about her, she bent down and pushed at a rock inside the railings, digging with her nails until she pulled out a key. It was her emergency park key, so she didn't have to go in to the house to get the one on the hook inside the kitchen door. Straightening up, she shook the key to dislodge the earth, before unlocking the gate and pushing past a makeshift barrier which had been placed across the path.

Hannah didn't like her walking in the park, she was afraid she might be mugged, but then, Lily thought, her daughter was afraid of her own shadow. Besides, how was she going to be mugged in a place where only those who had a key to the gate could get in?

Lily liked to sit under the old lilac tree. The seat was placed under the white lilac, but from here, she could see the purple flowering tree. Beautiful and green now, she closed her eyes to remember the lilac blooms, from mauve to deep purple, which heralded the beginning of the flowering garden. The carpels of tiny flowers clustered together, giving off a heady scent she could call up so easily now. This tree was important to her and she was glad, too, that she could see it from her drawing-room window. Representing the first emotions of love, it was a permanent reminder of Eamon: all the times they sat on this bench, sometimes daring to hold hands, other times like two strangers, happy that they could be together in whatever way was possible. In all the years since, when she looked through her window, and whether it was in bloom or not, this tree reminded her of a time when she had been so deeply loved, and it gave her strength. This tree was her haven, her quiet place, where she could remember happier times, where nobody could tarnish the memories she held dear.

When she heard the loud voice of Gladys, she jumped up and scuttled back to the gate, managing to get out and lock up before Gladys appeared around the corner.

'Lily, how are you? I thought I heard somebody opening the gate. You didn't see anything, did you?'

'No. I saw you at the funeral; they got a good send-off.'

'Strange there was nobody there from the States. I would have thought Jack had a lot of friends.'

'Maybe they are having something over there for him.' Lily said.

Gladys shook her head. 'Possibly. You should know, we are going to have an association meeting. I came across another hiding place today with a sleeping bag and a holdall. Somebody is sneaking into the park at night to sleep; it really isn't on.'

'Maybe they have nowhere else to go.'

'That may be so, but this park is for the exclusive use of the residents. Why do you think I've blocked off two of the four gates? It makes it easier to patrol.'

Lily didn't answer and turned to leave.

'You know you'll have to go round to the west side to enter or exit the park?'

'It's all rather inconvenient. I hope it doesn't deter people, it's nice to see so many using it.'

'If it stops all those office types, it will only be a good thing.' Gladys huffed as she walked off, stopping along the way to pick up a piece of rubbish and push it in her pocket.

Lily stood looking across at No. 22 and No. 23. You could pick them a mile off as private residences. The top windows coated in a film of dust, the flowers at the front. The window box on No. 22 hadn't been watered in a long time. Her front door could do with a lick of paint. The curtains were pulled across, because she hadn't time to draw them back before leaving for the funeral.

Jack and Amelia's house had the look of a place that had been recently done up. Tears bulged inside her, to think of the lovely young woman lost. She felt anger too that Jack had insisted on driving so far into the countryside, to a restaurant in the next county, when they could have got a cab into the city and back instead. Her phone pinged and she checked her email, a welcome distraction from her thoughts. It had only been fifteen minutes since she had seen Gladys and in that space of time the woman had managed to fire off an email.

From: **GladysSpencer@gmail.com**
To: **all De Courcy Square Association members**

Dear residents and tenants,

It has come to our attention the new resident of No. 29 De Courcy Square is very unhappy at the suggestion that cyclists can lock bicycles on his railings. As a result of the recommendation from the business in No. 10, which was taken on board by the Association in good faith, No. 29 has been inundated to such a degree that at one stage its frontage resembled a bicycle park.

The Association never knew so many read these notices and while we are very heartened by this vote of approval, we ask those who thought they had authority to lock their bicycles to the railing of No. 29 to please desist.

We ask for your co-operation and hope the gentleman new to No. 29 can continue to enjoy the peace and quiet of this beautiful square.

Gladys Spencer,
Chairperson

# SEVEN

Cora stepped out of the taxi and looked up, squinting in the bright sunshine. Three floors over a basement, the house stood strong against the blue sky. The front door was painted bottle green, the stained glass of the ornate fanlight glinting a rainbow of colours.

'Are you sure you are at the right address?' she asked the taxi driver as she fished in her purse for the money to pay him.

'23 De Courcy Square, a fine address,' he said as he pocketed the bunch of euros.

She didn't reply but he laughed, shrugging his shoulders. 'As long as you have a ringside seat on the park.'

He pulled his car out into the midday traffic as she turned to climb the granite steps to the door.

She pulled two keys from her purse. One was a big iron key, dark and ancient-looking. The other was a small silvered Yale key. She hesitated. Was she mad wanting to see inside Jack's secret home? A voice inside her told her to turn back, forget about this place, have it cleared and sold, go back to the States, cash in hand. But if she did that, she'd be faced with the constant question in her head that would forever be unanswered. For her own peace of mind, she needed to walk into Jack's life, to live it and to find out who exactly he was here. Steeling herself, she pushed the long jailer's key in the bottom lock and twisted hard. Nothing happened until she used the small key and turned the top triple lock. Gently, she eased the door open, beams of sunshine pushing past her in to the hall. She stood as if on a precipice. Behind her, she heard a mother and child scurry past in the street, chatting as they hurried. Somewhere a car braked. Taking a deep breath, Cora stepped over a small mound of letters and junk mail. The house was still, two bicycles stacked against one wall in the hall. She stared at the man's bike; she had never imagined Jack could even cycle. Tentatively, she edged around the bicycles, into the front room.

Originally meant to be a sitting room, it had been turned into an office. Her chest tightened when she saw the two desks snug in the bay window. Jack's was on the right; she knew it was his by the level of chaos and disarray, papers piled in stacks, two abandoned mugs, the contents now a grey gelatinous sludge. The only clear space was where his laptop should have been. In the stillness of the room, she felt her every movement was loud, that she was a trespasser in Jack's other life. Running her hand lightly along the desk, she wondered if he hunched over his desk or, here in this other world, did he sit straight for all the world to see through the window?

Slipping into Jack's chair, she swung slowly from side to side. Closing her eyes, she could imagine him here, the stale aroma of his Captain Black tobacco hanging in the air, making her imagine for a moment that he was close. Jack occasionally liked to smoke a pipe to help him relax. Opening her eyes, she slowly took the room in, the other desk neat and tidy, swatches of fabric in a small stack, two picture frames placed at an angle, a small bowl of roses, once blush pink, now faded, dropped and brown. Dead roses, an appropriate adornment to this space.

When Jack had presented them to his wife, they had been a symbol of love, that love now disappeared, decayed.

On the couch in the corner a light blue cardigan had been draped as if the wearer intended to return.

Her hands shaking, she picked up a notepad thrown on top of a pile of newspapers on his desk and flicked through the pages. There were normal, everyday notes, much like he'd made back in the States: *pick up the dry cleaning, Amelia's birthday cake, ring C about dinner plans.*

She dropped the pad, letting it fall on the floor. Pain crept up the back of her neck, taking over her brain. How could he so casually put their names together? How could he live these two lives so fully? Had he felt any pangs of guilt or remorse?

Unable to contemplate it further, she stalked out of the room, not stopping until she was back out the front door and had banged it shut behind her. An older woman standing on the top step next door called out: 'You startled me. I didn't know there was anybody inside. Are you a friend of Jack and Amelia?'

Cora, her head thumping, stopped what she was doing. 'I'm...' Her throat dried up and her voice sounded hoarse. 'I'm Jack's sister from the States.'

'Oh, you didn't make the funeral.'

'Sadly, no,' Cora said attempting to smile.

The woman pulled her raincoat around her. 'Oh dear, you poor thing, I'm Lily. I live next door, I'm so sorry for your loss.'

She grabbed Cora's hand in a firm grip. 'Are you staying at the house?'

'Yes, I thought I might.'

'Well, if there is anything you want, don't hesitate to knock. We are practically on top of each other, sharing the frontage.'

'Thank you.'

Lily made to go back inside her own home, but hesitated before turning again to Cora.

'There's a key to the park and gardens, they usually have it hanging up by the noticeboard in the kitchen. We're lucky, the park is for residents only. It's a little bit of heaven in the city, far from the madding crowd.'

'Thank you.'

'Don't be a stranger and if you do come knocking, don't leave after the first knock. I'm not as agile as I used to be, it takes me a while to make it down the stairs from the first-floor sitting room.'

Cora smiled, but pretending she was in a rush, hitched her handbag under her arm and pushed quickly down the street, lest she get caught in further conversation. At a small coffee shop, she stopped. Ordering a cappuccino, she sat inside the window. Jack must have sat here; he liked to linger in coffee shops. For a brief moment, she thought maybe they knew Jack and she shrank back to the wall. She was his partner for almost a decade, but on this side of the world, she didn't even exist.

A wave of anger surged through her, not at him or this secret wife, but at herself. Why hadn't she noticed? When he started to take more frequent trips to Europe, why didn't she go with him? People always said you could tell from a change in behaviour, a smarter way of dressing, but with Jack she could not say any of that had happened. Jack was always Jack. Why was she here? She could have stayed at home, cross-examined their friends, but what would be the point? They would have refused to be caught up in this. She didn't blame them; she would have backed away as well.

When a young woman came in to the café, there was a flurry of attention at the desk. She was handed a sandwich wrapped in foil and a takeaway cup of coffee.

'Remember what we agreed, you don't sit anywhere near the entrance,' the man Cora thought must be the owner said as he steered the newcomer towards the door, stopping to watch her as she walked back up the street. Cora saw her tear the foil from the food and take a bite, before slurping the coffee.

The café owner caught Cora's eye as he turned from the door. 'It's the only way to stop her begging on the doorstep. At least we are giving her a bit of food. We shopkeepers and café owners are doing the Government's job for them.'

Cora nodded, not entirely sure how to answer. She took a few sips from her cup, before getting up to pay.

'Was everything all right?' he asked, eyeing the coffee cup left almost full on the table.

'Yes, thank you, I just need to get back to my house.'

'Do you live around here?'

Cora felt her mouth dry up. 'I'm just visiting,' she said primly, as the café owner turned his attentions to another customer.

Cora crossed the road and walked up one side of the square, past the Georgian houses, many converted into swish offices. As she neared No. 23, she noticed that the young woman who had been moved on by the café owner was sitting on the ground outside. Her legs scrunched up underneath her, a few sheets of cardboard between her and the pavement, she held out the now empty takeaway cup and smiled. 'I'm looking to make the price of a hostel for the night, if you have any change?'

Cora reached into her pocket and took out a euro. 'Why are you sitting outside this house?'

The woman, who looked to be in her early twenties, smiled. 'It's okay, I have the permission of the owner – he sometimes helps me top up, so I can get a bed for the night. He might be away, he's often away.'

Cora climbed the first two steps before swinging around. 'Haven't you heard?'

'Heard what?' The young woman stood up. 'Jesus, has something happened?'

Cora found herself in the unusual situation of having to break the news and stand while tears rushed down the face of this stranger, who had only a passing acquaintance with Jack.

'He was very good to me, he let me keep my cardboard and sleeping bag in the coal shed in the basement. He was decent at doling out the cash too, though he always said not to tell his wife.'

Spotting keys in Cora's hands, she pulled away. 'Who are you?'

Cora hesitated. 'I'm Jack's sister.'

The young woman gripped Cora's hand. 'You must be in bits. He was such a good man.'

Cora pulled away, muttering thanks as she did. She made for the door as the young woman called after her. 'I'm Stacey. Is it all right if I keep this pitch?'

'I suppose so, for now anyway.'

Using only the small key on the top lock, she let herself into the house. Standing for a moment in the hall, she was unsure where to go next. She should go to the kitchen, make tea or pour a brandy or whiskey; Jack surely had some here. But instead, she climbed the stairs.

Outside the master bedroom, she delayed, moving from one foot to the other, making the floorboards creak. She need not go in, she could leave this place and never see where they lay as man and wife, but somehow she knew she would be forever haunted by that lack of knowledge. It was not an option.

Gently, she turned the doorknob and stepped in. The room was dark, as though on that last time here they had rushed about, not bothering to open the blinds, because day had not yet filtered through. In the half-light she could see the bed, the duvet curled back, cushions piled on the floor, clothes draped over a nearby chair. The silent stillness surrounded her; there was a feeling of walking in on two lives, an indecent interruption. She regretted her decision, felt she was intruding, even now, when both of them were dead. Switching on the light, she watched as a glow built up in the bulb and slowly illuminated the room. Walking to the dressing table, she picked up a bottle of Chanel No. 5. Automatically, she sprayed some on her wrist. It was her favourite scent. Had it smelled any different on his latest love? Had Jack ever compared the two of them when he breathed in the fragrance?

She could not look directly at the bed; instead she sat at the dressing table and viewed it in the mirror, as if its reflection somehow gave her the distance she needed.

An Ikea bed, it looked out of place in the grand Georgian room with two long windows overlooking the square. She would have it as a sitting room, where she could sit and watch the city street, unseen. The pillows were scattered, the sheets wrinkled, underwear stepped out of and discarded on the floor, his shoes pushed under the chair beside the window. She saw him walk across and slip off his leather loafers, bending down to clutch them and push them exactly halfway under the bottom rung.

Automatically, she looked to the mantelpiece. She gasped when she saw his watch laid out on top. She wanted to pick it up, but she couldn't even contemplate touching it. What hurry was he in, that he forgot his watch? She had bought it for him when she had sold her first painting, a delicate watercolour of daisies, a sunny portrait of a time forever in the past. Life had been simple back then. There were many more expensive watches he could have purchased since, but he told her he loved this timepiece, because it reminded him of their love for each other, which was growing deeper as the days and years went by.

Anger pierced through her, jealousy clouding her brain. She pounded the dressing table with her fist. Running to the window, she tugged fiercely at the blinds, so they curled up with a screeching noise, letting the daylight flood the room, dispersing the ghosts of the past and leaving only an untidy bedroom behind. Stalking out of the door, she ran downstairs, not sure where she could hide in this place where Jack and his wife had set up home. Moving to the kitchen, she noticed the big iron key hanging on a nail beside the noticeboard covered in takeaway menus.

Snatching it, she rushed from the house, crossing the road to the entrance to the park. She was trying to turn the key in the gate lock when Stacey called out to her from her pitch on the pavement, 'Push and turn. That's the way to get it open.'

Cora wanted to shout out how did she know, but she saw her neighbour watching from an upstairs window.

Stacey got up and bundled up her cardboard, throwing it over the railings to the basement below before crossing the road. 'Let me do it for you.'

Cora stood back and Stacey turned the key, pushing the gate open. 'Be sure and lock it properly, you don't want people like me getting access to the park,' she said, without a hint of a smile.

Stacey turned to go back to her pitch. 'I'll be here if you have any trouble getting back out; that's if I haven't been forced to move on.'

Cora set off down a shaded path which led out onto a lawned area surrounded by flower beds. A woman tending to the flowers looked at her suspiciously as she walked past.

Straightening up, she took off her gardening gloves. 'Excuse me, have you one of the keys given out to the offices?' Gladys called out.

'No, I own a house on the square.'

Gladys smiled broadly.

'We residents can't be too careful. So many companies have set up offices in these old houses, there are so few of us living on the square anymore. Dublin is dying, the heart will stop beating one of these days, but nobody cares. Gladys Spencer, pleased to meet you.'

'Cora, thank you.'

'You're not from around these parts.'

'The States.'

Gladys looked surprised. 'Are you in number 23, Jack's place?'

'He was my brother.'

Gladys stepped from the flower bed and gripped Cora's hand, shaking it fiercely. 'We were in the residents' association together. I was so shocked to hear of the accident. You must be devastated. Jack was a one-off, and so generous.'

Cora didn't respond, but Gladys barely noticed. 'We thought the house was going to go on the market and we would lose another fine property to business development. Please tell me you are keeping the place on.'

When Cora didn't answer immediately, Gladys drew in her breath to signal her impatience.

'I'm going to live there, for the moment anyway.'

Gladys clapped her hands. 'Splendid news, you must come to the next residents' meeting. I didn't see you at the funeral.'

'No, I couldn't cope with it. I sent yellow roses.'

'A beautiful bouquet, I remember. The mystery of the sender "C" is now solved.'

Cora fiddling with the key reminded Gladys of her original enquiry.

'I'm sorry for rabbiting on, let me show you the gates.'

She set off down the path, with Cora following, to the other side of the park.

# EIGHT

Lily was sitting on a chair in her hallway, her door open, when Gladys spotted her. 'You're from a bygone era, sitting taking in the street from your vantage point, but do you think it's safe?'

'I'm waiting for a delivery, I think I can chance it for five minutes,' Lily called back across the street. Gladys waved, before continuing her patrol of the square.

Cora, returning from the bakery with fresh bread and a bag of oranges from the small grocery shop two streets away, smiled at Lily as she walked up her steps.

'A little harsh, I know, but Gladys does that to me sometimes,' Lily said, winking at Cora.

Cora didn't answer, concentrating instead on balancing her loaf and the bag of oranges in one hand as she rummaged for her keys and unlocked her front door.

Lily got up from her seat. 'Would you care to drop in for a chat? We should get to know each other better, two women living on our own in substantial city-centre properties.'

Cora hesitated. 'I have my hands full at the moment; maybe another time?'

'Amelia's brother asked me to pass on his number. I think he wanted to get some of her things. I must get you his card,' she said, moving away from Cora a moment to rummage on her hall table.

Lily turned to her new neighbour as the Brogans Restaurant van pulled up. 'There's enough for two: chicken chasseur, salad, a bottle of decent red wine and American-style cheesecake,' she said as she told the delivery man to go through to the kitchen. Cora was not sure how she should answer.

'Please join me. I will dine just after one, if you reconsider,' Lily said, pushing the card into Cora's hand.

Cora muttered something about her schedule and getting back to Lily, before she scuttled inside.

Leaning against the front door to close it, she pulled in deep breaths to try and keep calm. Was she mad coming here, where over-friendly people wanted to know her? Dropping the shopping bag, not bothering to follow the oranges when they tumbled along the floor, she moved to the office. Scrunching the card that Lily had given her, she tossed it onto Jack's desk, not caring where it landed. Sitting in Jack's swivel chair, she found some comfort in the familiar feel to this place, his desk as disorganised as the one in the home they'd once had. She was annoyed at herself for thinking that; there was no home any longer, there was nothing back in the States, only shattered memories.

In an effort to distract herself, she pulled at the drawers, fingering through the contents like a detective looking for clues. Envelopes were neatly stacked on one side, old credit card bills taking over the middle section. She made to pick one up, but dropped it back, too afraid of learning more of Jack's secret, charmed life.

Yanking out the bottom drawer, she saw it was empty except for a small box. Lifting it out, she held it in her hands. Made of oak, it was lightly polished. Pushing up the lid, she took out a small key. Turning it over, she glanced around the room, looking for a cabinet or a lock where it belonged. When she saw a mahogany box on the top shelf of the bookcase, she stood on her tiptoes to reach it. Easing it down, she was surprised it weighed so little. The key fitted neatly and turned easily in the well-oiled lock.

Inside were two pieces of paper and a dried pink rose. She took out the first piece of paper. Sweat prickled on her temples. Gingerly, she unfolded the marriage certificate of Amelia Hooper, dress designer, and Jack Gartland, company director.

It had been so important to him, he'd carefully locked it away with his wedding-day buttonhole.

The pink page, folded in two, she picked out next.

*On this our wedding day,*
*1 3 June 2015.*

*My Dearest Jack,*

*As we start on our journey together as man and wife, know that I love you completely.*
    *There are not enough stars in the sky to show how much.*
    *This pink rose is a symbol of our love for each other. To live in peace and love with you is my honour. Let us grow old together, and when we die, let them bury us under a locust tree to show the world that even after death our love continues.*

*Your Amelia*
    *Xx*

Cora bundled everything back in the box, banging down the lid. Was their love so precious to him that he kept these mementos in a fancy box, locked away, so no others could taint the words by reading them? He was dead, she was dead; and yet reading this declaration of love from Amelia to Jack gave life to the love, making it vibrant once again. The bruising in her heart flared once more, making her feel a small and insignificant part of Jack's life.

Marriage, he'd always said, was for those who were afraid their love would not withstand the everyday challenge. It hurt at first and then she had believed him, luxuriating in the longevity of their union. It was only in the last few years that it had become an issue for her, as she found herself wanting the greater security that their marriage would bring. Jack had laughed it off, pretending to be offended, but had made a big deal of telling her that if and when he died, she would not be left short. He hadn't exactly left her short, but she felt a fool, a sad, defeated fool. Not only were her memories of their togetherness tainted, but she had also lost any dreams she had of a future together. Her head hurt. All she knew was she felt bruised, her heart squeezed too many times.

Feeling drained, Cora went upstairs to the bathroom to sluice cold water on her face. She couldn't help stepping into the master bedroom. Lingering at the dressing table, she picked up the Chanel No. 5 and sprayed it liberally around her neck and down her cleavage. Pulling open the wardrobe doors, she saw Amelia's collection, jeans, sweaters and tops folded neatly, dresses, skirts and blouses hanging up. Flicking through the hangers, she stopped at an ivory silk blouse. The fabric was soft in her hands, the sleeves gathered into a high cuff.

It was the type of blouse that would make anyone feel good. She pulled off her sweater and slipped it on, taking time to close the mother-of-pearl buttons, which shimmered when she moved. Standing looking at herself in the mirror, she thought Amelia must have been the same petite size. She had expensive taste: Cora loved silk but had only ever had one dress made up from a bolt of multicoloured silk Jack had brought back for her from a business trip to Beijing.

When the doorbell buzzed, Cora jumped. She thought of

not answering but when the bell was pushed again, she felt she had to answer. Not bothering to take off the blouse, she went downstairs. Peeping through the office window, she saw Lily, a coat over her shoulders, loitering on the top step. The doorbell rang again and she saw Lily bend down as if she was going to peer through the letterbox. Afraid she was going to shout through it, Cora went to the front door, only opening it a few inches.

All she heard was a jumble of words. Lily laughed and moved a little closer. 'You've no idea what I just said, have you?

'I'm afraid not.'

Lily pushed the door gently so she could see more of Cora. 'I know I'm being pushy, but frankly you look as if you could do with a bit of company, and I have some lovely food and wine. We can eat here if you prefer.'

'I'm not sure...'

Lily looked at Cora in alarm. 'Shite, you're not vegetarian, vegan, or somebody who only eats egg whites when the sun has gone down?'

Cora shook her head. 'I'd love to eat the chicken dish, it's just I'm not sure if I'd be very good company right now.'

'Don't worry about that. No offence, but any company is better than having dinner for two while staring at a blank wall.'

'When you put it like that, I can hardly refuse. Let me tidy myself up and I'll follow you in.'

Lily rubbed her hands in excitement. 'It might be time to get out the good china dinner service.'

Cora watched her carefully go down the steps, holding on to the railing all the time.

'Give me fifteen minutes,' she said and Lily waved a hand without turning around.

Cora stood in the hall berating herself for accepting the invitation, but maybe Lily next door would be able to tell her something about how Jack and Amelia lived their lives. She went upstairs intending to take off the blouse, but instead she pulled out Amelia's jewellery drawer. Picking a plain gold chain, she put it on over her head. Gathering up her hair in a chignon, she used a navy scrunchie from the dressing table. She should have baulked at wearing a dead woman's clothes, but they had shared a man; clothes seemed such a trivial sharing after that. Besides, she could hardly accept the kind invitation and turn up in the jeans and top she had been wearing since she arrived from the States.

Before she left for next door, Cora grabbed a bottle of brandy from Jack's stash in the kitchen. Lily had left her door ajar by stuffing a teddy bear between the door and the jamb. When she heard Cora's step, she called out from the kitchen. 'Just pick up the bear and leave it on the hall table and the door will swing shut.'

Cora stood awkwardly as the door swished into place. Lily stuck her head out from the kitchen. 'Come on in, for goodness sake. I hope you don't mind eating here, but I have taken down the china service in your honour.'

Cora stepped into the kitchen, where Lily had soft music playing and the food in the oven warming. 'You look lovely; that colour complements your auburn hair,' she said, as she offered a glass of wine.

Cora leaned against the worktop as Lily fussed, transferring the chicken from the silver heating trays to a serving dish. 'Brogans are so good to me. I like to walk there at weekends. I wander down and get a taxi home, but there are times, during the week, I like to have a meal or two delivered. Hannah, my daughter, thinks it's a waste of money, but then she's not the one who cooked three meals a day, every day of every month of every year, while I was married to her father. Reg was strictly a meat-and-two-veg man, he considered curry an abomination.'

'How long were you married?'

Lily motioned Cora to sit. 'Too long to a bully; we were not a happy union, which is why, since he died, I have made a decision to do things my way. And that is why plain meat and two veg will never be on my menu.'

Lily raised her glass. 'To us women, and to you, Cora. I imagine all this hasn't been easy.'

They clinked glasses, Cora forcing a smile. They ate in silence for a little. Cora, finding herself hungry after all, declared the food delicious. She enjoyed being in this old kitchen, which was full of reminders of past times: China tea sets on display, postcards from afar pinned to a noticeboard and the table covered in a flowery oilcloth. It reminded her of her grandmother's kitchen in Ohio.

'Maybe I can ask them to do the same for you, if you so wish. Brogans don't normally run a takeaway service,' Lily said, breaking into Cora's thoughts.

'That's very kind of you.'

'Cora, you have to look after yourself, it mustn't be easy walking in to Jack and Amelia's.'

Cora gulped her wine. 'It isn't; maybe if I could have made it in time for the funeral.'

Lily reached over and took her hand. 'I'm sure you had your reasons. If you need any help, just ask, please don't be a stranger.'

'I don't know where to start. Is it right to clear away all their stuff?'

'I don't see why not, you have to get on with living.'

'Easier said than done.'

Lily took the cheesecake out of the fridge and got down some small china plates. 'It was a little different for me. Reg's passing was a blessed relief. I can say that now but even so, I had to push myself to get out there and catch up on all the living I had missed. I still am. It makes my daughter furious of course, but who cares.'

Cora put down her glass of wine. 'Lily, would you think me very rude if I didn't stay for dessert?'

Lily looked at Cora. 'Stay, you got dressed up. Amelia's blouse looks well on you.'

Cora jumped up. 'It was a mistake to come, I'm very sorry.'

'It's never a mistake to carry on living.'

'I had no clothes of my own.'

'I'm not judging you.'

'I know; pardon me, I haven't been sleeping well.'

'Link up with Amelia's brother, he's a detective. I'm sure he will be able to tell you a lot about Jack and Amelia. He'll be sorry he wasn't able to inform you of the funeral arrangements. Be sure to ring him. He has asked if he could have certain family items of Amelia's; it might help you find closure as well.

Cora trembled, her mouth dried up as panic rose up inside her. She had never thought this wife had other family. She was Jack's sister, she had better get used to that.

'Thank you for being so kind and considerate,' she said.

Lily smiled.

'Why wouldn't I? Amelia and Jack were as good as family to me.'

She tipped Cora on the elbow, 'Stay for a bit longer, share the brandy with me.'

Cora quietly said she would and Lily got down two tumblers and poured out a measure in each. 'It helps me think,' she said, downing hers in one. Cora followed her example, spluttering and gasping.

'I'm a seasoned hand, it sounds like you need more practice,' Lily said, making Cora laugh.

'I'm more of a fan of whiskey,' she said with a small smile.

Cora was walking to the door when she turned around to Lily. 'Do you think I am very strange, wearing a dead woman's clothes?'

Lily shook her head. 'You do what's right for you. She had a fine long, light blue silk coat. Wear it next time. She designed clothes, worked in a small studio off George's Street. Had her own label.'

'Did she design this blouse? It's beautiful to wear.'

'Yes, she was named a rising star in the *Irish Times* last year. She really was very stylish.'

'Did you know Jack well at all?'

'Jack, not so much. He was a funny fish, never let anyone get too close. I can hardly believe you two are siblings. You seem to be more like Amelia than Jack.'

Funny that Lily should think that, Cora thought. She wanted to tell this kind woman the truth, but knew it would lead to too many questions that she was not able or ready to answer. She hugged Lily before she left to return to No. 23. Once inside her own hall, Cora sank to the floor. Her head was throbbing again and she was shaking. Served her right, she thought, for wearing a dead woman's clothes.

After Cora left, Lily brought her cheesecake upstairs to her sitting room. She checked her phone, smiling when she saw an email from Gladys.

From: **GladysSpencer@gmail.com**
To: **all De Courcy Square Association members**

URGENT NOTICE.

It has come to the attention of the Association that key holders to our lovely central gardens and park are not entirely living up to their responsibility. It is not under any circum-stances acceptable that the designated key holders for each house in the square should give out the key, willy nilly. A representative of the Association has on three occasions recently been forced to stop unknown people entering the park. These people had a key, but could not even name the designated key holder for the address they claimed to represent.

This Association takes a very dim view of those who think they can hand out park keys to all and sundry. If we allow this practice to continue, it will be as good as opening up the park 24/7. In the coming weeks, our Association chairperson Gladys Spencer will call on each property to check on keys and named key holders. We trust we will get your co-operation on this matter.

Gladys Spencer,
Chairperson

# NINE

Lily sat in the sunshine outside Brogans restaurant. Every Friday she strolled here, ordered an Irish coffee and settled her bill for the week. She wasn't in much of a mood to be out and about after the death of Amelia, but routine brought its own comfort. It was a warm summer evening, but still she had the Irish coffee. She didn't care that it was expensive, Reg had left her enough to be comfortable and finally it was time to enjoy the small treats in life. The new waitress tried to persuade Lily to change to an iced coffee, but the manager called her aside. When the waitress returned ten minutes later with the creamy mixture of hot coffee, cream and whiskey, Lily pushed a two-euro coin into her hand. 'I know it seems odd, but this is my treat and I have it on Friday afternoons, come rain or shine.' The young girl giggled. 'It's all the one to me, but I thought it would leave you pumping sweat.'

Lily laughed out loud, making the manager glance over at the table. 'I'm gone past all that, dearie, and even if I wasn't, it would be worth it.' The waitress, feeling a little embarrassed, backed away.

Lily sat in her favourite seat, under the awning at the front of the restaurant, watching the street. Across the way was the small hotel where she and Reg had stayed on their wedding night. She gulped her drink as if she needed a reminder she was in the here and now, where nobody was going to tell her what she could and could not do.

A select few had been invited for a luxurious wedding breakfast in the hotel dining room with a large oval mahogany table under crystal chandeliers. She couldn't remember if she ate anything, only her husband complained she had the bad manners to leave her plate untouched. When everybody had drunk their fill and wished them well for their future together, they had retired upstairs.

Lily looked up at the two windows on the second floor, which had been their bridal suite. She remembered that day and night as if it was yesterday. As they'd walked up the stairs, Reg had pushed past her, pulling at his tie to take it off, letting his jacket fall on the floor just inside the door. She shrank back to the wall, steeling herself for his advances, but he had dragged on his workday pullover over his head and said he was going out.

'I've arranged to meet a few clients and a few guys from work. Be ready for me when I get back.'

He had grabbed her roughly and kissed her hard, hurting her lips, before he ran down the stairs to the pub on the corner of Baggot Street.

She remembered she had locked the bedroom door after he left, slipped off the blue dress to sit in her satin petticoat watching the street from her seat by the window. There was a restaurant there then too, but a more formal premises with heavy linen napkins. Eamon had wanted to bring her there, he had promised to save up. He said they would have a table for two by the window, so everybody passing in the street would see them and feel envious. She had replied that she would be green with envy if she saw anybody she knew dining at the Imperial

Restaurant. Eamon had laughed out loud and said he didn't mean that at all, everybody would be envious of him, sitting in the company of such a beautiful young woman. She tingled with excitement and when he kissed her on the lips, she responded.

This memory still threw up so much sadness for her. She had sobbed bitterly and sometimes angrily that he had left her, left her to this fate with a man she not only did not love, but she despised. For so long, she worried what had she done wrong to make Eamon leave without a word.

On her wedding night, she must have sat for hours by that window, because when she moved, the room was dark, the street lights on outside. She had got into bed, not bothering to change into her nightgown. Her head hurt and her eyes were puffy from crying. She'd curled up on one side of the bed and, exhausted, she fell asleep. When the pounding on the door began, she had sat bolt upright, not even sure where she was. When she heard Reg shouting, she began to shake.

'Open the door now or I will kick it in,' he roared.

Quickly, she got out of the bed and turned the key, letting the door swing open. Reg had pushed in on top of her, catching her hair and pulling it out of its bun. Tugging hard, he didn't let go when she screamed. Out of the corner of her eye, she saw the hotel night manager slowly close the bedroom door.

'Thought you could lock me out and deny me what's mine,' he'd growled, the whiskey on his breath almost smothering her. She didn't answer because she was crying so much, a fact that appeared to anger him more.

'Go clean yourself up. Is this the way to present yourself on your wedding night?' he snapped, letting go of her hair like he'd suddenly got an electric shock.

Propelled towards the washbasin, she'd tried to splash water on her face, before setting the towel under the tap and pushing the wet cloth against her eyes to reduce the swelling.

Sitting on the bed, Reg had observed her every move. She shivered, deliberately slowing down as she tried to buy time in her head. She wanted to run away, but they were joined together forever. Her stomach felt sick. She turned on the cold water again and was about to slurp some from the tap when Reg, throwing his pullover off and undoing his braces, had marched across the room. Grabbing her satin petticoat so hard it ripped up the side, he pulled her towards him. She'd squealed in anguish, but he caught her wrists tight and shoved her to the bed. She'd called out, telling him she wasn't ready, but he'd laughed and said he couldn't wait, as he pulled off her stockings and panties.

Lily closed her eyes tight, remembering only the pain and the heavy smell of whiskey from his breath and every curse he flung at her, telling her she was only a whore. The next morning, he'd apologised profusely, blaming the drink and pledging to give it up from that day on. Lily had been surprised when Reg kept his word, stopped going to the pub and instead became a vocal advocate of abstinence from alcohol.

When a man approached her table and politely asked if he could sit there, she was, for a moment, confused. She glanced about; every other table was full.

'I have disturbed you,' he said. 'I apologise, but I like to sit outside and this is the only seat left.'

She took him in: the old-fashioned pinstripe suit that had seen better days, the worn brown shoes, the grey rucksack on his shoulder. 'I'm so sorry, please sit down. I was quite lost in my thoughts.'

He pulled out a chair as the waitress set down a cup and saucer on the table along with a small pot of tea.

'My apologies for interrupting your thoughts, I hope they were happy ones.'

Lily smiled. 'I was thinking back to my wedding day. We had the reception in the hotel over there.'

She nodded at the building across the road. 'It looked a lot better back then,' she said.

'I remember it. My family, for big celebrations, liked to hire out the function room. The food was good. You know they got it all from the kitchens of the restaurant that used to be on this site; quite a fancy place, from what I remember.'

Lily laughed out loud. 'And I always felt hard done by that I never had the brass to eat there. Little did I know.'

'It wasn't something they wanted to advertise, there was quite a price difference.'

He poured his tea and dropped two cubes of sugar in his cup, stirring slowly. 'Hot, sweet tea is best on a day like this.'

'I'll stick to coffee laced with whiskey,' Lily answered, raising her glass to her table companion. He raised his cup and they both laughed.

'I've seen you here before, on Fridays,' he said.

Lily eyed him up and down, the longish silver hair brushed neatly behind his ears, clean shaven, his eyes friendly. 'Really? I haven't seen you, where do you usually sit?'

'I like the bench over there on the canal, but today I wanted some shade.'

'Do you live around here?'

He hesitated and began to fiddle with the spoon. His fingers were long and slender, but his nails were ingrained with old dirt. When he felt her eyes on him, he scooped his hands under the table. She felt awkward and gathered up her bag, getting ready to leave.

'May I be permitted to introduce myself?'

She dithered, letting her bag drop back to the ground.

'Samuel Carpenter, my friends call me Sam.'

He extended his hand and she shook it, noting his firm grip.

'Lily Walpole from De Courcy Square.'

'I know it, one of the finest squares in the city. My aunt had a house there once, we loved to play in the park and it was quite safe, because it was residents only.'

'I have lived there all my life. I couldn't imagine living anywhere else.'

'We might have played together as children.'

'I don't think so; my mother was very strict and quite insistent I only play with other girls.'

'Now I can place you, you and another girl, always helping out with the flower beds.'

'You have a good memory. Yes, that was my cousin, the only time we got a bit of peace and were allowed out in the park. We envied the rest of you.'

'Spring, when the daffodils and crocuses push their way through, is my favourite time in that garden.'

'Do you have a garden?'

'I don't even own a window box, but I have access to quite a lovely garden. I just wish they would plant some lavender.'

Lily pushed her Irish coffee glass to the side. 'Lavender isn't my favourite. It has a certain cachet now, but it's really quite overrated. There was a a time it was merely thought useful to mask the bad smells, because of its strong scent. These days, people seem to think it is the bee's knees.'

'Remind me if I ever have a garden and you visit, I should hide the lavender,' he said, making Lily regret her outburst.

Samuel stood at the same time as Lily. Reaching into his pocket, he took out a sprig of rosemary. 'I may not be as obsessed as Napoleon, who adored the herb's perfume, but I like to carry this aromatic herb.' He handed the sprig of rosemary to Lily. She smiled, holding the herb gently in her right hand.

'If you are going back to De Courcy Square, I would be delighted if I could walk with you?' Sam asked.

Lily nodded and they strolled side by side down Baggot Street.

'At this time of the evening, I like to wander in St Stephen's Green.'

She didn't know if it was an invitation, so she didn't say anything. Instead, after a pause, she asked him, 'Where exactly do you live?'

'I have a small place off Leeson Street at the moment.'

'Like me, you have the convenience of the city on your doorstep.'

He smiled. 'Yes, I know every inch of the streets around here. It's different from my childhood days, but my life is not the same now either.'

She thought there was a wistfulness about him. She stopped when they got to the corner of the square. 'I'm down here a little way. Thank you for your company, and maybe we will meet again at the restaurant.'

He took her extended hand and kissed it softly. 'It will be my pleasure.'

She gently pulled away and walked down her side of the square, afraid to look back, because she knew Sam Carpenter was watching. She was so busy concentrating on walking tall, she did not see Gladys spy her and scurry across to her side of the street.

'Have you heard, not only have we the American lady at number 23, but the new owner at number 29 is some big developer?'

Lily stopped and under the pretence of talking to Gladys looked back to see Sam turn away in the direction of St Stephen's Green. 'This is good news.' Lily said.

'About time we had good news. I saw his furniture being moved in, he's clearly a man of taste.'

'Or his wife is a woman of taste, Gladys.'

Gladys looked put out. 'Of course, I didn't mean anything else. We may have lost poor Jack and Amelia, but we have gained a whole house in number 29 for residential living. Those in the offices can put that in their pipes and smoke it.'

'As long as he lines up with the rest of the residents and joins our association,' Lily said and was immediately sorry she had, as she saw her friend's face fall.

'I hadn't thought of that. I'll pop around with a welcome basket to butter him up.'

Lily, who had reached her steps, smiled broadly at Gladys. 'A splendid idea and if you want flowers in there, some violas for their window box.'

'The language of flowers is beyond most, Lily. Maybe home-made biscuits and some of my marmalade and strawberry jam.'

'It makes me want to move out and back in again just to get a De Courcy Square welcome basket.'

Gladys rubbed her hands together in anticipation, but suddenly stopped. 'I had better do two, we can't have number 23 finding out number 29 got preferential treatment.'

She almost skipped back across the square to her house, no doubt to make batches of biscuits.

Lily made her way indoors. In the kitchen she popped the sprig of rosemary in a small vase of water and placed it on the table. It was fitting that rosemary symbolised remembrance and friendship, she thought. She liked the rosemary and her new enigmatic friend. Reaching across, she bruised a couple of the bladed leaves, letting the pungent aroma tickle her nose. She must get out and walk more and dawdle around Brogans, she thought.

# TEN

Cora woke up to the bins being collected at De Courcy Square. For a moment, she lay where she was, listening to the sound of the machinery. As the refuse truck revved on to the next pick-up point, she realised her back was aching and her left side was cold, because the blanket she had pulled over herself as she lay on the sofa the night before had slipped. She stayed for a while on the couch in the front room, eavesdropping on the city. Fast footsteps clacked past as women in high heels scuttled by. She sat up to stare out onto the street, where young men in tight-fitting suits and shouldering man-bags traipsed to work. When she heard the creak of a gate and footsteps on the stairs leading to the basement, she stiffened, concentrating intently. There was no attempt to be silent, the person muttering loudly as the coal-shed door was wrenched open. Remembering Stacey, she relaxed for a moment, blocking out the sound of her heavy foot-fall as she went back up the stairs and shut the gate with a loud rattle.

Jack would never have allowed such an invasion of their space in the US, but what did she know about him anymore? Cora got off the couch and stretched, rolling her left shoulder, which felt stiff. She should have gone to a hotel last night; she'd had every intention, but a loneliness overcame her as night glided in. After returning from next door, she had found a bottle of whiskey and the wedding album of Jack and Amelia. She hadn't been searching for it. She was in the front office, aimlessly shunting back and forth in Jack's swivel chair. She hated most of this house, because it reflected so much of its owners, and yet she needed to be here.

In the office, though, she could feel some distance, the filing cabinets, desks and office paraphernalia all allowing her to pretend this union was somehow verging more on the convenient than an emotional bonding. She had concentrated on the outside as a little girl skipped along the street beside her mother, her hand trailing along the railings. When they had passed out of earshot, the city sounds twisted around Cora, so she began to shift in the chair, searching for a distraction to chase away her darker thoughts.

Spying a box under the couch, she had walked over and bent down to pull it out to the middle of the floor. White, covered in artificial blush-pink roses, she wanted to pretend she had never come across this box, and yet she desperately needed to look inside. Carefully picking it up, she had carried it wide in her hands and placed it on Jack's desk.

Lifting the lid, she had pulled away two sheets of white tissue paper, under which lay the album, bound in ivory silk. The inscription on the cover read 'Amelia and Jack's Wedding 13 June 2015'.

That date. Her chest tightened, her mouth was dry. She had been so looking forward to her party. Two days before, she'd been in the basement trying to untangle fairy lights, when Jack had called. 'Sweetheart, I have bad news, I can't make it home for the party.'

'You're kidding with me.'

'Baby, I'm not, there's a glitch which could jeopardise the

push into new markets. Underwood is insisting I stay an extra week to smooth things over.'

'You told him our plans?'

'Honey, you know personal plans mean nothing.'

'I have a good mind to call Underwood and tell him what I think of him.'

'That would make things a lot worse, baby doll.'

She had sat on the basement floor and cried. Jack made soothing noises down the phone, but nothing could stop her sense of desolation.

'Jack, I have invited about sixty people, the food is ordered, the music, everything. People from your office are coming.'

'Have the party, darling. I'll be there in spirit, just don't say anything to anyone from work. Underwood doesn't want anyone to know this deal is touch and go. I've said I can't get a flight back in time, so stick to the same story.'

She didn't want to have the party without him, but neither did she want to cancel, so she had gone ahead with it.

The house had never looked so beautiful, the food by the new caterer was delicious, but she spent the night explaining Jack's absence. She pointed to the huge bouquet of roses and sighed that he was with them in spirit. She did her best to ignore the pitying glances of her guests. She felt foolish and as the evening went on, she became angry in her head at herself. All evening, she had watched the driveway, expecting him to suddenly turn up, having flown over specially to surprise her. When the last of the guests had gone and she was clearing paper plates into the garbage, she still thought he might turn up. When he didn't, she'd sat on the front porch, necking back a bottle of champagne as she waited alone for the dawn of a new day. When the darkness faded away and the sun crawled into position, she had gone to bed, glad her birthday was over.

She felt the same desolation now and a deep anger, that she had allowed herself to be hoodwinked for so long. He hadn't even rung her on that birthday and when he had made contact a few days later, he'd appeared distracted and stressed.

'Everybody missed you at the party,' she'd said, trying not to cry.

'Did you get the flowers?'

'I would have preferred you to be here.'

'Cora, you know I couldn't turn down my boss. There aren't many jobs like mine around.'

'It better not happen again.'

'I will make it up to you, I promise.' He appeared to turn and speak to somebody in the room, before he had to rush off the phone.

When he got back to the States, Jack had taken her out to lunch at Jordan's Lobster Bar and presented her with a Chanel necklace. She wore it every day. Some told her that was a silly way to treat an expensive piece of jewellery, but she wanted this prized gift he had sourced and chosen specially for her to be close.

The necklace had come in a beautiful box presented to her with champagne. As she popped open the lid, Jack was beaming with pride. 'When I saw it, I knew you had to have it. I love you more than you will ever know,' he said. Other diners had clapped as she sat full of love for this man, who could break her heart and mend it again in one day.

Placing the album on her lap, Cora gently lifted the sheet of tissue from the first page and photograph. They were walking hand in hand, laughing together, sharing a secret joke, Amelia's head tilted towards Jack. Her blonde hair in a messy bun, a bunch of blush-pink roses in her hands, she looked happy. The bride's smile was broad, trusting. She was everything Cora wasn't. Confident, with an easy style, this was a woman sure of herself and of her husband's love.

Cora admired the simple style of her dress, a small string of sparkle at the waist. She was cross with herself that she was taking in such details when she should be ripping the pages apart, but it was her strange way of coping.

It was as she studied Jack's wife that she noticed the necklace, vintage Chanel, the same thick gold chain leading down to a rhinestone-encrusted medallion with a single drop pearl. It was a chain meant to go longer than the neckline, but she saw Amelia wore it high. Cora fingered the knot she had put in the back of her own chain. Amelia, Jack's wife, must have done the same.

Anger surged through Cora for herself and also that Jack should have done this to the woman he was prepared to marry. Was this what Jack liked to do, deceive the women he loved? Did Amelia have any inkling or was she, like Cora, too caught up in a life with Jack to notice the cracks?

Remembering how he had placed the necklace around her neck, she smarted with anger. He had gently closed the clasp, before kissing her softly and whispering, 'I love you to the moon and back.'

Had he fingered the neck of this woman who had become his wife? What sort of a man could be brazen enough to purchase two identical pieces of beautiful jewellery at the same time? Cora put her hand up to the pearl drop of her necklace. She'd considered whether to leave it behind when she'd left the States, but she couldn't bear to take it off. Now, she wished she had fired it into the old box she'd left for Donna to clear away.

Stretching her fingers behind her neck, Cora managed to unclip the clasp, letting the necklace drop into her lap. Balling the chain up, she threw it so that it hit the window, cracking against the old bevelled glass. Quickly, she shoved the album back in its box and pushed it under the couch. Pulling a bottle of whiskey towards her, she'd stayed on the couch, swigging from the bottle as the night drew in and the city noises lulled for a while.

. . .

Now, the morning after, she got off the sofa and stretched. She was still in her jeans and jumper, but she felt uncomfortable. Standing looking out the window, she saw Stacey, who gave a friendly wave. Cora pulled away to open the front door and shouted out an invite.

Stacey shook her head. 'Did I hear you right?'

'Yes, I wondered did you want to come in and have a coffee?'

'You hardly want the likes of me in that fancy house.'

'It's just for a coffee.'

'I don't want to seem ungrateful, but I don't have time to sit around drinking coffee. These hours before lunch are the best to be holding out my empty cup, if you get my drift.'

Cora felt flustered. 'I hadn't realised.'

Stacey walked up the steps. 'Are you all right? You don't look very well.'

'Just a rough night.'

She reddened when she realised what she had said. Stacey laughed. 'I know all about those sort of nights, and days, too.'

A group of well-dressed older men turned the corner into the square.

'I'm not being rude, but I have to get back, the older geezers are often the most generous.'

Cora stepped back into her hall and gently closed the door. From the front window, she watched as the men stopped and dipped in their pockets for loose cash, before pushing notes into Stacey's cup. When she was sure they had left her side of the square, Stacey climbed the steps and knocked on the door of No. 23. Cora took her in from her vantage point behind the office curtains. Stacey, her hands in her pockets, scraped her feet on the door scraper as she waited. Her navy tracksuit was ingrained with dirt at the seams, her shoes worn, with black scuff marks. When Cora pulled back the front door, she noticed the sleeves of her tracksuit were badly frayed at the cuffs.

'Look at this, they gave me a tenner each. One started them off, the others just followed.'

Cora laughed. 'Will you have that coffee now?'

'As long as you're sure.'

Cora led the way to the kitchen. Stacey whistled under her breath.

'Jack sure had a nice place.'

'You haven't been in here before?'

Stacey grinned. 'Don't get me wrong, Jack was a pet, but he never invited me in.'

'Is decaf OK?'

'Do you not have the real stuff?'

Cora began to search in the kitchen cupboards and found a jar of coffee. 'Instant?'

Stacey nodded.

'You must think I'm a right one, turning up my nose at decaf.'

Cora concentrated on making the coffee.

'I try to hang on to the little things. If I let those go, I will lose every bit of what I am.'

'I understand, I think.'

Cora sat opposite Stacey, who was busy looking all around her. 'Do you mind if I ask a question?'

'Fire away.'

'Why have you never visited before?'

'I never had the time, I guess.'

'You have plenty of time now, when…'

'It's too late. I know.'

An awkward silence followed as Stacey quickly gulped down her coffee. 'I'd better get back to my spot or some other bugger will have squatted there, or else the busybody at the other side of the square will have binned my cardboard.'

'Gladys wouldn't do that, surely?'

'And she would call the cops, if she thought she would get

away with it. With Jack gone, I'm not so sure I'll be allowed to stay here.'

'Why, what had Jack to do with it?'

'Jack was great at laying down the law to Gladys. He said that as long as he lived on the square, Stacey Mullen was allowed to sit outside his house. Gladys had a lot of time for Jack and it ensured I had a good spot. It just made life a little easier.'

'I can tell Gladys I'm following the tradition.'

'You can try, but that woman has a bee in her bonnet about us lot at the moment.'

Stacey got up from the table. 'I'd better get along. What's your name? You never said.'

'Cora.'

Stacey stared at her. 'You're not pissing me, are you?'

'What do you mean?'

'Jack told me about you.'

'Surely not.'

'The time you... you're the artist, right?'

'Yes.'

'Jack mentioned you, he said you had him pose nude on a beach one morning and next thing the police came and he had a hell of a time explaining it was your idea and it was all for art.'

'I remember. It was a very long time ago,' Cora said a bit too sharply, making Stacey look at her oddly.

'I've spoken out of turn, haven't I?'

She stepped into the hall. Before she pulled the front door open, she swung round.

'Thanks for inviting me in.'

'It was nothing.'

Stacey eyeballed Cora, making her take a step back. 'Don't say that. It was everything to me.'

'Call in again, another time.'

'For dinner, I'll nick a bottle of vino, specially.'

When she saw the look of horror on Cora's face, Stacey burst out laughing. 'I'm only joking.'

Cora watched as Stacey got herself ready on the cardboard, tucking her legs under her, bowing her head so she didn't have to look into the eyes of those who passed her by. Funny that Jack had mentioned that incident such a long time ago. Maybe he didn't forget her entirely when he entered his secret life. As she walked back to the kitchen, she resolved it was time to begin clearing the house of that other life.

# ELEVEN

Lily had taken to rambling along the canal banks most afternoons, breaking for tea at Brogans. She had waited two days before starting off this routine in the hope of bumping into Sam Carpenter again. She wrestled in her head whether it might just be a little bit nonsensical for a woman her age to be wandering the streets in the hope of encountering a man she barely knew. But a stroll along the canal was a nice distraction to her day, because ever since Amelia had died, she had felt unbelievably lonely. She missed her calling by, throwing herself into a chair at the kitchen table, stretching out her legs and chattering on about her fussy clients and her husband. Sometimes Lily paid close attention, but mostly she enjoyed the lilt of conversation, which blew the dust off the house and made Lily feel part of somebody's world again. Funny how she never felt like that when Hannah visited these days, but a fear pressed in on her in case she said something that might be taken down in evidence to be used to make her downsize and move out of De Courcy Square.

Amelia came by most days up until about a month before the accident. Lily didn't want to appear too needy and ask why, but when she hadn't seen her for a whole week, she had steeled herself and rapped on the door. She knew Amelia was on her own; Jack had taken off in his car twenty minutes earlier.

She'd waited several minutes, but when there was no sound on the stairs and the hall, she turned away. Half an hour later, Amelia, in her pyjamas and dressing gown, stood at Lily's door. 'Can I come in?'

'Of course. Is everything all right?'

Amelia didn't answer, but waited until she got to the kitchen, where she had burst into tears.

'Hey, what's the matter, did you and Jack fight?'

Amelia looked at Lily. 'I think Jack is having an affair.'

Lily had gently pushed Amelia to sit down. 'You're only together a short while and married a wet week, that's a few bare years in my books. What makes you think that?'

Amelia shivered. 'I just know.'

'Are you sure?'

Amelia had slapped her hand down on the table hard. 'I thought you would believe me, Lily; I thought you were my friend.'

'I am your friend, but you need to take this slowly.'

'What do you mean?'

'You've settled down together, you have to ask yourself, do you want all this disruption? If you are going to accuse him, you'll need to have your facts right. Otherwise it's going to heighten the tension even more, and for what? I always picked my battles with care and only when I was on solid ground.'

Amelia put her head in her hands. Lily moved away to rinse her glass and plate from last night's dinner under the tap at the sink. She was reaching for a tea towel when Amelia raised her head again. Wiping away the tears with the back of her hand, she'd got up from the chair, saying, 'I'm sorry for the outburst, Lily. It won't happen again.'

Lily had watched her step out into the hall. Throwing down

the tea towel, she called after her: 'Amelia, wait, I don't want you leaving like this.'

'I know, I have to sort out my own marriage problems.'

Lily had pushed past Amelia and stood at the front door, blocking her way. 'What are you talking about, girl, of course I'm on your side. Now, you come upstairs, we will sit in the comfortable chairs and talk.'

Reluctantly, Amelia had allowed Lily to take her by the hand. In the sitting room, they sat either side of the fireplace. Lily switched on the electric heater when she had seen Amelia shivering.

'The words came out wrong, I want you to take it slowly, weigh up the evidence, that's all.'

'I just know, Lily. When I agreed to marry him, I told him we had to be together full time, but he says being away for weeks on end is what his job requires. I can't bear it anymore.'

'He could switch companies or freelance, sort something out here; you're Irish so he's surely all right visa-wise?'

'He says he's too old to be looking for a job here.'

'Or you could move to the US with him.'

'He's never suggested that,' Amelia said, her eyes glistening with tears.

In the park, children played hide and seek, their squeals of laughter carried by the wind.

'I found a notebook, it said: "arrange flowers for C. Book C's favourite restaurant for dinner." It was for back in the States, the dates he was there. I confronted him, but he laughed it off, said C was an important client.'

'You don't believe him?'

'I did. Well, I tried, but then he started taking off for one night a week and sometimes two, saying he had to meet clients in the UK.'

'Maybe he's trying to get business this side of the Atlantic.'

'Or he's having an affair.'

They'd sat and listened to the children's laughter, fainter and further away as the kids chased off to the far end of the park.

After a while, Lily had got up and begun to rummage in the drawer of the mahogany sideboard.

'My husband was in banking and I know, on occasions, they called in a private detective to follow people. Once, there was a woman who sued, claiming she slipped on the tiled floor of the bank. She said she couldn't walk again. The investigator got pictures of her playing with her dog in the local park.'

'You think I should have him followed?'

'I think you have to be sure of your ground if you want to confront him about an affair.'

'I don't know if I want to go that far.'

Lily had rooted further into the drawer. 'Aha, I knew it was here. I hope he's still in business. Take it, do what feels right.'

Amelia had scanned the card, before slipping it into her dressing-gown pocket. 'Do you think I'm mad?'

'I think you know your own marriage.'

'What will he do if he finds out I went to a private investigator?'

'He needn't know, unless you tell him.'

'It's a big step; whatever he tells me can't be untold. I love Jack, the last thing I want is to lose him.'


At that moment, Lily saw Sam walking towards her and broke off her reverie.

'So you like to linger by the canal as well, I see,' he said, lightly tipping his cap. Lily, a little taken aback, stood off the path, almost falling over the root of a tree pushing up through the ground. He leaned over and took her by the elbow. 'I rather hoped I would bump into you, I so enjoyed our chat the other day.'

'Me too. Would you like to go to Brogans? We could have tea.'

She surprised herself she was so forward and worried she might have been pushy, so she quickly added: 'That's if you haven't already made plans.'

He laughed out loud. 'Lily, I have all the time in the world. But first, may I bring you to my favourite seat?'

She nodded and they walked on together along the south bank, pausing only to watch a pair of swans glide past. They stopped near the lock gates at a simple wood and granite seat. 'It's not near as grand as the famous seat that was specially commissioned to commemorate Patrick Kavanagh, but I like it. I imagine Kavanagh used to sit at this spot and these days, I like to do the same,' Sam said, indicating to Lily to join him.

'Peaceful, I like it,' she said, making sure to sit close.

'Do you sometimes feel the world is just passing us by?' Sam asked.

'I think we're supposed to begin feeling like that at our age, but I think we're lucky too, we don't have the terrible pressure of today's world.'

'You think?'

'And we are lucky to have a roof over our heads.'

'Yes, some a finer roof than others.'

Lily looked at him oddly, but a large Labrador at that moment ran past them and jumped into the water. Its frustrated owner was on the canal bank shouting at the dog, trying to coax it back. She looked around for help. 'I'm only looking after him for a friend. She told me not to let him into the water. What will I do?'

'He looks as if he's enjoying himself; he'll come out in his own good time,' Lily said.

'Except his owner returns in half an hour. I brought him down for a walk, so he would be tired and therefore calm when she came in the door.'

Sam opened his rucksack and took out a half-eaten sandwich from its wrapper. 'Maybe you can entice him with this, they say that Labs will do anything for food.'

The young woman took the sandwich, calling out to the dog, who swam to the grassy bank.

'That sandwich, if you don't mind me saying, looks the worse for wear. Best the dog eats it,' Lily said. She saw Sam's eyes narrow as they turned to talk to the young woman, and she was afraid she had offended him.

'Snip on the lead while he gobbles that, then stand back, he'll shake himself dry,' Sam said to the young woman as the dog pulled itself from the water.

They all quickly sidestepped when the dog shook himself vigorously.

'Can I give you anything for the sandwich?'

'Don't be silly,' Sam replied.

'You are a kind man, Sam Carpenter. Now may I treat you to a cup of tea and a slice of lemon drizzle cake in Brogans?' Lily said, lightly linking his arm.

The woman, who was still within earshot, smiled at the couple.

When they arrived at Brogans they were shown to a table where they had a view of the canal bank, the yellow irises gone out of bloom, showing off their green, blade-like leaves, the water shimmering silver in the afternoon sunshine.

'I hope I didn't offend you back there when I commented on the sandwich,' Lily said softly.

'No, you were right, it was past the sell-by date,' he said. They both fell silent and Lily was glad when the waitress interrupted them. She made to place a tray of tea and a selection of small sandwiches and cakes on a pretty cake stand on the table but Lily waved her away. 'I think you are at the wrong table, we haven't ordered yet.'

'No, right table. The lady with the Labrador asked us to serve you, she said you were so kind to her and Coco.'

'What a treat,' Sam said, indicating to Lily to go first. She took a salmon and cucumber finger sandwich, cutting it into two neat squares. Sam surveyed the plate.

'This is some spread,' he said, reaching for a buttered scone. 'I haven't had food this good in so long,' he added, beaming. Lily took small bites of her food as Sam tucked in, slathering strawberry jam and a huge dollop of cream on his scone, before biting in to it. Lily watched as he munched with relish, calling for more cream for the top section of the scone.

'I'm glad I met you today, I lost my neighbour, a young woman, recently in a road accident and today I was feeling particularly sad,' Lily said.

'I'm sorry. Were you very close?'

'Years between us age-wise; she was just starting out in married life. But we understood each other; she brightened up my days no end.'

'You're lucky to have been friends.'

She detected a wistfulness or something she couldn't quite put her finger on in his tone, but she continued. 'You would have liked her, she loved her flowers. Friday was her flower day. Even when she was a student and she could only afford a bunch of brightly coloured blooms at the service station forecourt, she bought a bouquet without fail. Her husband, Jack, showered her with roses, lilies and orchids. Once when he was away on business, he had a single red rose delivered to her every day he was out of the country.

'She was a lucky lady.'

'She felt that way, for a while anyway.'

Lily sat back, her tea cup in her hands. 'Tell me about yourself, Sam. Are you retired now?'

'You could say that, but it wasn't something I wanted to happen. I used to buy and sell property. The quick turnover was important, but the Celtic Tiger gobbled me up for a while, before spitting me back out. I lost everything, and have been trying to find my feet since.'

'Everything? What about your family home?'

'It's my one regret that I put it up as collateral on the loans. I believe a government minister owns it now.'

'But you, are you all right?'

'I'm here, I'm still standing,' he laughed, but she saw a strange sadness drift across his eyes. Later, as they got ready to leave and she picked up her handbag, she noticed him slipping the last slice of cake on the plate into his pocket. She thought it odd he should do so, but was afraid she was making too much of it in her head. Linking arms once more, they wandered down the street together.

'You don't mind, do you?' he asked and she smiled at him.

At De Courcy Square, not feeling so confident, Lily pulled away slightly. When she saw Gladys, she dropped her hand quickly. Once she came onto Gladys's radar, there was no escape.

'Lily, I'm glad I caught you. An unseemly set of events has come to my attention. That homeless girl, Stacey, has ingratiated herself into the affections of our American friend. Can you please alert her to the dangers of letting her stay in the square? Bad enough that she feels entitled to beg under our noses, but we cannot have her going in and out of one of our homes. I would rather do this quietly and not get the association involved.'

Lily shook her head. 'Gladys, if you have something to say to Cora, at least have the guts to say it to her face.'

'She's your friend, and I have bigger challenges to attend to,' Gladys said in her hoity-toity voice, before turning on her heel and marching off.

Lily turned to Sam. 'There is a good side to Gladys, it's just hard sometimes to see it.'

He took Lily's hand and kissed it lightly. 'I thank you for being such wonderful company. Maybe we could do the same again another day?'

'That would be lovely.'

'In that case, I will say goodbye here, in case my presence outside your home draws unnecessary attention.'

Pulling a single red rose, tightly furled, from inside his jacket, he presented it to Lily.

'Hide it, in case Gladys sees it.'

'We might as well give her something to talk about,' she said, twirling the flower so that Gladys couldn't but see it.

'I have had a really lovely time,' she said, offering her hand again. He took it, kissing it gently, something she liked very much.

# TWELVE

Cora had no intention of ringing Amelia's brother when she first took the card from Lily. She could hardly remember where she had tossed it. But the idea of talking to someone directly connected to Jack and his wife burrowed deep in her mind, agitating her brain, until several days later she returned to Jack's desk in a rush to find the card. Pushing a mound of old newspapers out of her way, she found it wedged between a discarded and dusty pen holder and a giveaway newspaper magazine nobody had bothered to take from its plastic wrapping.

It was the late evening, but she sat at Jack's desk and punched out the mobile number on the old office phone.

When he answered, Tom Hooper seemed a little distracted.

'I'm sorry, who is this?' he asked impatiently.

'Jack Gartland's sister.'

'From America?'

'Well, I'm at the house in De Courcy Square now, the lady next door gave me your card.'

'Thank you for ringing me...'

'Cora.'

'Cora. I'm sorry for your loss. This is one fine mess.'

She wanted to answer, but the tears rising through her stopped her getting any words out. Detecting her confusion, he spoke softly. 'You know I'd like access to the house to retrieve some of my sister's possessions?'

She welcomed the change of subject. 'I don't have a problem with that.'

'I'm working at the moment, but would tomorrow morning early, around nine a.m. suit?'

'I guess.'

'I'm sorry, I'm at work, can we talk more tomorrow?'

'Sure.'


Cora got up three hours early for her appointment with Amelia's brother. She stood inside the ground-floor office window staring out into the stillness of the park, waiting to meet this man who could tell her about the couple who were Jack and Amelia.

Jack had once suggested they vacation in Ireland; she could paint, he would get a little business done. She should have taken him up on the offer a few years ago: maybe she would have noticed something, become suspicious, been able to see off this young woman, before she became a permanent fixture in her partner's life.

Feeling nervous, she began to pace the width of the rug in the front room. Outside, people glided past like early-morning ghosts, too preoccupied to witness Cora's anguish. She wished she was a smoker and she could pull on a cigarette. Wandering to the kitchen, she snatched a chocolate biscuit from the packet she had bought the day before, but only nibbled it before firing the rest in the bin. Tom Hooper was due at nine, so half an hour beforehand, she showered and grabbed her jeans and T-shirt. Today was not the day to wear Amelia's clothes. She squeezed a blob of Amelia's foundation onto her fingers and applied it to her skin before tying her hair back from her face with a plain black scrunchie.

She was in the kitchen when he rang the doorbell. Slowly she walked up the hallway and opened the front door.

'Tom Hooper, pleased to meet you, Cora,' he said, flashing his ID card at the same time.

'You'd better come in,' she said. She pulled back the door, noticing as he stepped in that he was tall, with a slight hunch at the shoulders, as if he was used to leaning down to accommodate the lesser height of others.

'There was no need, I would have let you in,' she said nodding at the ID still in his hand,

'My sister was the same, way too trusting. I never knew why they had to live in the city centre. You make sure you're careful, it's rough enough not far from here.'

But then he grinned. 'I'm acting too much like a cop.'

'I guess.'

She beckoned him to follow as she walked to the kitchen.

'We never got to meet anybody on Jack's side. Nice to finally do so, despite the terrible circumstances.'

Cora cleared a chair of junk mail she had dumped there the day before. 'Please take a seat,' she said and muttered something about needing a *no junk mail* sign. Her nervousness was making her voice tremble and she hoped he wouldn't notice.

'This is difficult for you,' Tom said gently.

Cora took a deep breath, dropping the bundle of mail onto the worktop. 'You might as well know from the start, I'm not Jack's sister.'

She saw his eyebrows arch, the look in his eyes change rapidly.

'What the f—? Sorry, but who the hell are you?'

She hesitated, staring past him to the gravelled garden with tubs containing basil trees and tea light lanterns hanging along the side walls. Maybe she had been too hasty with her revelation, but there was little she could do about that now.

'Are you going to tell me?'

Tom Hooper stood taller, as though this gave his question more authority. Cora looked at him. He was thickset, like a lot of detectives who had forsaken a proper breakfast for the bacon roll. He stared at her intently, waiting for her answer.

'Jack's partner.'

'What do you mean partner, business partner?'

Cora laughed a strange, low, gurgling sound. 'I was his everything partner, we shared a life, a home.'

She walked to the sink and lingered, watching a magpie drop down and jab at the gravel, one stone at a time, pecked and discarded.

'I thought you should know,' she said quietly.

'What the hell do you mean, "everything partner"?'

Cora turned around. 'Jack and I were partners, living together for just over nine years.'

'Before he met Amelia.'

'When he died.'

'He was married to Amelia.'

Cora guffawed out loud. 'Wasn't she the lucky one, to get that ring on her finger?'

'What the hell do you mean, why are you telling me this?'

'Because you should know what Jack Gartland really was, who he really was. For all we know there's another woman, another family stashed somewhere in the world.'

'Stop it.'

'Why, because the truth makes you feel uncomfortable?'

'How do I know you are even telling the truth?'

Cora looked at him. 'I don't much care whether you do or you don't believe me, but I felt you should know.'

'Is this some sort of revenge kick, because he married my sister?'

'Hardly, could I even make this shit up?'

Tom slumped back into a chair. 'I always thought he was too good to be true, but she told me if I started looking in to his background, she would never speak to me again.'

'I thought we were happy. I was the bigger fool, waiting back in the States for him.' Tears rose up inside her, making her voice quaver. 'Do you think your sister knew he had another life in the States?'

Tom put his head in hands. 'I hope to God she didn't.'

He got up to pace between the table and the sink. 'I always knew he was hiding something. I never liked him, I always felt the...'

Tom stopped. Cora felt sick. 'There's more isn't there, more crap I have to hear about him?'

Tom studied the floor. 'It's not my place to be telling.'

'Who else am I going to ask? You have to tell me.'

'Don't you think you have had enough heartbreaking news?'

Tom made to leave, but Cora stood in the doorway. 'We both know you have to tell me; get it over and done with, think of it as two heartbreaks for the price of one.' She tried to make her voice sound light, but she knew she only sounded pitiful.

When he spoke, Tom's voice was low. 'Amelia was pregnant.'

Those three words speared through her. Feeling dizzy, she slumped back against the fridge, hitting the filter tap, so water spewed over her jeans. She felt Tom's arms around her, guiding her to a chair by the table.

'None of us knew either, the post-mortem showed it up.'

'Jack never wanted children.'

'Pathologist said she was about ten weeks.'

'Is that why Jack bought this place, for his family?'

'Amelia wanted lots of children, I know that.'

She saw Tom, but she wasn't listening to him anymore. She was back on their deck the last time she and Jack had sat and chatted over a beer. He had cracked open two bottles and they'd sat for a while, in a familiar companionable silence. Jack had reached over and squeezed her hand. 'You don't regret not having kids, do you?'

She'd smiled and taken a swig of her beer before responding. 'It's probably a bit too late for either of us, I don't know if I want to be an older mom.'

He'd laughed out loud. 'Jeez darling, we're lucky. I'm not complaining. Life's good as it is, thank you very much.'

They'd sat and listened to the neighbours on the right side arguing over colour shade cards for their living room and the old man on the left watching his TV, which was blasting out jazz music. She was glad Jack had not pursued it further: she would never tell him about the miscarriage, just two years earlier, when he'd been away on business. When he'd returned she should have confided in him, but she'd been afraid it would lead to a huge row. She knew Jack liked to be in control and an unplanned pregnancy was never going to be welcome.

The sound of Tom speaking jolted her back into the present.

'I'm sorry, I'm going to have to get to work. Can I ring later and come around another time for Amelia's things?'

She nodded.

'You won't throw it all away or smash it to bits before then?' he asked gently.

'I think if I was going to do anything crazy, detective, I would have done it before now.'

'Maybe so,' he said as he made for the front door. She followed, standing on the top step as he left.

Watching Tom's car turn out from the square into a long line of traffic, she heard Gladys call her name before beetling across the road towards her.

'Do you mind if I have a word?'

'Can it wait?'

Gladys was out of puff by the time she reached the top of the steps.

'If I got a euro for every time somebody in this square said that, I would be a rich woman. I just want to fill you in on the way we do things around here. Now is as good a time as any.'

Gladys stood expecting to be asked in, but when Cora didn't move, she began her lecture anyway. 'I noticed your gentleman caller parked on the square without a permit. I didn't ring the traffic warden this time, because in fairness you may not know about the rules and regulations here in De Courcy Square.' Cora made to interrupt, but Gladys, in full flight, chose to ignore her. 'I am making some allowances for you, because of the tragic circumstances under which you took over the house, but you have to realise the rules of the square and in particular the gardens are important. First and foremost, no parking without a permit. Jack had one; if you don't have it, we can arrange a replacement.'

'Do we have to do this now?'

Gladys stepped back. 'I thought you wanted to be part of our little community.'

'She has a lot on her mind, Gladys, and she has promised to help with my back garden,' Lily's voice boomed from next door.

Gladys swung round. 'The sooner I get Cora on board the better; we permanent residents have to stick together. I hope you're not going to sell up,' Gladys said, directing a stern look at Cora.

'I have no solid plans.'

Gladys harrumphed loudly. 'Can I at least include you in the email notices from the association?' Cora walked back into the house and pulled her card from her purse. Gladys quickly read it.

'You should have said you were an artist, I would love somebody to capture the square for me on canvas. I would give it centre stage in my drawing room. You should show me some of your work, or where I can look it up, and maybe I can commission you.'

'I'm afraid I'm not painting right now.'

Shaking her head, Gladys muttered that she would put Cora on the mailing list, before turning on her heel and walking down the steps. Lily and Cora watched her go, marching over to a cyclist who was attempting to lock his bike on the park railings.

'Gladys is some ticket,' Lily said softly. 'She has a good heart, but you have to be in the mood for her,' she added.

'Thanks for rescuing me.'

'No problem, and when you are ready, I'm always here for a chat.'

Cora mumbled her thanks and stepped quickly back into her hall. She let the door bang shut, making vibrations pulse through the house. Bending over, she held on to the hall table. Up to this point, there'd been a distant hope this was a nightmare and she would wake up and be able to grieve the loss of the man she loved.

Today's news meant that man had disappeared a long time ago. This was a new situation. She could no longer trust any part of her memories of Jack. This secret life was his real life, full of future plans, a life looking forward, not back. There was no room for her in this life or this house, not even now.

Walking into the office, she sat at his desk. It was a stranger's desk. Jack, the man she loved, had died a long time ago, but nobody told her. She had moved in to this house expecting to learn more and understand him better, but instead, she found a stranger with a secret life, a stranger who had robbed her of every good memory she had left. There was no life to go back to in the States, none here that she knew of. The decision she had to make was whether to move forward and create a new existence in this new country or wallow in her past, discredited life. She knew what she should do, but only time would tell if she was able. Aimlessly she wandered upstairs, loitering in the rooms, looking out of the windows.

Fifty minutes later, she'd come back downstairs to hear Lily dawdling outside the front door, coughing before knocking quietly.

Cora opened the door.

'The sound of the doorbell is so grating, I took a chance you might hear my shuffling,' Lily said as she placed a bouquet of white and purple flowers in Cora's arms. 'Forgive me too, I never asked if you liked flowers, but I can't imagine you don't.'

'They are so beautiful.'

Lily leaned over the bouquet. 'I guess nobody has recognised your loss, I felt it was high time, I hope you don't mind.'

Cora pulled back the door. 'Won't you come in?'

Lily laughed. 'And invade your space? Not today. I have put rosemary for remembrance. It goes nicely with the small purple daisy. A late bloomer in the garden, it says farewell rather eloquently. The lilac-tinged bellflowers are for gratitude. I think that is gratitude for all the times spent together.'

'I never knew that flowers could say so much. I wish I'd known you when I got bouquets in the past.'

'I'll leave you to it. If you want a laugh, wait for the emails from Gladys. It's why a lot round here call her email communications 'A Giggle from Gladys'.'

Cora closed her door, losing herself for a few moments in the heavy scent of the rosemary.

From: **GladysSpencer@gmail.com**
To: **all De Courcy Square Association members**

Dear residents and tenants,

Following the key survey carried out over three days this

week, it has come to our attention that keys were missing from five properties. It is not known how this happened.

As a result, we have decided to impose a fine of €200 per property. The funds will all go towards the replacement of all four locks leading in to the square gardens. This is a costly business and every property is also being asked to donate €50 and in return the occupants will be provided with one new key.

Please remember this could have been avoided, if those already entrusted with keys had shown a level of responsibility in the first place.

Please forward all payments to me, until we can find someone prepared to sacrifice some of their time and take up the role of treasurer. We aim to have the new locks installed by early next week.

Gladys Spencer,
Chairperson

# THIRTEEN

Lily sat up in bed. Somebody was hammering on the front door, pounding urgently, alternating knuckle raps with fast palm of the hand slaps. She stayed perfectly still, afraid to move. Who came to the door at six in the morning, other than the bearer of bad news? Curled up in her bed, she shivered and pulled the duvet over her head. Her phone vibrated and buzzed on the bedside table.

Putting out her hand, she pulled the mobile towards her. When she saw the Gladys Gossip icon flashing on the screen, she turned the phone over, but it vibrated across her bedside table. Lily was angry when she sat up to answer it.

'What do you want, Gladys? Do you realise how early it is?'

'You didn't answer your door.'

'I live in Dublin, not Ballydehob, I don't usually rush to answer the door to unknown callers when it's practically the middle of the night. What's so urgent? Can't it wait?'

'Not if we don't want to still have our park by nine a.m. Look out your window first, then come downstairs.'

Lily reluctantly got out of bed and pulled back a curtain.

The railings on her side of the square had been taken down

and were lying across the pavement. Three men wearing high-vis jackets were walking about, kicking the ground and talking. One took out a tape measure and ran it along the remaining railing, calling out to one of the others, who wrote on a clipboard. Lily winced when she saw the patch of pink cosmos flowers being being trampled and the lupins already mashed into the earth.

She grabbed her dressing gown and rushed to the stairs. Pain shot up her right leg as she over-exerted herself, but she ignored it, gripping tightly onto the bannister. When she opened the front door, Cora was already there, Amelia's long grey cardigan over her pyjamas.

'Maybe the utility company is carrying out some drain work,' she said, but Gladys cackled loudly.

'Do you really think any legit workers would be out so early?'

Lily reached over to the coat stand; taking her raincoat in one hand, she grabbed her Wellington boots and stepped into them. 'Why don't we just go over and ask, then we can all get back to bed?'

Gladys, pulling her dressing gown tight around her, knotted the belt. Lily led the deputation across the road, gesturing to the men to stop. They ignored her as she stood foolishly waving and gesticulating, trying to get their attention.

'I've had enough of this. Look at the havoc they're creating. Who are they and what the hell do they think they're doing?' Gladys said.

She stepped forward, prodding one of the men on the shoulder.

'Would you mind telling us what you are doing in our park, please?'

'I'm sorry, but you'll have to take the matter up with the owner. Now please let us get on with our work.'

'What do mean, *owner*? Has the council plans for the park?'

'We don't work for the council,' the man answered sharply.

'Well, whoever you are, we have called the gardai to deal with this blatant act of vandalism,' Gladys said.

The man with the clipboard took out his phone. He called a number and spoke briefly, then handed the phone to Gladys. She refused to take it.

'Please, it's the owner of the property.'

Gladys pushed the man's hand away. 'You and your scam, you will be sorry you crossed the residents of De Courcy Square.'

Lily accepted the phone. Gladys shook a fist at the men, but Lily placed a restraining hand on her as she listened to the person at the other end of the line.

'Gladys, it's a man who says he owns the park and he can do what he wants to it.'

'The park is an integral feature of this square, no one person owns it.'

Cora wrapped her cardigan tighter around her. 'Doesn't the city?'

'Yes, of course, that's why what this man is saying is so preposterous.'

Lily gently pulled at Gladys's sleeve. 'Let's not do anything silly before the gardai arrive.'

The three women moved back to Lily's side of the street.

'I've never seen anything like it. He'll ruin my life's work, never mind seriously devalue our homes', Gladys said, making to go back, when the men resumed working.

Lily pulled her away. 'We need to know the enemy, before we fight it.'

Gladys broke free, rushing to the houses on another side of the square, and began to ring the doorbells. 'They're up to no good. We need as much support as possible to stop them before it's too late. We surviving residents have to stick together, those in the offices won't give a damn,' she called out to anyone who cared to listen. A Jeep pulled up at the same time as the garda squad car.

Gladys marched over to it. 'Can you kindly move on, we are dealing with a crisis here and you don't have a parking permit.'

A tall, elderly man wearing jeans and a grey sweatshirt got out of the car. Extending his hand to Gladys, he spoke in a loud voice. 'Pleased to meet you. Anthony Draper, the new owner of this patch of land. Thank you for your welcome basket to number 29, so kind of you.'

He had grabbed her hand in a firm grip before Gladys had time to answer.

'You can't be seriously saying you own the park. Where are the cameras?' Cora said, swinging around in an attempt to locate the jokers filming.

'This park is centuries old,' Lily said.

'All the more reason why it's time for a change,' Anthony Draper said, before excusing himself, so he could amble over to the two gardai.

Gladys, who had by now recovered her composure, marched after him. 'You surely don't believe this man?' she said to the gardai.

Cora and Lily could not hear the conversation that followed, but when Gladys turned round, it was clear this was one argument in which she had not had the final say. Anthony Draper called across to tell them he would be back later and beckoned his men to join him, before they drove away. Gladys watched the garda squad car drive off.

When she didn't move, both Lily and Cora went to stand beside her. 'Tell us what's going on,' Lily said.

Gladys stared straight ahead. Lily walked over to the corner of the park and pushed the loose cosmos back in the soil, pressing it into place with her fingers. 'Is that man going to pay for the damage and restore things the way they should be?' she asked.

'He bought the park and now he says he'll do what he wants to it. What are we going to do?' Gladys said, her voice unusually subdued.

Cora put an arm around her. 'You can't just buy up a city park. If that was the case, Central Park would have been built on a long time ago.' She laughed, but when she saw Gladys, tears streaming down her face, she stopped.

'There must be some mistake. They've left for now, so that's good,' Lily said.

Gladys marched over to the fallen railing and attempted to lift it off the ground. 'They're only gone because they were told they have to have a permit to carry out extensive works so early in a residential area. They'll be back, if not today, then tomorrow.'

She pointed at different houses on the square. 'There are only a few of us still living here. Those people in the offices don't give a rats whether there's a park here or not.'

'Why would he want to take away the park? He lives here, after all,' Lily asked.

'When we get an answer to that, we will know what we're up against. For now, we must alert as many as possible to the prospect of losing this beautiful park forever,' Gladys said.

She walked home, her shoulders slumped with the weight of a huge worry.

Cora was about to go back inside No. 23 when she realised Lily was still standing in the middle of the road, looking at the section of the garden which had already been trampled and churned about.

Softly, she called out to her, but Lily didn't move. Walking back, Cora touched Lily gently on the shoulder. 'Maybe you should get on home.'

'What?'

Lily looked confused, so Cora led her by the elbow to her steps.

'Do you want me to come inside with you?'

Lily shook her head. 'I'm sorry, I can't bear to think of anything happening to our park.'

'Maybe it won't come to that.'

Lily pulled away. 'It will come to a lot worse, I just know it.'

'Why don't I make some coffee?'

'I'm sorry Cora, all of this has really shook me. I need to be on my own.'

She walked up her steps and pushed her front door open. 'A rain check on that coffee?' she said, slipping into her hallway, letting the door close behind her. She didn't know how long she'd stood there before her phone pinged with an email from Gladys.

From: **GladysSpencer@gmail.com**
To: **all De Courcy Square Association members**

Extremely urgent notice

The De Courcy Square Association is begging the support of the many and varied residents, permanent and temporary, of the square for your unstinting support in our darkest hour.

Our beloved park has fallen into the hands of a private developer. His intentions are unclear, but already he has begun tearing up a section of the square. This developer claims to have purchased the land and be the legitimate owner of our park.

We of course dispute this and we will, at the earliest opportunity, seek a meeting with the City Council. We will also have to seek legal advice. What we need now are suggestions, ideas and funding so we can fight this threat. Our unique way of life in Dublin city centre is under threat.

This Association has always been at the forefront of keeping this beautiful square as it should be. Let us put the differences of the past behind us and fight this greedy attempt to rip out the heart of our community and destroy our beautiful Georgian square and gardens.

Gladys Spencer,
Chairperson

Lily deleted the email. Climbing upstairs to the sitting room, she stood and surveyed the park, her favourite section now desecrated, the earth torn up, the roses, lupins and sweet peas uprooted and already looking limp. Sinking into her armchair, she let the tears sweep unchecked down her face. Who knew what the next days and weeks would bring to the beautiful garden she had imagined would always be there, a reminder of times past and a comfort in the present?

Her phone pinged again. Another email from Gladys.

From: **GladysSpencer@gmail.com**
To: **all De Courcy Square recipients**

The Association in this follow-on email would like to add that we have suspended all other duties during the crisis, including following up on illegal parking and locking bicycles to railings. We want to concentrate our efforts on the battle ahead of us and humbly ask for any assistance you can offer.

Gladys Spencer,
Chairperson

Lily, despite her tears, smiled. Gladys and humble didn't go together, but she was right on one thing: they faced a huge battle ahead.

# FOURTEEN

Cora sat at Jack's desk and switched on the overhead lamp. Taking a jotter, she opened it at a blank page. Scrabbling in the top drawer she found a pencil. Tentatively, she held the pencil, all the time looking at Amelia's desk opposite, wanting to capture this small scene: the empty desk, the large office-like room which no longer had a function. Her pencil was poised, but she couldn't even stroke out a quick sketch. Maybe it was the subject matter – to commit anything associated with Amelia to paper was too much for her – or maybe it was because she had lost the ability to create. She tried again to sketch across the page, wanting to become so absorbed she could suspend reality, but it was as if her brain was paralysed and incapable of telling her hand what to do. Squeezing the pencil hard she pushed it into the page, the lead breaking, tearing through the paper. Frustrated, she flung the pencil on the desk, not bothering to pick it up when it rolled over the side onto the floor. Pushing back her chair, she quickly left the room for the kitchen, where she feverishly began to chop an onion and prepare dinner.

She was ladling some stock into her risotto and stirring when she heard the loud knocking at her front door. She dithered on whether to answer before she heard the unmistakable voice of Stacey cursing. Turning down the heat under the risotto, she walked smartly to the hall, shouting out when the pounding of the door began again.

Stacey was standing wringing her hands when Cora opened the door a few inches.

'Is there something the matter?' she asked, glimpsing a young man in a dark hoodie rush away.

'No, I thought I would visit,' Stacey said, her voice flat.

'Come in, it's chilly out there.'

'It's fucking freezing. Warm days, cold nights; summer is nearly over. I'm sorry, I had nowhere else to go.'

Cora looked at the young woman standing in ripped jeans and a flimsy T-shirt.

'What has happened?'

Stacey looked as if she wanted to say something, but she bowed her head to hide her face, which was pinched with anxiety. Cora gently pushed her towards the kitchen.

'Let's get you warm.'

'I can only stay a few minutes.'

Cora walked ahead and pulled over a chair in front of the kitchen stove. Next, she poured a whiskey and handed it to Stacey. The other woman shook her head. 'I have to stay away from that stuff; if I start drinking now, I'll never stop.'

Cora placed the glass out of sight, behind the bread bin and switched on the kettle.

'You seem rattled.'

'Is that what you call it?'

'I don't mean to pry.'

Stacey sighed loudly. 'I was fucking robbed, wasn't I?'

'What?'

'I know what you're thinking: who would want to rob a homeless person like me?'

Cora didn't protest that she was wrong in her interpretation. 'I was told I had to go to a different hostel. It was the only place they had a bed for me. I wasn't too happy, but I rocked up there.' She stopped to gulp from the mug of tea Cora had placed on the table in front of her. 'I was in the place two hours, when there was this big fight. I wasn't involved, but I was watching. Next thing I looked around and my rucksack, everything, was gone. The last tenner I had was in it and the photographs...' She looked away. 'You don't want to know.'

Cora reached out and gently stroked Stacey's arm. 'I do, if you want to tell me.'

Stacey looked Cora straight in the eye. 'I was married, I had a job and a place to live. I wasn't always like this, there was a time I was doing all right.'

Cora doled out some risotto into a bowl, placing it in front of Stacey. 'Eat now, there'll be plenty of time to talk later.'

Stacey took a mouthful. 'You have the seasoning just right, you're a good cook.'

Cora smiled. 'I have never been told that before.'

She filled a bowl for herself and sat opposite Stacey. They ate in silence, Stacey preoccupied with her own thoughts and Cora nervous of intruding. When Stacey was finished she brought her bowl to the dishwasher.

'I'd better be getting along, I've trespassed enough on your generosity.'

'Where will you go?'

Stacey hesitated. 'I'll find somewhere. They'll be coming around with sleeping bags; I should get one.'

'And then what?'

Stacey turned towards the hallway, but Cora stepped in front of her. 'I can't stop you leaving, but I can offer you a bed for the night and a nice warm bath.'

'Why would you do that for me?'

'I'm doing it for myself, Stacey. I can't, in all conscience, let you out into the city night with no money and nowhere to go. This house is way too big for one person, I don't fill the rooms.'

'You don't know me.'

Cora smiled. 'I'll take my chances. You're hardly going to murder me in my bed, are you?'

Stacey guffawed. 'I'd be too grateful to have a kip in a real bed.'

'That's settled, then.'

Cora beckoned Stacey to follow her upstairs. She showed her into the single bedroom on the second floor. 'I can give you some PJs and a dressing gown. Why don't you have a bath or a shower?'

Cora thought Stacey looked as though Amelia's clothes would fit her, so she went to the master bedroom. Jack might have been the nice fellow over here, but she knew he would never approve of Stacey staying over. What did she care? His opinion didn't matter anymore. He had lost that right to make a difference in her life, not by his death, but when he had decided to betray their love.

Rummaging through the drawers, she found a pyjama set, still in its wrapping. One hundred per cent cotton, cream with a light blue stripe. Cora grabbed it and left the room, taking the blue dressing gown from the back of the door as she left.

On the next landing, she heard Stacey humming a tune as she ran a bath. She knocked on the door and left the PJs and dressing gown in a bundle outside.

Cora went downstairs to the kitchen. Reaching behind the bread bin, she took the glass of whiskey and gulped down the contents. Pouring another drink, she wandered to the small sitting area overlooking the garden. Flicking on the outside lights, she surveyed the garden through the glass, peering into the dark shadows, suddenly fearful of an intruder. A cat, unaware it was being observed, ran along the top of the fence to the tree at the bottom of the garden. It stopped to scratch around the bird feeder, darting off when it heard a door bang next door. She heard Stacey on the landing upstairs, her footfall light as she came downstairs.

'I feel like a new woman.'

'You look like one.'

'Are you sure about this, me staying?'

'Don't be silly.'

Stacey flopped at the kitchen table. 'It's so long since I sat in somebody's kitchen, in a real house, if you get my meaning.'

'How long have you been on the streets?'

'You mean when did my life come to a standstill?'

'I suppose.'

Stacey picked at a tassel hanging from the tea cosy. 'I had a job, a house and a husband. Look at me now; some people don't even notice me on the streets. Once, a woman let her dog piss up against my sleeping bag.'

'What did you do?'

'I kicked out at the fucker and Mary Poppins said I was violent and should be locked up.'

Cora shook her head and tutted loudly, but Stacey hardly noticed.

'Mary Poppins doesn't realise that to be locked up on a winter's day could be a luxury in a weird sort of way.'

They were both silent, until Stacey began to recount her story.

'Jimmy, my husband, died in an accident at work. I was left with my low-paid cleaning job. I couldn't keep up the mortgage. The bank hounded me. I offered them a hundred and fifty euros a month, but they said I was hiding something. They rang me in the morning before I went to work, sometimes they rang me at lunchtime, the minute I got in the door in the evening. They were on the blower, threatening me I would be out in the streets, if I didn't pay what I owed. I got a night job cleaning at the local factory and I upped the offer to two hundred a month, but the bastards brought me to court. I woke up in that house one morning. My eyes were on stalks, I was exhausted, I couldn't take it anymore. I packed a small rucksack, with a few pictures of our wedding and my dress, because the day I wore that, I felt like a princess. I was first in the queue when the bank opened. Very politely, I gave them my address and handed back the keys. They tried to stop me leaving, said there was paperwork that had to signed or something, but I just walked out of there. They tried ringing me, but I threw my phone in the Liffey. I only kept Jimmy's pay-as-you-go. All I had was my rucksack, my dress and my wedding and engagement rings.'

'You're not wearing your rings?'

Stacey voice trembled. 'I pawned them early on, so I could have a deposit to rent a place, but once I defaulted on that weekly payment, I was out on my ear anyway. I tried to keep up my job, but I wasn't able to keep myself respectable or washed and I lost it. There was nowhere else I could sink: I've been floundering, in and out of hostels for the last seven months.'

'Was there nobody who could help? Family, maybe?'

'My mum died a while back. I have sisters, but we haven't talked in a long time. I saw one of them walking into Marks and Spencer last Thursday.

'Did she recognise you?

'You must be joking, she looked straight at me, but she didn't see me. Somebody sitting on the ground begging wouldn't be on her radar.'

'I'm sure if you rang up and told her.' Cora's voice was firm, as though she definitely wanted to persuade Stacey to take the first step towards reconciliation.

'As if I'm ever going to do that. Can I go to bed? I'm not being rude, but I'm fecking exhausted.'

'Of course, you get a good night's sleep. If you put your clothes in the washing machine, I'll transfer them to the dryer later.'

'I'm grand; they are clean, they're just old, that's all.'

Cora sensed a discomfort in Stacey, so she said goodnight.

When Stacey went back upstairs, Cora continued to look out at the garden, afraid almost to switch off the outside light and let the dark of the night close in.

She had this house and she knew she was lucky. Did Amelia ever guess? Did she ever question? Jack and Amelia's life in this house seemed so perfect, working and living together. Did Jack have his childish sullen moods with her, like the time he came home from a trip, handed her a gift and promptly went down to the basement, to put on his earphones and listen to the Rolling Stones? Two hours later, he emerged with no words of explanation. She tried now to go back in her head, to figure out the time of year. It was probably soon after his Irish wedding. Slowly, she got up from the couch and tramped upstairs to bed, maybe not to sleep.

# FIFTEEN

Unable to sleep, Cora got up around six a.m. and padded downstairs to Jack and Amelia's front office.

Up until now, she had avoided this tidy desk, the pens arranged neatly in a row, a box of charcoal sticks to one side along with swatches of material neatly pressed in squares in a tidy pile. Sitting in the modern rattan chair, she picked up a few pieces of fabric; silk, she thought, luxuriating in the softness slithering through her fingers. Opening a fabric-bound book, she slowly turned the pages. Sketches executed in swift charcoal strokes on the left page; on the right, snippets of fabric and instructions in a rushed hand. Fingering an azure blue silk, she traced the outline design of the intended shift dress with the simple short sleeves and a high neckline embroidered with beads.

There was a beauty in the simplicity of the design, the beads toning down the brashness of the blue.

The designer, she thought, had a keen eye for detail and colour. The dress would never be stitched now. Sadness welled up in Cora for this woman she'd always thought she could only hate. Turning the page, she noticed the date: Amelia must have been working on this sketch before they had left for the restaurant. An ankle-length, boho tiered maxidress with long sleeves and a prim collar. The sketch was unfinished, just broad strokes with no shading. Cora fingered the swatches, pulling out a silk that looked like swirls of different shades of blue and pink. The dress conjured up a lazy day in the sunshine and Cora thought that with it, she would wear a wide-brimmed straw hat.

What was she doing, playing dress designer? Bad enough she had rifled through Amelia's clothes, picking the best pieces for herself; was she now trying to steal her ideas?

Quickly, she got up from the desk. Grabbing a long cable-knit cardigan from the hook at the back of the kitchen door, she wrapped it around her pyjamas and tied the belt tight. She didn't bother changing her slippers before moving quietly out of the front door to the park.

Squeezing past the barriers which had been erected the previous day, she negotiated a bank of fresh earth, before making her way onto the footpath inside the park.

She was fighting for this park and she hardly knew it. She stopped to admire the lilac tree, spring crocus bulbs underneath it roughed about in the soil, their bare roots showing.

As she walked along the path, a blackbird whizzed by in a rush into the thicket; a robin sang a loud song from a high spot in the fuchsia.

Cora sat down, viewing snatches of the red-brick houses through the trees, fragments of domesticity among the park wildlife. It was easy to understand why Gladys wanted to fight so hard for this place. She imagined she saw her lingering at her upstairs drawing-room window and she felt sympathy for this woman, who ploughed all her hope into this patch of land.

When she saw Anthony Draper coming towards her, she made to get up and walk away.

'Please don't leave on my account, I understand you are also new to the square,' he said, offering his hand.

'Mr Draper, I know who you are.'

He smiled. 'My reputation precedes me. May I at least know to whom I have the pleasure of talking to?'

'Cora Gartland from number 23.'

'Ah yes, I was sorry to hear about Jack. I didn't know him myself, but a friend had business dealings with him. It must be very difficult for you, taking over the house.'

'It is.'

'Well, if there is anything I can do?'

'Thank you.'

He moved away and was halfway down the path when Cora called out to him.

'Do you mind if I ask what are your plans for this garden?

He looked around. 'I don't have much time for parks that members of the general public are banned from using. A park for the exclusive use of residents, when they are clearly in the minority, is outdated and old-fashioned.'

'I don't have a problem with this being a public park.'

'What this area needs is a good car park and that is what I'm going to provide. Of the sixty-nine houses in the square, only twelve are private residences. While some have parking at the back, the majority don't. It's a business opportunity I would be a fool to pass on.'

'I don't understand, you are a resident of the square. You surely don't want to be looking out over a parking lot?'

Draper clasped his hands in front of him.

'I am a resident for now, but my principal residence is in County Kildare. Until the building is up and running I will use number 29 as my HQ. It is not all doom and gloom, you know.'

'What do you mean?'

'The car park will be underground, three floors with a garden feature on top. A hell of a nicer garden than is here at present.'

'But from what I gather this is an historic garden.'

'That may be so, but I can't say this arrangement where Mrs Spencer tends to the flower beds is working for everybody.'

'The residents will never allow a parking lot, it's a preposterous idea.'

'Time, I'm sure, will tell. What an exciting time to be in the square,' he said without any hint of sarcasm and gave Cora a friendly wave, before heading back down the path. Cora shook her head. There was something rather endearing about Draper, even if he had the craziest plan ever.

Stacey was up when Cora got back to No. 23.

'I must go across to Gladys, I have important news on the park. I'm not sure how long I will be.'

'I'll leave at the same time.'

'There's no need. Stay, have a rummage in the fridge, get yourself something for breakfast.'

'I can't stay here if you're going out.'

'It's fine, take your time.'

Stacey looked agitated. 'I just can't, what if something went missing? I would be blamed.'

'That's dumb, I wouldn't do that.'

'You might not, but there are plenty who would. You were kind enough to take me in last night, but now I must go.'

Cora shrugged her shoulders. 'Suit yourself, you're welcome to stay another few nights.'

Stacey stopped on the stairs. 'You're kind, Cora, but I'll be all right.'

Cora tugged at the front door handle. 'Let yourself out in your own time. I have to get going.'

She rushed out. Gladys, wearing a high-vis vest and carrying a clipboard, waved as she scurried from her house to set up her pitch at the barriers.

'Come along, we need to get our act together. I have

everyone out bright and early. The more support we have from the office crowd the better. Best to catch them as they arrive for work. Go help Lily staple the signs to sticks.'

Cora stepped into a small group of people who were writing out slogans for placards: 'Hands Off Our Park', 'Don't Dig Up the Park' and 'We Love Our Park'.

'With any luck, this developer will run at the sight of a mob led by Gladys,' Lily said and everybody laughed. A number of people in the offices at the far side of the square wandered over.

Cora pulled Lily aside. 'He is going to build a parking lot in the square.'

'Who, what?

'An underground car park with a rooftop garden.'

'You mean he's going to destroy the place.'

Cora was about to make her way over to Gladys when she saw Draper walk towards the group.

Gladys stepped in front of him. 'Mr Draper, you have to know we will not tolerate any interference with our park.'

He smiled broadly. 'You all have to know I now own the park and what I do with it is my business.' He turned to a stout man in a suit. 'Isn't that right? Tell these good people, I bought the park last month and all the paperwork is in order.'

The man nervously approached the group. 'Michael Harvey from the council offices. What Mr Draper here says is true.'

Gladys straightened up. 'This park was never advertised for sale.'

Harvey nervously tugged at his shirt collar. 'The leasehold, after many hundreds of years, had lapsed. The council wasn't informed and Mr Draper here bought it outright in a private transaction. He is the new owner.'

'Without any thought for the residents and all those who use this park and live nearby?'

'It is out of our hands, I am afraid. We hope the park will

remain an amenity for all those on the square and its history will be respected,' he said.

Gladys turned around to the group. 'Well, that illusion has been well and truly shattered.'

'We didn't expect this situation,' Harvey mumbled.

A titter of laughter rose from the crowd and Gladys put her hand up for silence. 'We will not let anybody ruin our park. That's final.'

Anthony Draper stepped forward. 'You can wave your placards and be as indignant as you like, but there's little you can do. I have to warn all of you, take one step inside that park and you are trespassing on private property.'

Lily clapped her hands to get everybody's attention, but she felt quite nervous when she started to speak. 'I am Lily, I have lived all my life in number 22, I can't bear to think that this beautiful garden is to be turned in to a car park.'

Overcome with emotion, she gestured to Cora to continue.

'Mr Draper himself told me of his plans for the multi-level parking lot. I have to say I am only new to the square, but it sounds like a horrendous plan.'

'What in God's name is going on? Are the council going to stand idly by and let this happen?' Gladys said, directing her gaze at Harvey.

Michael Harvey mumbled his apologies, saying it was now the responsibility of a different department, before he scuttled quickly away, his leather folder tucked under his arm.

Anthony Draper said he had to get on with his work. 'Ms Gartland can fill you in on my plans. If there are any questions, I will be happy to answer them by email or if you want to schedule any appointment with my office,' he said, before tipping his cap at the group and walking off towards No. 29.

'What has just happened?' Lily asked.

'We have been put in our place, that's what has happened,

but that man has severely underestimated us,' Gladys said, her voice sounding a lot stronger than she felt.

'I think we have to get legal advice,' Cora said.

Gladys shook her head. 'We have no money for a legal battle, unless anyone knows somebody who could help us.'

'My Hannah is a solicitor, I'm sure she will be able to help,' Lily said.

'Can you ring her? We will have to put on our thinking caps on how we are going to finance this fight.' Gladys said, swinging round when she heard the front door of No. 23 bang shut. She watched Stacey go downstairs and collect her cardboard, before laying it on the ground and setting up her sign, to begin her begging day. 'You have done a foolish thing, letting the likes of her access your house,' Gladys said.

'She needed help for one night; she's a sweet person, just down on her luck.'

'Mark my words, you could end up regretting your kindness.'

'I think, Gladys, it would be best if you stayed out of it. After all, it's none of your business.'

Gladys did not appear in any way perturbed that Cora's tone of voice was cross.

Lily looked from one woman to the other. 'Come back to mine for coffee, the two of you. I'll ring Hannah to see if she can help.'

'I'm sorry, I have a lot I have to do today. Can I call you later, Lily?' Gladys said in her marbles-in-the-mouth voice. Taking off her high-vis jacket and gathering up the placards, she marched the short distance to her own house.

Lily beckoned Cora to follow her. 'We're going to need Gladys's fighting spirit, if we want to hold on to the park.'

'Why does she have to be so bossy?'

'Because she has little else to brighten her day. I think Gladys needs this square and this park to keep her sanity.'

Lily called across to Stacey.

'Join us for a cuppa,' she said kindly.

'Nice of you to offer, but I'm all right,' Stacey called back.

'I'll send Cora out with a mug and a few biscuits.'

Cora followed Lily inside. 'I didn't realise you knew Stacey.'

Lily swung round. 'I don't. To my shame, that's the first time I have even spoken to her, but if you can let that poor woman stay in your home, I can rise to a cup of something hot.'

'I was thinking of persuading her to stay with me for a while. I told her she could, but she won't.'

'She's a good woman. It's pride, or maybe she's afraid of messing it up. You don't know all the ins and outs of her life story.'

Lily made the coffee and poured some into a cup. Walking to the front door, she called out to Stacey.

'I have a cup of coffee here, I took a chance and added milk and one sugar.'

Stacey climbed the steps to the door. Lily held out the cup along with five chocolate gold grain biscuits.

'I'll keep the biscuits for later,' Stacey said, stuffing them into her pocket.

'Eat them now, they're best with a hot drink.'

Stacey smiled. 'They'll be even better later to take the edge off things.'

Lily leaned over and pushed a five-euro note along with her address and phone number into Stacey's pocket.

'Cora told me your name. Mine is Lily. If you ever need a cup of something, don't be afraid to ring or knock on the door.'

When she got back inside, Lily's head was reeling: Stacey had made her think of Sam, storing his half-eaten and out-of-date sandwich in his bag, the way he wolfed down the delicate finger sandwiches of the afternoon tea and the way he surreptitiously squirrelled away the last piece of cake left on the plate. Shaking the thoughts from her head, she put a smile on her face as she walked back into the kitchen. She saw Cora in the garden and decided to ring Hannah and leave a voicemail.

'Hannah must be very busy, though I'm not sure if she'll be able to help us or that she would want to become embroiled in the fight for the park,' Lily said as she stepped outside to join Cora.

'I'm sure she'll help if she can,' Cora said.

'I wouldn't be so sure. Hannah only wants me to move away, downsize. She's not going to be happy if I'm caught up in this situation. I'll have to do a bit of persuading.'

Lily sauntered around the back garden. Flopping down on a seat, she examined her hands.

'The trouble is I love this place and the square. That park has been my salvation. It has always been my refuge. Often, when my husband came home early or worked from home, I would escape there. I think when Hannah was young, I forced her into the park too many times. Reg hated it and because I had the only key, he couldn't follow me; he never tried either. He was a controlling man, but when I took off to the park, he let me be.'

'Reg sounds like he was difficult to live with.'

Lily held her face up to the sun. 'He was. We should never have married. Reg never in all his life experienced that heady in-love feeling and over time, I think that led to a bitterness in his heart, which, unfortunately, he took out on me. He adored Hannah, but I'm not sure he could even bear the sight of me.'

'Why did you stay together?'

'How easily an American asks that question. Because we had to. We had no option. The bank would have frowned on it for sure if we hadn't and the local priest would have had something to say. Anyway, even if I had the courage to leave, where would I go? We wasted the best years of our lives, pretending we were happy. How sad is that?'

'Very sad.'

Lily thought there was something strange the way Cora answered, but she continued talking to fill the gap. 'I was in love once; I think if we had been able to follow it through, it could have lasted. I still love him.'

'Where is he now?'

'Eamon disappeared out of my life decades ago. It's why that park means so much to me. He was the park superintendent's son and the gardener when I was a young woman. He planted all these plants and flowers beds in the square; it's the only reminder I have of our love for each other. It never was the usual type of public park with low-maintenance planting. De Courcy Square always had a homely cottage-garden feel about it, full of flowers chosen by the residents. Special requests were made and honoured: mine was the lilac. Eamon lived in your house; his parents were the caretakers for a wealthy couple who mainly resided in London. Eamon's family had quarters in the basement of number 23.'

Tears streamed down Lily's face and she swept them away with the palm of her hand.

'I wish this wasn't happening. The last thing I need right now is the past to be dredged up.'

Cora took Lily into a tight hug. 'I think with Gladys and maybe Hannah on our side, we have nothing to worry about,' she said as she made for the front door.

Lily climbed upstairs to the sitting room after Cora left. She switched on the light and pulled across the curtains, because even though she loved it when the room was full of light, she could not bear to look out on the park anymore. Why did the work have to start at that corner? It was as if they wanted her to suffer. Well, she was suffering.

Pacing the room, she stopped at the bookcase. Taking down the heavy old edition of *The Complete Works of Shakespeare*, she let it fall open at *Hamlet*, Act Two, Scene 1, where a long time ago, she had pressed a a small, yellow, wild primrose Eamon had placed in her hands.

Her fingers ran across the paper-thin flower with its petals tinged light to dark brown. It had been a perfect spring day, a day of hope. Sadness flooded her heart as she remembered those good times. He had plucked the wild primrose and placed it in her buttonhole.

She'd had to pull it out before going home, pressing it between the leaves of *Hamlet*, where she knew nobody would find it. Snapping the book shut, Lily slumped into the armchair.

The next days and weeks were going to challenge her greatly. A voice inside her head told her to bolt, but another told her to stand her ground. Without that garden, she faced the rest of her life without daily reminders of Eamon and that would be unbearable.

# SIXTEEN

Lily swished the clothes hangers back and forth, the scraping sound bouncing across the room, until she found the blue dress bordered with flowers. The dress with the long flowing skirt would get its first outing today; she had bought it in the week after her husband's funeral, but she'd never before had the courage to even consider wearing it. She took special care with her make-up and tried three different hair styles, before deciding to stay with her usual hairdo of a small bun at the nape of her neck. Every day, accidentally on purpose, they met, but Lily was still afraid they might miss each other. She would have preferred to meet at a set place and time, but Sam seemed happy to keep things on a more casual footing. The last time she'd seen him, she had invited him to a concert, but he had declined, saying he had a lot of things to attend to in the evenings. Today, she might suggest going as far as St Stephen's Green and maybe from there, she could persuade him to try for tickets at the Gaiety.

She picked a purple shoulder bag to complement the blue cornflowers on the border of her dress. Checking her reflection in the hall mirror, she pulled in her stomach tight, because she was conscious the dress was so unforgiving. She set off from No. 22 at a smart pace to the canal, where she slowed down to a stroll, scanning the bank on the opposite side for Sam. When she got as far as the Kavanagh seat, she sat in the sunshine waiting for him. What would she do, she thought, if he didn't turn up? She would have no idea where to go looking for him. She concentrated on the sound of the water lapping gently around an old discarded tyre, half in and half out of the water. Further down, a family of ducks squabbled loudly. A man called his dog to heel and a hooded young man boarded past, his skateboard scraping along the road. A young woman with a buggy negotiated the bumps on the canal path, as her child pointed excitedly at the ducks. At that moment, Sam tapped her gently on the shoulder.

'Lily, sorry, I'm a little later than I intended,' he said, sitting down beside her.

Lily smiled. 'I was thinking, I know so little about you, I would like us to get to know each other better.'

'I would like that very much also.'

'So, how do we do this, do we ask each other questions or what?'

'If you like. Be my guest.'

'What's your favourite colour?'

He seemed surprised at the question. 'When the sky at sunset turns to deep pink, that's my favourite colour. And you?'

'Blue, deep blue. I always wanted a sitting room with a deep blue colour on the walls.'

'Why don't you?'

'I've never been bold enough to try it, and when Reg was alive, he would not have allowed it.'

'Go on, another question.'

'Why do you always carry the rucksack?'

'I like to have a bag, otherwise my pockets will bulge out; that never looks good. Can I ask a question now?'

'Shoot.'

'Why aren't you asking me the question you want to ask?'

'What do you mean?'

'I will answer it for you anyway.'

She pulled away from him. 'I haven't asked you anything personal, I have no right.'

'I would like it very much if you felt you had that right.'

Lily didn't know what to say, but when Sam took her hand, she moved in closer to him. 'I just want to know you,' she said.

'The person in front of you now?'

'Yes. I like what I see, Sam, even though you are somewhat of an enigma.'

'Ask me whatever you like.'

She hesitated, stopping to watch a swan take the middle channel in the canal, which gave it an opportunity to glide forward uninterrupted by passers-by on the canal path.

'Is everything all right, Sam?'

'What do you mean?'

'I have noticed things and I just want to help.'

She felt him shift in the seat beside her.

'Are you down on your luck? I couldn't help but notice things, like the food you store in your bag, the shirts you wear.'

She stopped, afraid to go on. He pulled at one of his cuffs to show her.

'Frayed and ingrained with dirt. Are those the words you are looking for?'

Lily jumped up.

'This is coming out all wrong. I only want to help, Sam.'

'I have been down on my luck for quite a while, Lily. I used to have social standing, property and money; I have none of those things these days. I am merely a man in an old suit, carrying a rucksack.'

'But have you somewhere to live?'

Sam let his head drop onto his chest. 'No. I don't want to deceive you Lily, you mean too much to me for that.'

'Are you... Are you homeless?'

'If you don't want anything to do with me, Lily, I understand,' he mumbled.

Lily slapped his hand. 'Don't be daft, man. What makes you think I would walk away from you because of this?'

'I wouldn't think anything less of you, if you were reticent or afraid.'

'Why don't you just tell me the truth? The old Lily might have been scared, but that young girl Stacey has taught me a thing or two about being on the streets. I'm not as quick to pass judgement these days.'

Sam got up and walked to the water's edge. He picked a blade of grass and dropped it in the water, watching it float away.

'I wish you could have known me when life was good.'

'I like what I see now.'

'You hardly know me.'

She got up and pulled him back to sit down. 'I was married to a pig of a man. It gave me a great sense of relief when he passed. I'm not proud of that, but I can truly say that it's only in the last two years I have begun to live again. Meeting you has been a big part of that.'

Tears pushed from the corners of his eyes.

'I lost everything. I was lucky to be able to live with a cousin on Leeson Street, but I had to move out a while ago. His soon-to-be wife wants the house to themselves; I can hardly blame her.'

'Have you nowhere to stay?'

'I have a bed in a hostel a few nights a week, but mostly, all the spaces are gone by the time I get through on the phone.

'You don't sleep rough, do you?'

Sam shifted on the seat. 'I thought I had a lot of friends, but they disappeared, or maybe I avoided them, because of the shame I felt at not being able to make a living. I climb into parks on a summer's night; it's not so bad.'

'Tell me to stop if you like, but how can a well-spoken man like you end up homeless?'

He laughed. 'I'm glad you think I'm well spoken. I talk to so few out here, I sometimes think I have lost the art of conversation.'

'You don't fit into the picture I have of a homeless person. The only other one I know is Stacey, who pitches up outside the house with her begging cup.'

'I bet you have never invited her in.'

'No, to be honest I'm slightly intimidated by her, but my next-door neighbour, Cora, has had her in the house. I have talked to her and given her tea and biscuits. It's about as far as I can go, I suppose. She doesn't ask me for anything else, either.'

'I had a house like yours once, in Rathmines, and several other properties.'

'What happened?'

'I owed millions, the houses were sold from under me. I had to declare myself bankrupt, I began to drink. I lost my family as well; my wife threw me out, wouldn't let me see my daughter. I don't blame her, I let them all down.'

'But you don't drink now.'

'I'm an alcoholic, Lily, I don't drink, but it's too late. My wife has divorced me, my daughter Rosa is an adult and chooses not to see me. I have totally messed up, I have no way of making it better.'

Lily took Sam's hand.

'Let's walk together,' she said.

They walked side by side past the ducks, now squabbling over bread thrown into the water by a child in a buggy.

'What are you going to do when the weather gets colder?' she asked, a shiver running through her at the thought.

'In March, April when I had to leave my cousin's place, I went to a nice hostel run by a charity. I helped out and got a free room in return, but that place has since closed.'

'So what will you do?'

'What everybody else does: try and get enough money together to be able to afford a bed each night.

'But how?' she asked, but immediately regretted the question when she saw shame creep across his face.

Sam pointed over at two sleeping swans. 'Let's just enjoy the here and now,' he said softly.

They stood, both taking a break as they watched the swans, their heads tucked in to their wings as they slept and floated on the water, protected by the branches of a butterfly bush which was sprawled across one side of the bank. Lily took Sam's hand and squeezed it. She saw his eyes tear up and she stepped closer to him in a gesture of reassurance.

'I hate to see you like this,' she said.

'Please, no pity, Lily. I want you to know me as Sam Carpenter, not Sam who is homeless.'

'Sam, I'm only worried about you.'

'I know, and that thought sustains me an awful lot more than you think.'

Lily didn't say anything for a few minutes. She let her mind travel with the water, moving at that slow, gentle pace. It was so long before she spoke, she knew Sam was expecting bad news.

'Stay with me in number 22. I have plenty of room.'

He shook his head. 'I think your neighbours will have something to say about that, and what about your daughter?'

'I don't care what any of them think. You need a room to call your own and I have plenty of them.'

'Easy maybe to say, but it would be too hard on you. I'm not easy to live with, Lily,' he said, taking a step back from her. 'Don't pity me, Lily, I value your friendship too much,' he added, pulling away his hand.'

He walked down the narrow canal path. She watched him, his shoulders hunched, his gait slow. She knew if she let him go, they might never see each other again. She had experienced that same sense of desolation in the past and had no wish to go through that pain again.'

'What pity, and what are you talking about, man? Come back, please,' she shouted.

She thought he hadn't heard her, because for a moment it looked as if he might not turn round. When she saw him slowly turn towards her, revealing his face wet with tears, his arms outstretched, she stumbled towards him, sure she was doing the right thing.

'You can't be any worse than a man who put me down every day of the week.'

'I would never do that, but I'm used to being on my own.'

'Hush your mouth, I won't hear another word. Now, let's go home.'

Lily nudged Sam with her elbow.

'Let's give it a try. We're old enough to know the risks. I'm going to brave it if you are.'

'For somebody who is so kind and gentle, you can be very firm when you want.'

'When I want something, I usually get it. Let's give Brogans a slip today and get you back to number 22 and settled in.'

They walked down the canal path hand in hand, crossing over at Baggot Street. As they waited for the pedestrian light, Sam turned to Lily. 'Are you sure? What will people say?'

'I'm sure, and to hell with what people think.'

'Promise me one thing: if you ever regret this decision you will tell me.'

'I promise. Now let's get along,' she said, her voice sounding impatient, because she was nervous.

Back at No. 22, she sat Sam down in the kitchen and prepared a tuna salad sandwich which she put on a plate in from of him.

She told him to eat. He did what he was told as she went upstairs to make up the bed in the guest single room at the back of the house.

When she came back downstairs, Sam was in the middle of the kitchen, his cup and plate in his hands. 'Where's your dishwasher?'

'You're beginning to sound like my daughter. I don't have one and I don't need one.'

Placing his cup and plate carefully in the sink, he reached for the washing-up liquid.

She took it from his hand. 'There's no need to do that today, but every other day, it will be expected. Let's have some coffee in the sitting room upstairs and I will show you around too.'

'Lily, maybe I should get going.'

She opened the back door and pointed to the rain spitting across the garden. 'I won't let you out in that. I have plenty of room here. Don't be an idiot; enough of the foolish attitude.'

'You have been more than kind, but I shall not trespass on your hospitality any longer,' Sam said.

'Sam, you are obviously a bright man, so stop being so stupid right now. You are staying and that's it. I wouldn't make the offer if I didn't mean it. But why don't we do it on a trial basis for a week or two, then we both have an opt-out option.'

'I don't know what to say.'

'Pour out some coffee for both of us, put it on a tray and follow me to the landing on the first floor.'

She walked out of the kitchen before he could answer, calling out that she liked her coffee black with two lumps of brown sugar. When Sam arrived upstairs with the tray, she had a fire-log lighting in the fireplace. He sat on the armchair opposite her.

She pushed a wooden box across the coffee table to him. 'Cuban cigars; they were my husband's. He saved them all these years, but the time never seemed right for him to smoke one. I have no idea what they are like after all this time, but you are welcome to try one.'

Sam lifted the lid and opened the box, his fingers lightly brushing over the cigars. He breathed deeply, taking in the rich aroma before quickly shutting the box.

'I can't have one, much as I want to. I can't hold one in my hand without a glass of whiskey to accompany it. This is so kind and thoughtful of you, but regrettably, I have to decline.'

Lily took the box of cigars and pushed them into the sideboard drawer. 'Forget I ever offered them and drink your coffee,' she said firmly.

They sat on either side of the fireplace.

'You did well just now. I'm sorry about the cigars.'

'You weren't to know. I will always do well, until I don't. Unfortunately, when I fail, I do so spectacularly and more often publicly. I am a drunk, Lily. Maybe if I wasn't, I wouldn't have been so stupid in the past and I would be sitting by my own fireplace right now, having a very fine cigar.'

'Deal with the here and now. Flashing back to the past isn't always the best course to take.'

'You sound as if you are speaking from experience.'

She didn't answer and he didn't press her. She added a few briquettes to the fire and they watched the flames take hold, swirls of smoke rushing upwards.

Sam sighed. 'The last time I was this comfortable was over a year ago.'

He patted his clothes. 'These things still looked fresh and I suppose I had spent so little time on the streets, I still felt some entitlement to comfort. As bold as brass, I pushed the revolving door of The Shelbourne. I shot down to the men's and had a good wash and splashed on the free eau de toilette. I remember, I picked up a newspaper and sat in a wingback chair very similar to this one, in front of a roaring fire and inside the door. It was busy and I got to sit there for quite a while, before a young lady offered me a menu and asked would I like to order.

'I managed to snatch some more time by saying I was waiting for somebody, but the third time she came back to me, I knew I was rumbled. I saw her talking to a man in a suit and I got up to go. He came over and pressed down on my shoulder. "Sit down sir, have a pot of tea on the house, it's cold out there," he whispered. Not only did they bring tea, but also a plate of biscuits.'

Sam paused, remembering the taste of the biscuit, the richness of the Darjeeling tea.

'I promised that day if I ever improved my circumstances, I would go back to The Shelbourne and thank them for such generosity, when I was so low.'

'I bet you will get to do it, too.'

Sam guffawed. 'Not any time soon.'

Lily giggled and he looked at her, taking in the soft look in her eyes.

'You are a kind person, Lily Walpole.'

'I'll show you to your room,' she said, beckoning him to follow her.

On the second landing, she opened the bedroom door. 'I've made up the bed and I've left a pair of pyjamas for you as well. Just make yourself at home.' She loitered in the doorway.

'Just so you know, I'm telling people on the square, especially Gladys, that you are an old family friend.'

'And your daughter, what about her?'

Lily shook her head.

'I will tell her everything when the time is right, but I need to mull it over first.'

She walked downstairs. She was glad those silk pyjamas would finally be worn. She had, in a moment of extravagance, bought them for her husband many years ago. Reg had said he wouldn't be seen dead in them. She had pushed them to the back of her wardrobe until today. No doubt Sam Carpenter wouldn't complain about wearing silk.

# SEVENTEEN

From: **GladysSpencer@gmail.com**
To: **all De Courcy Square Association members**

Consider us on a war footing.

If you love our beautiful square, know that we face the biggest challenge yet.

The developer Anthony Draper is not for turning. A new resident here at No. 29, he insists he has bought the park and is determined to rip up our heritage and replace our beautiful gardens with a car park, a vandalism beyond our wildest thinking.

A meeting to discuss our overall strategy for the campaign to save the park takes place at the home of Gladys Spencer at No. 64 at 4 p.m. sharp on Thursday. If you can't attend, email any ideas you have or assistance you can offer on this most important and difficult situation.

Gladys Spencer,

Chairperson

Cora was on her way back from the shops when she saw Tom Hooper parked outside No. 23. He jumped from behind the wheel as soon as he saw her cross the road. 'Ms Gartland, do you think you would have time for that chat about my sister's belongings?'

'Please call me Cora.'

'Gartland was Jack's name as well.'

'Yes, I was the fool who took his name without the benefit of a ceremony. I will eventually go back to my own name, but at the moment, it's too much hassle. I think I have enough to contend with right now.'

She showed Tom Hooper into the office. 'The wedding album is here and you're welcome to have a mooch around. How exactly did you want to do this?'

He stopped at his sister's desk, fingering the multicoloured pens in a pot. 'I keep asking myself why didn't I notice? Maybe he made Amelia so happy, I didn't want to suspect any—'

He stopped in mid-sentence. 'I'm being insensitive. Please forgive me.'

Cora sat down at Jack's desk. 'You can't hurt me more than I already have been.'

She stretched out her legs. 'It must have been nice working side by side together like this. I envy her that.'

Tom laughed. 'Don't; she complained bitterly about his shuffling, his constant grazing on snacks, crackling paper and his loud voice on the phone. They were lucky they could work from here. She had a studio in town, although she did a lot of her sketches here, sitting inside the window. But he was a major distraction for her.'

'I can understand that; even when he was in the basement I could hear him. Funny, I always thought Jack was the last man who could run an affair successfully, he would talk himself into being found out.'

'You sound as if you are handling this mess better.'

'Who knows? Good days, bad days, it's only been a few weeks.'

Cora took the vase of dead roses.

'I'm going to get rid of these. Call me if you need me.'

She drained what was left in the vase down the sink, before gathering up the roses to fire them into the bin. The message card had slipped between the stems.

*'Amelia, my light, my love. Your Jack.'*

Crumpling the card, she tossed it in the rubbish after the roses. When Tom sauntered into the kitchen a few minutes later, Cora was washing out the vase at the sink.

'Can I take her stash of pens and the pen holder? I thought my daughter might like them. She's just like Amelia, very organised, knows what she wants from life and loves her stationery.'

Cora nodded. 'Take what you want, and you don't have to do it all today.'

'The wedding album, a few photo frames. My mother asked me about her jewellery, too.'

'I saw it in the bedroom, she had some lovely pieces.'

'Funnily enough, most of them are from a rich aunt in the States.'

Cora led the way upstairs. In the bedroom she opened the dressing-table drawer.

Tom picked out a silver bracelet. 'Mum and Dad bought her this in Weirs, Grafton Street, for her twenty-first.'

He dropped the bracelet back onto the felt lining. 'I'm sorry, it's so raw, I thought I could do this.'

Cora eased out the drawer and placed it on the bed. 'I'll get a box for this lot. I don't have any claim over another woman's jewellery.'

Tom got a handkerchief out and mopped his brow. 'All the things I see in the job, but when it's family, it's different.'

'Take a break, have a coffee.'

'I need a cigarette.'

'You can smoke in the garden or the street, but not in the house.'

She heard him go out the front door as she lifted three fine gold chains into an empty shoe box. Peeping out the window, she saw him exchange a few words with Stacey and throw a few coins in her cup, before crossing the road to survey the corner of the park which had been partly dug up during Draper's survey. When he looked back at the house, he spied Cora at the window and waved. She concentrated on the jewellery. It was easy to see which were the family pieces from the States, the Weiss brooches glinting in the sunlight, the chunky silver jewellery, the pearl choker, all of a certain era.

She was putting the last piece in the box when she noticed a navy velvet pouch. Opening it, a heart-shaped locket on a chain popped out, the gold heart covered in seed pearls. Running her hand over the grainy exterior, she gasped at the beauty of the simple piece, her fingers feeling at the side to see if she could open it. Her heart tightened as it clicked open.

Enclosed in a gold border, a small photo of Jack and Amelia. Side by side, him smiling broadly, her head leaning in to him. She had seen the wedding photos, but this was almost as if she was observing from afar two lovers who could finish each other's sentences. On the other side of the locket, an engraving:

'My Love Forever, Jack.'

She wanted to throw the locket far away, so nobody could look upon it again, but instead, she pushed it back in its velvet pouch and shoved it deep under the other jewellery in the box.

When the doorbell sounded, she ran from the room to let Tom in.

'Is there something wrong?' he asked as he stood in the doorway, his hands in his pockets.

'It's weird handling the jewellery Jack gave his wife, that's all.'

'I'm sorry, I shouldn't have let you do it on your own. There I go, being insensitive again.'

Cora guffawed out loud. 'It's probably insensitive of me to even be here.'

Tom clapped his hands together. 'What else can I do?'

'You have to decide on her clothes and I haven't checked the attic.'

'I don't know what to do with the clothes. It might be a step too far to bring them home. Maybe there's a thrift shop or a shelter. If there is any furniture, I can get St Vincent de Paul to collect it.'

'I like that idea and maybe Stacey would like some of the clothes.'

'She seems to have made herself a permanent fixture. Amelia moved her on a few times, but Jack kept telling her it was all right. He was always soft around a pretty face. I can tell her to find another spot, if you like.'

'No, Stacey is fine where she is. She provides a layer of security for anyone trying to get in to the house, especially if I'm not here.'

'I could think of easier ways, like installing a good alarm system.'

Cora shivered.

'I can finish off another day, if you prefer,' he said.

Cora shook her head. 'I have a few calls to make, so why don't you wander through the house, just pick up whatever you want.'

'Can I come back and look in the attic another time? But there's a print in the kitchen and a few of her old toys I saw on the windowsill on the landing.'

'Take them, take anything you want.'

Feeling suddenly tired and upset she moved past him to the kitchen, leaving him to go upstairs to gather up the last few of Amelia's possessions. Cora cleared the table and pulled off the oilcloth, stuffing it in the bin. She wasn't sure why she did this, only she hated that Amelia had probably picked it. She took down the Andy Warhol print from the wall and put the espresso machine beside it. When Tom came down the stairs, she called out to him.

'The print, and do you want that fancy coffee machine?'

'Amelia didn't drink coffee, she loved her herbal teas.'

'Jack couldn't live without strong espresso. Now, I even hate the smell of coffee.'

'You could sell it.'

'No, I could sell the house. Please take it, give it to somebody who will use it.'

Reluctantly, Tom picked up the machine. Cora followed behind carrying the Warhol print.

'What were they like, the two of them together?'

'Do you really want me to answer that?'

She nodded.

'They appeared to be great together, though Amelia was fed up of all his travelling to the States.'

'Were they ever going to get around that?'

Tom perched the coffee machine on the hall table. 'The last time I talked to Amelia, she told me she had issued an ultimatum to Jack, to give up the job which required him to be away for so long or she would go it alone.'

'Jack was never a man for ultimatums.'

Tom hesitated as if he wanted to say something else, but instead he picked up the machine and, taking the big print in his other hand, he said he had better get along.

When he had everything piled into his car, he hopped back

up the steps, dropping a few more coins in Stacey's cup on the way.

'We don't know what Jack thought of the ultimatum she was giving him at dinner that night. She was right that if they were starting a family, either he had to change his job, or they had to decide where they wanted to live.'

'But they had this place.'

'Amelia insisted this was home and she wanted to bring up her child around her family.' He swallowed hard. 'I'd better go, I've said too much already.'

Cora looked at him, his face scrunched up, his eyes staring like he was trying to stop the tears. 'Don't hold back on my account.'

He shook his head and pushed his hands deep into his jacket pockets. 'I'm a detective, I ask questions and I sure as hell would like to know why their car went off the road on a straight stretch on a summer's night.'

He stopped to take out his handkerchief and pat his brow. 'Except there's no black box in his bloody car.'

Cora studied the ground. 'Jack was always one for speeding.'

'Amelia was driving that night and she never went over the speed limit, ever.'

He was moving from one foot to another like an anxious child. When he put out his hand for her to shake, she took it. 'Come back if you want to go up to the attic or if you think you've forgotten anything.'

'You will look after her clothes, send them to a charity shop?'

'I'll arrange for them to come around and collect.'

He was halfway down the steps when he turned back. 'Don't mind what I said just now; she had so much to live for, it's damn hard to believe she's gone.'

'I know, it's easier if we blame somebody, anybody. This is so exhausting.'

He nodded before getting in to his car and driving off.

Gladys, spotting Cora at the door called out to her and beetled across the street. 'Any chance that detective would help us?'

'Gladys, he was here to pick up some of his sister's possessions.'

'Sorry, I was just hoping he had some influence.'

Gladys leaned against the railings. 'Hannah, Lily's daughter, says we will have to go to the High Court and that's going to cost a fortune. Nobody around here has that money and the big companies in all the offices don't really care what happens to our park.' She ran her hand along the railing. 'If the park goes, the square is nothing.'

'Maybe you should call in the press, tell the newspapers what's going on, get some publicity.'

Gladys's face brightened. 'I might even know a journalist who can help. No hack worth his or her salt would pass on this story when they hear about the plans for the car park. Brilliant idea, Cora. I'm even willing to overlook that Tom Hooper insists on parking his private car here without a permit.'

She shot off, with a spring in her step and a determination to get the plight of the square into the national news headlines.

# EIGHTEEN

Sam and Lily settled into a routine. Each morning he made a pot of Earl Grey tea and put it on a tray with a china cup and saucer, a small sugar bowl and a jug of milk, and brought it upstairs to the sitting room. Knocking gently on her bedroom door, he announced her tea was served.

'Just how you like it and where you can enjoy the goings-on in the square,' he said before going downstairs to potter in the back garden. She liked that he left her to savour the peace and quiet. This morning, on the fourth day of their share arrangement, she couldn't settle to enjoy her tea, pacing instead around the sitting room, wringing her hands with worry. She had to tell Hannah about Sam today. Gladys had set up a meeting at her house in the late afternoon and had invited Hannah to discuss possible court action against Draper and his plans for the park. Lily must sit down with her daughter before that.

She stood looking out at the park as she rang Hannah on her mobile.

'Hi Mum, are you OK?'

'Yes darling. Do you think we could meet before the Association appointment this afternoon?'

'I'm up to my eyes; can it wait until afterwards?'

When Lily didn't answer, Hannah pressed her mother softly.

'Is everything all right?'

'I have something I want to discuss with you, it's important.'

'You're worrying me, Mum. What is it?'

'Hannah, I know I'm sounding mysterious, but just fifteen minutes at lunchtime.'

She heard her daughter sigh heavily.

'All right, can you meet me in the coffee shop beside my office at one-thirty? I won't have long though, I'm getting pretty backed up and I have to be in De Courcy Square for four.'

'Thanks, darling.'

She heard her daughter mumble something and she knew she was a little annoyed to have to fit Lily in to her day, but too worried not to.

Lily put her phone away and sat watching the park. Where the railings had been taken down looked untidy and already people she didn't know had climbed over a makeshift barrier to have a gawk at the private gardens.

When she heard Sam hoovering downstairs, she returned to her room to get dressed. She was careful in her choice of clothes, opting for her usual skirt and blouse and button-up cardigan rather than the newer, flashier garments she wore around Sam. Lily wanted to tell Hannah in her own way and not have her daughter jump to conclusions before she could even speak.

Sam was putting away the hoover when Lily walked into the kitchen.

'Is there something wrong?' he said.

'Why do you ask?'

He shoved the hoover flex into the cupboard and turned to Lily.

'Because when something is bothering you, you pull at your fingers, and you're doing that now.'

Lily immediately stopped and pushed her hands in her skirt pockets.

'You're too observant,' she mumbled as she stepped out into the garden.

'It comes from my time on the street, plenty of time to observe others.'

Lily paced around the garden, stopping to deadhead the puce-pink dahlia.

'I was thinking of planting some spring bulbs under the lilac; it will give a nice splash of colour,' he said.

'Tulips, all colours would be lovely.'

He cleared off the bench where the spent fuchsia blooms had fallen, creating red streaks on the wood.

'I'm going to tell Hannah about you when I meet her at lunchtime,' Lily said as she sat down.

'I'm glad,' he said quietly sitting beside Lily and throwing crumbs in an attempt to entice the robin, who was watching them from the branches of the lilac.

'How do you think she will take it?' he asked.

'I suppose it depends on what I tell her. I'm not sure I'm brave enough to say you have moved in.'

The robin fluttered down and snatched a fluffy segment of bread before flying into the scrub underneath the lilac.

'I don't know Hannah, but I'm not sure it's a good idea not to to tell her the whole story. She deserves to know.'

Lily got up to pull at the seed heads forming on the sweet peas.

'It's just Hannah loved her dad so much, I'm not sure how she will handle another man living here at number 22.'

Sam didn't answer but took his spade and went to the far corner of the garden, where he began to dig out a foundation for a small raised patio so Lily could sit out and enjoy the sunshine in the late afternoons.

Lily closed her eyes. She liked the sound of Sam working in the garden. It reminded her of her stolen time with Eamon when she would sit out on one of the park benches as he dug and weeded a flower bed nearby. She had pretended to be reading *Pride and Prejudice,* at times holding up the book so she could steal a glance at Eamon. Sometimes he walked past with a wheelbarrow, making sure he could stop beside her so they could exchange a few words. They had been innocent times. When her phone rang, she didn't want to answer it and leave her daydreaming behind.

'Mum, I have a cancellation and I'm very near De Courcy, can I call over?'

Panic streamed through Lily.

'I'm not dressed, just give me a few minutes.'

'Are you sure you're all right? It's not like you to be still in your dressing gown at near eleven in the morning.'

'I'm fine; am I not allowed a pyjama day once in a while?'

'Well, as long as that's all it is; don't dress up for me. I'll see you in ten.'

Sam was standing in front of Lily.

'Maybe it would be a good idea if we met.'

Lily shook her head.

'Sam, please, she can't meet you, not before I have had time to explain things to her.'

He shook his head and pulled off his gardening jacket.

'I'd better go for my walk then,' he said, his voice low.

'Do you mind?'

'I'm not happy, but you're the boss,' he said, taking his coat from the hall stand before going out the front door, letting it thud shut behind him.

Lily felt a fool and she was annoyed at herself for putting

Sam out of the house. When she heard the key in the lock, she pulled the door back so quickly, she nearly fell over.

'What's the matter, Mum?' Hannah said, her hand holding her key, still suspended in the air.

'The wind caught me by surprise. Come, we'll go through to the kitchen.'

'You got dressed. I thought it was a pyjama day.'

'Old habits die hard, I guess. Your father would never have approved of me answering the front door in my nightdress and dressing gown.'

'Daddy was a silly stickler. Mum, why did you want to meet, when we're going to be at the same meeting later?'

Lily sat at the kitchen table opposite her daughter.

'I have something to tell you, and all that I ask is that you hear me out.'

'Oh God, you aren't ill, are you?'

'Nothing like that, I wanted to tell you about my new friend Sam Carpenter.'

'What friend, how long has this being going on?' Hannah leaned her elbows on the table.

'It's not like that, we are simply good friends.'

'Mum, I'm happy for you, it's nice to see you finally get a life of your own.'

Lily took her daughter's hand.

'It's nice for me to have Sam around. I have asked him to stay here, I hope you don't mind.'

'For a few days, or what?' Lily took a deep breath.

'He has moved in to the spare room on the second landing.'

'My old room.'

'Yes, but you haven't been in that room for a long time.'

Hannah stood up and switched on the kettle.

'Isn't this all a bit rushed? What do you know about this man?'

'I know he's the kindest man I have ever met. When you meet him, I'm sure you will think the same.'

Hannah threw a teabag in a mug and poured the boiling water from the kettle on it.

'All fraudsters are good at projecting a genial image. Where is this guy from? I have a friend who is a garda and he may be able to check him out.'

'Don't be silly, Han. Sam is the sweetest man and the best friend. You were always complaining I was vulnerable on my own. I'm not on my own anymore. Surely, you can be happy about that.'

'How much is he paying in rent?' Hannah, who was about to sip her tea, put the mug down carefully on the table. 'Don't tell me he's not paying any rent,' she said, her voice high-pitched with worry.

'He was down on his luck and I just offered him accommodation to give him a chance to get back on his feet.'

'Down on his luck? For God's sake, Mum, what sort of person have you let in to our house?'

'No worse than has been here in the past, I assure you.'

Once Lily had spoken the words, she regretted them.

'I hope you're not talking about Daddy. That man worked night and day to give us a good life.'

Lily, her hands under the table, grabbed a bunch of the oil-cloth and squeezed hard.

'Hannah, of course I expect you to defend your father, but things were a little different from this angle.'

'What do you mean?'

Lily shook her head.

'Your father loved you, but he wasn't the easiest man to live with.'

Hannah put down her cup.

'It doesn't mean you can shack up with the first man you meet.'

Lily stood up. 'Hannah, I won't have you talking to me like that. If you met Sam, you would know he is a good, kind man.'

'I have no intention of meeting this man.'

Hannah dragged her handbag towards her. 'I have to get going, we will have to talk about this another time.'

'I've told you, I don't need to talk about it further, unless you would like to meet Sam.'

'Mother, I have to go, I don't have time to fight about this anymore.'

Lily let her daughter go. If she attempted to stop her, she knew there would be an even bigger row. She wasn't sure if she would go to the meeting later; Hannah needed her space and distance right now.

Lily climbed the stairs to the sitting room after Hannah had left. Her heart was heavy but she was determined in her resolve not to be swayed by Hannah's fears over Sam. Reg would have been horrified, but a dead man's opinions didn't count anymore. She had finally met a man she liked very much, a man who was a very good friend and a man she trusted more than anyone. She was not prepared to let that go, not even for her daughter.

When she heard Sam's key in the lock, she called down to him. She heard him hang his coat on the rack before making his way upstairs.

'How did it go?' he asked softly.

'I told her you had moved in. She needs time to adjust. I think I'll give the meeting this afternoon a skip.'

'Gladys won't be happy.'

'All Gladys needs is Hannah. With my daughter on her side, she is sure to win.

# NINETEEN

Cora wasn't sure if she should go to the meeting Gladys had arranged in her home, but she was curious. As she walked up the steps, she heard Gladys talking in a shrill voice, fussing about how many biscuits to put out with the flasks of tea and coffee. Sighing, Cora made to turn back, but it was too late to reconsider as Gladys opened the front door.

'You're the first one, fair play to you. Lily hasn't bothered to show her face yet, though she promised to be here in time to set up.'

'Just give her a few minutes. Is Hannah here yet?'

'Thank goodness she isn't, because I haven't decided whether to go with china cups and saucers or plain mugs for the beverages.'

Gladys showed Cora into the front ground-floor sitting room. A dark room, it had heavy velvet drapes and net curtains on the large window looking out on the square and an embossed wallpaper on the walls. The furniture had been pushed back and light foldaway chairs set up in front of a table at the fireplace.

'I've no idea how many are coming or if anybody is coming. This is all so stressful, I don't know why I do it.'

'You do it because you love where you live. It's a mighty fine reason,' Cora said and she noticed Gladys appeared suddenly a little taller.

'Thank you, Cora. I am one of life's worriers. Not that anyone who sees me fighting this latest threat will realise. I was up half the night wondering if I should go for the bright sitting room upstairs. It's much larger, with two long windows over-looking the park, but it would be a huge disruption for my Tony.'

'Tony?'

'Yes, my husband. He's in a wheelchair and I don't think he would like strangers traipsing through the house; he can just about cope with us using the formal parlour. Tony loves the park, he hates what's happening but he's not one for agitating.'

'I'm sorry, I thought you lived here alone,' Cora said.

Gladys took a silver tray and terrine off the top of the side-board. 'We'll need space for the mugs and biscuits,' she said as she opened the sideboard and pushed them in on a shelf. She turned to Cora.

'You know, just like Amelia, when I moved in here all those years ago, I thought this house would be soon teeming with kids, but it didn't work out that way. Poor Tony ended up in a wheel-chair and we live in this lovely house that is too big for us and totally impracticable for anyone with a disability.'

'I'm sorry, I didn't know.'

'I didn't tell you. I don't until I get the measure of a person.'

Cora wandered to the fireplace where a watercolour in a white frame was hanging. A canal view, it was strangely at odds with its surroundings.

'I know what you are going to say: we should have an impor-tant oil painting hanging there, but I like that canal scene.'

Gladys walked over and pointed at the painting. 'You see the bridge and canal lock, that's where Tony proposed to me.'

She stopped and swallowed as if the memory of decades ago stirred up pain inside her.

Shaking herself and straightening her dress, she walked away from the fireplace.

'Don't mind me, I'm rabbiting on because I'm nervous.'

'I think it's a lovely story and a great reason to have that work on prominent display,' Cora said gently.

'Do you really think so? Others have laughed at my little watercolour, but I love it.'

The sound of people arriving at the front door stopped their conversation and Gladys clapped her hands in anticipation.

'Let the fun begin,' she said as she marched to greet her visitors, stopping to fix her hair in front of the hall mirror before she swung back the door. Three residents from across the square and two managers of the offices on either side of Gladys's home trooped into the hall.

'Our solicitor will be here shortly. In the meantime, my good friend Cora from number 23 will serve tea or coffee,' Gladys said, throwing a glance at Cora who immediately put the waiting tray of mugs and biscuits on the sideboard beside the flasks.

'Even if we only get five more, it will be enough to show Hannah we're serious,' Gladys whispered to Cora.

When the doorbell chimed again, Gladys scooted to the door expecting it to be Lily. When she saw Anthony Draper, she was shocked.

'Mr Draper, I realise you are a resident of the square and you are on the Association mailing list, but it is not appropriate for you to seek admission to this meeting,' she said in her prim voice.

'It would be nice if I could address the meeting in the interests of fairness.'

Gladys stepped back to allow old Mr Foley and two residents she only knew by sight into the hall. When she was sure they were out of earshot, she stepped out onto the top step directly in front of Draper.

'What was fair about you buying the park? What is fair about your plans for a car park? Don't dare insult me on my own doorstep like this. You don't even know the meaning of fair.'

'Mrs Spencer, I'm merely asking to address the meeting and answer questions. I'm not here to cause trouble.'

'That may be so Mr Draper, but you are not welcome. What do you take me for, a complete fool?'

'I would never make such a presumption. But I did think you had a sense of fair play and your blocking me from the meeting disappoints me greatly,' Draper said as he turned to walk down the steps.

He was on the street when Gladys called out to him.

'Your opinion of me, Mr Draper, does not matter one jot. I hope the next time we see each other will be in court.'

Anthony Draper did not reply, but waved cheerily at Gladys, which made her feel very cross.

Hannah, who was locking her car, called out to Gladys.

'Mrs Spencer, sorry I'm late.'

Not sure how much of the exchange with Draper Hannah had heard, Gladys smiled weakly and held the door open for the solicitor. She stood back as Hannah, a briefcase in her hand, walked into the sitting room and took a seat at the table.

'I think you had better introduce her,' Cora prompted Gladys, who was all of a sudden feeling very nervous.

At the table she leaned over to Hannah.

'Maybe we should wait for Lily, she assured me she would be here.'

'I'm tight for time, you can send a briefing email later.'

Gladys thought she detected a clipped tone in Hannah's delivery, but she ignored it and instead stood up and rang the little bell normally used by Tony, to call the meeting to attention.

'Thank you all for coming. As you know we have to devise a strategy to fight the plans for a car park in the site of our beautiful private gardens. You all know what has happened and I thank you for your unstinting support and ask you to give a hundred and fifty per cent now as we go deeper into battle. Solicitor Hannah Walpole is here to advise on the legal route.'

A few people at the front clapped as Hannah stood up.

'As some of you know, I grew up at number 22 and I know how important the park is for all those who use these houses, those who live here and those who work here. Mrs Spencer is correct, you all know the troubled history and the fact that the local authority took its eye off the ball, so to speak, and Anthony Draper who is the new owner of number 29 bought out the leasehold in the park and is the legal owner.'

'Can't we sue over that?' a woman at the back asked.

'I'm not sure what you mean exactly by that, but why don't I outline what I think is the best course of action,' Hannah said politely and firmly.

'Hear, hear,' Gladys said, ringing the bell again for effect.

'In my opinion, I think the Association should apply for an injunction. Mr Draper has publicly declared in a newspaper interview today that he intends to apply for planning permission for a multi-storey car park, most of which will be underground. However, in the meantime, because we know the planning process can take such a long time, he intends as of this Friday to open De Courcy Square park as a car park, charging ten euros a day.'

'Surely, he can't do that,' Cora said.

'Never underestimate the lengths a person like Draper will go to. I think it would be foolhardy to ignore him,' Hannah said.

She waited until the room quietened down before continuing.

'I have given this a lot of thought and I think that by showing his hand in relation to his car park plans, Draper may be doing us a favour. I intend to draft papers and go in to court to seek an interim injunction against the use of the park as a car park until there can be a full hearing of the case for a permanent injunction.

'It will buy us time and hopefully Draper will see sense and a deal can be struck. I have a meeting with the council next in an attempt to unravel the mystery of how Draper got his hands on the lease in the first place.'

Hannah said she would happily answer any questions if they were emailed to her but she would have to leave the meeting as she was required at the Four Courts.

Gladys walked Hannah to the door.

'I am very disappointed Lily didn't make it. Do you know, is she ill or something?' she asked.

'I really don't know, Mrs Spencer. I suggest you talk to the meeting about how you are going to fund the legal action and I'll begin drafting the papers – with a view to going into court as soon as possible.'

Gladys nodded and stood in the doorway as Hannah made her way back to the car.

A number of people from the offices pushed past, calling out 'thank you', so when she went back into the front room there were only a few residents still there.

'Any ideas on how we are going to fund this court action?' Gladys asked.

When there was no response, she flopped down at the table.

'Can I just ask everyone to put on their thinking caps and email me any ideas.'

Gladys knew she hadn't pushed hard enough, but maybe she could wrestle donations out of each house so they could give some sort of down payment to the solicitor. She made a mental note to delete No. 29 from the Association email list.

Cora waited and helped Gladys fold away the chairs and restore the sofa and armchairs to their rightful place in the front parlour before she left to return to No. 23. As she walked down the side of the square, she noticed a small group had gathered at the corner directly opposite Nos. 22 and 23.

Lily backed away from the crowd when she saw Cora approaching.

'Did Gladys miss me?'

'We all did, what's going on here?'

'Draper is only publicly advertising car parking spaces in the gardens from next Friday.'

'Hannah says it will help us get an injunction; you should ring and tell her.'

Cora thought Lily looked a bit put out at the suggestion.

'I'm sure Gladys is on top of it,' she said before making to go back inside No. 22.

# TWENTY

De Courcy Square needs you.

Residents and friends, I implore you not to use the abomination of a car park being advertised at our beautiful square.

We have got to come together to fight this threat. We need
every skill, every idea and all your strength and support to
fight this battle.

Please help in any way you can.

Gladys Spencer,
Chairperson

When Lily woke up, Sam had already gone out, leaving a note
saying he would be back before noon. After breakfast, wanting a
little time on her own, Lily set off for a stroll by the canal. She

walked out of the square, hoping Gladys wouldn't spy her and start a long conversation. Meandering down the uneven canal path, she kept her head down, to make sure she didn't trip and fall. She sat at a low bench hidden behind a tree and watched the water, the sounds of the city fading as a family of ducks glided past, the ducklings proudly in convoy after their mother. She used to meet Eamon at this very bench. She would sit gazing at the water, waiting to hear his footstep. She always carried a book in case anybody saw her and word got back home that she had been seen gallivanting down by the canal.

Sometimes Eamon had stolen up on her, placing his hands over her eyes and whispering in her ear. She loved it, but she'd always pretended to be cross, in case somebody had seen them together. When she saw Sam strolling further down the canal, her heart fluttered. When he saw her, he waved, quickening his pace to a brisk walk. Two women in tracksuits, their hair in high ponytails, power-walked behind Sam, gaining ground on him. Ducks squawking and kicking up a racket further up the canal caught Lily's attention and she craned her neck to see what was happening, laughing when she saw they were squabbling over a sinking empty crisp bag.

When she heard the thud of somebody falling heavily, she swung round anxiously. Fear gripped her heart. Sam was on his hands and knees as the two women in tracksuits stood over him laughing. When he shouted, the woman in grey pushed down on his back, rolling him over. Lily heard the words 'money' and 'cash'. She frantically looked all around her. Nobody else was on this stretch of canal.

Dialing 999, she spoke urgently into her phone as she pretended to look the other way.

'I need help, my friend is being beaten up, mugged.'

'Where are you, caller?'

'By the canal, on the city side of Baggot Street bridge. Please hurry, I think they are going to kill him.'

'Help is on the way.'

'One of them just kicked him, please tell them to hurry.'

'Stay calm, help will be with you very soon.'

Lily put the phone down. Her heart was thumping. She saw Sam on the path pull hard at the legs of one of the women and unbalance her. In the confusion he got to his feet and hobbled towards a group of buildings. The two women, squealing with delight, ran after him. Lily knew they had caught up with him, because she heard their angry shouts telling him to hand over his money.

Leaping from the bench, she chased after them as well as she could, ignoring the stiff protests from parts of her body. Just before the side street, she stopped, straightened up and, gathering her handbag in front of her, turned the corner, singing a song at the top of her voice. Sam was on the ground, his assailants standing over him. One aimed another kick at his upper body as he cried out in pain, covering his head with his hands before steeling himself for another blow.

'You're are wasting our precious time, what do you mean you have no money?' one of the women screeched in his ear.

Lily let a jumble of words tumble from her mouth so she sounded like a mad woman.

She didn't know how she belted the words out or how she walked towards Sam and his attackers with an arm outstretched as if she was striding across the stage, but she did, singing a song at the top of her voice.

The two women turned around. Sam, whimpering on the ground, waved his hand, signalling to Lily to stay away. The girl in the grey tracksuit stepped in front of Lily.

'What have we here, a bleeding songbird?'

Lily put on a 'mad staring eyes' look and continued singing.

'What do you think? I'm on stage at the Gaiety tonight,' Lily asked, when she stopped to catch her breath.

The girl started to laugh. 'And I'm a bleeding top model.'

She placed her hands on her hips and swanked about. The woman in black pushed her. 'Shut the fuck up, let's get out of here, that nutter is trouble,' she shouted.

The woman in grey dithered in front of Lily, who sang the only line which she could muster, she was so afraid.

'Would you ever shut up, you looney,' the girl in grey shouted in Lily's face, before trotting off, whooping into the air as she tried to catch up with her friend.

Lily stood still for a few seconds, terrified to move, feeling the wet of the woman's spittle as it dried on her face. Sam's low moaning jolted her back to the present. Quickly, she rolled him onto his side.

'Lily, you could have got yourself killed,' he choked.

'And so could you,' she said, her voice full of concern as she saw blood gush from a gash on his head. 'Help is on the way, best not to use up your energy talking.'

She hummed the refrain from 'My Way' over and over, because she was so afraid of the women returning or Sam taking a turn for the worse.

'I never knew you could sing,' Sam said and she was oddly relieved at his comment.

When two security men from the office block opposite ran over to help, she stood up and shouted at them. 'Where were you when this poor man needed help? Were you going to let them kill him first?'

One of them stopped in his tracks and shrugging his shoulders, turned back. The other walked over to Lily. 'You could have been killed, you know that; those two are trouble with a capital T.'

Lily ignored him, stepping out into the road, ready to flag down the ambulance and gardai when she heard the sirens in the distance. She protested when the paramedics insisted she be checked out as well, but travelled in the ambulance holding Sam's hands.

'You will get through this, you will be fine. You have to be, for us,' she said, holding his hand gently in case she hurt him. He could not respond, because he was wearing an oxygen mask, but he ruffled her fingertips.

At the hospital, they were placed in separate cubicles. Lily thought she should ring Hannah, but there was no point alarming her. Her daughter had a heart of gold, but there was no doubt she would use this incident to exert even more pressure on Lily to move out of De Courcy Square. Taking a deep breath, she dialled Gladys.

'Oh my God, I knew you shouldn't be out walking each day. You have been ambling around with a target on your back.'

Lily ignored the last remark. 'We just need to get home, Gladys.'

'I'm leaving now and will be with you in thirty minutes. Do you want me to ring Hannah?'

'No, let's not get Hannah all worried.'

Gladys wanted to say something, but thought better of it. 'Give me a half an hour,' she said.

After the phone call, Lily felt quite jaded and she lay back on the pillows and closed her eyes. A doctor gently touched her arm to wake her about fifteen minutes later. 'Sam says you saved his life. You were brave, but for a woman your age, I wouldn't advise intervening in street rows. You got off lightly this time; that might not happen again,' the doctor said severely.

'Will Sam be all right?'

'Bruising mainly and a fracture to his lower arm. He needs lots of rest. You two are going to have to find a safer place for your daily walks.'

'Can I see him?'

The doctor called a nurse, who brought a wheelchair and insisted Lily be wheeled to Sam's cubicle.

Sam, his skin grey with blotches of bruising and his arm in a sling, was sitting up in bed.

'My brave songbird,' he said, holding his hand out to her.

Stepping out of the wheelchair, she kissed him gently on the cheek, before sitting down at the bedside and laying her head on his chest.

'If you hadn't been there, Lily…'

She put her fingers up to his lips. 'Hush, from now on it's the two of us against the world.'

She sat up and got a tissue from her bag to blot the tears as they slipped down his face.

'Are you all right, did they check you over?' he asked.

'A little bit of singing never hurt anybody,' Lily smiled, sitting at the edge of the bed.

'You saved my life.'

'Don't be silly, it was just right time, right place.'

'Like it was wrong place, wrong time for me.'

Sam pulled himself up higher on the pillows. 'There was no rhyme or reason to it. They thought I had money. The gardai think they saw me leaving the bank nearby and thought I had cash on me.'

'What were you doing in the bank?'

'I went to enquire about opening an account, now that I have an address. Sorry, I meant to discuss it with you. I was going to ask about using your address, if you thought our arrangement was working.'

'You probably should have discussed it with me first, but I forgive you.'

'Those women didn't do their homework, I had the sum total of two fivers in my pocket.'

'It was the suit, no doubt, gives off an aura.'

'It might have at one time, but not anymore,' Sam laughed.

'The doctors say you are good to go. Gladys is on her way to bring us home.'

They sat quietly until they heard the familiar clack of Gladys's heels as she walked down the ward. 'Yoo hoo, Lily, where are you?' Gladys whispered as she patrolled the length of the ward.

'Two down on the left side,' Lily said, without even moving.

Gladys pushed back the curtain. 'My good lord, look at you two.'

'We are fine, Gladys, really,' Lily said, helping Sam as he swung his legs to the ground.

'Let this be a lesson to you both, not to be wandering around Dublin city.'

Lily turned on Gladys. 'Not now, please.'

'I suppose all's well that ends well. I'm so grateful you are both all right. But can we go? I have to get back to the De Courcy Square Association business.' Feeling it was necessary to explain herself, Gladys added, 'I'm rather busy, I don't like to leave the park unsupervised. There are some fine specimens of old trees there; it would break my heart if any were felled in my absence.'

Sam was humming a song.

'Are you sure he's all right?' Gladys said.

'It's our song,' Lily said and Gladys gave her a funny look. 'Excuse me?'

Sam laughed. 'She started singing it, that's why my attackers ran away.'

'You could say I did it my way,' Lily said.

They giggled and Gladys shook her head, saying they had better get on.

'I think I'll ring Brogans to send chicken chasseur for two and dessert. That will do us a lot more good than sitting around this bloody hospital,' Lily said as they made their way out. She phoned the restaurant and placed the order from the car, so when the doorbell rang soon after they arrived at De Courcy Square, she thought it was her food delivery.

'Can you carry it in to the...' she started to say as she rooted in her handbag for change for a tip.

'Mum, are you all right? How is Sam?' Hannah asked.

Lily couldn't answer. Sam, who had gone upstairs to lie down came out onto the landing.

Lily pushed her bag onto the hall table. 'It was Gladys, she told you.'

Hannah threw her arms around her mother.

'I'm so glad she did. You two could have been killed.'

Sam began to walk down the stairs. Hannah pulled away from her mother.

'Mr Carpenter, I'm very glad you are all right. What a nasty experience for you.' Lily watched as Hannah extended her hand to Sam.

'Thank you dear, I'm glad you're here,' she whispered to Hannah.

'Your mother was the hero, if she hadn't tackled my attackers, I might just be another name on the crime statistics,' Sam said as he firmly shook Hannah's hand.

'What?'

Lily immediately put her arm around her daughter's shoulders.

'Brogans are sending round a fine lunch. Stay and we'll tell you all about it.'

'You'd better, and I don't want to hear of either of you walking by that canal again,' Hannah said as they walked to the kitchen.

When the doorbell buzzed, Sam turned back to the front door to collect the food.

'Sam is a good friend, I want you to get to know each other,' Lily said and Hannah smiled, sitting down at the table as her mother set a third place.

# TWENTY-ONE

From: **GladysSpencer@gmail.com**
To: **all De Courcy Square Association members**

URGENT NOTICE.

Dear residents and tenants,

Now is the time to come out and show how much you care
for our beautiful park at De Courcy Square. Join us for a
huge rally on the square on Wednesday morning, starting at
8 a.m. We have picked the time to coincide with the most
traffic on the square.

Let's get the word out on social media that Anthony Draper
wants to ruin this beautiful green area, which is so important
to the Dublin landscape. Tell the newspapers, talk about it on
Twitter, everything will help in this battle to save our park. We
will not allow this car park under any circumstances.

On a separate note, we send our good wishes to Mr Samuel

Carpenter who was viciously attacked as he walked in the
neighbourhood. Another reason why we need our private
park back.

Gladys Spencer,
Chairperson

Gladys used the loudhailer like a weapon. Standing on a
kitchen chair she had dragged across the road earlier, the
squeaky loudhailer gave her the confidence to begin marshalling
the crowd, which had been gathering since well before the
allotted time. Tentatively, she spoke a first few words, asking
those protesting to do so in a manner which was respectful and
polite, befitting this lovely old square.

'I knew we should have had a stage built. People won't stay
if they're not being entertained,' she muttered to Lily. As if on
cue, two women at the back sauntered off and another man
propped his placard neatly against a lamp post before slipping
away. Gladys was about to summon the man to return when
two men in suits joined the group, swelling the numbers to over
twenty. Mr Foley took out a hammer and nails and nailed his
placard across the sign advertising the car park. When two cars
made to turn in to the car park, he waved his stick until the
others joined him in blocking the entrance.

'There are enough people against the car park for us to send
a very firm message to that weasel Draper,' Lily said.

'And with that loudhailer, he has no choice but to listen,'
Cora said, making those around her giggle.

Gladys handed the loudhailer to Lily.

'You're not expecting me to talk into that, I hope?' Lily said.

'Don't be silly, I just want my hands free for a moment.'

Quickly, Gladys took out her powder compact and lipstick
from her skirt pocket. Angling herself so she got the light on her

face, she touched up her lipstick and slapped a little powder across her nose and cheeks.

'What in heavens name are you doing, Gladys?' Lily said.

'If there are any press photographers here, I want to look my best. Lipstick smudges on the teeth ruin everything,' she said, running her finger across her teeth, before hurriedly pocketing her cosmetics and snatching back the loudhailer. Before Lily had a chance to answer back, Gladys had called the crowd to attention.

'Ladies and gentlemen, thank you for gathering so early in the morning in our beautiful square. We are here to say no to development and hands off our park.' She shouted the last bit, so her words boomed across the square, making some working in the surrounding offices wander to the windows for a gawk.

'We are here today to send a message to developer Anthony Draper, the latest resident of De Courcy Square, that we will not stand idly by and let our park be vandalised and turned into a car park.'

The crowd cheered and Gladys, heartened by the reception, raised her voice even louder.

'Where will our children play? Where will we walk in this city, if we can't stroll in our own park? Who does he think he is, to take over our park and think he can turn it in to a car park? We won't let that happen, we will die first.'

Lily tugged at the hem of Gladys's skirt. 'Steady on girl, don't lose the run of yourself.'

Gladys gently kicked out at Lily, to push her away. When she spoke again, her voice blasted across the square, bouncing against the houses at the other side.

'Mr Draper has to know we will not rest until this threat to our beautiful square is gone. We will go to court, we will fight to the bitter end to protect this beautiful patch of green. We will not give up. If we have to lie down in front of machinery, we will. The residents and friends of De Courcy Square will not give up.'

A crowd of young men in shirt sleeves cheered loudly. Lily tutted her disapproval as Gladys, feeling a surge of adrenalin, shouted Anthony Draper's name through the loudhailer.

'Come out from where you are hiding, Anthony Draper; face the people of Dublin,' she said.

Her hand on her hip, she turned to the crowd and made a face, before raising the loudhailer again. 'Come and tell us why you want to destroy our beautiful park,' she said, to the whoops of the crowd.

Lily tugged hard on Gladys's skirt this time. 'Enough, wrap it up.'

Gladys bent down. 'Why? They're loving it.'

'That lot, Gladys, would cheer on a goat if it meant they were away from their desks. The real battle is elsewhere.'

Gladys was about to answer back, when a man at the back of the crowd raised his hands over his head and clapped loudly. Gladys hesitated. Lily saw her feet on the chair skip about as if she was trying to run on one spot. A quietness descended on the crowd, which parted to allow Anthony Draper, still in his pyjamas and dressing gown, through. 'Mrs Spencer, pardon my attire, but your early morning protest caught me while I was still trying to get my beauty sleep.'

Gladys shook her head, raising the loudhailer so she was shouting to the sky. 'Thank you, Mr Draper, for attending this protest. Know this: we, the members of the De Courcy Square Association and friends of the De Courcy Square campaign will not be intimidated in any way by your presence here. We are firm in our resolve.'

The group clapped in appreciation.

'I wouldn't expect it any other way,' he said, bowing to Gladys.

He made to walk away, but hesitated before turning to the crowd.

'The car park remains open. Tell your friends, just ten euros a day and you couldn't be nearer the city centre.

Lily grabbed the loudhailer from a surprised Gladys. 'Lily Walpole here. I have lived all my life at De Courcy Square. I beg you to give all your support to save this beautiful park. I too, am willing to occupy this park, day and night, to prevent its destruction. We ask the same commitment from all of you.'

One or two people at the front cheered.

She saw Anthony Draper return to No. 29, where he banged the front door so hard, a puff of dust rose up from around the lintel.

Gladys did a little dance, nearly falling off the chair. 'We have shown him up good, he knows we are no pushover now,' she whispered to Cora, who helped her to the ground.

'Was it wise, though? He must be very angry,' Lily said, but Gladys ignored her, turning her attention to a newspaper reporter who had asked her for an interview.

Sam shook his head. 'I knew Anthony in the past. This is exactly what he wants, plenty of publicity. I think negotiation and mediation would be better than confrontation.'

'Try telling that to Gladys,' Lily said as she beckoned to Cora to come over. Lily tipped her neighbour on the elbow. 'Sam is off into town. I would invite you for a coffee, but I would prefer to share a brandy.'

'This early?'

'What early? At my age, I have my tipple when I feel like it, not when somebody else decides. Besides, I want to show you something.'

'How can I resist, when you are being so mysterious.'

Lily looked over her shoulder. 'In that case let's lift our legs and disappear, before Gladys decides she wants to march on Government Buildings.'

When they got in the house, Lily led the way to the dining room. 'I know Amelia's brother has been to see you, and I have something you may want to share with him.'

She reached into the china cabinet and took out an envelope. 'Bear with me, Cora, but I have wondered whether I should leave well alone.'

'What do you mean?'

'I am in two minds whether or not I should be raising ghosts.'

'What are you talking about?'

Lily drummed her fingers across the envelope. 'Maybe the brandy first?' she said as if procrastinating would make the task easier.

'You're worrying me, Lily. Please tell.'

'Amelia asked me to keep this for her. She didn't want Jack to know about it.'

Cora stood up. She was trembling, but she tried not to show it. 'Can't you leave it? Do I need to know every single detail of Jack's life or marriage?'

'You didn't come for the wedding.'

Cora made for the door. 'You probably mean well, but like you said, they're both dead.'

'Even if there might be somebody else out there who should know he's dead?'

Cora froze. 'What do you mean?'

'I can't leave another person waiting for a man who is never going to return.'

Cora shook her head. 'Lily, take it to Detective Hooper yourself, I'm not sure I can deal with this right now.'

Lily stretched out and placed her hand gently on Cora's shoulder. 'I know you couldn't be Jack's sister. Amelia told me they didn't even know where in the US she was and she wasn't invited to the wedding. Jack didn't even like her, he was never going to leave everything to her in his will.

Cora shut her eyes and kept them closed as Lily gripped her tight. Tears pushed under Cora's eyelids and rolled down her cheeks.

'I'm here offering the hand of friendship. I think you could do with somebody on your side right now, Cora.'

'I can't talk about it, not yet.'

'Come, sit down. You don't have to tell me anything. I understand the feelings are so raw for you. Jack must have been a very good friend or relative to leave you number 23.'

Cora opened her eyes and looked directly at Lily. 'May I have that brandy after all?'

Lily went to the sideboard, where the brandy decanter was on a silver tray with four crystal tumblers.

She lifted the decanter and poured a decent measure into two glasses. Swinging round to Cora, she stopped as if considering what to say next. 'I guess you think I'm being an interfering busybody.'

Cora shrugged. 'I don't know what to think anymore. Life has fairly roughed me up.'

Lily guffawed loudly. 'Life does that, we all have those bruises.'

She handed a glass to Cora. 'Down it in one, let's drink to surviving and kicking life in the ass.'

Cora smiled and gulped the brandy.

Lily laughed and knocked back her own drink. She put her glass down. 'Do you want me to throw this envelope in the bin and we will forget about it?'

'No, I should know what's inside.'

'Are you sure?'

Cora gripped her glass tightly, because she was afraid she would do what the voice inside her head was telling her and fling it against the wall. 'I don't have much of a choice, do I?'

'It's your decision.'

'If I look inside, questions will be raised and problems

created; if I don't, questions will plague me, creating even more problems.'

Lily handed her the envelope. 'Amelia showed it to me, but if you don't want to talk about it it, that's fine by me.'

Cora turned the brown packet over in her hands several times. Lily sat watching her as outside they heard the handful of protestors shout at any cars attempting to get into the car park. Lily looked out the window. 'Gladys may yet get her wish to be on the evening news. I hope to God she doesn't get hurt. I'd better get across and give her support.'

She turned back to Cora. 'You can stay here if you like, or if you want to go home, you can nip in your door when I have Gladys nicely distracted.'

Cora, clutching the packet, followed Lily outside.

'Come in when you are ready to talk,' Lily whispered as she bustled down the steps to stand with Gladys, who was raising a clenched fist at a queue of cars backed up the street.

Lily noted those from the offices had drifted back to their desks. Mr Foley leaned on his walking stick near the lilac tree and Sam and a few residents carrying placards stood, looking uncertain.

Lily rushed across. 'What do you want us to do?'

'Most of these drivers have booked and paid for the parking online. They are determined to get into the park. We need to stop them,' Gladys said. Her cheeks pink with excitement, she shouted into the loudhailer.

'Come on everybody, after me: Get Out of Our Park.'

Lily stepped in beside her, chanting at the top of her voice.

Gladys turned to Lily. 'Hannah rang; she is nearly ready to go to court. That girl is a genius, she reckons we will be able to stop this.'

Lily stood looking into the park. She heard the others screeching 'Save Our Park', but she felt apart. This park meant so much to her, was such a large part of her life that she could barely believe somebody wanted to destroy it all. They might break up the earth, but they would shatter her dreams and memories in one swoop. Her heart hurt.

All the times she had hidden in this garden, sometimes looking to the sky for a sign, sometimes pushing into the thick bushes on the west side, so she could sit and cry alone.

In her darkest moments, this park was her sanctuary. A wave of emotion swept through her that her daughter might be instrumental in saving it.

Gladys tugged at Lily's sleeve. 'Here comes trouble. Thankfully the man looks decent; he has decided to put on some clothes. Remember, we need to stonewall him.'

'How on earth are we going to do that?'

'When the adrenalin is flowing, we'll think of something.'

Lily shook her head and picked up a spare placard. 'Why isn't Cora here?' Gladys asked, throwing her eye over at No. 23.

'She had a tummy ache, she did her bit earlier.'

Anthony Draper walked purposefully across the street towards the park.

He was about two feet away, when a garda squad car pulled up. Gladys raised the loudhailer. When she spoke, Lily detected a quiver which she put down to nervousness in the face of possible arrest. Draper clapped his hands in glee as Gladys called on the others to join with her as she led the chant, 'Hands Off Our Park.'

'What an awful racket you folks are making, maybe you will get arrested for disturbing the peace,' he laughed, pushing his hands into his pockets and humming a happy tune to himself as he waited for the two gardai to get out of the squad car.

Gladys turned her back on Draper, her body stiffening, but otherwise, she gave no indication of the tension slowly creeping through her and the fear and dread of being arrested, making her sound hoarse. Lily stepped closer and lightly took Gladys's hand. 'Stay brave,' she whispered.

'To the end,' Gladys said as the two uniformed gardai approached.

Draper stepped forward and introduced himself. 'I want these people arrested, officers, they are denying access to my car park.'

The first garda raised his hands and a hush descended on the little group. 'Who is in charge here?' he asked.

Gladys put her hand up. 'We're only trying to save our park from these vandals tearing it up.'

Mr Foley from No. 52 pushed his walking stick in the air and shouted, 'Lock the bastard up,' making onlookers giggle and the garda frown.

'It would be best if there were no more pronouncements likely to incite bad behaviour,' the garda said and the old man lowered his stick. Asking Gladys and Anthony Draper to step to one side, he questioned them before going away to talk on his radio and consult with his colleague.

Draper, a silly grin on his face, concentrated on scrolling up his phone, while Gladys joined the others a few feet away to wait.

'I don't think we have the law on our side at this particular moment,' Gladys said.

As if to confirm her fears, the garda called everybody together. 'This land belongs to Mr Anthony Draper. You are not entitled to prevent his access to the property. I will ask you now to disperse peacefully.'

'But we are going to court to stop this car park.'

The garda put his hands up as if appealing for calm. 'That is all well and good, but until you have a valid court order you can show me, you are not entitled to block the way.'

He looked directly at Gladys. 'You have done as much as you can, it's time to retreat graciously and prepare for your legal battle. Blocking up the road and shouting semi-abusive messages is never going to help you win the war.'

Gladys let the loudhailer drop down by her side.

'They will do untold damage to the flora and fauna. Is there no way you can stop this, officer?' Lily asked politely.

'Get legal advice and check with the local authority whether permission is needed. I can't advise you more than that.'

Gladys turned to the garda. 'What if I told you we are going to court this week to try and stop these groundworks?'

The officer pulled away to take another call on his radio. 'I will leave it at that. When you have a court order, we can revisit this.'

As the gardai walked to the squad car, Anthony Draper thanked them profusely.

'I just hope Hannah can stop this,' Lily said.

Some of the other members of the group handed their placards to Gladys, before drifting off.

'Why not come to mine; we can watch what's going on from my sitting room. Hannah will know where to find us,' Lily asked gently.

'I'm not sure I want to see it,' Gladys said, suddenly feeling very tired in defeat.

'We have only lost a battle, not the war,' Lily answered, guiding Gladys across the road to No. 22.

Gladys walked slowly to Lily's house, stopping to look around her when she heard cars revving as they parked. She shivered.

'Can we go to the kitchen? I'm not sure I can take a ringside seat on the destruction of our special space,' Gladys said.

At Lily's front door, they stopped as the cars filed in to park, churning up daffodil and tulip bulbs and the cute pink flowers of dianthus peeping from under the butterfly bush, which was showing its spikes of purple pink flowers.

'Hannah had better hurry up or there won't be a park left to save,' Gladys said.

# TWENTY-TWO

Cora was sitting on the floor of the hall, hugging her knees, black and white photos scattered all around her on the floor. Photos taken in secret: a couple smiling, laughing, holding hands and doing everyday things like they knew each other well.

The woman was tall with blonde hair and chunky jewellery. Jack, in jeans and the sweater Cora bought him last Christmas, looked relaxed and happy. The pictures were dated two months previously. She had not thrown them on the ground on purpose; they had fallen out of her hand. Even after she'd slit open the envelope, she'd hoped Lily was wrong. The black and white prints were in a bundle, some stuck together, tacky, refusing to come apart. There was no mistaking the relationship between Jack and this second other woman.

She saw his smile, his ease around her; she felt the bond between them. Halfway through, she had seen enough; spying brings its own pain. Slumping against the wall, she slid to the ground, letting the photos drift away, some flashing across the parquet tiles and settling into the dust under the skirting board. How much more could she take?

How much longer would this dead man continue to torture her, to tear her soul apart along the fault lines of the previous assault? She shifted, the damp from the tiles creeping up inside her. She welcomed the seeping cold because it diverted her momentarily away from the pain bulging inside her. She didn't cry. Were there any tears left for Jack's indiscretions? She was weary and felt so lost. She had moved here hoping to find excuses or even answers, but now she was faced with this abyss.

When her phone rang, it didn't at first register through the numbness of her mind. The sound twirling through the hall almost seemed to mock her stupidity in trusting this man, who had said he loved her.

The vibration of the phone in her pocket jolted her back and she scrabbled to answer it. When she heard the familiar, high-pitched voice, she felt guilty because she didn't feel like talking to Donna.

'Cora, is that you? I have been so anxious. Honey, you didn't ring after the text saying you had arrived. For all I knew you were dead in a ditch, the rain lashing down on you.' Cora threw her eyes upwards, holding the phone away from her ear as her friend continued. 'I have been so goddamn worried, you have no idea, honey. Are you OK?'

Cora sighed. 'Donna, so nice to hear from you.'

She knew her voice, which was syrupy sweet, would set off Donna again, so she held the phone a distance from her ear.

'You have no idea how worried I was. I said to Chuck I would give it two more days and if there wasn't an answer or a message, anything to show me you were alive, I was contacting the police or Interpol or anybody who would listen.'

Cora tried to stifle a giggle, but Donna heard it.

'I'm glad you find this so amusing, Cora. Honey, for all I knew, you were dead.'

Donna stopped talking and Cora thought she heard her

crying. 'I'm sorry, I was trying to get to grips with everything here.'

'You have no reason to be there, no good reason. Just come back to the States, where you will be among friends.'

'Donna, I'm sorry I didn't make contact, but I have to sort things out here.'

'It's not right you living in that house, where he was with another woman, a woman he had the audacity to marry.'

'It's a beautiful house in a lovely old square with a park.'

'But it's creepy, Cora. Let us help you work through all this.'

'Donna, I know you mean well, but I'm staying.'

'I bet you haven't told anyone over there the truth, have you?'

Donna didn't wait for an answer, because she knew she wouldn't get one.

'What good is this doing you? You're wallowing, Cora, I just know it.' Cora made to interrupt, but Donna, well into her stride, wasn't ready to stop. 'Everyone here feels sorry for you and we all only want to help. You don't have anyone over there. It's gross that you are living in their house. I hope to God you cleared it out before you moved in. Honey, how on earth are you going to mend your broken heart, staying over there?'

Cora felt the tears rise up, to hear so much emotion in her friend's voice. 'Donna, I can't pretend it's easy, but I have to do this.'

'Is there any way of persuading you to come home?' Donna asked, her voice low in defeat.

'No, I guess I just have to get through stuff first.'

'We all miss you, Cora.'

'I'll keep in touch, I promise.'

'OK, honey,' Donna said.

Cora slowly got up off the floor and gathered up the photographs, shoving them back in the padded packet. She stuffed it in the drawer of the hall table, before going upstairs.

In the bedroom, she kicked off her shoes and lay on the bed fully clothed. Donna was right; if she stayed in this place, she would never get free of Jack, never move on with her life. She was likely to spend her time constantly searching for an answer, an explanation she would never find. Reaching for her phone, she dialled her friend.

'Do you really think it's best if I leave here?'

Donna seemed surprised to be asked for her thoughts. 'It has to be your own decision, Cora. I guess you'll know when the time is right.'

'What's happened? I thought you would be booking the flight.'

'I know I'm never shy at giving my opinion, but only you will know when you are ready to leave there. Me, I think you should never have gone in the first place.'

'I had to know more.'

'But what good has it been? You don't sound good. It's pulling you down.'

'If I hadn't come here, the constant unanswered questions would have been worse.'

'Honey, I think you're mad.'

'Undoubtedly, but my reasons are valid.'

'Darling, if my guy did this to me, I wouldn't be able to function. You are strong and resilient.'

'Shut up, Donna, I don't want to hear any more of this.'

'Add ungrateful to that list.'

'There's more, Donna. His wife was pregnant and he had another woman on the side as well.'

Donna gasped. 'Whoa, back up a little bit, girl. One thing at a time.'

'Jack certainly didn't believe that,' Cora said sourly.

'His wife was pregnant?'

'Yeah.'

'But how do you know the rest?'

'I don't really. His wife had him followed by an investigator, I've seen the photographs. She was much younger than him.'

'Did you find the photos?'

'No, the neighbour gave them to me.'

'There's nothing like good neighbours. Honey, I think Oprah would fly to Dublin to talk to you.'

'It's such a bloody mess.'

'Come home then, honey. It's not doing you any good finding out about this.'

'It hurts, sure, but it's better than being the fool who doesn't know.'

'I'm not sure about that.'

# TWENTY-THREE

Hannah, her hair in a neat bun, her glasses placed just a little down her nose, was standing in the middle of the round hall when the delegation from the De Courcy Square Association arrived at the Four Courts. Gladys and Lily were dressed in their best suits, normally only taken out on special occasions. Cora lagged behind in her jeans and a navy blazer which was one of Amelia's designs.

'I have told the press about this; we want to make a statement afterwards,' Gladys said.

Hannah looked cross. 'No statements, nothing. Today we will hopefully get the interim injunction which will give us some breathing space to decide what to do next.'

'But if we get the order to stop works, that is a good thing, right?' Lily said.

Hannah didn't answer, but led the way down a side corridor to the courtroom. 'Sit at the back and don't say a word,' she whispered, before straightening her skirt and walking up to take her place in front of the judge's bench.

Gladys, Lily and Cora sat on the hard seats, straining their ears to hear. There were several cases before they saw Hannah stand up. Gladys, unable to contain herself, gave a little squeal of excitement, but Lily elbowed her in the side, hissing at her as she did so, 'Stop, don't make Hannah angry. Believe you me, that will be a lot worse than the wrath of the judge.'

They couldn't make out what was happening and not being able to see Hannah's face, they worried it was all going wrong. When Hannah bowed to the judge and swung round, a big smile on her face, they knew they had won the first round of a long battle.

Hannah beckoned to them to follow her out onto the corridor. Cora and Lily bowed to the judge and Gladys, in a dither, genuflected by mistake, causing those around them to snigger.

In the corridor Hannah was waiting, her foot tapping lightly on the ground.

'I have to get to another court. I'm hoping once news of this filters through to Draper, he'll seek to open some sort of settlement talks.'

'What settlement? He gives us our park back; it's the only deal we will accept,' Gladys huffed, with Lily interjecting, 'Hear, hear.'

Hannah shook her head fiercely. 'You leave the negotiations to me, do you understand? I want no lording it over Draper when you get home. Everything that is said and done now could affect the eventual outcome.'

Gladys made to speak, but Lily elbowed her again. 'You can trust us, I think we have had enough excitement for one day,' Lily said to her daughter, who nodded to the group, before rushing off up the stairs to another courtroom.

When she was sure Hannah was out of earshot, Gladys pulled the others to her. 'Haven't we rightly rubbed Draper's nose in it?' she said, her voice high with excitement.

'I think best take Hannah's advice,' Cora said as they walked out of the court building and hailed a taxi home.

At De Courcy Square, Gladys bolted from the car, saying

she had important association business. Lily and Cora watched as she marched over to the park and started shouting at those drivers parking on the grass to go home. When a door on the square banged loudly, Cora and Lily saw Anthony Draper run up the road. 'Where is that interfering Spencer woman?' he called.

'Gladys might be a bit previous, but the High Court has come down in our favour. You will have to stop work in the park,' Lily said.

'That's not going to happen.'

'I'm sure, Mr Draper, when you see the court order, you will realise you have no choice in the matter,' Lily said primly.

Cora laughed and Draper marched off to stop Gladys, who was shouting at the top of her voice.

'I'm sure you will be informed through the official channels shortly,' Lily called out to Draper, but he was too agitated to listen.

Lily announced that she and Sam planned to walk down to Brogans for a bite to eat. 'Why don't you join us?' she asked Cora.

'I'm not up to it at the minute.'

'We don't have to go out, Sam won't mind. How about a quick snifter at mine instead?'

Cora followed Lily inside.

'If we go upstairs, we might be able to see Gladys and Draper fighting it out in the park,' Lily said. Sam was washing his hands in the kitchen sink when they arrived and Lily told him about her change of plan.

'If we're not going to Brogan's, I'll go introduce myself to Anthony Draper. I will probably go for a wander to St Stephen's Green afterwards,' he said.

'Why would you want to talk to Draper?' Lily asked.

Sam dried his hands on an old towel, before putting on his jacket.

'Mediation, not a costly court battle, will solve this crisis. Maybe Anthony will hear me out.'

'I think it's worth a try,' Cora said.

'As long as you know what side you are on. I suppose it can't make things worse,' Lily said.

In the upstairs sitting room, Lily took out a bottle of Baileys. 'Easier on the stomach earlier in the day,' she said as she poured a measures into two crystal glasses.

'Do you think it is bad to drink in the middle of the day?

'Who cares if it is,' Cora said as they clinked their glasses gently.

'I was rather hoping you would say drinking around noon was disgraceful; it could have added a frisson of excitement.'

'I'll know the next time.'

In the park, they saw Sam stop for a few moments to talk to Draper, before walking away. Gladys made a beeline for Draper and stood in front of him gesticulating wildly.

'Gladys enjoys this too much,' Cora said.

'As long as Hannah doesn't find out. Gladys can be allowed her little pleasures I suppose; she has gone through enough.'

'What do you mean?'

'I imagine there's no harm in telling you, but her husband was shot in the back about five years ago, during a bank raid. He is paralysed from the waist down. She cares for him with a bit of help from his sister and a carer who comes in the mornings. These houses are not designed for anyone with a disability; for Gladys it has been hard. She relishes her time away from the house. They are a lovely couple, but Tony has never been able to come to terms with what happened.'

'Is that why she is so exercised by all this park thing?'

'It gives her a reason to be out and about. Gladys feels important and needed. Who can begrudge her that?'

'I always thought she was a lady of leisure.'

'She gives a good impression of it, but Gladys is just trying to fill the gaps where her life used to be.'

Cora saw her standing in the middle of the park, her hands on her hips.

'Do you think she needs help handling Draper?'

Lily stood up.

'Come on, I wouldn't like to think Gladys felt on her own.

They made their way to the park, tramping over the muddy grass, Cora catching Lily by the elbow when she slipped.

Anthony Draper laughed out loud when he saw them. 'Mrs Spencer, the reinforcements have arrived,' he said, a smirk on his face.

'And we have come with an important message,' Lily said, pulling documents from her coat pocket.

'I am all ears, ladies, but nothing will stop the work continuing. My JCB is carrying out further work and you ladies won't stop me,' Draper said as he directed the JCB driver to continue.

Lily stepped in front of the machine. 'Not so fast, there is an order of the High Court which stops the use of the park as a car park and also prohibits all work, digging or otherwise, until a full hearing of the case. I would warn you that it is a very serious matter to be in contempt of a court order.'

'What court order?' Anthony Draper laughed.

'Your papers will be served on you shortly, Mr Draper, but all works stop now. I have informed you of the court order and the clock runs from now.'

Gladys stepped in beside Lily. 'I warned you about this, maybe now you believe me.'

'And you expect me to take the word of a bunch of old ladies,' he said, clapping his hands. 'Great performance ladies, but you don't have the wherewithal to go to court. I sent Sam Carpenter off with a flea in his ear, so where does that leave you all now?'

'With the law on their side,' Hannah said as she walked up the far path towards them.

'Who are you, and what is your business here?'

'Hannah Walpole, solicitor representing the De Courcy Square Association.'

Draper's face soured. 'Ms Walpole, will you please talk sense to these women and can you all please get off my land,' he said as he pointed at his driver and told him to get back to work.

'There is a court order, Mr Draper,' Hannah said.

'Which has not been served on me. Never take your enemy for a fool, Ms Walpole. If you will excuse me, we have a lot of work to catch up on. Please get off my property, you surely understand you are trespassing.'

Hannah didn't answer but held her arms out wide, rounding up the others as though they were children on a school trip.

'We can't leave it like that, they will damage the lovely oak tree. Look how close they are,' Lily said, knocking Hannah's arms down.

'Mother, he's right; the server will be here soon and then he will have to stop,' Hannah said.

'And are we expected to just let him destroy a tree that has been there over one hundred years?'

'If it falls, it falls, there's nothing we can do at the moment.'

Mother and daughter swung round when Cora called out frantically to Gladys to get back.

'Divine Jesus, she's going to get hurt,' Lily shouted. Anthony Draper, who had been on his phone, ran towards Gladys.

'You stupid woman, I won't be responsible for you if you get hurt. Get out of the bloody way.'

Gladys, over the din of the JCB, either didn't hear or deliberately ignored their calls.

Draper radioed the driver to stop. The bucket dropped with

a crash. Gladys, who was only five feet away from it, winced, but continued to skirt past the machine and the deep hole dug out from the ground, to position herself alongside the tree.

Lily dragged on Cora's arm, telling her to follow.

Gladys picked her way carefully through the broken earth until she was standing directly in front of the tree. Hannah attempted to pull back her mother, but Lily, feeling a sudden spurt of energy, got beside Gladys in just a few strides, Cora right behind her. The three of them surrounded the tree, linking hands in a giant hug.

'What the hell are you doing?' Draper asked.

'If you want to uproot this fine oak tree, you will have to uproot us too,' Gladys shouted.

'We will stay here day and night if we have to,' Lily shouted, hoping others passing would be curious enough to investigate.

Hannah put her head in her hands. 'This is not the way to do things', she said, but Lily ignored her. Instead, letting go of Gladys for a moment, she took out her phone and rang the *Evening Herald* newspaper, which promised to send a photographer round straight away.

'Thank God I dressed up this morning,' Gladys said as she straightened her clothes and ran her hand over her hair, to make sure it was tidy.

'I don't think dressing to protest is about looking your best,' Cora giggled.

'Well, you may laugh, but when the media and their cameras come here, I would like to think I look well. I don't want the mortification of looking bad.'

'Forget that we are hugging a large tree,' Cora said in such a deadpan voice they all burst out laughing.

Draper, who was on his phone, looked their way. 'We will see who's laughing when you are hauled away from here and charged.'

Hannah stepped in front of him.

'Mr Draper, let me remind you there is a court order in existence; these works have got to stop.'

'Tell the tree huggers to get out of my way. Nothing is going to stop work on this project.'

As he spoke, a man in a suit called out from the far side of the square.

'Is Mr Draper of 29 De Courcy Square there please?'

Hannah answered yes and directed the man to the entrance.

'You fell that tree after you are served with the order, Mr Draper, you are the one who will end up in prison,' she said in her best officious voice.

'I never realised your Hannah could be so fierce,' Gladys whispered and Lily, at that moment, felt a huge pride swelling through her.

'Neither did I,' she said, beaming.

The man in the suit hurried down the path. Hannah pointed in the direction of Draper.

'I think you can consider yourself served,' she said to the cheers of the tree huggers.

Another man with cameras hanging from each arm approached.

'We have saved this tree. When we win the war, this Association will erect a plaque to the bravery of the women here today,' Gladys said, showing her winning smile.

Anthony Draper, after inspecting the papers, told his worker to go home. 'I would advise all of you good people to do the same. You are, after all, still trespassing on my land,' he said as he walked smartly away.

Hannah helped her mother around the hole already dug out by the machinery. 'You could have hurt yourself, Mum.'

'I didn't care, I wasn't going to let anyone chop down the tree which had my name and that of my first love carved on it,' Lily said.

Cora ran back to have a look, but couldn't find it.

Lily skirted the hole and ran her hand along the roughness of the bark, until she came to a smooth circle. She traced her fingers along the letters: 'E+L'. She remembered it was a warm summer's day when Eamon had carved those letters. She'd been a little worried somebody who knew them both might notice, but secretly she was thrilled.

'Nobody will find it unless they are looking for it, but we will always know it's here,' he'd said, kissing her softly on the lips.

'I've never seen this,' Hannah said.

'I reckon you didn't look hard enough,' Lily replied and the others whooped.

# TWENTY-FOUR

Lily crossed to the park. She left Sam asleep and was out early, because she did not want to be seen slipping by the myriad of signs saying 'Private Property Keep Out' as well as the car park signs Draper hadn't bothered to take down. There were also the more recently erected signs: 'Trespassers Will Be Prosecuted'. Some smartass had obliterated the word prosecuted and replaced it with shot.

All the gates were draped with chains and double locked; Draper had had the padlocks put on under cover of darkness and a new gate had been installed across the entrance to the car park. Lily went down one side, where she knew there was a weakness in the railings and she could push her way past and into the thick shrubbery around that side of the park. She scrabbled up a hill of soft damp earth, her feet slipping, mud sticking to her legs. She skidded down the other side of the mud slope, her hands catching the tough branches of a hazel tree.

Lily kicked some stones out of the way and stepped over a fallen fuchsia onto the path.

She had decided to walk here every day. There might be precious few days left to do so, and something inside her wanted her to show Draper he wasn't going to stop somebody who had lived all her life in De Courcy Square enjoying the park. She had become a grumpy old woman, she thought, but she liked this pig iron stubbornness she was suddenly displaying. She walked on, lingering at the dahlia bed to tend to a few of the flowers, which had been battered by the rain of two days ago. She pulled them upright, gently coaxing them in to the main plant, where they could be supported, propped between other stems.

She sat down on a bench looking across the square to where Nos. 22 and 23 stood, sombre in the soft morning light. She used to steal out this early to meet Eamon. They'd run barefoot through the dewy grass, not caring if a resident, casually glancing out of a top window, should spy them. She used to come and talk to him here after he had disappeared, sitting, often remonstrating with him about why he'd left her. Fear curled through her that his ghost might confront her, ask her why she had not looked hard enough for him. She was so deep in her worry, she did not hear the footsteps until the walker was practically on top of her.

'Sam what are you doing here?' she asked.

'Lily, I was worried, I hoped you hadn't gone walking on your own in the city at this hour.'

'I want to enjoy the park for as long as we have it. I'm not sure we're going to win this war. I can't fathom why any resident of the square would want to tear up this beautiful place.'

Sam sat down.

'Draper has so much in life, why doesn't he let us enjoy our gardens?' Lily said.

'Because there are those who get a high from the discomfort of others. Which is not to say he thinks of himself as a bad man; he gives to charity, things like that. But the pain and frustrations of others, I'm sure that gives him a kick.'

'Are you telling us walk away from this fight?'

'Good God, no. I'm saying fight him slowly and firmly in the right forum, the courts. Stop the protests and the media coverage, he feeds on that.'

'Are you sure about this?'

'I knew him in a past life. Punch him where it hurts, fight him in the courts, he would much prefer to be in front of the cameras.'

'Somehow, I think that would suit us all; even Gladys is getting weary. Did he indicate when you talked to him if he is prepared to have mediation talks?'

'The exact opposite, he was full of fighting words.'

Sam got up and walked over to the triangular bed where the trellis showing off the last of the sweet peas was in shabby shape. 'The longer this garden is left without anyone tending to it, the more work will be required when we residents get it back.'

Lily pursed her mouth. 'But if we have to buy it from him, we won't be able to do that. Coffee mornings and cake sales won't buy this land.'

'Draper is doing all this to make a profit. I reckon he got the land cheap, so someone will have to work a way around all this so that he makes a profit, the residents get the park back and the council saves face.'

Sam picked a bunch of sweet peas and brought them over to her. 'Hannah is well able to broker a deal like that. Trust that it will work out.'

She accepted the flowers, but looked puzzled. 'Are you leaving?'

'The first woman I met who knows the language of flowers. Yes, for a little while.'

The scent of the sweet peas tickled her nose. Tears rose up inside her, but she acted quickly to hide them.

'My daughter has asked to see me,' said Sam. 'Oh.'

'Yes, it came as a surprise to me too.'

'But, isn't it a good thing?'

'I have to see it that way, but with Rosa and her mother, it's hard not to suspect an ulterior motive.'

'What do you mean?'

'They would have nothing to do with me when I was sleeping in hostels or parks, but once I move in to number 22, they get in touch, send a message via my cousin.'

'Invite them over, I don't mind; you don't have to meet them off-campus, so to speak.'

'I think it's better if I travel to meet them, it's just a train journey to the west and back. They said I can stay over.'

'It's up to you,' she said, but she was surprised at herself that she felt a bit put out he would consider staying with his ex-wife. To hide her confusion, she said she thought of something she needed to do.

He caught her hands. 'Don't worry. It will only be a day or so. It will be good to reconnect with Rosa and if that means having to put up with my ex-wife, I will.'

Lily gently pulled her hands away. 'I'm glad for you, I really am, but...'

'I don't understand.'

'Don't mind me, I'm being silly. I had better get along. I wish you'd told me this at home.'

He made to catch her hand again, but she sidestepped, pushing off down the path, so he couldn't see her crying. He had been upfront and honest, but for some strange reason she felt let down and afraid. The cold wind blowing in from the River Liffey was all around her again, she was back standing and waiting on O'Connell Bridge, the same fear gripping her heart. She knew she was being unfair on Sam, but she couldn't help it. She pushed her way through the bank of fuchsia and nipped out on to the street via the gap in the railings. Sam called after her, but she ignored him. As she stood pounding her feet on the pavement to knock off the earth from her shoes, she saw Cora watching her from across the street. She waved and Cora lingered on the steps, waiting for her.

'Were you in the park?'

'I refuse to let that petty man at number 29 stop me from enjoying it.'

Cora saw the tears had mixed a little with the mud, making brown streaks on Lily's face.

'You don't look so good.'

Lily shook her head as she unlocked her door. Sam passed by and went in the door of No. 22 without saying a word.

'Come in to mine,' Cora said gently. Lily gratefully accepted the invitation, following Cora through to the kitchen.

'Did something happen over there, did Draper threaten you? Did you and Sam argue?'

'No, nothing like that. I was given flowers.'

She got the bunch of sweet peas and placed them on the table.

'Pardon me, but I don't understand.'

'I have been stupid, Cora, I met a man who was kind and sensitive and we became close. Sam makes my heart sing. I haven't felt like that since I was going out with Eamon, when I was only a slip of a girl. I allowed myself to dream that maybe all these miserable years with a man I didn't love and who didn't love me counted for something; that now was finally my time.'

Lily stopped to observe a wagtail as he landed on the sill, his black and white head tilting from side to side as if he had been listening to her sad story. Quickly, he pecked at the paint on the window sill, before launching into the air, bobbing over the back wall.

Cora made to say something, but Lily put her hand up to stop her.

'Sam even knows about flowers, so when he picked the sweet peas, I knew what was coming next. I cursed myself that I knew he was going; I could not even have the pleasure of receiving the flowers.'

'But he may not be gone for long.'

'Don't you think I want to believe that? He said a day or two.'

'Isn't that your answer?'

'But this has happened before, promises are made, but I end up being left behind. I just can't take it.'

Cora reached out, taking Lily into her arms. Lily sobbed, leaning on her shoulder. When she finally pulled away, she took a tissue and blew her nose. 'I'm sorry, I know you have enough problems of your own, without listening to my silliness.'

'To love somebody is never silly.'

Cora pulled down the brandy and without asking Lily, poured a measure into each of two tumblers.

'Why is it we women never learn?' she asked, handing a glass to Lily.

Lily gulped the brandy, before speaking out. 'I am glad you invited me in because I have a question to ask. If you're not up to it, I understand.'

'Shoot.'

Lily twiddled with her glass, trying to find the words. 'What exactly were you to Jack? There's something about you, the way you ask about Amelia. Are you going to tell me your relationship to Jack? He certainly thought enough of you, to leave you everything he owned. What would have happened to poor Amelia, if she had survived that accident? Could she have lost her husband and her home?'

Lily grabbed her glass and gulped down the last of her brandy. 'There, I have said everything. I know I'm not entitled to any answers, but I would like to know, because I loved Amelia like she was my own daughter.'

Cora got up and began to pace the kitchen, back and forth in the small area between the sink and the table. Her arms wrapped around her, she stopped to study the ceiling, before the words gushed out.

'I've been Jack's partner for the last nine years. He gave me a diamond ring and said we didn't need to marry, only to continue loving each other. I never knew he stopped.'

Lily snorted, but Cora hardly noticed.

'The first I knew was when his company was informed of his death and that of his wife.'

She stopped to lean against the worktop, the pain of when she had first been told still burning in her heart.

'I might have inherited number 23, but he destroyed my life back home, left me with nothing, not even our house.'

Lily covered her face with her hands, shaking her head because this latest news was more than she could bear. 'Almost unbelievable.'

Cora smiled. 'Wasn't he a lucky man to be so loved?'

She laughed a strange laugh and took the bottle of brandy, pouring two more large measures.

'To the bastard men in our lives,' Cora said.

They pushed their glasses together, relishing the dull thud of the heavy crystal.

Cora sat down and stretched her legs under the table, reminding Lily of Amelia.

'What is wrong with me? I can't stop loving him. In a way, I wish he had told me he was marrying Amelia, we had fought and split up and I could have put my energy into hating him. This way hurts, more than hell.'

'You're not on your own.'

'He's dead and yet he continues to torture me. You know Amelia was pregnant, just a few weeks.'

Lily let out a shriek, tears spilling down her face. 'Jesus Christ, poor Amelia.'

'Was he ever going to tell any of us? It's eating me up.

Maybe he was always like this. When we first met, he flew to LA weekly on business.'

'You're going to go mad, if you keep thinking that way.'

'Why did Amelia leave the envelope of photos with you? Do you know, did she confront Jack?'

'I only know she left them with me because she wanted to confront him at her own bidding. I think she was afraid of him finding them. She was trying to take it all in, which makes sense now, considering she was pregnant.'

'How long did you have the envelope?'

'Only a week before the accident.'

Lily didn't let on to Cora, but in her head she reran the conversation she'd had with Amelia, after she'd rushed into the house, her eyes red from crying: *There's somebody else in his life. It's all here.*

Amelia had thrown the envelope on the table, the pictures slithering out. Lily had tried to push them back in, but Amelia had shouted at her: 'Look at every one of them, tell me now he's not having an affair.'

Lily's stomach had turned to see her friend in such pain, alternating between tears and anger.

'What are you going to do?' she'd asked quietly.

'I want to make him pay, but I just don't know how. Can I leave the envelope here? I don't want him to find it.'

Lily shook the memory away as she straightened up in her chair.

'Did you hear my question?' Cora asked gently.

Lily shook her head.

'Do you know the woman in the photographs?'

'No, I don't think Amelia did either. She said they were taken in Dublin and Kildare but she said the investigator said they were staying in a hotel, so the woman must have travelled into the city.'

'We don't have to know, it hardly matters now,' Cora said.

Lily stared at her. 'But there's a woman out there who must be pining for him, has no idea he died.'

Cora stood up. 'I can't handle that right now. What I have to decide is whether to tell Amelia's brother. A part of me says her family has a right to know, but another part says, why pile more suffering on their grief?'

Suddenly she turned to Lily. 'I apologise, you have your worries about Sam.'

Lily got up and kissed Cora on the cheek.

'I'm going home to tell him I am a stupid cow who cares about him deeply. Hopefully he'll return when he's ready.'

Back in No. 22, Lily sat at the kitchen table and waited for Sam, who was packing his rucksack upstairs. Pinching the sprig of rosemary in the vase, she breathed in deeply its heavy aroma as it enveloped her. She prayed for the strength to let him go and she prayed he would want to return to her.

# TWENTY-FIVE

From: **GladysSpencer@gmail.com**
To: **all De Courcy Square Association members**

This is an extremely urgent communication.

Anyone who can come out into the square, please do so, this minute. We have to do something. It appears not even a court order can frighten this man. Anthony Draper will stop at nothing until he destroys our most beautiful park. He knows he could go to prison for this and what does he do? He tears up more of the park.

Please help, in any way you can.

Gladys Spencer,
Chairperson

Gladys pounded on the front door. 'Lily, get your clothes, we must protest, he has started digging up another section of the park.'

'Hannah will deal with this.'

Gladys threw her hands in the air. 'Yes, but look at it, the eucalyptus is in danger.'

'I was talking to Hannah last night, she is pretty confident of stopping Draper for good this time.'

'Draper knows that too. That's why he's trying to vandalise the place, so it becomes a complete eyesore.'

'Just give me a few minutes and I'll come out.'

'Don't be too long, I've told Cora she's needed as well.'

Lily made her Earl Grey tea and carried it upstairs.

She pulled her chair clear of the window in case Gladys spied her, and she sat looking as a JCB scraped the ground first, before digging in deep. Gladys had already gathered a few residents and was handing out placards. Lily closed her eyes, but her thoughts and reminiscences were interrupted by the drone of the machine as it continued to clear more vegetation. She said a prayer the courts would step in and come down heavily this time. The more Draper messed about in the park, the more anxious she became. She must steel herself and stay strong for whatever the future brought, but without Sam, she was finding that difficult.

When her doorbell rang, she thought of not answering it as she figured it must be Gladys, trying to chivvy her along. On the second ring, two sharp bursts, she detected a certain impatience and headed downstairs. She was halfway down the stairs when the bell sounded again.

'I'm coming, where's the fire?' she shouted.

Swinging back the door, Lily was about to give out, when she saw two gardai standing on the top steps. 'Excuse me, are you Lily Walpole?'

Lily's knees weakened; she stared at the uniformed officers. Her mouth dried up, she could hardly speak. 'Is there something wrong, is it Hannah or Sam?'

The female officer smiled. 'We just called to ask your help.

Your name and address was on a young woman we came across this morning.'

For a moment, she could not concentrate on what the officer was saying, because she was steeling herself for bad news. Slowly, it dawned on her that this visit was not personal.

'My name and address?'

The garda handed a torn piece of paper to Lily.

'I gave it to Stacey, the young homeless woman, who used to beg around here. Is there something wrong?'

'Do you know if she has any family?'

'I can't say I know her very well, Cora next door knows her better. Let me get her for you.'

'That's OK, we can try next door. Thank you,' the female garda said in a firm voice.

When they had gone, Lily climbed the stairs to get dressed, but she opened the windows of the sitting room upstairs, in the hope of hearing what the gardai wanted to know about Stacey.

She heard nothing, but when there was a knocking on the front door ten minutes later, she knew it had to be Cora. 'Stacey is dead,' she blurted out when she saw Lily.

Cora's face was grey in colour, her hands shaking.

'What happened?'

'She was found in the canal, nobody knows exactly, the police say she drowned.'

'Ah no, did she slip maybe in the dark or was she... God, I can't bear to think of it.'

'The police didn't say. They're trying to trace her family. I asked them to let us know about her funeral arrangements.'

Gladys marched across the street.

'What are you two up to? We need you on the picket line.'

Lily went down the steps to meet Gladys halfway.

'We've got bad news, the young woman, Stacey is dead.'

'The homeless girl?'

'Yes.'

Gladys blessed herself. 'Lord have mercy on her soul. The streets are a hard place to try and live your life.'

'It sounds harsh, Gladys.'

'Factual, the reality of life in this city,' she answered, before turning back to the protest.

Cora joined them.

'I knew she should have stayed with me, but there was no persuading her. She just disappeared,' she said.

'I reckon she had to deal with things herself. Don't be blaming yourself.'

'I let her down, Lily. She told me her story and I didn't do anything to get her off the street. If she was in trouble, why didn't she come back?'

'I think it's more complicated than that. We should go to the funeral, send flowers,' she said, steering Cora inside No. 22 as Gladys returned to her small group of protesters.

'Wouldn't that be a bit hypocritical of us, to be so concerned when she's dead?' Cora said, taking up a seat in Lily's front room.

Lily grabbed Cora's hand. 'You can't save the world, Cora. You should know that by now. You did more than any of us for Stacey. Hell, I didn't even know her name, until you came along.'

'Do you know, five weeks ago today, near lunchtime in the States, I was putting on my nicest outfit to have crab and champagne with my Jack, at the best seafood restaurant on Long Island. Look at me now.' Lily didn't answer, but even if she had, Cora wasn't listening. 'I reached out so far and then, no more. I'm ashamed of myself, Lily.'

'You have no reason to be. You saw Stacey for what she was, a pleasant young woman – it's the rest of us who should be ashamed. She sat at the bottom of my steps for nearly a year and I never even asked her name. I suppose you're right, it's hypocritical to be thinking of sending flowers.'

'It's not, I shouldn't have said that. I apologise, it's been a rough few days. Have you heard from Sam?'

'He said he'll be back in a few days. He's gone to visit his daughter on the west coast.'

'Hang in there, he's one of the good ones,' Cora said.

# TWENTY-SIX

From: **GladysSpencer@gmail.com**
To: **all De Courcy Square Association members**

Please join us at the Four Courts to see greedy developer
Anthony Draper jailed. There surely is no other course of
action for a man who can so swiftly turn his back on a High
Court order. Today is the beginning of the end for Draper and
his outrageous plans for our park.

Gladys Spencer,
Chairperson

Gladys decided it was an occasion to wear a hat. She didn't care
what the others would say or that people may stare, this was a
day to celebrate. She would have a nice gin and tonic afterwards, but today was definitely a hat day. Hannah had found a
barrister willing to go in to court and seek the jailing of Anthony
Draper for contempt of a High Court order. Gladys didn't think
he could wriggle out of this one. It gave her satisfaction, to think
that by this evening, he would be on his way in a prison van to

Mountjoy jail. She liked to think that as he was sent down, Draper would look all around him, but because of her hat, his eyes would rest on her, and he would see in her the satisfaction that came with winning the battle of De Courcy Square.

The hat was a discreet black colour, a jaunty feather with a dash of red and peacock blue sticking into the air, with a light netting she pulled down over her face. She'd last worn it at the Curragh races, when her Tony could still stride out on his own two legs, his binoculars swinging off his right shoulder as he inspected the horses in the ring before the race.

How she longed for those days, when every weekend they did something together. She used to complain she would love a weekend at home, a day she didn't have to dress up.

She whined too much and the good Lord listened to her. Now, she rarely got past the square. Even doing the grocery shopping was denied her, because her sister-in-law, when she drove to one of the busy supermarkets in the suburbs once a week, bought for both households.

When Hannah rang and said she was going to apply to have Draper committed to prison, because he had sent in the JCBs again and had continued to offer car parking in defiance of a court order, Gladys insisted she and some of the Association members would have to be in court.

It was sad, she thought, for a woman who used to have a diary full of social engagements to regard a trip across the Liffey to the Four Courts, to sit on a hard bench and not understand one iota of what was going on, to be the highlight of her week. She searched in her dressing table drawer, until she found the ruby-red lipstick which, worn with the hat, she thought gave her a diva look.

When she called in to peck her husband's cheek, he told her she looked beautiful.

'I hope you're going somewhere nice,' he said, trying to sound neutral, but before she had answered, he had turned his face to the wall. She stood in the room, looking at him lying on the bed the hospital had given her all those years ago, tears rising inside her. Doreen, her sister-in-law, told her to get along, she was going to read the *Irish Times* to Tony. Grateful to be dismissed, Gladys made her way downstairs and across the square to stand outside Lily's, waiting on whoever was coming to the courts.

Lily looked out to see who was joining Gladys, but when nobody turned up, she threw on her coat and grabbed her handbag. 'Are we on our own, Gladys?' she said, closing her front door.

'Should I knock for Cora?'

'She probably has enough on her plate right now. The two of us will do fine,' Lily said, putting her hand out to hail a taxi.

At the Four Courts, Gladys felt conspicuous. She saw Hannah eye the hat and pull a cross face, but she said nothing. Instead, she introduced a young barrister, Martin O'Leary. 'Martin here has been kind enough to offer to help us out. Have you seen Mr Draper this morning?'

Gladys nudged Hannah and pointed to the far end of the corridor, where Anthony Draper was talking loudly on his phone.

'He doesn't appear to be legally represented, a foolish move on his part,' Hannah said as she led her party in to court. The courtroom was packed, the only seats available were towards the front. Lily and Gladys were just seated, when Draper sat down beside them.

'We will have to stop meeting like this, Mrs Spencer,' he said and Gladys changed position, so a large part of her back was facing him. They sat perfectly still, listening to the myriad of applications, words said, decisions made as barristers and solicitors stood up and addressed the bench.

'I wish they would hurry on,' Lily whispered.

'The wheels of justice turn at their own speed, but we're so lucky to be here,' Gladys said primly.

'It's just I have to be somewhere. I hope it comes up before lunch.'

Gladys grabbed Lily's hand. 'It must be very important to you, if you put it ahead of our fight for the square.'

Lily pulled her hand away. She wanted to give a sharp answer, but she knew if she did, she would regret it.

When the case was called, Anthony Draper stood up and stayed standing, while the barrister on the side of the residents put his case. The judge looked out over her glasses and addressed Draper directly.

'Mr Draper, it is a very serious matter to ignore an order of the High Court.' Draper, gripping the seat in front of him, spoke in a loud, clear voice.

'Judge, I'm sorry, but I wasn't sure that piece of paper was authentic. I thought it had to do with the campaign of intimidation against me by the local residents.'

'Mr Draper, my concern is your defiance of a court order. Ignorance is no defence. We also know you were properly served with the order of this court.'

Gladys made to stand up, but Hannah glared at her. Emboldened, Anthony Draper continued. 'I own that piece of land at De Courcy Square and I intend to turn it in to a space for everybody, not just for the privileged few who live there.'

'You are privileged, you live in number 29, you hypocrite,' Gladys shouted.

The judge's tipstaff left his seat and stood between Gladys and the bench. The judge looked severely over her glasses again.

'I would ask that legal counsel convey to his clients that I will not tolerate disturbance of court proceedings.'

Hannah left her seat and hissed in Gladys's ear, making her

cheeks burn a deep red under the netting. The judge asked Draper to step closer.

'Mr Draper, I have a good mind to send you to prison. Not abiding by an order of the High Court is a very serious matter. This is your last chance, do you understand me?'

He nodded, but when she stared at him again, he replied, 'Yes, your Honour.'

'Do you understand, no work of any kind is to take place on the land at De Courcy Square, until there is a full hearing of the case and judgement is made? And that also includes the use of the land as a car park.'

'Yes, but how long will that be?'

The judge handed the papers down to the registrar.

'I have given you quite a bit of latitude, because you are a lay litigant, Mr Draper. I am not here to answer your questions.'

The judge called next case and the tipstaff told them they could leave the court.

Mr O'Leary took Draper aside as Hannah waited in the corridor with Lily and Gladys.

'Mrs Spencer, you are lucky you are not the one to be sent to Mountjoy for the night, with that display in there.'

Lily, detecting a big upset in Gladys, signalled to Hannah to be quiet. When her daughter made to say something else, Lily told her to hush.

'What does it mean for the park?' Gladys asked quietly.

'It means the digging stops until the full case is heard. The park can't be touched until the court has decided all the issues and neither can a car park be operated there.'

'But is he going to leave that awful machinery in situ?' Gladys asked.

'A very good question,' the barrister said, making Gladys beam with pride.

They huddled around O'Leary as he spoke. 'I have agreed with Mr Draper, he can move the machinery from the park tomorrow morning, which I'm told will involve the loosening of some earth, or where they have already broken ground, they will have to complete the manoeuvre before exiting. I would advise somebody to be on hand, to make sure he keeps his word.'

'I will be there, I would not trust that man as far as I could throw him. And with that lump of lard, that wouldn't be far,' Gladys snorted.

Lily elbowed Gladys gently as they both eyed Hannah to see if she would react. Hannah was deep in thought, frowning as she strummed the elastic band around her files like a guitar. 'Did he give any hint he might be open to negotiating a deal out of this mess?' she asked Mr O'Leary.

'Quite the opposite, he said that land is potentially worth an awful lot of money, he wants to be properly compensated to walk away.'

'What do we do?' Gladys asked.

'Hold tough and pray for a miracle,' Lily said.

'Mother is right, let's concentrate on getting the machinery out of the park first. I have a meeting with the City Council during the week, so something might come of that,' Hannah said, before saying she had to rush off to another court. The barrister also said goodbye, leaving Gladys and Lily to make their own way home.

'We won the battle today, I just hope we don't lose the war,' Gladys said, pulling her hat off, because she suddenly felt foolish.

Lily put her arm around Gladys's shoulders. 'I think we should celebrate this success, don't you?'

'I thought you had to be somewhere.'

Lily looked embarrassed. 'That was just me being nervous, fussing about nothing.'

Gladys linked her arm. 'Aren't we the right pair?' They managed to flag down a taxi.

'I don't feel like going home, wouldn't it be nice to have a cuppa or something stronger?' Lily said.

Gladys's face brightened. 'Could we go to The Shelbourne? It's been so long since I darkened the doors of that hotel.'

When their taxi pulled up outside the hotel, the doorman opened the door for Gladys.

'It makes me sad I took off my hat,' she whispered as they went in, veering to the right in search of afternoon tea.

The girl at the desk said although they didn't have a reservation, she could manage to squeeze them in at a small table beside the fireplace, which was not in use but instead had a vase of white lilies in front of the hearth. They picked afternoon tea with a flute of champagne each on the side, taking off their coats and settling into the comfy armchairs.

'My Reg would not approve, which makes this very special indeed,' Lily said.

'I texted Tony and said the case is taking longer than I thought. Is that very bad of me not to want to rush back to the square?' Gladys laughed.

'Sometimes, we need to think of ourselves.'

'I've almost forgotten how to do that,' Gladys said.

They watched as a woman sat down at the piano and began to play.

'When I moved to the square, I imagined a life like this with Tony. We were quite the socialites, all to do with his work, but I was so looking forward to when he retired, striking out on our own.'

'How is he?'

'In a lot of ways, he's still the same old Tony, but he has lost so much confidence, he talks little these days. Don't get me wrong, he is cared for so well. We manage it against the odds, but there is no quality of life. Tony loved the theatre, visiting galleries, the races; you name it, he did it. We have tried to do those things and managed in some way, but he just can't take it, he says it's a reminder of all he has lost.'

Lily reached over and squeezed Gladys's hand. 'The next campaign will have to be to get Tony to take more of an interest in life,' she said quietly.

The waitress came with the crockery and a silver pot of Earl Grey tea. Lily placed the strainer on Gladys's teacup and poured. 'I see him at the upstairs sitting room window, when I'm in the park.'

Gladys wiped away a tear as she dropped two cubes of sugar in to her tea. 'He likes that spot, there's a great view of the park. It's why I've set up so many flower beds in that section, he loves the colour.' Gladys watched as Lily poured her own tea. 'We can't let Draper turn it in to a car park. It would kill Tony, he says the only enjoyment he has left in life is listening to his Mozart and Bach, while looking out at the trees and flowers.'

They sat in silence, sipping their tea for a few moments until Lily spoke. 'I feel so bad it happened on Reg's watch.'

'Don't be, you have been kindness itself over the years. I won't pretend I feel the same way about your late husband.'

'Maybe we could include Tony more. I like Tchaikovsky, we could listen together.'

Gladys put her cup carefully down on her saucer. 'Would you really do that for me, Lily? I know I can be a bit of a wagon at times.'

'True, but this park business has taught me one thing: we are better when we work together.'

She raised her champagne glass and they clinked, the tinkle sending a frisson of excitement through them both.

Neither of them noticed Anthony Draper, a tumbler of whiskey in his hand, making his way towards them. 'Ladies, ladies, don't you think this celebration, this toasting of victory is grossly premature?' He laughed as if he had cracked a funny joke.

'What we do in our own time is our business. Kindly leave us alone,' Gladys said.

'With pleasure, dear ladies, but remember: best to celebrate victory in the war, rather than fall after the first battle,' he said, before turning smartly on his heel and heading for the lounge bar.

'The bloody cheek, now he has turned me off my food,' Lily said.

'Me too; do you think they could give us a doggy bag?'

The waitress looked surprised, but agreed to pack the sandwiches and cakes in two boxes.

When they asked for the bill, she said the gentleman had already paid.

'What is he up to? The nerve of him,' Lily said.

'Nothing good, that's for sure,' Gladys said as they quickly left for De Courcy Square.

They were nearly home when Gladys began to giggle. 'That Draper is some ticket, it's going to be a great pleasure beating him into the ground.'

Lily agreed and the two of them laughed heartily as they passed No. 29.

# TWENTY-SEVEN

From: **GladysSpencer@gmail.com**
To: **all De Courcy Square Association members**

The sound of silence. We have stopped Anthony Draper in his tracks. But this is not the time for complacency, we must continue our fight and prepare for the most important court battle ahead.

We want our park back in exactly the same condition as it was, before it was so grossly vandalised. We won't have it any other way. No Surrender.

Gladys Spencer,
Chairperson

Sam was gone two days. Lily felt a fool for having doubted him. He rang both evenings; they didn't talk for long, but both knew they missed each other terribly. On the Thursday morning, she was waiting on the platform when he arrived by train at

Heuston Station. They hugged and she thought he might kiss her, but he didn't and she felt a little disappointed.

They sat close together in the taxi back to De Courcy Square.

'Do you think we could go into the park first?' Sam asked.

Puzzled, Lily agreed and they went round to a far gate and used a key.

'They are moving out the JCB and any other machines today. It's just a pity we can't start working on the flower beds; the fuchsia looks quite stressed. I threw a jug of water on its roots the other day, but I think it is going to need more than that.'

'Maybe I could ask Anthony Draper if we could do a small bit of maintenance,' Sam said.

'Best not to ask him anything, I don't want to be beholden to that man in any way.'

Sam caught her hand.

'I hope you missed me, Lily, as much as I missed you.'

She shrugged and he knew she must have.

'How did it go with your daughter?'

'It's hard to know. There were a lot of questions as to why I have moved in to number 22. My ex-wife was rather disappointed to hear I don't own the building, but Rosa and I, we reconnected, I hope.'

'Then it's a win for you.'

'She promised the next time she's in Dublin, we will meet for a coffee, so let's see.'

'I'm very glad, Sam. You haven't missed much here, only Gladys is impossible because the court has come down in our favour. For now, at least, and the works have to stop.'

'I asked to come into the park because I wanted to ask you something, and this place is special to both of us.'

Sam would have said more, but just then, Gladys bustled

across the grass. She gave a loud whoop. 'The dear Lord is looking down on us after all; not only has the vandalism been stopped, but we have been thrown a lifeline. I know now, we will win the war.'

'The big machinery leaving, isn't that what is supposed to happen?' Sam said.

'There has been the most delicious development. This is huge news.'

'What news?' Lily asked, her voice clipped with impatience. Gladys took a deep breath, looking all around her to see if anybody else might be listening.

'Come on, woman, the suspense is killing me,' Lily snapped.

Gladys smiled broadly. 'The JCB has stopped.'

She waited as if she expected an excited reaction from Sam and Lily.

'So?' Lily interjected.

Gladys stared at the two of them. 'So all works in the park have stopped and Draper can kiss his car park goodbye.'

'This is what was decided at the Four Courts, and it's only an injunction for the moment. So what's new?' Lily snapped.

'Draper is screwed, pardon my French,' Gladys said, red creeping up her neck.

Lily leaned toward Gladys. 'Just tell it straight, please.'

Gladys chuckled. 'My Tony always says I'm the most frustrating storyteller.'

'Gladys,' Lily said crossly, rapping her on the wrist.

'Oh, all right, the gardai have been called, a section in the middle of the park where the spring bulbs are planted and the delphiniums are on their last show has been cordoned off. They have found something.'

'What do you mean?' Sam asked.

'Bones. Draper hasn't a hope now of ever having a car park here.'

'You mean human remains?' Lily asked.

'The gardai are sealing it all off. They are not going to do that for a dead dog. I had better get along in case they need my input,' she laughed.

Lily felt strange, her knees were weak and her mouth was dry; a tension ache was crawling up the back of her head.

Sam, detecting her fear, took her arm.

'Let's go home,' he said and she leaned into him as they made their way down the path between the two rows of box hedge, which badly needed to be clipped into shape.

Men in white forensic suits passed them by and a uniformed garda asked them to please leave the park.

'Who do you think it is?' she asked Sam as they climbed up the steps to the house.

'Whoever it is, I hope it brings closure for their family or maybe it's one of those skeletons from centuries past.'

'I hope so,' Lily said as she walked to the kitchen and switched on the kettle.

'You don't look so well; let me make the tea,' Sam said gently as he pulled out a chair at the table for her to sit.

When the mug of tea was placed in front of Lily, she jumped, her hand jerking forward, knocking against the handle, making tea splash onto the table and the floor.

'I'm so sorry, I'm not myself this morning.'

'Has something happened, something while I was away?'

'I'm just finding things hard. This idea that human remains have been found in the park is awfully upsetting.'

'Well, I'm here now and willing to help in any way.'

Lily looked at Sam. 'I'm sorry, I completely forgot, what were you going to ask me?'

Sam looked at Lily. 'It can keep, right now you need to relax, go out and sit in the back garden and enjoy the flowers. It will take your mind off what's happening in the park.'

When the doorbell sounded, Sam groaned.

'I'll try and get rid of whoever it is,' he said. Lily heard the loud voice of Gladys and she hoped Sam could keep his word.

When she heard Gladys coming down the hall, she almost burst in to tears.

'Lily, I just came round to tell you gardai have confirmed it is human remains. I think a murder investigation is underway.'

The pain on Lily's face was plain to see.

'I thought you would want to know; and they will want to talk to long-standing residents of the square. I hope you don't mind, I gave them your name.'

Sam, when he saw Lily's face, tapped Gladys on the shoulder.

'I think it might be best if you left, Gladys. Let me take care of Lily. She's just not feeling one hundred per cent.'

'But I was hoping we could have a chat about where we go from here. This has to be good news in the long run for the Association campaign.'

'Let's hope it is, but Lily needs her space right now.'

'Of course, I didn't mean to intrude. I'd better be getting along anyway. I have so much to do. Now, we need to pile even more pressure on Draper,' Gladys said, walking back to the front door.

Sam waited a few moments in the hall after Gladys left, to give Lily time to compose herself. Lily took a piece of kitchen roll and blew her nose, wandering out the back door as she did so.

She stepped into the garden. Sam had potted up the lilies in two terracotta pots and placed them either side of the door. She hadn't noticed until now because she hadn't bothered with the garden when he was away, preferring it when he was there with her. When Eamon and his family lived in the basement next door as caretakers, this boundary wall had been so important to her. Stumbling along the wall now, she thought of Eamon, a good memory which calmed her heart.

Out of sight of the houses, Eamon had hacked out a small hole in the brick wall so they could see each other and whisper late at night. He would push through his fingers and they would touch. Sometimes he just left a flower there, anything from a buttercup to a rosebud to tell her he was thinking of her. It seemed silly to look back on it now, but on days when there was no excuse to be made for them to meet, they relied on this as their only way of communicating. If there was greenery placed in the crevice, it meant she should quietly slip out the house to the back garden when her parents were asleep.

Feeling the stonework with her fingers, she tried to find the spot in the wall, knocking at the stones in case the piece camouflaging their little porthole loosened. It was foolish to think after all these years that it would still be there. When a stone flicked out, she jumped back. It seemed such a small, insignificant hole. Tentatively, she pushed her fingers past the cobwebs; a spider flitted for cover. She felt the roughness of his hands, the gentle touch as he spoke in a low, soft voice. Eamon had to bend down because he was tall. How many times had they stood, either side of this stone wall, comforted by each other's touch.

Realising she looked as if she had gone daft, Lily quickly pulled back her fingers and replaced the stone, before returning to flop into the old wicker chair, its cushions dusty and scattered with spent flower petals. She prayed that Gladys was wrong, but she knew she wasn't. Hannah would insist she sell up and move away. She deserved all of it. How Sam fitted in to all this, she had no idea.

When she saw Sam anxiously peering out the kitchen window, she waved to him.

'I'm sorry, you deserve an explanation, but I'm not up to it at the minute.'

Sam came out and sat beside her. 'Lily, I'm not in a position to judge anyone, nor do I want to. I'm sure you will tell me when you are ready and when you want.'

She watched a snail trail across the paving slab. 'If I stood on that snail, the shell would smash to bits. I feel like a snail, but there's nothing I can do about it.'

The snail stopped moving, tucking itself away as if it felt it was under observation.

'Are you sure it's as bad as all that?'

Lily stood up, making sure to avoid the snail.

'It's worse.'

'How can be that be? And whatever it is, I would like to help.'

'I think on this one, I may be past helping,' Lily said.

'I'm here when you want to talk about it,' Sam said, moving off to pluck some seed heads from the sweet peas. Brushing past Sam and into the house, she thought he was a patient man and she was being unfair on him, but at the moment, she could do little about that.

When an email from Gladys pinged in to her phone, she read it, making her chest tighten again.

From: **GladysSpencer@gmail.com**
To: **all De Courcy Square Association members**

Dear residents and tenants,

This is a brief email to let you know that gardai have now cordoned off our park, because it is believed the bones found are human remains. We will update as soon as we have been informed further.

It is hard to loudly celebrate our victory in the circumstances, but thank you to all who have supported us this far and please note, the battle continues until the fate of De Courcy park and its ownership are changed to our satisfaction.

Gladys Spencer,
Chairperson

# TWENTY-EIGHT

When the garda leading the investigation into the death of Stacey made contact to pass on the funeral arrangements, Cora felt she should go along.

'Can you tell me how to get to Glasnevin cemetery?' she asked Lily when they met on the front step later that day.

'A good place to go to get to grips with the history of Dublin,' Lily said.

'I don't know about that: I want to go to Stacey's funeral.'

'When is it? I will go along as well.'

'Tomorrow at eleven.'

'I will order a taxi for ten-thirty,' Lily said.

Cora was about to go back indoors when Lily called after her.

'Do you think I should make up a small bouquet of flowers from the garden?'

'That's a lovely idea,' Cora said. She saw Lily in the garden later instructing Sam on the blooms to pick. She wanted to sketch the two of them as they mulled over the flowers, carefully considering each choice in the sunshine. The urge to capture the intimate moment when their two heads lightly touched as they bent over the dahlias was strong, making Cora shudder and want to busy herself elsewhere. All she could do was store the image in her head, because she could not make her hands do her bidding.

---

When Lily and Cora arrived at the crematorium chapel in Glasnevin the next morning they were not sure they were in the right place. Lily walked up to a small group of people wearing black.

A tall woman in a jacket with a pinched-in waist twirled round as Lily approached.

'This service is private, you do understand, don't you?'

Lily put out her hand to sympathise, but the woman stepped back.

'Strictly private,' she said as she pulled at the sleeve of a man who was standing beside the basket-weave coffin. 'Tell them to go away, Sean, please.'

'If people want to pay their respects, let them,' he whispered, before leaning over to kiss the small name plate on the coffin.

'Sean, I don't want anybody here from this other life of hers, only those who knew the real Isabelle.'

'Isabelle?' Cora said.

The woman glared at Sean as she drifted away and he, muttering under his breath, approached Lily and Cora.

'I'm sorry, but you heard the lady, this is a private ceremony and you haven't been invited.'

Lily, holding a bunch of tea roses, made to hand them to Sean. 'No flowers either, I'm afraid, just the family wreath.'

'We knew Stacey this last while, helped her out,' Lily said.

'We only want to pay our last respects,' Cora said, stepping forward with her hand extended.

Sean pulled the two of them to one side. 'It's not that it isn't appreciated, but the family has been through enough. Let us be, please.'

Cora made to say something, but the man raised his hand as if asking for quiet. 'I know you mean well, but she isn't Stacey. Her name is Isabelle, Isabelle Moloney.'

Cora looked at Lily. 'Are we at the right funeral? The gardai said Stacey's funeral was here.'

Sean shook his head as he answered. 'Look, you two look like nice, kind women and whatever you did to help Isabelle is very much appreciated, but you don't know the whole story.'

He checked behind to make sure he could not be heard by the small group standing to one side of the coffin. 'My sister called herself Stacey on the street, so if she was arrested she wouldn't bring shame on us all. Isabelle hated what she had become, we tried everything to help her, but she always went back on the drugs.'

'But she wasn't using, that's what she told us,' Lily said.

'We know she had a hard life losing her husband and then her home,' Cora said.

Sean snorted so loudly, the group of mourners glanced over at them. 'Isabelle was expert at lying, weaving a story, so she got maximum sympathy. Believe what you like, but that is precisely why we want this to be family only. We knew her, saw her grow up, picked her up every time she fell. But once she abandoned us, there was nothing we could do to stop the inevitable. Now can you please go, let us get on with this.'

Lily and Cora walked out of the chapel into bright sunshine. 'I think we have been a pair of fools,' Lily said as they wandered in to the café to sit down.

'I don't care, I liked the bit of Stacey I knew. Who knows what pushed her to hide from herself?'

Lily grabbed Cora's hand. 'Maybe best not to let on to

Gladys, she couldn't resist crowing about it. And if Hannah heard, she would get very cross about me being conned.'

'I seem to spend my whole life being taken in by liars.'

'No point thinking like that. What Jack did and what Stacey— I mean, Isabelle did, they did. There is nothing wrong in loving somebody or believing in somebody. We can't give up on that.'

'I really am going to take a step back in the future.'

'Don't. If you did, we wouldn't have become friends.'

'Thanks, Lily. At least I know you aren't hiding anything from me.'

Lily smiled faintly and said they had better get along.

'What are you going to do with the flowers?'

Lily looked around the café. Walking over to a woman who was sitting on her own, staring out the window, she presented her with the bouquet. Cora saw the woman embrace Lily.

'What was that all about?' she asked Lily, who was smiling broadly when she returned to the table.

'She lost her daughter two months ago and was sitting thinking about her. She said I'm the angel who found her.'

'Over the top, surely.'

Lily laughed. 'It brought a smile to both our faces and saved me from a cross-examination by Gladys.'

They walked out together to hail a taxi to De Courcy Square, Cora enjoying the journey through the old part of North Dublin City, crossing the Royal Canal and passing streets and streets of single- and two-storey red-brick houses which she thought all looked the same.

When the taxi pulled up in front of No. 22 and No. 23, Detective Hooper was leaning on the railings outside Cora's house. 'I hope you don't mind,' he said. 'I have a bit of time on my hands and thought I would chance dropping by.'

Lily, who seemed edgy, said she would leave them to it and quickly let herself in to her house, though she was so nervous, she thought everybody must notice her fumbling with the keys. Cora opened her door and invited Tom in.

'Is the old lady all right?' he asked her.

'We had a bit of a shock at Stacey's funeral. It turns out Stacey didn't even give us her real name.'

'She wasn't the worst. She had a lot of problems. Shame is a terrible thing, she was just trying to protect her family.'

'Someone at her funeral said the same thing. But now I'm not sure anything she told us was true.'

Tom reached out and put his two hands on Cora's shoulders.

'Did you like her?'

'Yes.'

'Did she do you any wrong?'

'God, no.'

'Then think of her kindly, she probably had her reasons.'

'I didn't think that type of empathy came with the job description.'

'For someone like Stacey, yes.'

Tom looked around. 'You've started the clear-out.'

'Yes. It's time, I think. Please, if there is anything you want to take, go ahead.'

Tom shook his head.

'We only ever wanted the reminders of Amelia before she met Jack. We have no place for anything that includes him.'

'That makes two of us.'

She walked into the office and pulled down the envelope from the top shelf, where she had hidden it. 'Lily was holding these for Amelia. Have a look and see what you think.'

Puzzled, Tom took the thick envelope and opened it. Cora slipped upstairs, knowing Tom would want to look at the photos of Jack's deception of Amelia on his own. Gathering up a refuse sack, she went into the bathroom. She remembered looking in the cabinet on the first night and smiling at the rows of vitamin containers. They were all Jack's. She pulled out the tub of B complex and fired it in the bag, rushing to throw out the others, one after another. When she moved the electric shaver, little specks of black stubble fell into the wash basin. It made her stop what she was doing for a moment as a pang of grief and loneliness at his death swept though her.

Jack liked to preen himself in front of the bathroom mirror. Even if he was running late, he had to spend time on his shaving, smacking on the aftershave loudly, before slicking his hair to the right. Cufflinks next, if he was going to a business meeting, and a straightening of his tie, before he slipped on his jacket and checked himself in the long mirror. She pulled the cap from his bottle of aftershave and breathed in, but as quickly turned away before replacing it. When she heard Tom on the stairs, she hurriedly closed the cabinet doors and stepped onto the landing. 'We need to talk,' he said and she followed him downstairs. He stood in the hall, the pack of photographs in his hand, his face red with anger, perspiration glistening on his forehead and neck. 'The bastard is lucky he's dead.'

'I thought you should see them.'

'Did she confront him?'

'We don't know, only that she had Lily keep them, while she decided what to do.'

'Why didn't she tell me, ask for help?'

'Maybe she was just trying to get her head around it.'

'Amelia wouldn't stand for this sort of thing.'

'Lily said she was very upset. She just needed time to process it, I guess.'

'I was talking to her in this hallway two days before she died and I asked her was everything all right. She didn't look good, but she insisted everything was fine. Why the fuck didn't she ask me for help?'

'Shame. I know I was ashamed, when I found out about Jack's other life.'

'Did Amelia know this woman, does Lily know?'

'I don't know about your sister, but Lily doesn't know. She thinks if Amelia had any idea, she would have said as much to her.'

'Can I take these photos with me?'

'Of course, but please, if you find out more, will you tell me?'

'You're a sucker for punishment.'

'There's nothing left to hurt anymore, Tom.'

Reaching over, he pulled Cora into a big hug. 'Ring me anytime if you need me, and the moment I get anything on this, I will be back to you.'

She stood at the door as he left, watching him get into his car and turn right at the end of the square. She didn't feel like staying in the house, so she grabbed her jacket and keys from the hall table and set off walking. She tramped along, passing Government Buildings and The Shelbourne Hotel, crossing over to St Stephen's Green and entering by a side gate. Avoiding the larger crowds around the lake, she set off on the quieter path along the side of the green. It was shaded here, a cool spot in the busy, throbbing city. Sitting down, she closed her eyes. She could be anywhere: every city sounded the same, the same simmering tension, the strange noises that nobody notices as they go about their day. There was a time she and Jack had loved to ramble around Manhattan, dipping into Central Park on a Saturday morning. In truth, they had not done it in a long time. She was back wandering up the little hill where the ice rink was and he was holding her hand. It was where they had met, on a cold December day. She had been standing watching the skaters on the ice down below, when all of a sudden she'd been sent flying. Jack, who had been on his phone and arguing, never saw her as he backed out of the way of a woman and her buggy. He was so apologetic, helping her to her feet. 'I can't believe I did that, I'm so sorry. Are you hurt?'

Her hand was bleeding, from where she had scraped it along the path. He'd insisted on calling a paramedic and waited with her. After she'd been checked over, he'd introduced himself.

'Jack Gartland. Can I please take you somewhere nice right now? We can sit and get to know each other.'

He'd taken her to the Plaza and ordered a rum cocktail without even asking her what she fancied. 'For the shock, and much nicer than taking the spirit straight,' he'd explained as they clinked glasses.

When she rang Donna from the washroom, her friend had warned her to leave there and then.

'How do you not see somebody standing right in front of you, and why ask you for a drink? I bet he has done this before. Way too slick, if you ask me.'

'Donna, you read too many crime novels.'

'Like you believe it was all an accident. Leave now, tell him you're busy.'

'I'm enjoying his company.'

'Which hand did you hurt?'

'My painting hand, but it's just bruised and grazed.'

'Tell lover boy you might sue and see if he sticks around.'

They had laughed at that so many times in the intervening years, even telling Jack, who had seemed to be in a huff that they should have doubted him.

A part of her wanted to be back there, to sit in the leather tub chairs in the Oak Room at the Plaza, refuse the rum cocktail and find some excuse to leave.

# TWENTY-NINE

Lily fumbled around the back of her wardrobe until her hands touched the cold metal of the USA Assorted biscuit tin, hidden under the refuse sacks she had filled with her husband's shoes after his death, but never dropped off to the charity shop. She yanked the box from under the weight of the black bin bags. She had not looked inside it since that night she had grabbed it from kitchen table, thrown out the last of the biscuits and shoved the letter in, fixing the cover on tight.

Patrolling the room, she wrestled with whether or not she should open it or just throw the box away. Walking to the window, she stared down at the park; one of the lilacs was tipped over, its leaves crinkled brown.

She tried to ignore the white tent the investigators had erected in the middle of the park, the flowers trampled, the paths overrun with weeds; there was no comfort in this view anymore, only anguish.

Concentrating on the biscuit tin, she attempted to prise open the lid. Digging her nails underneath, she tugged, but it didn't budge. Taking her tweezers, she burrowed them under the lip of the seal, applying pressure until one side of the box opened with a pop.

Her head was thumping, her hand shaking as she saw the letter placed across the base of the box. Slowly, she picked up the envelope addressed to 'My Wife Lily, Only'.

Even in his last words, she thought, her husband sounded so formal.

She'd only read it once before, but that was enough for her to know that nobody else must set eyes on it. She persuaded herself that she'd done it for her daughter, but was this secrecy for herself? When she'd locked away her husband's suicide note, she thought it would prevent her past secret life being analysed, commented on and thrown to the mercy of the gossips. Tentatively, she reached for the envelope, tugging it free. Turning it over in her hands, she was back in the house she shared with Reg. She could smell the aroma of his Fox Ardagh pipe tobacco, the strong whiff which caught in the back of her throat and made her stomach sick. Even the memory of it now made her gag and check behind her, in case he had in some way stolen back into her life. *Had he ever left her?* would be more accurate. These last two years, she had worried that by not immediately declaring the contents of the letter, she had somehow been an unwitting accomplice in a wrong which could never be righted.

She was lost in the moment she had first digested the contents of the letter, the raw pain flaring inside her, blood coursing through her, making her want to bolt from the house and never be heard from again. She should have returned to the box before now and burned the letter, let it melt to smoky blackness in front of her eyes. Why had she kept it, risked everything by keeping this last act of confession? It was too late to regret it now.

Slowly, she took out the envelope and pulled out the single sheet of Basildon Bond writing paper.

*Avalon*
*22, De Courcy Square*
*Dublin*
*27 March 2016*

*My Dearest Lily,*

*I know I have not been a good husband but I hope and pray I have been a good enough father to our daughter. No doubt my death will be marked down as a casualty of the recession, and let it be that way.*

*I cannot bear the burden of guilt that weighs down my very existence any longer. I know those first years you must have hated me. I saw it in your eyes. When that passed, there was a loneliness l knew could never leave you. If it wasn't for our lovely Hannah, I doubt there would have been an iota of happiness in either of our lives.*

*I committed a wrong in making your father agree to our marriage. But the burden of a greater wrong lies on my shoulders and haunts me day and night. I was a stupid and foolish man to think if my competition was out of the picture, you would be more amenable to me.*

*My shame prevents me divulging the horror of the details but I know this: I offered your young man thousands of pounds to leave the country and he wouldn't. His love for you was real and was deep.*

*Mine on the other hand was fuelled by the need to have a wife to start climbing the ladder at the bank.*

*No words can express my sorrow and shame. Don't think I have not suffered, looking out on the park, watching his poor mother and father tending to the flower beds he had dug out before he disappeared. Looking at your face every day and feeling your desolation at being abandoned broke my heart in two.*

*I often wondered why you were so drawn to the park, why*

*you never wanted to move from the square. I have gone mad with shame and know no other way out. The guilt has made me a difficult man to live with. You did not deserve that, you did not deserve any of it.*

*I wronged you, Lily, but I have left you well provided for. Thank you for being such a great mother to our daughter. Please, if this confession means anything to you, speak kindly of me to Hannah.*

*Try and find happiness now I am free at last and you too have been set free.*

*With affection and love,*
*Reginald*

With one hand, Lily crumpled the letter into her pocket. She'd never told anyone about it. There were times she wandered to the park and sat near the lilac tree, talking in her head to Eamon, but not for a minute did she consider showing anyone else the letter. There was no excuse for what she had done, only a pathetic fear of being found out and caught up in a mess that could forever stain her family. Was it time now to assess the contents of the letter again, to right a wrong about which she had stayed silent? She needed time to think.

# THIRTY

Cora was reading the email when Tom Hooper rang.

'I'm outside the house, can I come in?'

'Give me a minute, I'm still in bed.'

She pulled on a dressing gown, worrying he would recognise it wasn't hers. She checked the time on her phone, it was just after seven.

'I'm sorry,' he said, 'I was working nearby, my sense of

timing is off, but I wanted to tell you what I have found out about Jack and his other secret life.

She flinched, pain drifting across her face.

'Me and my stupid mouth. Forgive me, I hate the fucker, but I forget you still love him.'

Did she still love him? She wasn't sure anymore, she thought.

'No point staying on the doorstep or Gladys will be over to cross-examine you about your pattern of parking. If you're hungry, I can do scrambled eggs on toast.'

He followed her to the kitchen, sitting down at the table, while she cracked the eggs into the saucepan.

'I did this once or twice with Amelia, calling early, but Jack didn't like to be disturbed at breakfast time, so I never arrived unexpectedly again. On that last day, I passed here really early; I wish now I had knocked on the door.'

'Life can't be full of our regrets.' She smiled. 'I'm great at giving advice, it's just a pity I can't take it myself.'

Quickly stirring the mixture, she reached for the plates and tipped the scrambled eggs out on to them, when it was fluffy ready. Popping two slices of bread in the toaster, she took orange juice and butter from the fridge. 'I hope you're all right with this, I'm afraid I have no bacon.'

He went to the cutlery drawer and got two forks and knives. 'I know you may not want to hear this, but you are so like Amelia.'

'From what I've learned, she was a gentle person.'

'Good inside and out.'

When the toast popped up, he took it and buttered a slice and put it on Cora's plate. 'She had that same generosity and kindness I see in you.'

'So is that what Jack saw in us, women easily taken in?'

'Don't be so hard on yourself.'

He downed a few forkfuls of the egg and drank half a glass

of juice, before pulling a sheet of paper along with the envelope of photos from his inside pocket. 'Do you want to read it yourself or will I tell you what I have discovered?'

'Who is she?'

'I knew you would ask that, but I don't know.'

He scanned down the page before he continued: 'Amelia was recommended the private investigator by your next-door neighbour. He doesn't usually do marital stuff, but Amelia started crying and offered him twice his normal rates. My sister always did have a way of persuading people.'

'How come we have no name for the woman?'

'I'll get to that. Jack must have told Amelia he was away on business, when in fact he was in a hotel in Kildare. He had some cheek.'

He stopped to pour some more juice.

'They booked in as Mr and Mrs Gartland?'

'Yes, the investigator followed them around, but mostly they stayed in the hotel. Early on Sunday morning, he drove her to the airport and she got the London Gatwick flight.'

'Don't tell me he didn't follow her. What name had she checked in under?'

'The trail is cold. He had established Jack was having an affair. It's what he was asked to do. Her identity didn't appear to matter so much to him.'

'Damn it.'

Tom reached across to Cora. 'There's nothing more we can do.'

'But it's like Lily said, there's another woman out there, one who may not even know Jack is dead.'

'His laptop was in the car. I got a guy to have a look at it, but it was purely work stuff. He only had work-related contacts on his phone. I tried random numbers he had dialled but nothing useful came up.'

Tom placed his fork and knife on the plate and pushed it in

from the edge. 'I can't do any more, Cora. Whether we like it or not, it might be time to move on.'

'Do you think Amelia was going to let it go?'

Tom shook his head. 'She had it out with him or she was going to, we'll never know. Ask yourself, though, what good it will do you. It's a wild goose chase.'

She got up and stacked the plates in the dishwasher. 'Nothing can make anything right, but I just want to know.'

'Have you been through Jack's papers? There might be some clue, a location or a surname.'

'Every time I have gone near his desk with that exact intention, I haven't been able to carry it through.'

'It's only an idea.'

He pushed back his chair. 'Thanks for the food, I had better get home and get some sleep, I'm due back in work later.'

Cora let Tom out, just as Gladys opened her door for a newspaper delivery. She waved, but Gladys, unnerved because she had been caught gawking, pretended not to notice.

Cora turned back to the office and Jack's desk. It would have been an idiot who had left such incriminating evidence in plain sight, but Jack was arrogant. She never went near his office at home. Now as she pulled open the top drawers, she was wary of invading his privacy. She smiled to herself; a dead man can have no privacy.

Taking out the first bundle of papers, she scanned the contents, looking for something other than business. When she saw a pink sheet peeking out from under a pile of credit card bills, she pulled it free.

*'You are my everything. Love, Amelia.'*

Sadness rolled through her at this simple declaration of love, a love that on Jack's part could so easily be set aside. What was it about him that earned the love and trust of such beautiful women, yet he continued to inflict small stabs of pain, until he wore down and challenged that love. The truth was she hated and loved him in almost equal measures.

The credit card bills were in a neat pile. She picked out the bundle, running them through her hands like a deck of cards. She took some from the top, middle and bottom, but they were all from his office business account. She pushed down to the next drawer, her hands spanning across stationery supplies, looking for anything unusual. She was about to close the drawer when her fingers felt the ribbed outside of Jack's cigarette box. Silver, with a flat bottom; she had had it engraved many years before: 'From me to you'.

Cora remembered she'd bought it for Jack four weeks after they'd met. They had a date for the Oak Room at The Plaza. She thought she had embarrassed him at first when she gave him the package, until he had pulled out a small Tiffany box from his coat pocket. A silver bead bracelet. She had no idea where it was now; she felt a pang of guilt that he had kept her first present to him.

Turning over the box, something inside rattled. Opening it, she stared at the gold band, the one she had given him. How had she been so silly, to think he would be still wearing it, when he had married one woman and had a fling with another. She slipped the ring on her finger. It was too big; she remembered it had always looked tight on his pudgy fingers.

What was she going to do with it, other than put it back in the cigarette case? She would never know when it all went sour for Jack. Had it already begun to decay, only she hadn't noticed, when she had handed him that cigarette box in The Plaza? She had to believe it hadn't. She had to believe they had once had something. She took the box and slipped it into her handbag. It might be the only reminder she would keep of Jack, from a time when she considered what they had was good and right.

She slipped off his ring and let it roll across the desk, until it hit a mound of newspapers and rested there. She let it stay there, to begin its journey again to an unwanted place when the newspapers were moved. When her phone rang, she was grateful for the interruption.

'I couldn't sleep. Are you OK?'

Cora laughed. 'I'm not OK, Donna, I never will be. But yeah, I'm still standing.'

'I felt you might need to talk.'

'You have impeccable timing.'

'Oh no, what's gone wrong now? I keep saying to Chuck, you should come home. Stay with us, the kids love you.'

Cora laughed.

'They're teenagers, they don't love anyone.'

'That's true, but you are top of the list of people they will tolerate. I don't think I'm even on that list.'

Cora giggled.

'I miss you, Donna.'

'Good, when are you coming back, honey?'

'It's not as simple as that.

'Get a plane, darling, leave that damn place, get a realtor to put it on the market.'

'I've had an email from a friend in a gallery downtown asking if I had enough paintings ready for a small exhibition in Manhattan.'

'What? I hope you said yes...'

Cora heard her friend turn away for a moment and tell her husband to wake up, there was news.

'...This could be the break you are looking for. And of course you will have to come home. So, all is good.'

'I haven't decided; it may be too big a commitment at this stage.

'You have to finish the one painting, that surely is not going to tax you too much. Chuck will make a little studio for you, you can stay as long as you like.'

When Cora didn't answer Donna got cross.

'Jeez, girl, isn't this what you always wanted?'

'Like I said, it's not that simple.'

'Honey, you can't let this opportunity go. When do they want to run the exhibition?'

'Some time in November.'

'Plenty of time to finish that painting and sort out your affairs in Ireland.'

'Donna, I'm not sure I can even paint anymore.'

'Nonsense darling, it's like riding a bike, you never forget. Hell, if an exhibition space downtown wants your work, I'll help you finish that last painting even if I have to do it myself.'

Cora laughed out loud. 'Which is exactly why you're such a lovely friend, but this I need to decide on my own. Jack has left me so much to deal with here, I can just about manage all that at the moment.'

'Jack, Jack, he has so much to answer for. I knew he was going to be trouble some day.'

'I thought you were his biggest fan.'

'I think over time, I was taken in by his charm but remember, I said stay away from him at the start, when he bumped into you in Central Park. Oh honey, I didn't want to be right about this.'

Cora pushed back the chair and got up from the desk, in the hope it would distract her enough not to sob.

'Are you there?' Donna asked, her voice softer now.

'Yes.'

'Honey, staying in that house is no good for you. Maybe a few days in Vermont or Nuala's place in Cape Cod; the offers remain open.'

'I don't even know this third woman's name.'

'Why on earth would you want to know that? What would you do, invite her to lunch?'

Cora giggled through her tears. 'It might help towards understanding any of this mess.'

'What's to understand, honey? He was a shit who did the worst thing a man can do to a woman, after rape and murder.'

'But why? Why do it to his wife of only three years? She was beautiful.'

'Hold on a second, girl. Just because she was a looker doesn't give him any excuse for what he did to you. Sounds like Jack was a serial adulterer, a bad egg, a horrible character masquerading as the all-American nice guy. All of which I warned you about, when you had known him less than an hour.'

'But you liked him when you got to know him.'

Donna harrumphed. 'He was charming, slippery like a snake. He was your guy, you loved him. That was enough for me.'

Cora looked out at the park where the herbaceous borders were in full bloom, the dahlias muscling the smaller flowers out of the way. This was such a lovely place to live, peaceful like the countryside early in the morning and late at night. Yet she was so unhappy here, her head and heart in constant turmoil as she tried to find answers where there were none. All that was here were riddles and puzzles that she would never be able to solve.

'Cora, honey, are you still there?'

'Yeah, just feeling a little down.'

'Of course you are, that cad knows to keep kicking you, even when he's dead. You have to stop this search in the abyss that was his complicated life. Extricate yourself, come home, darling.'

'Soon... I don't know.'

'The house has been cleared.'

'Tell me, please.'

'Threw all Jack's shit away. All your pieces are in storage.'

'I forgot to ask, thank you.'

'You've had enough on your mind, I didn't take offence. By the way, that guy Rich was true to his word; he and two friends helped us to clear the place. In a weird way, we enjoyed throwing out Jack's stuff. On the last night, we had a barbecue, some of the neighbours came along too.'

'Donna, that's why I didn't want to be there.'

'I know. Everybody was on your side, darling. After a few beers we named the event the "go to hell Jack barbecue".'

When Cora didn't respond, Donna laughed. 'Maybe it's too early for you yet, but it sure helped all of us. You need to rage and get drunk and get that bastard out of your system.'

'Another time. Right now, it's all about getting through.'

Donna rang off and Cora was left in the silent house in this strange city, where Jack had brought her. A person walked by the window and in the distance, she saw Gladys patrol the perimeter of the park.

What was she doing here? All that was this side of the Atlantic was pain on top of more pain. There were no answers, only more questions. She checked her email. Even if she stayed, what would she do in this house full of reminders of Jack and his wife? No questions would be answered for her, but her wound would be pulled back and left to fester and never heal. Her only way back was to start painting again and that had to happen soon. She needed new subjects, new ideas and a new outlook because all her other work was so intricately linked to Jack.

# THIRTY-ONE

Lily stepped carefully down the front stone steps. She was nervous, as if she shouldn't be out and about in the dark. Slowly, she stepped across the road and around the park to an entrance gate Draper had forgotten to padlock. Burrowing into her pocket, she pulled out her key and pushed it in the lock, checking all around her when the gate squeaked as she pushed it open. She was glad her old key still worked, because she needed so badly to pretend the garden was as it always had been. She stayed away from the area where the remains had been uncovered. The garda crime scene tape was in place, surrounding the grave at a distance of several metres. Her head began to throb to think it might be Eamon and what might have befallen him. She sat on a seat from which she could just about make out the shape of the fallen lilac tree.

She thought of the years before she'd read Reg's letter; all the times she'd sat here screaming in her head to Eamon, asking him why had he left her behind.

Gladys said the park would be forever haunted. What did she know, Lily thought. Her and her stupid emails. She took out her phone and called up the latest missive from Gladys.

.   .   .

From: **GladysSpencer@gmail.com**
To: **all De Courcy Square Association members**

We are all beside ourselves with what has happened. We are beyond horrified that a grave has been unearthed in our beautiful park. The gardai have removed the remains and soon the area will no longer be cordoned off.

Rest assured that when we retake possession of the park, this Association will have that section restored back to its former glory in a matter of weeks. It is our intention to use the funds left over from the key fiasco to pay for the necessary groundwork. Some have mentioned erecting a plaque to remember the dead person when their identity is known. It the view of the Association that this episode is best put firmly behind us, so we may concentrate all our energies on the battle to save our beautiful park.

Gladys Spencer,
Chairperson

Gladys and her pompous attitude. A snuffling in the bushes made Lily start. She didn't relax until she saw the shape of a fox creep from under the fuchsia and wander down the path. Lily needed to sit here. In her heart she wanted it to be Eamon because it would explain everything. Men in plastic suits had scraped away earth with small trowels, unpicking the bones in an effort to solve the mystery of whose they were and what had happened, to finally piece together the story of that person's life and death.

It said on the TV news they were still trying to identify the remains. Lily mourned Eamon while also dreading the final confirmation. All this time, she had looked to the lilac tree, hoping by the time it bloomed each year her circumstances would have changed, that the new season would bring him back. She never gave up hope. Ten years ago, when Mr Barry in No. 34 said he had heard the young lad managed to get as far as Australia, she had written to the newspapers in all major cities there, saying how much she wanted to reconnect to her good friend before she died. A newspaper in Perth had rung her asking for a photograph, but she had nothing. She had rushed off the phone, pretending to be confused, unable to talk about Eamon and irrationally afraid her family would find out about her quest.

Getting up off her seat, she carefully picked her way across the uneven ground to stand close to the crime tape on the cold earth turned over by the forensic investigators. Loneliness crept through her, to think what might have been. All the times she had come to this garden, the space where she felt closest to him, to create alternative storylines in which they both starred. She cursed Draper, who had started all this park trouble. He not only had robbed her of the peace of mind here in this garden, but he had tarnished her memories forever.

Pushing her hands into her pockets, she felt the letter. If she produced it now, what would happen? If it was Eamon here in this grave, then this letter directly incriminated her husband and her family. She would have to explain why she had not shown the letter before this, why she had not sought justice for the man she loved. Dragging the bench back to its old position closer to the grave, she sat down. Closing her eyes, she remembered the last night she and Eamon had sat here, sure they could not be seen, because he had earlier managed to throw an old coal bag over the street corner light.

He'd held her close, whispering into her hair as they made plans to meet on O'Connell Bridge the following night.

'I have booked the ferry, arranged a guesthouse in London.'

She'd shivered in excitement as he told her not even to bring a case, so as not to arouse suspicion walking through the streets. 'Your father knows too many people, so best dress up as if you are meeting a girlfriend to go to the pictures,' he said.

He had kissed her softly and told her to stay brave, before shepherding her to the gate and watching as she crossed the street to her home and went in the front door.

The next evening she had left early, running around her mother as she tried to cross-examine her in the hall. The conversation was strained, her mother asking her to stay home, as if she knew her daughter was not telling her the truth. 'Lily, it's cold out, you don't need to be going anywhere.'

'It's just the pictures.'

'There's still time to cancel, we could sit and talk.'

Lily had pretended to laugh, but she was worried it sounded hollow, so she kissed her mother on the cheek. 'I don't want to be late, I'll be back soon.'

She had rushed from the house, before her mother could say anything more. Tears had stained her make-up and she had to go to the ladies in Buswells Hotel to clean herself up before hopping on a bus to O'Connell Bridge. As she walked across the bridge to the GPO side, a photographer snapped her, but she shunned his card. Others queued up to pay for a photo on O'Connell Bridge, but she had no inclination for a memory without Eamon. This was the start of the rest of her life; she didn't need a photograph to remind her she was leaving her past behind.

She was ten minutes early, so she'd sauntered down O'Connell Street, straying a short distance from the bridge, to look in the window of the *Irish Press*, where people were gathering to read the headlines, displayed on the front page of the newspaper. She did not stay too long, but walked back to the bridge, quickening her pace, lest Eamon be worried she wasn't going to show.

She wasn't concerned when she did not see him immediately, and was almost relieved she had made it back before him. Standing up against the quay wall to shield herself from the harsh cold wind spewing in from the sea and up the River Liffey, she turned up the collar of her coat, dipping her head down as the bitter cold rested on her eyelashes and made her cheeks prickle. She had worn her high, going-out shoes to avoid igniting the suspicion of her mother and she wobbled now as she attempted to stay standing on the uneven ground.

All the time, she expected him to come behind her, catch her two shoulders and swing her into his chest. All the time, she wanted to glimpse him stride across the bridge, forcing his way through the cold wind as if he did not feel it. Her small toes were crippling her, her back was sore. She had started to feel unsure, when she thought she glimpsed him. Quickly, she had shaken away the doubts, stretched to her full height, a smile on her face – to see the man walking towards her wasn't Eamon. Feeling stupid and unsure, she moved onto the bridge. The man with the cameras across his chest smiled kindly at her. When she didn't respond, he came and stood beside her. 'I see it a lot, you know.'

'See what?'

'Go home. If he really wants to find you, he will.'

She'd trudged on, angry at the little man who spent his life observing others go about their business.

It had been nearly two hours and she did not know what to do. She crossed to a phone box, but how could she ring his house and ask for him. She had never done that in her life. They had always arranged to meet and turned up. There was never a question about that, until this time.

She remembered leaning against the door of the box, wondering had he been in an accident, should she trek around the hospitals? When a man stopped to ask was she all right, she ran down Westmoreland Street, only stopping when she turned over on her ankle as her foot caught the edge of a manhole cover. Her ankle stinging, she jumped on a bus to Merrion Square, cutting up past Leinster House to get to De Courcy Square. Anger overtook worry, her ankle throbbed with pain. She walked past their corner of the square, checking the seat near the lilac tree. She looked up at his window on the second floor.

She refused to cry, taking out her powder compact to check her face in the mirror, before going up her own steps and ringing the doorbell.

When her mother swung back the door, she eyed her daughter up and down. Ushering her into the sitting room, she had gently asked what was wrong.

The sight of Sam approaching brought Lily back into the present. She felt a little annoyed he had not let her come home in her own time.

'I am all right,' she called out. Sam slowed his pace, unsure of approaching.

A light came on in Gladys's house.

'What are you doing here?' Lily asked, trying to compose herself.

'I should ask you the same thing. What's wrong?'

'I needed to think.'

'Is it helping?'

'Not really.'

Sam looked up at the stars. 'Can you see the Plough?'

She let herself be diverted as he sat down beside her.

He leaned his head beside hers.

'Can you see the handle? Now follow down, to the slightly irregular rectangular shape.'

'Like a saucepan?'

'If you like. Now, follow up the far end of the saucepan in a straight line. Can you see the North Star?'

Lily laughed.

'I can.'

Sam pulled Lily close.

'It's a good way to put things in perspective, get lost in the stars.'

'Can you pick out others?'

Sam laughed. 'You have caught me out. The stars remind me there is another world out there. Troubles get smaller, the longer you stare at the stars.'

'I had better do a lot of staring then.'

'I'm ready to listen, if you think it would help.'

'I wouldn't know where to start'

'The beginning is usually a good bet.'

She smiled. 'I'm not ready, not yet anyway.'

He brushed her cheek lightly with his hand. 'Why don't we go home?' Then he said, 'You're a good person, Lily.'

'I'm not,' she said, leading the way as they crossed over the road. They were passing by Gladys's place, when her door swung back.

'Lily, are you all right? I heard a commotion in the park.'

'We're fine, Gladys. Probably some young people messing on the way home from a night out.'

'I called the gardai. You can't be too careful. We can't have antisocial behaviour in the park. We have had enough of trouble there.'

When they got back to No. 22, Sam gently took Lily by the hand and brought her upstairs. He helped her into bed and when she asked him to stay with her, he held her in his arms, humming the only song he could remember, *My Way*, until she fell asleep.

# THIRTY-TWO

Lily's head was thumping. Sam was asleep, so she slipped out from under his arm and padded to the sitting room. She needed to be on her own. As the night melted away, she stayed sitting in her armchair, inside the sitting room window. She didn't welcome the pink spear of morning light that slowly opened up the dark sky. In the city's blackness, she felt safe; there were no questions she had to answer, no decisions she had to make. She sat peering into the half-dark, the trees lining the perimeter of the park making strange silhouettes in the low-level street lighting. A fox sidled up the middle of the road, stopping to listen intently before veering into the park. A cat ran for cover as a door opened at the other side of the square, light flooding the steps of Gladys's house. Gladys let her pug out, shooing it away from her section of path and sending it across the road, where the city bicycles were parked. The dog squatted in the street and Lily leaned forward to see if Gladys would follow to clean up after her dog, but she only stood on her top step and watched. Lily wished she could have shouted at Gladys, the same woman who gave old Mr Barry hell last year for letting his

Jack Russell wander on his own because the old guy was laid up with a bad leg.

All of this was a nice diversion, but it was short-lived. She could not get Eamon out of her head.

There was no doubt that she had loved Eamon, loved him still, but the pain of not knowing all these years, and marriage to Reg, had taken their toll. Would that she could be back to those days when the love between her and Eamon was all-consuming. They'd never had a chance to move from those giddy first days. Maybe they would not have stood the test of time, but her well of regret was that they had never had an opportunity to try. Theirs was a forbidden coupling. Easy to see in retrospect how it could never have happened, but their youth and innocence and the fog of love they'd inhabited meant they were unaware of the strength of feeling against them. When she had gone to her father days after Eamon went missing, spilling out her fears for him and admitting how much she loved him, her father had said nothing. Once she had left the room, she knew now, he had set the wheels in motion for a wedding in the shortest time possible.

It was easy to sit and judge from this distance. She knew whatever ruminating she did, she could never justify her own actions. Hannah would feel so let down if she found out. Lily felt the tears run down her face, but she didn't bother to tidy herself. She wanted the cold discomfort of sitting in the half light feeling her tears soak deep into her collar. The letter was back in the tin. She could still tear it up and nobody need know. The problem was she would know. As the city woke up to another day, Lily was no closer to deciding what she should do. The buzz of the doorbell made her jump. Wiping her hands across her face, she listened for the caller to ring again.

Unsure as to whether she wanted to entertain a visitor, she tried to peep out of the top window, but the person was too close to the front door to be easily observed and identified.

The doorbell buzzed again, the caller pressing urgently on the bell.

Groaning, Lily made for the stairs, carefully making her way down to the landings and then the hall. The person outside coughed loudly as she opened the door.

'Mrs Walpole?'

The man in front of her had a friendly voice, but she took in the grey serge trousers, the badly fitting shirt, a tie that was too narrow for his build and a grey-flecked tweed jacket. She knew, too, by his neat haircut, he was a detective.

'Is there something wrong, officer?'

'Detective Inspector Michael Reid. What gave me away?' he asked, smiling at her embarrassment.

She wanted to say 'the well-cut clothes' and shut the door in his face, but she didn't.

'I apologise for calling so early, but I understand from Mrs Spencer that you have lived in the square for a long time.'

'Yes, all my life.'

'Could I come in, chat to you about life in the square in the last decades?'

'Don't you have better things to do?'

'It's all part of the investigation into the discovery in the park.' She stepped to one side.

'Come in, but I'm not sure how I can help you.'

She led the way to the kitchen and switched on the kettle. 'Do you know yet who is buried in the park?'

'Not for sure, but we did find a few things, including a key to the house next door, near the body.'

'You think it has something to do with that house?'

'Mrs Spencer said you knew the family. You used to be friendly with a young man there?'

'Gladys is only in the square about twenty years. For a blow-in, she knows the gossip from way before that.'

Lily took down two mugs and plopped the tea bags in. She concentrated on getting the milk out of the fridge.

'We have to follow up on all information.'

'I knew the caretaker's son. The house belonged to a London family, but the caretaker Thomas Griffin and his family lived there too.'

'What about the son?'

'He was a bit older than me. He went missing. Everybody said he went off to England. I don't know what happened, we never saw him again.'

'What happened to the family?'

'The house was sold and they moved away months after.'

The detective stirred two heaped spoonfuls of sugar into his tea. 'Strange a person could just disappear like that. You were friends, weren't you?'

Lily hesitated. Sitting up straight, she looked the detective in the eye. 'If you have something to ask, fire away. Too many years have passed for me to care what anyone thinks anymore.'

'I have to ask the question, were you in a relationship with the young man?'

Lily smiled. 'Did I love him? Yes. I still do. Do I know what happened him? No.'

She got up, and asking the detective to wait she went out and plucked some white achillea. Taking the scissors from her pocket, she walked to the end of the garden and snipped her best red rose and some bramble. Pushing her bunch together, she took a deep breath, walked back into the kitchen and handed the arrangement to the detective.

'You think it's him, don't you?'

'We think so, yes.'

'Would you place this on the ground where they found him? There's a story in that arrangement, of love and the suffering of a broken heart. I imagine the last bunch of flowers handed over to a uniformed officer must be quite faded now.'

'Can you tell me more about the two of you?'

Lily sat down and took a sip of her tea. 'We were young and in love, life was good, then he left. I thought my parents had a word, told him to leave. Within a month, I was married off to my husband; he was from a banking family. He had money and social standing, that's all that mattered to my parents. That they were tying me to an angry, rage-filled man who was so cold, he could freeze hell over with his stare, was an unfortunate consequence.'

'I take it he's not still around.'

'He died a couple of years back, but by then, my good years were well and truly behind me.'

The detective concentrated on tracing the pattern of the oilcloth covering the kitchen table as Lily let tears wet her face. 'I'm sorry, I didn't mean to upset you,' he said quietly.

She got up and, pulling a kitchen towel from its holder, she blew her nose noisily. 'Life upsets me, detective.'

He stood up and walked to the sink, throwing the dregs of his tea down the plughole, before rinsing his mug and placing it on the worktop. 'Is that a lilac tree at the bottom of the garden?'

'Yes, why?'

'It looks about the same age as the one in the park.'

'Eamon planted it there. There were two purple trees earmarked for the park, but he said one was enough and the lilac tree would remind me forever of our love.'

She stood by the detective, looking out at the garden. 'The flowers burst forth and then are gone; it's like what happened to us, we blossomed together and were no more. At least for the tree, the lilac blooms return, as lovely, as innocent and as beautiful. Maybe I was lucky: ours was an in innocent, sweet love, it never had a chance to grow weary and tired.'

The detective checked a message which flashed on his phone screen.'

'I'm embarrassing you...'

He put away his phone and smiled. 'Not at all, but I had better get back.'

She got some tinfoil and placed it around the stem of the flowers.

'Can you place them nearby for me?'

'Of course.'

He walked in front of her, stopping by the hall mirror to let her pull back the door.

'Will you promise me one thing?'

'If I can.'

'If it is Eamon buried there, will you tell me?'

'I will.'

She was going to say something else, but her mouth dried up.

She stood on the top step as the detective crossed the road and entered the park.

Turning away, she thought of the letter. Panic waved through her but she tried to ignore it.

Slowly she climbed the stairs back to the upstairs sitting room, where she sat in her chair to watch that corner of the park now so desecrated, so untidy; the lilac tree at half tilt, half dead against the railings. At one stage the detective looked up at the window and waved before placing her posy of flowers to one side of the crime scene tape. Shrinking back, she closed her eyes, letting her fingers run across the thin silver chain on her wrist. When he had given it to her, Eamon had made her promise to wear it until he could replace it with a wedding band.

'Until then, this is the symbol of our love. Wear it, so we may show the world the bond between us cannot be broken.'

Tears flowed down her face now. All the times her husband had told her to stop wearing that silly, trash trinket. 'You are the wife of the most important bank manager in this city, please at least look the part. It's not as if you are wanting for anything,' he had said.

She had to wear long-sleeved blouses that Anne Kelly, the dressmaker, ran up for her, because it was the only way she could ensure her husband did not notice. Sometimes, she wore a gaudy, gold bracelet low down on her wrist, so he did not suspect anything.

Once, he had gripped her so fiercely as he flew into a rage about some perceived slight, she felt the thin silver chain slip off her skin into the gathered folds of her sleeve. Two days later, when the bruises to her cheeks had yellowed and could be hidden by make-up, she had taken the chain to Weirs on Grafton Street to have it repaired. The man behind the counter asked was she sure, the chain was not worth it and he could offer her much nicer alternatives.

She had refused, asking how soon could the chain be fixed. Gently, she pulled the chain past the cuff of her left sleeve. Even now, she wore long sleeves, the years when she could show the sheen of her smooth skin long gone.

She no longer deserved to wear the bracelet. If she called back the detective, she could right a wrong, but how many more problems would it create? What would it do to Hannah to read that letter? When the doorbell rang again, she made her way downstairs, sure it was the detective returned to grill her.

Gladys was standing, a clipboard in her hand. 'Can I come in, Lily? This hullabaloo about the park has upset us all so much, I have been neglecting my usual duties.'

'I'm sure everybody understands, Gladys.'

Gladys stepped into the hall. 'We are going to win that war, Hannah said it's a matter of the terms of the agreement. When the police will be finished on the square is another question. I saw the detective called on you. Any developments?'

'He's hardly going to tell the likes of me.'

'I hope you don't mind me sending him your way, I knew you used to be sweet on that young man, donkey's years ago.'

'That was a long time ago.'

Gladys took out a pen. 'I thought now that all the park situation is nearly sorted, I would take a poll of the burning issues for the square residents. What is your number one?'

Lily stared at Gladys. 'I'm so glad you asked. Last night, I couldn't sleep. I happened to be looking out my window. Somebody on the square let their dog out unattended and never even bothered to clean up afterwards.'

Gladys stopped writing, Her cheeks reddened. 'I will certainly put it down as an issue. Of course it will depend on whether anyone else is equally concerned.'

'If one person says something, others will follow. Isn't that what you always tell us?'

'Really, I can't say I remember.'

'At least we know where the culprit lives.'

'Really?'

'Right beside your house.'

'It must be the young people in the flats further up.'

'No, I thought it was nearer your place.'

Gladys put away her pen, her cheeks colouring. 'I have just realised Hannah asked for a full written report on the park dispute for her files. Let's take a rain check.'

Lily laughed out loud, her face and sides hurting with the exertion. Gladys turned on her heel and marched out of the house, picking up speed as she hurried along. Lily watched as Gladys pressed the clipboard under her arm, never once looking back as she beetled across the road to her side of the square.

Lily, exhausted by the laughing, slumped against the bannisters, unable to climb up the stairs. She sat down on a step, her laughter turning to tears.

Sam, on the landing, watched her, uncertain at first whether he should go to her. She wept, her shoulders almost buckling as she let the pain take over. Unable to stand on the sidelines any longer, he ran down the stairs. Lily jumped up at the sound before he reached her.

'I'm all right,' she said, her voice almost challenging him to dispute her claim.

He stopped on the second last step. 'I was thinking we should get out and organise the back garden today, get a start after breakfast.

She nodded, letting him come down and enfold her in his arms.

'Always remember, I'm here for you. You saved me once; let me try to do the same for you.'

She dipped her head onto his chest. They stayed like that until she said it was his turn to make the tea.

# THIRTY-THREE

When Sam knocked on the door of No. 23 and asked Cora if she had time to join him for a stroll in the park, she was intrigued.

'Thank you, Sam, but can I ask why?'

'Can I show rather than tell,' he said, a big smile on his face.

There was an old-world charm about Sam, she thought, which made even an invitation to walk around the park sound like a special thing to do.

Pulling her cardigan around her, she grabbed her keys from the hall table and stepped out onto the front steps.

They walked side by side across the road.

'The gate in the south side is not padlocked and it means with the key we don't have to suffer the indignity of pushing past all the keep out signs or slipping through a too-tight gap in the railings. This way is like entering the garden of old,' he said.

When they got to the gate, he took the key from his waist-coat pocket and turned it in the lock, holding the gate open for Cora.

'I am told you're an artist of some repute and I hoped by

showing you the park of my childhood, it may inspire you to begin a painting at De Courcy Square.'

Cora stopped on the path.

'Did Lily and Gladys put you up to this?'

'Not exactly.'

'Sam, you're not very good at lying. I can see it all over your face.'

'I wasn't discussing you with Gladys, but Lily is worried. She says you have to get back to painting.'

'I'm sorry Sam, but painting is the last thing on my mind right now,' Cora said as she made to turn back towards the gate.

'Won't you hear me out?'

'Hear you out? Have you been pulled in to some sort of a plan which involves getting me back at the easel?'

Sam threw his hands in the air.

'All right, we thought if you could do a painting of the square, we could auction it and get some money for the campaign.'

'You think it's that easy?'

'Of course not. I apologise, but we thought if you were inspired, then maybe you would want to paint.'

Cora kicked at a dandelion in the middle of the path.

'Sam, you are a lovely, sweet man and I know you and Lily want the best for me, but I don't think I can even do the initial sketches or anything like that right now. My head is not in the right space.'

'Well, it was worth a try. Can I at least show you my favourite view into the square?' She nodded and they set off down the path, veering to the far corner. He pushed into the fuchsia and beckoned Cora to follow.

'It's my secret spot, an old potting shed even Gladys doesn't know about and an old tree stump which is covered in primroses in the spring.'

Cora took it in; the shed was practically falling down, the timber cracked, half the roof tilted at an angle. Sam reached in under the structure and pulled out an old folding chair. Shaking it before opening it up, he offered it to Cora.

'Don't worry, it's quite comfortable,' he said and she sat down, so as not to offend him. He leaned against the tree stump.

'Humour me, please, and close your eyes.'

Hesitantly, she did as he asked.

'Now open them and describe to me what you see.'

'The trees, reaching high, the houses playing peek-a-boo, a bird floating in the branches of the rowan tree, the clouds pushing onto the roofs, the sun slanting down like it's pointing out something or somebody.'

He clapped lightly.

'Excellent! I see my aunt's house, the window where I used to sit and watch over the park below and the stars above, the place where I could dream and nobody said it wasn't possible. If I could paint, I would capture this view, this vignette of a previous life.'

Cora stood up.

'Sam, you are so kind, but I can't do this, not right now when my head and heart are in this turmoil.'

He got up and pushing back the fuchsia, he used his body to hold it to one side so she could make her way to the path.

'You're a lucky man to be back living in the square,' she said.

He smiled. 'I would live in a tent with Lily, that is what makes me the luckiest man in the world.'

Cora looked at him.

'Can I ask a question?'

'Fire away.'

'What's your background? You seem to have an understanding and empathy that only adversity brings.'

'I wasn't always like this, I was more like Draper, wheeling and dealing and winning. My luck ran out and I lost everything, my family, my home and my reputation. I had to go into bankruptcy and I ended up homeless. Lily has been my salvation.'

She made to say something, but he put up his hand to stop her.

'Cora, you're going through the worst patch right now. I'm here to offer you the opportunity Lily gave me, a sense of purpose, a reimagining of yourself if you like, a chance to regain your self-worth.'

'Lily has told you.'

'Only because she wants to help. She thought we might connect at some level.'

Cora pushed past the box hedging and out into the central grassed area of the park.

'Sam, you are so sweet to try, but I can't even hold a pencil and even if I wanted to paint, I don't have any brushes.'

'Gladys said she can help on that front. Tony used to love painting and she still has all his gear.'

Cora laughed. 'But Gladys knows nothing about this.'

Sam shook his head. 'I confess there was a brief discussion with Gladys about commissioning a painting, but that's all.'

Cora sat down on a bench.

'I have a chance to have an exhibition in Manhattan. It's a big deal. If I was going to paint, it would be towards that. Jack left me money, too. I'm not short, I can donate to the campaign and the legal fees.'

Sam sat beside her.

'From here you can get a full view of Gladys and Tony's home. No doubt, if we could see past the net curtains, we would see Tony at the first-floor window, looking out on his whole world here in this park.'

'And Gladys trying to figure out if you have persuaded me.'

'Possibly.'

Cora stretched out her legs, throwing her head back to watch the clouds curling past the trees.

'Sam, I'm not sure I can do what you ask, but I do appreciate that you care so much and that you showed me these snatches of life from the park.'

'Maybe, if it doesn't inspire you now it will in the future.'

'Who knows? First I have to make a decision on this Manhattan exhibition.'

Sam got up.

'Give yourself time. If they really want you, they will wait for you. Now, if you will excuse me, I must report back to Lily and she can tell Gladys.'

'They could have come to me themselves.'

'They could, but for some reason they thought I might be able to persuade you.'

Cora stood up. 'Sam, if I was going to say yes to anybody, it would have been you. I'll stick around here a while. I'll get back out through the gap in the railings further up.'

He bowed to her and she watched him as he ambled across the grass, stopping to pluck a pink rose she was sure he would present to Lily.

Curious, she doubled back to the old gardening shed. Pushing open the door, she stepped inside. It was dark, but she could make out shelves at the back, a small table and a stool. A sleeping bag wrapped in plastic was on one of the shelves along with plastic bags folded as if somebody expected to use them again. Other plastic bags and old newspapers had been used to stuff gaps in the shed walls. Cora sat on the stool, listening to the sounds of the city around her. Dublin had taken her in when she was at her lowest; for that she would always be grateful.

The question now was would she ever be able to paint in this place?

When her phone rang she resented the intrusion.

'Cora, I have a favour to ask, but I will understand if you say no,' Tom Hooper said.

'Shoot.'

'Amelia had a small upstairs studio off Grafton Street. I hadn't even thought if it until now, but the owner has made contact to explain the lease is up.'

He sighed heavily. 'I need help to clear it out. I know you should be the last person to ask but I don't think I can face it on my own.'

'When did you want to do it?'

He blathered on as if he had not heard her question.

'The lease is up, all the employees have scattered. My wife is away with the kids and to be honest, I don't want to go in there on my own. I can't really ask another detective to come along. What do we know about this creative lark anyway?'

'Just because I paint doesn't mean I know anything about dress designing.'

'Some things will be sold on and I will try and keep a few mementos, but mostly I need the company, I hope you don't mind.'

'OK, but don't expect me to know much about any of this stuff. When do you want to do this?'

'Would Wednesday afternoon be all right?'

'Can I meet you there? Text me the address.'

'Thank you. It means a lot.'

'That's OK, it will be interesting to see somebody else's studio.'

'I was in it once before. It seemed a messy and busy space, but now it's only a room that has to be cleared. Amelia had three employees but at least two of them have found work with another designer, so that's something.'

'She must have been doing well to be able to employ three people and herself.'

'I think Jack was bolstering the business up quite a bit, but she had some valuable clients; one or two of them were at the funeral.' His voice choked up. 'I just don't think I can do it on my own,' he said once more.

'Don't worry, I'll come along,' she said.

# THIRTY-FOUR

Sam wore Reg's clothes, which was an odd feeling for Lily, but there was little point throwing out such good outfits, when there was a need for them.

When she first threw back the wardrobe doors and showed the rows of trousers, shirts and jackets, Sam shook his head. 'There was a time I had a collection just like this. It has been so long since I have worn freshly creased trousers.'

Lily saw his shoulders droop and she kissed him gently on the lips. 'You can take it the trial period is over.' He kissed her back and they stood, her head resting on his chest, his arms around her. Lily was the first to pull away. 'Sam, this is your home now and those are all your clothes. I think you and Reg were about the same size. Thankfully, it appears to be the only thing you two had in common.'

The first time he came down the stairs in the blue cardigan Reg had always worn when he pottered around the house at the weekend, she thought of asking Sam to take it off, but she didn't. Somehow it looked better on Sam's tall frame. When Reg pulled it on, she knew she would have no respite from his insistence on dinner at five, to be finished in time for the television news at six. He insisted they sit together looking at the news. Once the weather came on at the end of the bulletin, he switched off the television set, declaring those lucky enough to live in the city didn't need nor care about a nightly weather report. He would then take the *Irish Times* from his briefcase, shake out the broadsheet and instruct her to read the letters page out loud. He said in his line of work, he needed to be close to the pulse of the nation, especially those from the right side of the tracks.

Sam rolled up the sleeves of the cardigan and, using a fork and a shovel he found in the shed, he began clearing away brambles and weeds which had accumulated along the boundary wall with No. 23.

'This is a little sun trap. The sweet peas and a climbing jasmine will be perfect along here next summer.' Lily deadheaded the roses near the back door and cut back the scraggly blooms from the white lace hydrangea.

'Do you think Hannah will mind about us?' Sam asked.

'What she doesn't know won't hurt her, for the moment anyway. I want this to be our time; I don't really care what others think, even Hannah.'

'But it's something we will have to confront eventually.'

'This park business and all her other work is keeping her very busy, so at least we have some breathing space.'

He held up a bunch of cornflowers. 'They will look nice in a jug on the hall table.'

Lily took the bunch of deep blue blooms, smiling coyly when Sam reached for her hand and kissed it. In the two years since Reg had died, she had never been brave enough to place a vase of flowers on the hall table. If she even thought about it, she heard Reg's disapproving voice, telling her he didn't want the pong of bloody flowers when he walked in after work. She arranged the cornflowers now as she hummed a happy tune.

After a while they decided to go out for a coffee. As they left the square, they bumped into Anthony Draper. Delighted to see them, he wished them all the happiness in the world. Lily attempted to smile but once Draper had moved further down the street she rounded on Sam. 'I can't be seen chatting and being all pals with Draper.'

'It could be a good time to put that nasty chapter behind us all.'

'Forgive all the things he said and did, are you mad?'

Sam laughed out loud. 'You do realise, we are having our first row about Anthony Draper?'

Lily refused to find the situation funny. 'And we will continue to row, if you insist on cosying up to that man.'

They walked, a space between them as they made their way along the footpath.

At the coffee shop, Sam ordered two coffees and pancakes. Lily, still quite cross, pushed the plate of pancakes to one side.

'Anthony Draper has been good to me, Lily,' Sam said. 'He has put out a few feelers for me for consultancy work, I can't ignore that; but please, am I forgiven?'

'Yes,' Lily answered, sticking a fork into the pancake and cutting up a small piece, which she then proceeded to eat.

'Thank goodness for that. I'm used to being on my own; being us, I realise is going to take much more.'

The café owner strolled over. 'I hate to interrupt, but will I give the gentleman the remainder of his food and drink for takeaway?'

Lily looked perplexed. 'Why, do you have to close?'

'No, but you know the rules, I will serve you. but your gentleman friend is not allowed to sit at the tables.'

Lily stared at him. 'Whatever do you mean?'

Sam stood up and tried to hush Lily. 'Maybe we will just go.'

'No, I want to know why are we being throw out of this establishment?' Lily said.

The café owner appeared unperturbed. 'Like I said, I don't allow the homeless to take up the seats; the gentleman can have the rest as takeaway.'

Sam tugged at Lily's arm. She looked directly at the owner, who was fiddling with the ties of his apron. 'This is Mr Samuel Carpenter, resident of De Courcy Square. I'm sure The Shelbourne won't turn down our custom. We are leaving now. We have no intention of darkening the door of this place ever again. Neither do we have any intention of paying for the swill you pass off as coffee.'

She raised her voice even louder. 'I wouldn't be eating anything here if I were you. Ask him why he's always brushing up mouse droppings from the kitchen floor,' she said, before turning on her heel and marching out of the door, Sam trotting after her.

After they rounded the corner, Lily fell back against the brick wall at the end of the terrace.

'He must have recognised me as homeless. I'm very sorry you had to put up with that,' Sam said.

'You silly man, don't dare apologise for that moron. I have a good mind to put a brick through his window.'

'We haven't paid, so I think it best to rush home.'

They beetled along to No. 22, rushing to get in the door when they saw a garda patrol car turn in to the far side of the square. 'Fugitives from justice,' Lily said and they laughed together.

'I think we had better not go out all day,' Sam said and Lily agreed, taking Sam by the hand and leading him upstairs to her bedroom. She kissed him and he kissed her back. She let him unbutton her blouse and she slipped off her skirt as he gently caressed her neck.

'Can I get into bed first?' she asked and he watched her as she undressed and got under the covers. When she held out her arms to him, he pulled off his clothes and got in beside her. 'It's been so long,' she said.

'For both of us, but we love each other,' he said gently.

They made love and afterwards she lay in his arms, happy and safe. When they heard another garda car passing, sirens sounding, they laughed like teenagers. They fell asleep, waking up in the late afternoon. Sam pulled on Lily's dressing gown and went downstairs to make omelettes.

He placed two plates of omelette and green salad on a tray along with a glass of white wine for Lily and an orange juice for himself. Before he went upstairs he snipped three or four long stems of cosmos and pushed them into a blue bottle he found on the kitchen window sill. Lily was sitting up when he got to the top of the stairs.

'Flowers, too. I have never been so royally treated,' she said. After they had eaten, Sam stroked her hair.

'Isn't it time to tell me what has been bothering you? You can trust me, Lily.'

'I do trust you, but I don't want anything to spoil this mood.'

'There will be plenty of time for us, but please don't bear this burden on your own. You don't have to anymore.'

Lily gulped down half her wine before telling Sam about Eamon, her husband and the letter. She noticed he listened intently, at times reaching over to pick up her hand and kiss it softly.

'The letter is in the tin under the bed,' she said.

'Do you want me to read it?'

'Why wouldn't I, aren't we together now?' she said.

She watched as he got the letter and sat down near the window to read it. When he was finished, he folded it carefully before handing it back to Lily.

'What are you going to do?' he asked. She shook her head. 'I simply don't know.'

'I think there is only one way and that is show this letter to the detective on the case.'

'How can I explain that I have had it for the last two years?'

'Tell the truth.'

'That I have avoided that letter, afraid of what a deeper analysis would reveal.'

'Nobody is perfect, Lily, but now that a body's been found, it's time; you have to show the letter.'

Tears streamed down her face. Sam went to her, enfolding her in his arms once again.'

'I'll come with you,' he said.

'No, this is something I have to do on my own. Just tell me you love me no matter what.'

He held her tighter. 'There aren't enough stars in the sky to show how much I love and adore you,' he whispered in her ear.

# THIRTY-FIVE

Cora planned a day out, a walk around the National Gallery, lunch in a cosy pub. It was time to be a tourist in this city. She picked a pair of jeans cut out at the knees, a crisp white blouse and a long silk summer coat from Amelia's pile in the bedroom. When she saw a multicoloured scarf which had slipped off the clothes mountain to the floor, she picked it up, knotting it at her neck. The night before, she had cleared out her handbag so it wouldn't be too heavy, swopping over her passport for a map of Dublin.

The square and park were unusually busy; young people in yellow high-vis vests were weeding flower beds, cutting the grass with two petrol mowers and clipping the box hedges. Cora tried to slip by unseen, but Gladys spied her. 'We need all the volunteers we can get. Draper, as a gesture of goodwill, has allowed us in to work in the flower beds and tidy up the grass. Just for today, mind,' she said.

'I'm afraid I have plans today; maybe another time,' Cora said.

'Lucky for you and every other resident, these young people were spending a day in the square at the English school next door to mine. Otherwise, I would have been knocking on doors looking for volunteers.'

Cora said she had to catch a bus and trotted off, in case Gladys caught her up in any more chat. She saw Lily peering out of her top window and retreating quickly when she saw Gladys directing operations.

Outside No. 29, Anthony Draper was standing looking up at his roof.

'Do you think if I ask Gladys nicely, will she let me sell advertising, neon lights on the top floor?' he asked Cora as she passed.

When she didn't answer, he called after her.

'Only joking, but it would give the old bird a new focus.'

At the gallery, she didn't bother taking a map. She finally had the confidence to step inside the doors, thanks to the kindness of Sam. She knew what she wanted to see and asked the security man for directions, not stopping to look at any other paintings until she got there. Jack had told her that when he saw the painting of Lady Hazel Lavery, he had wished she could put her love for him on a canvas. She stood now in front of the huge canvas of the artist's studio, Lady Lavery with the fine cheekbones and the smoky look sitting resplendent in purple. Who had Jack brought to see this painting: his wife or his lover? The woman in the painting wearing satin and velvet looked like both, her artist husband revelling in her beauty. The look in Hazel Lavery's eyes was hypnotic. When she walked a few paces away, Cora found herself turning to gaze again at this enigmatic figure, one hand around her daughter, a greyhound at their feet.

Jack never went to look at this painting on his own. She had teased him he had not enough work to keep him busy, if he had time to loiter in front of a painting in the National Gallery. He'd got angry, because she was so ungrateful. When she protested he was overreacting, he'd taken a postcard of the Lavery painting out of his breast pocket and torn it in two.

'I don't know why I bother, Cora, you really know how to make a guy feel swell,' he'd said, before storming out of the house and into his car, the tyres screeching as he had rounded the corner.

She had picked the two pieces from the floor and sellotaped them together, sticking the card up on her studio noticeboard. Stress prickled through her again to think back, and she suddenly felt small as if the troubles on her shoulders had pressed her further down. Nobody here knew what Jack had done. She looked around her, wanting to shout out that life for her was bloody unfair.

She rushed from the gallery, unable to avoid a man handing out leaflets who pushed a piece of paper into her hand. Without looking, she stuffed it in her coat pocket. A man with a map stopped to ask directions and she calmed down for a moment, feeling a sense of belonging in Dublin as she directed him to the canal, without even having to consult the map.

The encounter set her up nicely and she walked on towards Grafton Street. Standing looking at the display in the window of Knobs and Knockers, she took out her phone to ring Donna, but realised it was still too early in the States. Donna collected door knockers, strange, beautiful and silly knockers on every door in her house. When she ran out of doors, she had her husband create a panel of fake doors down the sides of their back yard. Cora went inside to pick an old-fashioned brass knocker and arrange for it to be shipped. Feeling happy as she left the shop, her head tilted to the sun. At Grafton Street, she stopped to buy carnations from the sellers on the corner, before heading towards St Stephen's Green, where people were lying out on the grass, enjoying the summer sunshine. She found a space at the end of a bench, setting down her handbag and bouquet of flowers beside her. When an elderly lady joined her, she nodded a greeting and smiled. Stretching out her legs, she watched the children cavort around the fountain, letting the water bounce off their hands, creating rainbows of colour in the sunlight. One little boy tore off his sandals and jumped into the water, splashing like he was in a swimming pool. When another child joined in, the park attendant ran over, ordering them out as others laughed and shouted, 'Lock them up!' She wanted to paint that scene, to create the carefree moment, when the boy felt the sensation of the fountain water through his toes as the heat of his body was calmed. In her head, she was framing the scene. The itch to sketch, when it came, surprised and excited her. She had not carried a sketching notebook since before Jack died. Rummaging in her bag she picked out a pen.

Remembering the paper crumpled in her pocket, she pulled it out. Flattening the blank side and placing it on her bag for support, she quickly stroked the page, capturing in a few deft movements the innocence and joy of the young boy splashing in water on a late summer's day. The elderly lady beside her watched as Cora's pen replicated the happy moment, which, for those looking on, symbolised a perfect summer's day in the city.

'You have a talent, you should do something about it,' she said to Cora who, feeling embarrassed, stopped and hastily put away her pen and folded the sheet of paper into her handbag.

'I didn't mean to interrupt. In my day I loved to work with watercolours and sometimes charcoal.'

Cora dithered, not wanting to be caught in a conversation she hadn't invited.

The old lady stood up. 'I'll go, stop distracting you. Enjoy working up that sketch.'

She was gone before Cora had time to respond. Momentarily feeling guilty, she thought of leaving too, but the pull of sketching some more in the sunshine appealed to her. In each stroke and consideration of angle, she found a peace she had not felt in weeks. The children were back at the fountain, the attendant had disappeared. Two of the kids were knee-deep in the water, two others sitting on the parapet, letting their legs skim across the surface, making waves of water slosh over the side. Passers-by laughed and gave the fountain a wide berth as the lad who had originally jumped in shouted 'Geronimo!' over and over as he flung rainbow-coloured droplets out onto the path. Cora felt happy, something she had not felt in so long. Lifting her head from the sketch, she was singing silently to herself, a smile on her face that the sun was shining warm.

She watched the boy at the fountain as she absentmindedly fiddled with the paper in her hands, turning it over as she did so. A woman had stopped to scold the boy and he was near tears. Cora hated that his carefree enjoyment had been spoiled by a person who cared only for rules.

Carefully she folded away her sketch and walked from St Stephen's Green.

# THIRTY-SIX

From: **GladysSpencer@gmail.com**
To: **all De Courcy Square Association members**

Dear residents and tenants,

An important update on the battle for De Courcy Square.

Delicate negotiations are under way. Our solicitor Hannah Walpole is representing the Association and with the negotiations chaired by an expert in this field, Samuel Carpenter, I am sure we can expect a more than satisfactory outcome. A series of meetings will take place with Mr Draper and the City Council.

The Association has been very clear it will accept nothing less than a handover of ownership back to the City Council and a return to the status quo.

Gladys Spencer,
Chairperson

Lily crossed over to the park soon after first light. A blackbird let out a shrill warning call as she moved along the path, past the lilac tree, which had been shoved back in to position, its leaves died-back brown. She wanted to be near where Eamon had been found, to find some way in her heart to set this whole episode to rest.

The grass had grown long in this part of the park, which Gladys's maintenance squad hadn't reached, and she knew that when the sun came down strong, splashes of yellow would appear where dandelions had pushed through and begun to spread. If the truth be told, Lily preferred it like this. She watched out for the fox, but she might have been too late and it had already slipped away to its hiding spot. What had been Eamon's grave for so long was now an unmarked, untidy mound of earth. His remains had been quietly taken away. Without a formal identification, she didn't think he could be buried. The newspaper said gardai were continuing their investigations.

Nobody but Sam knew of the letter. She could tear it into shreds, burn it or simply throw it in a bin and the murder would remain unsolved, Eamon's story filed under a cold case designation.

She had already held the letter two years too long. Cursing the shame and fear of public scrutiny that had prevented her showing it when Reg had killed himself, she knew her own weakness was most to blame. It was the same weakness that made her now hesitate to do what she knew to be right.

There was no choice here; no matter how she weighed it up, there was only one thing to do.

She came to the park, because in this quiet spot she could find the space to think. The repercussions for herself she accepted, but for Hannah, the hurt would be enormous.

A rabbit hopped across the grass to a spot that was a darker green colour and munched away at a patch of clover. When she shifted on the seat, he stopped, his nose twitching, but after a few moments of alert attention, the lure of the clover was too much and he resumed tugging at the leaves, which were wet with dew. A finch perched on a thistle seed head and diligently pecked at it. Somewhere, the blackbird called out again and flew low over the grass; the rabbit scooted off, and the finch fluttered into the air, leaving the seed head on its brown stem lightly swinging.

When she saw Anthony Draper walking along the path, Lily got up to leave. He gave a friendly wave and marched across to her, his boots leaving indentations in the damp grass.

'It's a beautiful morning, Mrs Walpole.'

'I was just leaving.'

He gave a small laugh. 'Please, not on my account. I enjoy the early morning quiet in this park. It gets the day off to a good start.'

She thought she should have a smart retort to his statement, but couldn't think of anything.

'I'm glad I saw you, I have an early appointment with your daughter.'

'Hannah?'

'Yes, she is some operator.'

'I'm not sure I understand what you mean.'

He sat down on the bench beside Lily, who shuffled to one side.

'Mrs Walpole, I don't bite. She and Sam Carpenter have brokered a very nice deal. I think all sides will be happy.'

'I don't understand. Sam was home so late, I was asleep when he got in.'

'Before the crash, Sam was known for this type of stuff. He's a man you can trust and he came up with a great idea.'

She leaned closer so as not to miss a word. Anthony Draper stretched out his legs in front of him. 'I think I will let your daughter fill you in; she might not appreciate me speaking out of turn, but you folks get your park back and I get a good financial return on my investment in this land. It's a win-win, although maybe not for the council, which has had to dig deep into the coffers to avoid the embarrassment of a protracted court battle.'

'You are backing off?'

'I call it a strategic withdrawal. The important thing in my line of business is to know when to get out. The time has come for this deal.'

Lily stared at Draper, not entirely sure if she should believe him.

'I understand your scepticism, but you have to know, I saw a business opportunity and I grabbed it.'

'What business opportunity?'

He laughed and slapped his knee. 'My big mouth is getting in the way again. I think you merry band of women will be equally happy with the deal.'

'We'll see about that.'

Draper got up off the bench. 'It will be nice to see this park back to normal: I have come to love strolling here, listening to the dawn chorus.'

Lily looked at him. 'You never intended to turn it into a car park, did you?'

He laughed, pushing his walking stick against a dahlia which had drooped, the flower head in the mud.

'Guilty,' he said as he slowly and gently raised the dahlia stem with his stick, until he could lean the flower head against another for support. 'If this place was a car park, the value of number 29 and all the houses on this square would plummet. Why would I want that?'

'You seemed to hate everything about living on the square.'

'I'm good at bluffing.'

'It was all a big joke to you.'

'Not exactly; there was a lot of money at stake, all mine.

Anyway, but for the JCBs, the poor bugger who had been put in the ground here would never have got a proper burial.'

Lily's chest heaved, tears rising inside her. Draper was right, it was no thanks to her that Eamon had been found. Maybe it was time to right the wrong and offer up the letter in order to help confirm the remains were Eamon.

Lily said she had to go and made to leave.

Draper offered his hand. 'In peace, maybe we can be neighbours and some day friends?'

Lily shook his hand lightly, not sure if she should even be doing so.

'I only have a small garden at number 29. This park I can see becoming very important for me,' he said.

'You're staying in the square?'

He laughed again. 'Go on, admit it, it wouldn't be half as much fun for Mrs Spencer if I left.'

She smiled, but as quickly stopped. 'You were unkind to us at The Shelbourne.'

He looked at his feet, like a boy caught stealing apples. 'My apologies. I was smarting from the ticking-off in court, I came within a hair's breadth of going to prison.'

'Which was all your own fault.'

'Mea culpa. I can be an idiot at times, especially in the middle of a tussle.'

She shook her head; there was something rather endearing about Anthony Draper, but she would never admit it out loud. 'I have to get back,' she said, stepping round him.

He reached into his pocket and produced a key. 'Use the east gate, you don't want to twist an ankle getting over all that earth at the entrance.'

She accepted the key and headed down the path, past the bank of fuchsia and out of sight.

Anthony Draper had provided a nice distraction, but she knew where she must go and what she must do. Tightening the belt of her raincoat, she walked smartly out of the park to Dawson Street and hopped on a tram to Westmoreland Street, crossing over and walking the short distance to Pearse Street Garda station. When she asked at the hatch for Detective Garda Michael Reid, they rang upstairs.

'He will be with you in a few minutes; will I give him your name?'

She said her name quietly. The uniformed garda said Michael would not be more than ten minutes. She sat in the plastic chair in the grey room, twiddling her fingers, slipping her hand into her pocket occasionally, to check she had the letter. By the time Michael Reid pushed open the security door leading into the public office, she appeared calm, a calm brought on by exhaustion from over-analysing her own situation.

'Mrs Walpole, is there anything wrong? How can I help you?' Michael Reid said, a friendly smile on his face.

Lily stood up, falling slightly back against the chair, because her knees could not fully support her. The detective stretched out his hand to steady her. 'Whoa, are you all right?'

He called for a glass of water and put Lily sitting back down.

'Has something happened, Mrs Walpole?'

Before she could answer, a glass of water was handed through the hatch and he collected it, giving it to Lily.

She gulped the water down. 'I'm sorry, but I have come here to show you something. I think it will tell you what happened Eamon.'

'Eamon Griffin?' 'Yes.'

Maybe we should go somewhere more private.' He indicated to the garda behind the hatch to open the door of interview room one and he escorted Lily there. When she sat down at the table, he asked her if she needed another glass of water.

She didn't answer, but pulled the envelope from her pocket and handed it to the detective.

'Read it, please.'

Slowly, he opened the letter and scanned through it. 'From your late husband?'

'Yes.'

'Are you all right, Mrs Walpole? We are only having a chat, but would you like anybody to be here with you. Your daughter, isn't she a solicitor?'

'Oh, God. Am I under arrest?'

'No, not at all. You are free to go whenever you want, but you have handed me a document that is relevant to a murder investigation. You understand this is a serious matter. I am going to ask a colleague to step in and we will ask you a number of questions about this document.'

He left the room, the letter and envelope in his hand. When he came back the letter was in a plastic seal. A female detective, introduced as Rachel Crawford, sat opposite her. Lily shifted on her chair, panic and fear rising up inside her.

'Have I done something wrong?' she asked weakly.

'Mrs Walpole, we will be asking you questions about this letter.'

Michael Reid placed a notebook and pen on the table.

'Mrs Walpole, why don't you tell us why you came here today and how you came to be in possession of this letter?'

She had it all set out in her head, but when she started to talk, it came out differently.

'My husband Reg killed himself. He hanged himself from the top landing, I found him when I came home from doing the grocery shop.' She stopped to take a gulp of water. 'It was March two years ago.'

The image of him hanging over the landing had stayed with her, often returning as she walked up to the sitting room. She had been so happy that day, as Hannah and Derry had put in an offer on a lovely house in Mount Merrion and she knew they would get it.

Michael Reid cleared his throat, jolting her back to the present.

'He was a bank manager. He had been down, because of everything happening with the banks. The week before, a man came in to the bank, threw the keys of his house at Reg and said he was responsible for making his young family homeless.'

'And the letter, where was that?'

It was on the hall table, but she hadn't seen it until she had raced down the stairs to ring for help. Did she know what was in it? She didn't, but as she waited for everybody to arrive, she had pushed the letter into the drawer. Whatever was in it should be for her eyes only.

Lily looked at Michael Reid. 'That's the funny thing, well the odd bit. I only found the letter last night.'

'Last night? Your husband died two years ago.'

'Where was the letter?' the other detective asked.

'I fell apart after Reg died. For ages, I couldn't even look in his wardrobe.'

Lily looked at the far wall. 'I couldn't sleep last night. You see I have met a nice man and I must make room for him.'

Her cheeks reddened when she talked about Sam, her voice was lighter.

'It has made me confront the past and the first thing I had to do was get rid of my late husband's clothes. Last night I started, putting every thing in bin bags to give them to the charity shop. I was checking pockets, when I found the letter.'

'Are you saying you never saw this letter before last night?' Michael Reid asked.

Lily looked directly at the two detectives. 'I know it doesn't make sense. Why write the letter and then not leave it out? Isn't that what people do?'

The female detective shifted on her seat. 'Why that jacket?' she asked.

'Reg was wearing his good suit when I found him. He was

always a neat and tidy man; he must have hung up his old clothes, before he changed to hang himself.'

'Sounds odd,' the detective said.

'Reg was an odd man,' Lily said quietly.

The female detective put her elbows on the table and leaned forward. 'Why would he go to all the bother of writing this letter, not to give it to you?'

Lily dropped her head. When she spoke, her voice was so low, the detectives had to lean their heads close to her to catch every word.

'I don't know, maybe it was the contents. Maybe he was trying to protect Hannah.'

'Hannah?' the female detective asked.

'Our daughter.'

'Have you told us everything?' Michael Reid asked gently.

'Yes. What happens next?'

'I don't know. Neither of the two men are alive. We haven't been able to trace any of the young man's family.'

'You never suspected anything?' Detective Crawford asked.

'I thought Eamon had gone off without me, I could never figure out why. I loved him, I still do.'

Tears flowed down her face and Michael Reid pushed a box of tissues her way.

'Do you have to tell my daughter? She has always loved her father, I don't want to destroy that memory for her.'

'You are going to have to leave it with us. We will take legal advice on this.'

'What do you mean?'

Detective Crawford sat back in her chair. 'If you are telling the truth, Mrs Walpole, you have nothing to fear, but if you have been hiding this information for the last two years, that's another matter.'

Lily felt light-headed and her stomach was sick. 'You don't honestly believe I would do that?'

'We can't rule anything in or out at the moment; we are just doing our jobs, Mrs Walpole.'

'Are you saying I could be charged?'

Michael Reid snapped the cover on his pen. 'Let's not get ahead of ourselves. Let us bring this upstairs, go back, look at the death of your husband and what we knew of the death of Eamon. Detective Crawford will take your statement in writing. I promise we will get back to you soon.'

He leaned back in his chair. 'We have not been able to positively identify the remains as those of Eamon Griffin. I know it's a long time and this is a long shot, but would you by any chance have anything belonging to him? We are thinking of trying for a DNA match.'

Lily lifted her sleeve and showed the bracelet. 'That is the one thing I have been able to keep all these years. That and a small lock of his hair.'

'Do you have that lock of hair still?'

Lily reached inside her blouse and pulled out a gold locket. 'It was my mother's. All this time I have carried the lock I snipped from his hair when we were messing around. That and a picture of my Hannah; they are both so precious to me.'

Detective Reid leaned closer to Lily.

'I'm not sure how successful or accurate we can be with a lock of hair. I know there is something about it having to include the follicle, but if it is all right with you, we could ask the lab to have a look.'

Lily nodded her head, silent tears flowing down her face. Slowly, she reached behind her neck and opened the clasp before taking the locket and handing it to Detective Reid.

'We will take very good care of it and get it back to you as soon as possible,' he said gently.

Lily got up to go but Detective Crawford said she had one more question.

'We found an item with the body. Maybe if I show you a

photograph of it, you might recognise it.' She reached in to a folder and took out two photographs. The first one showed a discoloured jewellery ring box. The second showed the box open, a white gold ring inside.

Lily swallowed hard. Pain shot through her and pride too that Eamon Griffin was a man of his word; he had wanted to marry her. He always said he was saving up for the finest engagement ring. She dropped her head into her hands, tears convulsing through her. Detective Reid inched the glass of water towards her. She pulled a bunch of tissues from the box.

'Do you recognise the ring?' Detective Crawford asked.

Lily nodded. 'I had brought him to the window at Weirs so many times. I loved its simplicity, the round diamond set into a classic square shape, the stones either side of the square. I never in a million years thought he could afford it. I never thought he was going to be able to buy a ring like that.'

'He disappeared when he should have been meeting you. Maybe you can take some comfort in knowing he had the ring,' Detective Crawford said.

'In time, I will, but all these years later it is so painful to contemplate,' Lily replied. She got up to leave, the chair screeching across the floor.

'Can we call anyone to come and collect you?' Michael Reid asked.

'I think I need to walk, get some fresh air. Thank you.'

A burden had been lifted from her shoulders, but as she walked along the city streets towards home, Lily felt an overwhelming sadness for what might have been.

The moment she reached the square, Gladys made a beeline for her. 'Hannah was looking for you. You'll never guess the news.'

'Don't tell me Draper has been up to his old tricks again.'

Gladys linked Lily's arm. 'Everybody, including your Hannah and Sam Carpenter, is over at number 23.'

When they got to Cora's, Hannah swept open the door, her face beaming.

Lily did her best to look surprised and hugged her daughter tight.

'I have never been more proud of you,' she said, happy when Hannah hugged her back.

'It was Sam who came up with the strategy.'

Sam stood smiling as Hannah continued: 'Sam here realised that one of Draper's many companies had gone into liquidation. The liquidator wanted the park sold off to meet Mr Draper's debts. Sam persuaded the council to purchase the park for a hundred thousand euros. Mr Draper's creditors get paid and we get the park back.'

Lily reached over and took Sam's hand. 'I never knew you were so wily. It was a great day for all of us when you moved in to the square.'

The others clapped loudly and Sam, looking deeply embarrassed, bowed.

Gladys patted Sam on the back.

'We couldn't have done it without your cool head and your yen for the small details which made all the difference. The only downer is the council will insist De Courcy Square be a public park from now on.'

'I think that is infinitely better than a multi-storey car park,' Hannah said and everybody laughed.


When Sam and Lily got home much later, she said she was going straight to bed as she wasn't feeling well. Sam rested his hand on her arm.

'You went to the detective, didn't you?'

Lily nodded.

'And?' Sam softly prompted.

Lily gulped hard before she spoke. 'They are investigating it, but Sam, I told them I only just found the letter.'

Her hands were shaking as she attempted to grip the bannisters to go upstairs.

'You did what you had to do. I'm not going to condemn you for that. But there's something else, isn't there?'

She knew he could see the pain in her eyes. 'He had an engagement ring in his pocket,' she said. Her strength gone, she fell on the stairs. Sam rushed to pick her up.

'My darling, darling Lily, let me help you.'

'He loved me, Sam, and I loved him. I can't get it out of my head what might have been. Reg stole all that from me and spent the next decades making me suffer. He killed him, Sam, and even then he was still jealous of Eamon.'

She let Sam put his arm around her waist and guide her to the bedroom.

'Don't ever leave me, I love you,' she said as they lay on the bed together.

'I love you, too. I'm not going anywhere. Let's look to the future together,' he said, kissing her gently on the lips.

# THIRTY-SEVEN

As she walked down George's Street, Cora saw Tom Hooper pulling on a cigarette as he waited in his car. He waved when he saw her and hopped out of the driver's seat, putting the cigarette out with his fingers before throwing it in the bin.

'Thanks for coming, Cora, it means a lot,' he said as he entered a key code on an electronic pad outside a high red-brick building.

The studio was up two flights of narrow stairs.

Cora stood to one side as Tom, using keys he had taken from the hook at No. 23, quickly opened the door and pushed it back.

They slowly stepped into a large room with a big window, the sun streaming across the floor highlighting the threads of different colours, the lint caught in the crevices between the floorboards. Lining one wall were mannequins, tall bare figures looking as if they were crowding a platform waiting for the next train. Trestle tables were covered in a pink fabric, a pattern pinned down but never cut out. Bolts of silk and satin stood against a far wall which was lined with shelves holding different reels of thread in various hues and thicknesses.

She watched Tom go over to a writing bureau at the window.

'Amelia liked to sit here and sketch; she said all you needed was good light, a long piece of charcoal and a cup of tea to help kickstart the day,' he said as he ran his hands lightly over her sketch pad.

'That's all you ever need,' Cora said as she fingered some royal blue silk.

'I saw the sketch for the dress she intended for this fabric. I just wish she'd had a chance to make it.'

Lifting up the bolt of silk, Cora bunched the fabric around herself and stood in front of the mirror.

'I don't know much about these things, but that looks mighty fine on you.'

'It would take Amelia's talent to turn it into something magnificent.'

When Tom didn't answer she slid the bolt back on the table and followed him over to the bureau.

'Look at this,' he said, handing Cora a handwritten note he had pulled from an appointments diary on the desk.

*'Book the restaurant in Wicklow. Neutral space to talk.'*

'Sounds like Amelia was going to confront Jack after all,' he said.

'Maybe, Maybe not. I don't know if it matters that much anymore,' she said.

'You are probably right,' he said rolling the note into a ball and throwing it in the bin.

Tom picked up the scrunched-up wrapper of a KitKat chocolate bar. He rolled the foil and red wrapper around his hand.

'I keep thinking she will ring, walk by, say "Don't disturb anything"; she never liked anyone touching her things.'

'I know, I feel the same about Jack,' Cora said as she moved to the window to give Tom some space.

From here she could see across into the upstairs storage rooms of the shoe shop across the way. Two assistants sitting chatting jumped up when another woman walked in to the room and appeared to tell them off. On the street a delivery van pulled up onto the pavement outside the shoe shop, its hazard lights flashing. She saw the two assistants and supervisor help unload several large boxes.

'I don't know what to let go or what to keep. Maybe I should have told the landlord to bin the lot. He offered, but I felt it would not be the right thing to do.'

'You would have regretted it. It helps the healing to tidy away the flotsam and jetsam of their lives.'

'When you put it like that.'

Cora leaned over to look at the sketch pad.

'She was really good.'

'Always sketching or designing with fabric. When I was a kid, she used to make me model for her. She would take one of Mam's old dresses and make me put it on. I had to stand so still while she nipped and tucked and turned a very ordinary dress into something quite extraordinary. Even when I was a teenager and she could afford to buy fabric, I modelled for her.'

'I would've liked to have seen that.'

'Let's just say, if the lads at work get their hands on any of those pictures, I'm finished. Shall we start with the shelves? I have bin bags; maybe we can offload a fair lot of this to the charity shop.'

Cora walked over to the first shelf, where boxes of vintage buttons, bobbins and rows of different-coloured thread were stored.

'There must be someone who could use all this stuff.'

'There probably is, but the landlord wants the place clear by five this evening, so we need to get moving.'

He held up a refuse sack and tipped the spools of thread in, row after row of blues, pink, green, different shades of white and black.

Cora turned back to the bureau. Picking up a pencil she turned the page of the sketch pad and began to draw in clear, broad strokes. Tom cleared the shelves, chucking out what had been so neatly compiled and stored. Puffs of dust punctured the sunshine, different sounds echoed through the room as he filled the bin bags. Cora sketched, the pencil capturing the sadness of Tom, his back bent as he worked without a break, tearing his sister's dream apart.

Almost as if he knew he was being keenly observed, he straightened up and stopped.

'I thought that maybe something here would give a clue as to Amelia's state of mind: a diary, notes on a marriage; maybe it's too much to ask, I don't know.'

Cora put the pencil down.

'Sounds like you need a break. I can take over for a bit, clear out the filing cabinets.'

'I'm afraid if I don't go through everything, I will miss out on anything that could explain what was happening between those two.'

'Tom, there are no answers and even if there were, it might not be what you want to know. It might not settle your mind. What good would it do at this stage?'

'No good. I'm sorry, it's not easy, this whole grief thing.'

'I know.'

'You were sketching?'

She handed him the sketch pad, the man in jeans and a jumper pulling items off shelves, the stoop of the shoulders, the frantic clearing away conveying a sad urgency.

'You have a talent, just like Amelia. She can't use hers anymore, but you must.'

Cora signed the sketch and dated it before carefully ripping it from the pad and rolling it up. She tied it with a small length of ribbon and handed it to Tom.

'For you.'

He took it, turning it over in his hand.

'I thank you, I will frame it and hang it up in my home office, but first I want to see it framed as part of your exhibition. With a red sticker mind, because it's mine.'

Taken aback, Cora turned away to stand at the bureau.

'I have one more thing to say and then I will shut up and mind my own business,' Tom said as he walked up and stood beside her.

'What Amelia wouldn't give to be able to let her creativity loose one last time. We are left behind, Cora, but please let us take heart now and look to the future. I have to do it with my family and you have to do it with the one thing that brings you the greatest comfort, your artistic talent.'

Tears stung her eyelids as she fingered the rolled-up sketch.

'It could be a long time before you get this back.'

'When you are ready you will paint again and wherever you are in the world the Hoopers will be honoured to attend your exhibition. Deal?'

'Deal.'

'Now, let's put some elbow grease into clearing this place,' he said, shaking out an empty refuse sack.

They worked side by side, clearing the shelves, placing bolts of fabric and five sewing machines to one side.

When the buzzer sounded, Tom pressed the access button to allow the caller in.

'There's a fashion design business after setting up and I called in to them yesterday; they will take all this stuff,' he said as he opened the door to a man in a suit.

'Sorry, I was looking for Amelia,' he said.

'Who are you?' Tom asked, Cora noting his voice sounded firm and strong.

'I'm a friend of Amelia's, I come by every month and we discuss what fabric she will need, what will suit her designs. Is something wrong?'

Cora stepped forward.

'You haven't heard the news?'

'What news, where's Amelia?'

The man stepped further into the room and Cora noticed he had a holdall bag with him full of fabric sample books.

Tom put his hand on the man's shoulder.

'I'm afraid my sister Amelia died in a car accident along with her husband Jack.'

The words flitted around the room, the impact of the old news as strong as the first time people heard it.

The young man buckled and Cora led him to Amelia's chair. 'I know it's an awful shock.'

He nodded, tears washing down his face.

'I always looked forward to the third Wednesday in the month, it's my Dublin day and lunch was always with Amelia when we had the business done.' He looked at Cora.

'Sorry, I'm forgetting my manners, my name is Dave,' he said, extending his hand first to Cora, then Tom.

'I'm very sorry, I was very fond of Amelia. In a few years, she would have been...' He stopped. 'I don't mean to sound insensitive, but she really was something as a designer. I always kept my best swatches for her.'

When the doorbell buzzed again, Tom went to answer it.

'Are you part of Amelia's family?' Dave asked.

'Yes, in a way,' she answered, looking away when she caught Tom's eye. A few minutes later a heavy man, his face red from exertion, walked in the door.

'I have a few of my team following in, we should have most of this stuff gone in no time,' he said.

Dave tugged Tom's elbow. 'Those books on the top shelf, don't let them go, they are all of Amelia's designs.'

Tom reached up to the top shelf and took down three hard-back journals. Handing one to Cora, he opened another.

Sketches in pencil with some coloured in; others, bare outlines in black charcoal, the elegance, style and cut of the outfit conveyed in a few well placed lines and shading.

A number of other removal men began clearing away the mannequins, carrying them shoulder high as they trooped down the stairs. One man lifted a heavy machine in his two hands and staggered downstairs and out on to the street.

Cora shook hands again with Dave as he sought out Tom and gave him a sympathetic hug, before saying he had to get on and meet other clients. Cora stood to one side of the room watching as many as six people clear away the heavy rolls of fabric, machines, irons and ironing boards. Two removal men lifted the bolt of royal blue silk between them.

'Sorry, but we are keeping that,' Tom said. He pushed it to one side as Cora held the door for the last people to leave with bits and bobs. Afterwards, Lily and Tom stood in the almost empty room, the bolt of silk at their feet, the shelves empty except for the sketch pads where Cora had left them and Amelia's bureau still in position at the window.

'The bureau belonged to my grandmother, so I'll take that home. Would you like to borrow the sketch books to have a look through them?' Tom asked.

'I would like that very much,' Cora said.

Tom nudged the bolt of blue silk with his foot.

'You liked it, so I thought if anyone knows what to do with it, it's yourself.'

'It's so beautiful.'

'Come on, let's throw it in the car and get you home.'

The bolt of silk on the back seat, Tom drove Cora back to De Courcy Square. When he pulled up outside No. 23, Sam was standing next door tending to new pots of flowers.

'You look like you could do with some help,' he said to Cora, gently pushing her aside and easily lifting her end of the fabric bolt. She directed them into the front office.

They placed the bolt across the couch. Cora invited them both to stay for a coffee but Sam said he'd better get back or Lily would have her say. Tom lingered for longer, leaving the sketch books on the hall table.

'Let me know what you think of her body of work,' he asked quietly.

'I will,' she said and smiled when she saw he had placed the sketch she had given him on top of the stack of books.

# THIRTY-EIGHT

From: **GladysSpencer@gmail.com**
To: **all De Courcy Square Association members**

Dear residents and tenants,

As you all know the De Courcy Square Association won the battle to save our beautiful park. We would like to thank each of you who helped, whether it was making posters, attending protests or donating funds and giving valuable legal advice.

A deal was struck, the details of which have to remain confidential, but suffice to say, we are extraordinarily happy to have our gardens back. There are no hard feelings between us and Mr Draper who as the owner and resident of No. 29, is automatically a member of this organisation.

We wish to acknowledge also that Mr Draper kindly donated funds towards the replanting and stocking of the gardens. The City Council will this week restore the damaged railings around the square, and as the new owners of the park, are committed to its upkeep.

As part of the purchase and agreement, it has been laid down that the gardens will now be open to the public and the locking of gates will only take place after sundown. The Association will remain heavily involved in De Courcy Square park.

Gladys Spencer,
Chairperson

Lily and Gladys had booked a table for afternoon tea at The Shelbourne. Several days after the resolution of the park battle, Anthony Draper had called at Lily's house looking for help. 'Believe it or believe it not, but I feel bad about spoiling your afternoon tea. I was wondering if you would pass on this voucher for two to Mrs Spencer.'

'How very kind of you, but I think she would really love to get it from you herself.'

'You mean she wants to see me grovel.'

'I wouldn't use those actual words, but yes.'

'I would have thought with the liquidation of one of my companies, there had been enough grovelling, but I'm glad to say I'm still standing.'

'From what I hear, you are not doing bad at all.'

'I can't deny it, but isn't that the fun of the deal. Still, credit where it's due, your Sam was the star of the show, he made everyone including me a winner. Now, if you will excuse me, I am off to the lion's den to talk to Mrs Spencer.'

When Gladys rang and said she had booked afternoon tea for the following day, Lily couldn't upbraid her for not consulting with her first. She didn't want to go, but Sam persuaded her.

She arranged to meet at the hotel, because Gladys was getting her hair done earlier.

Lily, who had walked to The Shelbourne, sat in the lobby waiting. When a taxi pulled up and a woman in a royal blue suit got out, she knew it had to be Gladys.

The doors swung open. Gladys looked so different in a tight skirt and a fitted jacket that showed off her figure. Her hair was highlighted with blonde and swept away from her face.

'What do you think?' she asked Lily, an anxious look crossing her face.

'I think, wow girl, but it's only afternoon tea.'

Gladys laughed and a number of people turned to look at the woman in blue, who seemed so happy. 'I have decided I'm not just going to be Gladys Spencer, carer, anymore, I'm going to make time for myself as well. This is just the start.' This time, they were shown to a table by the front windows. 'My life is changing already,' Gladys laughed as she accepted a flute of champagne.

'And all thanks to Anthony Draper,' Lily said, raising her glass.

'I'm not sure I would go that far,' Gladys replied in her posh voice, making Lily giggle some more.

'Well, it's very kind of him to fund this treat for us.'

Gladys snorted. 'You know he made tens of thousands from his prank, buying up the park.'

'Sam tells me he's like a shark waiting in the deep water. He said what happened was classic Draper. When he was buying number 29, they did a search and they realised the title of the land was in the gift of an old man who lived somewhere near Monkstown. He got it from him for just a few grand, but the council had to purchase it from Draper for considerably more.'

'He's the winner all right but what do we care, we have our park back. Tony is delighted.'

'How is Tony?'

'Would you believe he has struck up a friendship with Draper. When he called in with the voucher, I introduced him. Turns out, they knew each other years ago. As students, they used to have chess tournaments and put a lot of money on the table.'

'Small world.'

'They are planning a tournament, going to play every Friday night.'

Lily poured the tea and handed a china cup and saucer to Gladys.

'It gives me Friday evenings to myself, I can go to the cinema or the theatre. I can have my time away from running errands or on bloody Association business. It's a new lease of life for me. I can thank Anthony for that.'

'Anthony now, is it?'

Gladys reached over, slapping Lily lightly on the wrist. 'I was hoping somebody else might take over as Association chairperson. I have been doing it for so long, I guess I really need a rest.'

'You have put in the hard graft all right.'

'My sentiments exactly. Would you or Sam be interested?' Lily smiled to herself that a man who was previously homeless should be asked to be chairperson of the De Courcy Square Association.

'Sam brokered that deal to save the park and he's such a kind man. Cora is another choice, but I'm not sure she's with us for the long haul.'

'Maybe you will have to consider Anthony Draper.'

'He does love the square now, so if Sam or yourself can't do it, I will ask Anthony.'

After they had sampled all the sandwiches and cakes, they had an Irish coffee each, before asking for a taxi home.

As they approached De Courcy Square, Gladys got out her compact and renewed her lipstick. 'I want to look my best for Tony, give him a nice surprise,' she said, excited at the prospect of showing off her new look. Lily got out at Gladys's house.

'It looks like you have a visitor,' Gladys said as she went in her front door. Lily heard her calling out to her husband as she went upstairs.

Detective Garda Michael Reid, his hands in his pockets, was leaning against the railings waiting for Lily.

'We need to talk,' he said, when she got to where he was standing.

'Can we go into the park?'

He crossed the road with her, holding the gate open as she stepped onto the garden path. 'I'm glad the residents managed to save this place.'

'Am I going to be charged? Are you here to arrest me, Detective?'

'What do I arrest you for, bringing a letter to our attention as soon as you found it or solving an old case? No, I am here to tell you that we are closing the investigation and you don't have to worry about anything.'

Lily clapped her hands together. 'Thank you, Detective, I am so relieved. Does this mean my daughter need never know the contents of her father's letter?'

'That is between you and her; she will never find out from us.'

She caught his hand. 'Thank you. I have a favour to ask. Can you tell me where and when is Eamon being buried? I would like to place flowers, maybe even plant some bulbs in the autumn.'

'There's a plot in Glasnevin; I will text you the details. We are satisfied it is Eamon, but unfortunately, we have not been able to trace any family,' the detective said as he reached into his pocket and took out a plastic bag containing her locket.

'There is some of the hair lock intact. Thank you for your help. While the DNA test we could carry out could only tell us so much, it was another piece of the jigsaw.'

'I'm glad,' she said.

'There was one other thing, and I have cleared this with my superior officer.'

'Yes?'

Detective Reid pulled a small jewellery box from his pocket.

'We thought you would like to have this,' he said, pushing the box into Lily's hand.

She curled her hand around it, tears flowing freely down her face.

'That is so kind,' she said, patting the detective lightly on his arm.

Michael Reid said his goodbyes, leaving Lily in the park watching the children playing tag.

When she saw Sam walking towards her, she got up and hurried to him. He held his arms wide and she sank into them.

'What has brought this on?' he said, kissing the top of her head.

'I missed you, that's all.'

'Well, next time I will be happy to accompany you to The Shelbourne,' he said.

She kissed him again.

'The detective was here just now. Everything is fine. Eamon can finally be buried properly and with some dignity. Will you come with me to the funeral? They can't trace any family.'

'I would be honoured.'

Lily reached into her pocket and took out the ring box. 'The detective gave me the ring.'

Sam opened the box. 'May I put it on you?'

Lily gave him her left hand and he slipped the ring onto her finger.

'A perfect fit,' she said, holding her hand up to the light, the diamond flashing in the sun.

They walked together back to the house. Sam said he would get on with cooking dinner.

'Do you mind if I lie down? Afternoon tea with Gladys and then meeting Detective Reid was exhausting.'

Sam said he would call her when dinner was ready. Climbing the stairs, she could hear the tension creak of the rope as she had that day, Reg's lifeless body straining its fibres. She had been afraid to touch him in case the rope snapped. Instead, she had run to the phone in the hall, before waiting outside until the ambulance and gardaí arrived.

She had one more thing to do and today was the day she was brave enough to do it.

Reg, in a separate note, scribbled and left on the bedroom mantelpiece, had asked that the watch he'd been given by his parents for his twenty-first should go to a good home. Michael Crimmons, the young bank clerk who had been his able assistant, he thought to be a good choice. If Hannah had ever found out, Lily knew she would be devastated Reg could not leave his watch to a woman and had preferred a male stranger to have the family keepsake.

Opening her bedside drawer, Lily took the watch from its box. She called to Sam that she would be back in a few minutes and she walked smartly to the park. Turning the key in the new gate, she let herself in. She walked to the earthen rectangle that had once been Eamon's grave. When she was at school she had been good at the long put. She twirled, swinging her hand until it almost fell off. Releasing her grip on the watch, she saw it soar through the air, crashing into the high branches of the old oak tree, making a group of crows rise noisily into the air. Gladys, glancing out her window thought Lily was waving and she waved back.

Lily straightened her clothes and walked briskly from the park.

When she got in the door she called out to Sam.

'What's for dinner? I'm starving.'

# THIRTY-NINE

Cora washed and ironed the jeans and sweater she had been wearing that first day she arrived at De Courcy Square ready for this morning, because she thought it would be strange and a bit creepy to be wearing a dead woman's clothes at her grave-side. But she felt out of place in the tight-fitting cable sweater and bootleg jeans, as if they somehow didn't suit her anymore.

When Tom Hooper had called by to collect the sketch books and asked her if she wanted to visit Jack's grave, she'd been strangely grateful. She'd had the sketch books ready for him on the hall table and was handing him the stack when he'd suddenly stopped. 'This is a mad thought and if I'm stepping out of line, please tell me.'

She'd looked at him, wary of what he was going to say next.

'Every Saturday if I'm not working, I go to Amelia's grave and leave fresh flowers. It's a nice drive and I go down to the sea afterwards. Jack is buried there too; would it help at all, if you visited his grave?'

'I don't know, I never imagined I would go there, even if I knew where it was.'

'You could dance on his part of the grave, I suppose,' Tom had smiled.

'I don't even have the inclination to do that anymore.'

'Come this Saturday morning for the spin and if you don't want to visit the grave, you can sit in the car.'

'Should I bring flowers?'

'What flowers have you got? Amelia always liked informal bunches of flowers so I bring some from my own garden, purple and pink colours usually; they are the colours my wife, Frances, prefers.'

'Do you think I should bring some from the pots here? There's pink carnations and some lovely roses, and the big blue agapanthus out the back still has lovely long blooms.'

He'd smiled once more. 'In another life, you and Amelia could have been such friends; you both have that same kindness and generosity of spirit. From this garden would be very special,' he'd said.

She waited for Tom to arrive to pick a small bouquet of roses and the last of her tall blue agapanthus, wrapping tinfoil around the stems and tying it all together with a pink and white striped ribbon, which Cora had found when she had cleared out a small drawer the day before.

Tom fingered the satin ribbon. 'Amelia bought this the last time we met for a coffee. I was cross, because she was late meeting me. I'm ashamed to say, when she showed me that ribbon and said she had to stop and buy it because it was so pretty, I laughed at her.'

'Our memories have ways of pulling us down, if we let them.'

Tom took out his keys. 'Come on, let's hit the road, if the old bat Gladys hasn't arranged for my car to be clamped.'

They were talking and laughing as they got in the car. Lily, who spotted them from her sitting room window, wondered where they were going. Cora got into the leather front seat as Tom pulled rubbish out of her way.

'I'm sorry, it's like I live in the car. My wife refuses to travel in it and my daughter makes me promise I won't use it when I pick her up from school.

'If it gets me away from De Courcy Square, I'm more than happy.'

The car started and he revved out of the square, causing Lily to lean forward and look out the window again. 'I think we have set the tongues wagging,' Tom said as he turned to take the coast road through Sandymount.

'Gladys will just be happy to see the car out of the square.'

'After all that has happened, maybe she should give it a rest.'

'I don't think anyone is brave enough to take on Gladys,' Cora giggled.

When they stopped at the lights, Tom put the roof down.

'If it gets too blowy, let me know,' he said and she sat back enjoying the wind ruffling the top of her head as they sped along the N11 to Greystones. Just before they got to the town, he pulled up at the cemetery gates.

'Are you still OK with this? We haven't put up a headstone yet, so it's just the grave.'

She got out of the car, carrying her bunch of flowers. They walked down the hill towards the sea. The grave was at the far end.

'I'm glad to have you here, it can be a lonely spot. It's almost as if the grave is apart, but I guess those who have bought plots here don't expect to be using them any time soon.'

When she saw the grave at the edge of a new field acquired by the cemetery, she stopped.

Tom reached out and took her hand, slowly guiding her along the newly laid gravel path.

She felt herself stiffen as if this suddenly was the realisation within her that Jack was finally gone. When they reached the grave, Tom pulled away his hand and picked up the vase of sodden, decayed roses. He walked over to a nearby bin to throw out the faded flowers, before filling the vase with water from a plastic bottle he took from his pocket.

'I forgot, I have only the one vase. Maybe we can fit both bunches in here.'

She got down in her knees to help, carefully arranging the flowers in a way she instinctively felt Amelia would appreciate.

'What do you think happened? The car smash I mean,' she asked.

Tom looked startled.

'I can only think of it as an accident. Amelia was driving.'

'But the weather and road conditions were good.'

Tom kicked at a weed growing in one corner of the grave.

'What are you saying exactly?'

'I'm not, but don't you want to know?'

Tom dragged his hands down his face and groaned.

'I wanted to know. In the beginning, I was desperate, quizzed the gardai who were at the scene, the expert who had a look at the skid marks on the road.'

'And?'

'It could be either of two explanations.'

He paused as if considering whether to speak further.

'Accident or deliberate?' she asked gently.

'You have been wondering too.'

'When you said Amelia was driving, it didn't make sense. Jack was the speed junkie.'

'The garda report came down in favour of an accident caused by excessive speed. The car skidded, came off the road.'

He shook his head and dug his hands deep in his jacket pocket. 'It's hard to align that to my sister and the way she normally drove, but who knows, maybe they were having a blazing row.'

'It probably doesn't matter anymore.'

'It's not going to change anything. Frances and I were talking about it the other day and we have decided that we have to accept that it was an accident. It was all-consuming, and I have my family to think of. If I managed to establish it was more than an accident, it would put the spotlight on Amelia and I honestly don't think I could handle that.'

'Best to look to the future with your family,' Cora said.

'And you, what about you?'

Cora laughed. 'I only have myself to think of.'

'That brings its own challenges.'

She nodded and he took the hint that the conversation was closed.

'I usually stand for a while. I don't say any prayers, but I talk to Amelia, tell her my news,' he said.

They fell quiet, their heads bowed.

What had she to say to Jack that she had not already screamed into the dark of every night since she'd got the news he was dead?'

When Tom shuffled to indicate he was finished, she raised her head.

'I will eventually have to decide on a headstone, but I haven't a clue.'

'From the little I know of Amelia, I'm sure she would have been very particular.'

'She would like some flowers, I just wish I knew what flowers to ask for,' he said as he gathered up the tinfoil and ribbon. He tied the ribbon in a neat bow around the vase, before throwing the ball of foil in the bin.

'Do you fancy a walk by the sea to blow the brain cobwebs away?'

They walked briskly from the cemetery, both glad to be finished with that Saturday ritual.

When they got in the car, Tom said he knew an isolated

stony beach a few miles away. 'Kilcoole beach and bird sanctuary, my favourite spot far away from the madding crowd,' he
told her and she was glad of the suggestion.

At Kilcoole, they parked the car and crossed the railway
tracks to the beach. They tramped along the shore, the waves
crashing in around them, pulling out the smaller stones, making
smooth what was once rough.

'In the evening, I sometimes drive down here to watch the
sequence of beacons across the Irish Sea from the lighthouses,
Wicklow to Howth. It's good to let the eyes feast on distance.'
He tapped Cora lightly on the shoulder to get her attention, and
pointed.

'Here they are, the three swans moving from that one part
of the marsh to the lake just over the tracks from us. Come on,
we might be in time to see them land.'

They rushed together over the sandy dunes and across the
tracks to a path overlooking the marsh and lake.

Cora heard the rhythmic beating of their wings, like a
whistling noise through the sky, before she saw the swans. They
passed overhead, the air full of their humming, their wings
effortlessly propelling them towards their goal. At the lake they
dipped down, slapping the water hard, their wings batting the
air around them as they skidded along the top of the water, until
they folded their wings, quietening down, to glide without even
causing a ripple.

'Why three?' she asked.

'They mate for life. I guess the third one is the hanger on.'

'I was the hanger on but I never even knew it,' Cora said.

'Christ, what am I saying, I wasn't alluding to you.'

'I know,' she said and he figured by the lightness in her voice
that she did.

Cora stood taking in the marsh lake, the mountains in the
distance, the rhythmic sound of the waves pulling on the shore.
Calm washed over her and she felt content. Tom walked back to

the sea to skim stones across the waves; a Labrador ploughed into the water, leaving its companion, a collie cross, behind. She wandered along, stopping every now and again to pick up a pretty stone or shell.

After a while Tom waved and walked towards her. 'I'd better get back.'

She nodded and they trudged up the beach towards the train platform, where a tiny house was built in the small patch between the tracks and the car park.

'This place is good for the soul,' Tom said.

'There are so many days after I came to Ireland when I could have done with a walk along here. Thank you for bringing me.'

'How are you now?' he asked and she didn't mind the question.

'Better most days. I think he loved us all. Strange, but possibly true.'

'Amelia adored him, said the reason he was so attentive was that he was busy trying to make memories because his childhood was so deprived of love: losing his parents when he was very young and just being moved between different relatives, none of whom invested any time or love or developed a relationship with him.'

'It makes sense as an explanation, I guess; or maybe he just enjoyed the intrigue, living life on the edge.'

She stopped to look at the Sugar Loaf mountain. 'Solid as a rock, that's what I thought our partnership was. There's only so much pain a person can take, only so much more I can hear about Jack and other women. I have reached the endgame.'

'I understand,' he said, leading the way to the car. He turned on some classical music and they drove back up the motorway to the city.

At De Courcy Square, she turned to Tom.

'Thank you for taking me to see Jack and Amelia. It really

did help. I'm afraid I have to do something important, so I can't ask you in for coffee, but please don't be a stranger.'

He said he had to get home and he would check in on her one of the days when he was passing. Cora stood on the steps and waved Tom off before walking down to Reads of Nassau Street to purchase an easel, paper, brushes, a palette and an array of different coloured paints in tubes.

'You are going to be busy for a while,' the assistant said.

'I certainly hope to be,' Cora answered, a smile on her face.

# FORTY

Sam woke up early and decided to go for a walk. He left a note on the kitchen table and let himself out of the house, carefully closing the front door, so he didn't wake Lily. He had crossed over the road and was on his way in to the park, when Gladys called him.

'You're out early, Sam.'

'I have a lot of thinking to do and early morning is a better time for it than late at night.'

'That sounds serious. Is there anything I can help you with?'

Sam hesitated.

'My bark is worse than my bite. I'll gladly help, if you want,' Gladys said.

She faltered, worried she had been too pushy. 'You know, a lot of people around here might think I'm a bit of a busybody, because I'm so passionate about the park and follow up on every transgression. Gladys Spencer, when she does a job, does it right.'

Sam stepped back to allow Gladys to walk through the entrance first.

'I'm looking forward to the spring, when the garden renews and we can finally put this sad chapter behind us,' Gladys said as they ambled up the path, trying to tread softly, so as not to disturb the birds. 'I'm glad I met you, Sam. Since the park was opened to the general public, I'm too nervous to come in on my own late in the evening or too early in the morning.'

'The wildlife won't do anything to you, Gladys.'

'I know of your past life, Sam, and may I say straight away, you are a perfect gentleman, but there are others who climb in to this park and frankly they are up to no good.'

'Who would bother climbing over when it's locked at night? Sure how would you sell drugs in there, how would people get to you?' Sam laughed.

'You think it's funny, but from my sitting room window, I have in the half light of late evening or early morning seen the goings on in here. I imagine it's a good spot for all sorts of criminal activity; gardai are hardly going to patrol this park.'

Sam led the way to a small bench in front of the bank of fuchsia. 'Do you think there is some way we could remember the man who was buried here?' he asked.

'I thought we all wanted to forget about that.'

'Lily said he planted a lot of the plants here and the bulbs you are waiting for in spring.'

'Remember him that way, rather than the crime committed?'

'Yes, that's what I mean.'

'We have a few bob left over after Mr Draper's donation; let me have a think about it.'

A thrush, its head down searching for worms, hopped out into the central grassed area and Gladys and Sam sat quietly watching. A wagtail was braver and dropped down beside their feet, but when Gladys leaned for a closer look, it took off into the air, fluttering furiously.

'So what has you in the park so early?' she asked him.

Sam chuckled. 'You know, I have something on my mind.'

'Is anything wrong? You're not ill, I hope?'

Sam shook his head. 'Nothing like that.'

He cleared his throat. 'Do you think if I ask Lily to marry me, she would?'

Gladys squealed in excitement. 'Fantastic, of course she will. This is such lovely news.'

'Please, not a word to Lily or to anyone.'

Gladys sat back, her face beaming. 'Mum's the word, I promise. This gladdens my heart so much, you are such a lovely couple.'

Sam jumped up. 'But I'm nothing, only a failed business-man. She took me in, I love her so much, but her first husband was a banker.'

Gladys guffawed out loud. 'And a proper pig of a man, who made everybody around him miserable. Thankfully Sam, you are nothing like him. We wouldn't have this park but for you. I for one will never forget that.'

'I guess everybody ended up hating anyone high up in banking during the crisis, but many were just carrying out orders.'

'My husband worked directly under Reg Walpole for a number of years. I can assure you Mr Walpole was a nasty piece of work.'

'I don't want to hear any more, I really shouldn't be discussing Lily's business.'

There was no stopping Gladys, once she had started. 'As it happens, it's very much my business as well. When my Tony suffered his injuries, Reg Walpole wanted nothing to do with him.'

'I don't understand.'

'Tony was in the bank when armed robbers burst in. The fool Tony wouldn't open the safe and they shot him in the back.

He has been paralysed from the waist down ever since and confined to a wheelchair.'

'I'm very sorry to hear that, I had no idea.'

'How would you?' Gladys stopped to swipe away tears. 'There are some times Tony says he's sorry they didn't finish him off. Life can be so unbearable, but it was made a lot worse by the way the bank and in particular Walpole dealt with him.'

'How do you mean?'

Gladys got a tissue out of her pocket and noisily blew her nose before continuing. 'Don't get me wrong, none of this is directed at Lily; I have never met a finer, more loyal woman, but Reg Walpole was the exact opposite. He only came to the hospital once, but Lily sat with me every day. He never came to the house either, when Tony was allowed home. I think the worst bit was almost a year later, Tony rang him at the bank and said he was ready to return to work. His was always a paper pushing desk job, but Walpole said no way.'

'Why, he was surely entitled?'

'He was, but instead the bank offered him a pay-off. Walpole said he would only be a reminder to everybody of that day when the bank was cleaned out of all its cash, and he couldn't be dealing with members of the public.'

'I'm sickened by that.'

'Tony got a great redundancy and a monthly stipend for life. We are comfortable but what Reg Walpole did was tell Tony he was nothing, worthless, and he has never got over it.'

'I'm sorry, Gladys.'

'Don't be, just never ever make out you are in any way inferior to Lily's first husband. It was a good day when you came in to her life.'

Sam stood up.

'You have helped a lot, Gladys, thank you. Can I ask you to keep our conversation and its contents secret? I want Hannah to be the first to hear our news, if Lily says yes.'

Gladys jumped up and kissed Sam lightly on the cheek.

'As long as I'm invited to the wedding, and don't worry, I will be suitably surprised when I'm told the news.'

Sam said goodbye to Gladys and walked back along the path to the gate. He wasn't quite ready to meet Lily yet. It was too early for the florist on Baggot Street, so he headed off in to the city centre, where the women were beginning to set up the flower stalls on Moore Street.

'You're out early luv, give us a half an hour or so to set things up,' one stallholder laughed as she put out vases of roses.

'Do you want a hand?'

He carried boxes of sunflowers, bouquets of lilies and buckets of roses from the van parked down the side street.

'You are keen, it must be a lucky woman who is getting flowers from you,' the stallholder laughed, after Sam had arranged everything and stood back to survey his handiwork.

'I'm looking for pink roses, they have to be pink.'

'You are a funny one, I have every colour under the sun and you want the one I don't have.'

'Pink roses have a particular message.'

'And what would that be?'

'A love that is constant, serene, fulfilling and all-encompassing. It says I'm happy and secure in your love.'

The woman laughed. 'Be still, my beating heart; forget about her and stay here with me.'

Sam blushed and the woman laughed louder.

'Go along to Marge two stalls down, she has pink roses.'

As he walked down the street, she called out to Marge.

'Give that lovesick man a good price on the pink roses. He's a keeper.'

The other women chuckled and Marge began to wrap as many pink roses as she could in cellophane.

Sam made his way quickly back to No. 22. At the door, he stood, suddenly worried that Lily might not be happy with him.

When he heard steps behind him on the street, he pretended to be fumbling for his keys.

'Get on with it, man, I'm dying to spread the good news,' Gladys said, a huge grin on her face. Nodding to Gladys, he pushed the key in the lock. Taking a deep breath, he turned the key and opened the door of No. 22. He called up the stairs, but Lily, already up, was in the kitchen.

'The coffee is just brewed, perfect timing,' she said without looking round from where she was spreading out some crumbs on the window sill.

Sam swallowed hard. 'Lily, I have something for you.'

Wiping her hands on a tea towel, she swung round. 'Oh my, where did you get them? They are so beautiful.'

'You know what they say, how I feel when I am with you.'

Reaching out, she gently ran her fingers across the petals. 'I don't think I have ever seen so many pink roses in one bouquet,' she said, taking the bunch and holding it close. 'I'll put them in a big glass vase in the hall, that way I will pass them by at different times of the day.'

She was scouring around in a drawer for some scissors to cut the cellophane, when Sam softly called out to her. 'Lily, there's something else.'

Feeling suddenly nervous, she stopped what she was doing.

'If I could get down on my knee, I would. Would you do me the honour of marrying me?' Sam felt a stab of panic as he tried to read her face. He thought she went a little pale.

'Sam, we're old.'

'I understand, if you don't want to.'

He saw her face redden. 'God, no, I'm just so surprised... Yes, yes, yes.'

He pulled her into his arms, smothering the top of her head with kisses.

'I won't have a church wedding, though,' she said, her voice muffled because he held her so tight against his chest.

'A civil ceremony in the park, as soon as we can?'

'Perfect,' she said and he held her even closer.

He reached down and picked up her left hand.

'I would be honoured if you wore Eamon's ring as a symbol of his love, but also of mine.'

'Thank you, Sam Carpenter. You are a good man,' she said and he kissed her again.

When she pulled away from Sam, Lily looked anxious. 'I'm not sure how Hannah will take this.'

'We'll go tell her right now. She's bound to have questions. I'm not going to hide anything from her.'

'She rang, she's on Grafton Street. How am I going to tell her?'

Sam gently pushed Lily to sit down. 'We will tell her together. She deserves to know everything. Now, go get dressed and I'll put the roses in water.'

As she climbed the stairs, Lily felt a peculiar mix of excitement and dread.

She only just had got her clothes on and was patting a little powder on her face when she heard Hannah's key in the door. 'Only me; where did you get the lovely roses?' she called out as she walked through to the kitchen. Lily could hear the murmur of voices. She gazed in the mirror, steeling herself for what was to come.

When she got to the hall Hannah waved to her. 'Sam here has been telling me about the language of flowers. You are a lucky woman.'

Sam caught Lily's hand.

'I got them for your mother, Hannah.'

'Oh, how lovely. Is there a special occasion? Shit, I haven't missed Mother's Day or something?'

Lily couldn't answer, so Sam stepped forward. 'Actually, we have news and we want you to be the first to know.'

Hannah looked at her mother. 'Mum, what's going on? I don't understand.'

'I asked and Lily has agreed to marry me,' Sam said as clearly as he could.

'What do you mean, marry?'

Sam chuckled.

'Lily has done me the honour of accepting my hand in marriage.'

'What? You hardly know each other. Mum, what's going on?'

'Hannah, we are hardly spring chickens,' Lily said.

'It's a shock, but a very nice one,' Hannah said as she first kissed her mother on both cheeks and then Sam.

'This calls for champagne and I know just the bottle of bubbly to crack open,' she said, rushing out of the kitchen and up the stairs. 'Is that old bottle of champagne still in the drinks cabinet?' she called out from the sitting room landing. They heard her whoop in delight before tearing down the stairs brandishing the bottle.

'Sam, you will have to open this,' she said as she came back into the kitchen.

Lily made to take the bottle.

'Is there something wrong?' Hannah asked.

Sam shook his head. 'Lily, I will open the bottle, you two have the champagne, I can fill my glass with orange juice.'

He turned to Hannah. 'I haven't touched a drop in years and it's best to keep it that way.'

'I'm so sorry, I had no idea,' Hannah said her face pink with embarrassment.

Sam took the bottle and, using a tea towel to shield the cork, he opened the champagne with a loud pop. Lily poured his orange juice into a champagne glass and the three of them clinked glasses.

'Happiness always, you both deserve it,' Hannah said.

## FORTY-ONE

Cora filled two glasses of water and brought them to the front office. The night before, she had pushed the desks away from the window to make room for her easel.

She didn't care that those passing would see her working; she needed the best light. Her brushes were in a row down along the top of Jack's desk, the palette beside the tubes of paint which were bundled together in key blocks of colour, blue, green, red, yellow, black and white. On the wall, pinned up with drawing pins, was the sketch of Tom clearing shelves in Amelia's studio. Quickly and deftly she washed the light faded brown over the canvas. Dipping one of her brushes in the water she followed the slant of the sun in the studio room that day. The shelves were slightly wonky as if somebody had done their best when they'd put them up, but hadn't got it quite right. Tom, his shoulders rigid, had swept his hand, knocking some items to the floor. She felt his pain, the stoop of his back indicating a worry that was eating him from the inside out. The spools of thread, pops of bright colour, were strewn at his feet as if he was the one destroying the dreams of the designer. In the corner, bolts of fabric were stacked against the wall, while nude mannequins silently watched on. Cora felt for this man who did not understand the world of dress designing and now remained excluded from it after the death of his sister. 'Clearing Amelia's Studio' was the title of the work.

She mixed the colours and painted until the morning sunshine was too much for her. She was wiping her hands on an old tea cloth when her phone rang.

'Perfect timing, I was just thinking of calling you. I have news,' Cora said.

'Wonderful, hon, when are you coming home?'

Cora laughed out loud.

'Donna, you never give up. I have started back painting. In fact I'm nearly there, with my first work here in Dublin. I'm standing looking at it now.'

'That's so great, honey, does that mean you will include the Dublin pieces in your downtown exhibition?'

Cora hesitated.

'Honey, you are getting ready for the exhibition?'

'I emailed them, asked could I defer on the offer for a while. I want to stay here, paint, and who knows?'

'But who defers on exhibition space in The Village. Have you thought this through, honey?'

'I have to do what feels right for me, and staying here feels right.'

'In that house?'

'It's a beautiful space. I'm clearing away their stuff. I want to make it mine. For a while, anyway.'

Donna clicked her tongue because she was frustrated and annoyed.

'I hate to think you will miss out on the exhibition.'

Cora watched Sam and Lily come out of their front door and she waved to them, before they made their way across to the park.

'This is going to sound mad, Donna, but I'm thinking of having an exhibition here.'

'In Dublin, when you could have New York?'

Cora ignored her friend's sarcastic tone of voice.

'Here at number 23, I am thinking of a studio and exhibition space.'

'Are you serious?'

'The ground floor is a perfect space and I can live upstairs.'

'You really are going to do this.'

'I'm certainly going to try. Donna, I'm going to need your help.'

'You know I will, but across these miles, what can I do?'

'The Long Island paintings, can you get them over to me? I have a specialist courier company that can do it all, you just have to point them in the direction of the paintings.

'Are you sure, honey? They are going to drag up a lot of memories.'

Cora pretended she hadn't heard that and continued.

'There's one of Jack that was hanging on our top landing. He's in a suit, his tie undone on a lounger in the garden in Southampton. I called it 'Home from Work'.

'I know it, Rich really liked it when he was helping with the house clear-out.'

'Can you send that too?'

'Of course, but honey, why that one?'

'Jack is part of my life and part of this house. Of course I want to have a painting of him.'

'It's in storage with the others. As long as you're sure.'

'Donna, I'm excited, I'm painting and sketching like a mad woman. It's like I have been set free.'

I'm glad for you, honey. Looks like you're going to make your name that side of the world first. The States will be crying out for you in a while.'

'You guys must come over. I'm hoping to have the exhibition up and running for late October.'

'Honey, Chuck says there is a world to see in the good old US of A. He won't budge. I may have to insist I come over to help you.'

'That would be so perfect.'

Donna said something else, but Cora, distracted by a leather holdall stuffed behind the heavy brocade curtain in the front window, didn't catch it.

'Are you still there?' Donna asked.

'Yeah, sorry. I would love it if you came over for my first exhibition.'

'I'll certainly try. I have to see this house and square for myself. Now I have to rush. Talk soon, and I will get on to the company and arrange to have those watercolours shipped to you. You look after yourself, honey.'

'Thanks, Donna.'

'You can thank me in the exhibition brochure, darling.'

Donna rang off, leaving Cora smiling as she reached for the leather bag. She recognised it: Jack had bought it in a sale in Bloomingdale's not long after they met and used it when he travelled back and forth to LA.

She was surprised to see a small padlock on it. She wondered whether to ignore it and throw it in the pile at the far end of the room, which she had ready for the skip that was arranged for the following Monday. She went to the kitchen and threw three oranges in the juicer and made a glass of juice. To keep busy, she brought her drink out to the back garden. Next door, she could hear Lily and Sam, returned from the park, preparing an outdoor table for coffee and cake. The low murmur of their voices, the happiness in Lily's laugh, speared her heart. She was glad for those two, but the sound of their contentment somehow hurt her.

She and Jack used to sit on their back deck, chatting over

morning coffee. It was stupid talk; she couldn't remember any of its content now, only the feeling of companionship, moments shared and forgotten. If she didn't open the leather holdall, she would regret it. Grabbing some scissors from the kitchen drawer, she marched into the front room and lifted the bag onto the table, pushing her palette and paint tubes out of the way. Stabbing with the scissors, she broke through the leather until she was able to cut a hole big enough to pull out the contents.

There were three wooden boxes, all with labels. Prising open the box with her name on it, Cora saw Jack's wallet. She flicked through it. His US dollars, credit cards and store cards were there. Lifting a flap, the picture of the two of them the night they had celebrated nine years together dropped out. She traced their happy faces, frozen in that time. His US car keys and house keys were in the box along with a thick piece of cardboard labelled *phone back-up*, where he had written all the mobile numbers he could possibly need in the US, including Cora's. At the end, he had put the date they met and her birthday, with 'roses (yellow)' written after her name.

Amelia's box did not have so much, but a note of the key dates in their lives and the phone numbers back-up for Ireland.

A third box did not have a name on it but it contained a wallet full of sterling notes, credit cards and a picture of Jack and the woman with blonde hair. They were smiling in the selfie, Buckingham Palace in the background.

She could barely take it in, the happy faces, Jack looking more content than she had ever seen him. She didn't feel any pain anymore. Arranging the three boxes on Jack's desk, she took out the different cash and credit cards from the wallets and placed them in front of each box. The identical wallets she stacked to one side. Reaching for her sketch pad she took a pencil and began to sketch the scene in front of her, noting in the sketch the credit card colours, the sequence of the phone numbers on other cards. 'One Man, Many Lives' she called it and decided she would hang this painting beside the one of Jack, her own statement which few would understand. Checking her sketches, she added notes on the colour for when she worked at her easel. Snapping her sketch pad shut, she scooped up the money, cards, wallets and boxes. Dropping everything but the boxes in the bin, she went upstairs to the top floor. Pulling up the sash window to open it, she checked that Lily and Sam were not in their garden.

She lined the boxes in a row on the outside sill. Standing back, she flicked each one off, one after another. She didn't flinch when she heard them smash to pieces on the ground. Pulling the window down to shut it, she thought she should clean up the bits from the back garden, but she didn't feel like doing it. That was a task for another day.

Instead, she pulled on her jacket and grabbing her keys, pencil and sketch pad, she left No. 23 and crossed the road to the park to begin her series of sketches from there.

# FORTY-TWO

Sam and Lily stood by the grave of the Griffin family, where Eamon's coffin was ready to be lowered into the ground.

Lily held her homemade bouquet of peonies, rosemary and tea roses from the park, to say *I'll always remember*. A single white bud she had placed in the centre of the arrangement to remember the innocence of their young love. Sam carried a simple posy of white zinnias to signify goodness.

'You did a good thing bringing the letter to the detective, otherwise Eamon would not have been reunited here with his family,' Sam whispered as prayers were said and the coffin lowered.

'Can we visit sometimes, plant some bulbs for the spring? I would also like primroses, lots of them,' she said.

'Perfect choice to remember a beautiful young love,' Sam said and they walked away hand in hand, the only mourners at the funeral.

'Lilac too, when in bloom,' she said.

Sam put an arm around her shoulder and held her tight as they left the cemetery and got a taxi home to De Courcy Square.

When Hannah rang later that day and suggested she and Lily meet up, Lily was delighted.

'Let's go for a spin out to Wicklow like we used to when I was young,' Hannah said. Lily had always loved the freedom of those days, when Reg, too busy concentrating on his driving, made no demands on her at all. She had watched the city streets give way to wide roads with grand houses and gardens, then smaller housing estates and finally country lanes; and past fields where sheep grazed until they came to the base of the Sugar Loaf mountain.

'If the weather is good, we might be able to climb the Sugar Loaf,' she said to Hannah now.

'Are you sure, Mum? You never climbed it before.'

'Everything is quite different now, Han.'

'Don't forget you're older; we'll see when we get there. Will I bring a picnic, for old time's sake?'

'As long as it's not like the picnics we used to have; all that was to suit your father.'

Hannah laughed and said she thought she could do better than ham sandwiches and chocolate digestives with sweet tea.

Lily picked a deep purple trouser suit she had bought the week before and put her runners in a plastic bag, in case she decided to climb the mountain. Sam insisted she take a hat and scarf, saying if she did go up the mountain, she might be glad of them.

'What will you do with yourself when I'm gone?' she asked.

'Cora's skip was put in place early this morning, so I'll help her fill it. They are back to collect it this evening.'

'You'll have to work fast. Don't take any chances with the heavy stuff.'

'I told Cora to get rid of the skip as soon as possible, otherwise the whole of Dublin will use it as a dumping ground.'

'I hope there's more than you helping her.'

'Amelia's brother Tom is there already and Anthony Draper promised to give us a bit of time as well.'

'Sounds as if you have it all sorted,' she said, making for the front door when she saw Hannah's car pull in to the square.

'I hope that skip is not going to be there too long,' Hannah said as Lily got in the car.

'Going tonight. Make sure you wave to Sam,' Lily said.

Hannah waved and gave a short beep before they turned out of De Courcy Square.

'Your Sam is a sweet man. I'm glad, Mum, you deserve this,' Hannah said.

'Thank you, dear, I'm beginning to think I do, too.'

They laughed and then fell quiet as Hannah negotiated the busy streets around the canal, before turning out onto the N11.

'It brings back memories. Reg always made sure the Sunday spin included the N11.'

'Would you prefer to go by Dun Laoghaire and the sea?' Hannah asked, her voice anxious.

'Maybe on the way back,' Lily said. As they turned onto the back roads of Wicklow to get to the car park at the foot of the mountain, Lily asked her daughter why she had chosen this location for their time out together.

'You've never suggested it before.'

'I was never sure I should. I didn't know if it would upset you, raise too many ghosts.'

'It may have. It has been a hard time, these last few years.'

Hannah reversed into a parking spot and turned off the engine. 'I wanted to get out of De Courcy Square so we could spend a bit of time together, talk about things.'

Lily leaned over and grabbed Hannah's hand. 'Are you worried about me and Sam?'

'God no. Can I talk to you about Dad?'

Lily steeled herself for what was to come next.

'It's just I think I blamed you a lot when I was younger for his anger and I suppose I realise now it wasn't that simple.'

'Reg wasn't the easiest to live with. He tended to bring his exacting standards from his work at the bank to family life, and that wasn't going to go down well.'

'I have been thinking a lot about the way you two were, the way he treated you. I'm sorry I always seemed to take his side.'

'You loved your dad. There's nothing wrong with that.'

'I particularly remember that time he got so cross when you put a vase of flowers on the hall table.'

'You know your father, he could get incredibly angry at the smallest thing; leaving on room lights, towels on the bathroom floor, when he couldn't find the comb. I seemed to cause him major irritation. I don't think he was totally at fault. I should never have married him, I was in love with another lad at the time.'

'Who?'

'I was eighteen years old, it was a local boy. Who knows if it would have come to anything.'

'What happened?'

Lily hesitated. 'He moved away, I got married, but I think Reg knew he always had to compete with that big love of mine.'

'Was he your big love?'

'Yes, and to be honest I still do love him. Sam knows and he knows I love him so much as well.'

Hannah let out a deep sigh. 'It's a lot to take in, Mum.'

'Why don't I get my runners on and we tackle this mountain?'

'Are you sure?'

'Didn't I sit here for long enough and look at you and your dad do it together?'

Hannah, who had got out of the car, guffawed out loud.

'It was torture, he was so competitive. Dad was constantly

in a rush to get to the top, often leaving me to clamber across the stony ground on my own.'

Lily walked around the car and hugged her daughter. 'Well, that's not going to happen today.'

Lily pulled on the hat Sam had given her and pushed the gloves in her pockets. 'Come, let's conquer the mountain,' she said to Hannah and they walked on side by side.

'You always closed your eyes, your head was tilted to the sun, and he knew that. He rushed on. Maybe he wanted to be on his own.'

Lily linked arms with Hannah for this flat stretch before the real climb.

'I used to pretend not to mind and I'd stop, sit and enjoy the peace, letting my eyes stretch across the land to the sea, watching the boats bobbing out of Greystones harbour, like tiny boats in a tub of water.'

'I used to go off into a dream world, I suppose I enjoyed that quiet time. I didn't know any of this; you should have stayed with me,' Lily said.

'Mum, even though I was young, I felt you needed that time. Dad wasn't an easy man to live with. I know that now, and I felt it back then.'

Lily gripped her daughter's arm and squeezed it.

'Thank you, sweetheart.'

Hannah stopped in her tracks.

'Do we have to climb? I mean why are we doing this? I never did it before.'

'What do you mean? You did it every Sunday in the summer.'

'Dad always got to the top; me, I just hung around out of sight. Why do you think he always gloated he was the only one with the stamina and the willpower to make it to the summit? I wanted to shout at him it wasn't Everest, but I was never brave enough.'

Lily remembered she never challenged Reg either and there was always the tension as they sat and had their tea and sandwiches, followed by bourbon creams for something sweet. Sometimes, Hannah got to hang out with kids her age, if her dad got caught up in a big political debate or joined somebody listening to a match on the radio, but more often than not, they drove straight home after eating, Reg in a hurry to be on time to see the TV news.

Lily and Hannah started the climb, their feet slipping on the stony ground. Hannah was the first to call a halt. She could have gone to the top, but she stopped in the same spot she always had done, the place where Reg used to whip past her. She could see far out across the fields and the towns to the blue grey of the Irish Sea.

'Mum, I'm sorry,' Hannah said.

'For what, darling?'

'I've been a cow to you, blaming everything on you. I think I've finally grown up. I'm glad you have Sam. He's so different to Dad, so sensitive and kind.'

Lily took her daughter's hands. 'You loved your dad, of course you didn't understand. We tried to make it work, they were different times. It was a travesty that we stayed together.'

Lily looked at her daughter, 'I've had enough of this mountain, let's go to a nice café and sit and chat... Oh, but I forgot, what about your picnic?'

'In the end, I couldn't face trying to get it together. Sorry.'

'What sorry, I never want to have to eat another picnic in my life,' Lily said, and they both laughed as they dashed back to the car.

Hannah drove back towards the N11 to the Avoca restaurant, where they sat out in the garden with coffee and chocolate fudge cake.

'Mum, I want you to know I threw out Derry and I've changed the locks at home.'

Lily reached across to her daughter. 'Bravo my girl, I wish I had been brave enough to do it decades ago. When did this happen?'

'Last week. I've been meaning to tell you.'

'And I have been so preoccupied, I never noticed. I'm sorry Hannah.'

Hannah leaned over to Lily, who took her weight, softly stroking her daughter's head while she sobbed like a child.

'Have you banished Derry for good?'

'Yes, he's already shacking up with a young legal assistant with bouncy hair.'

'You can stay with me and Sam for a while, we can cook all your favourite food and eat cake whenever we want.'

'I can't leave our house, I won't give the bastard the satisfaction of moving Bouncy Hair in. He'll have to fight me tooth and nail for even a brick from that property.'

'That is the fighting talk I want to hear. Don't make it easy for him.'

'You never liked him, did you?'

'No, I always thought Derry loved himself enough, he didn't need my adoration as well.'

'You never said.'

'You loved him, what good would it have done?'

'I suppose.'

Lily, lightly rubbed her daughter's hand like she used to do when she was a child and came home from school with a tale of woe.

'I always thought if I was as happy as you and Dad, I would be OK. Now I know how wrong I was about that.'

Lily squeezed Hannah's hand. 'What is happiness? Back then when a couple got married it was for life. It was better not to dwell on things, but just get on with it.'

'You're not saying I should have stuck with Derry?'

'What do you honestly think?'

'I'm not sure Bouncy Hair is the first and I don't think she will be the last. I guess I have finally copped on that he's never going to change.'

'I'm proud of you, Hannah.'

'You and Sam though, you seem happy.'

Lily smiled. 'He is everything to me. You and Sam make my life complete.'

Hannah started to cry and Lily offered her a packet of tissues. 'Have a good cry, it will help to get him out of your system. Only then will you be able to fight him properly.'

Hannah pulled out a tissue and dabbed her eyes. 'It's not good, is it, to last only a few years?'

'Better than a lifetime of being treated as second best.'

'I know Dad was hard to live with.'

'Reg loved you, Hannah.'

'I know.'

Lily squeezed her daughter's hand. 'De Courcy Square will always be your home, Hannah. Me being with Sam is not going to change that. And now you are the one who saved De Courcy Square. You are smart, Hannah, and some day you will meet a man who appreciates that.'

At that moment, Lily banished any guilt she might have felt for not telling Hannah about the letter. Hannah, she decided, had enough on her plate.

# FORTY-THREE

Hannah was at the door early. When Lily answered in her dressing gown, her daughter threw her eyes skywards.

'What's with you? We have so much to do today. The ceremony is in a few days.'

Lily laughed. 'We have to get an outfit and a few bits and bobs, stop your fussing.'

Lily led the way to the kitchen, where she put on the kettle and and began to crumble bread for the birds. 'Watch closely, because this is what I want you to do when you're looking after the place.'

Hannah giggled. 'Can people your age have a honeymoon, Mum?'

'Cheeky missus, I will have you know...'

Hannah put her hand up. 'Mum, I don't want to know, too much information and all that.'

They chuckled, Lily enjoying the easy companionship between the two of them. When she opened the window to spread the crumbs, she spied the robin watching her from the boundary wall.

'You won't forget the birds, will you? They depend on my little offering.'

Hannah smiled at her mother.

'You always were a soft touch. I bet that fat robin has different houses lined up for different times of the day.'

'And you always were the tough one.'

'More like Dad, I guess.' Hannah stammered on the last two words. 'Mum, I'm not getting at you. I can see how happy Sam makes you and I'm glad.'

'I know, darling, but I would never ask you not to mention your dad, you surely know that.' Hannah took a Jaffa cake from the box on the table. 'Do you mind if I ask you a question?'

'Go ahead.'

Hannah, leaning against the worktop, examined her feet as Lily tried to find the words. 'Do you want to know more about me and your father?' she asked quietly.

'Were you always very unhappy?'

Lily sighed. 'I accepted the situation. I had to. Your dad loved his job; he didn't have room for anything else but the job and you.'

'I have blamed you all these years, for not loving him enough.'

'Somebody else's marriage is impossible to judge. There were times I could hardly gauge it myself.'

'Did your marriage have anything to do with his...' Hannah's voice wavered again.

'His death, no. That was all to do with the job. The Celtic Tiger robbed Reg of any pride he had in his work. He really did feel customers were personally blaming him for the decision to lend recklessly. He implemented the decisions made at a much higher level than himself. He felt totally powerless.'

'I don't understand why he didn't take a leaving package like so many others did.'

'Your dad and I might not have seen eye to eye on a lot of

things, but he was a man of principles; taking a package to leave the bank at a time of crisis was to him, unthinkable. Reg opted to go down with the sinking ship, rather than abandon it.'

'He always seemed such a proud man, failure wasn't a word in his vocabulary.'

'You're like him in that way, always having to be the best at what you do.'

'There's nothing wrong with that.'

Lily stroked her daughter's hair. 'I know,' she said.

Hannah looked directly at her mother. 'And Sam, does he really make you happy?'

Lily nodded. 'He's everything to me, which is why I'm glad you have accepted him into your heart.'

'He makes you happy; that has to be enough for me.'

'Know that I am happy, more than I have been in my entire life.'

Hannah hugged her mother. 'I really wish I could have the same.'

Lily stroked her daughter's hair. 'You are a fine woman, beautiful and intelligent. Somebody out there has probably already noticed.'

'Enough of talk about me, go get dressed, Gladys will be here soon,' Hannah said.

They heard Sam come down the stairs. He stuck his head around the kitchen door.

'Ladies, have a great day, I'm off. I will be gone for most of the day. A firm on the square requires an independent chair-person for their mediation talks.'

Lily called him back to kiss him on the cheek as Hannah rolled her eyes to the ceiling.

Lily walked Sam to the door. They kissed again and he took her hand, pressing his lips to her engagement ring. 'In a few days, my love, we will be married,' he said. She leaned in to him, until he said he had to go.

Lily felt a mounting excitement about the wedding as she went upstairs to get ready for their shopping trip. She wanted an outfit with a nice, floaty skirt which fell to somewhere just above her ankles. This time she wanted to put a rose in her hair to show her love for Sam. This time too, they would dine afterwards in The Shelbourne. This time it would all be so different. She heard Hannah open the front door, the sound of voices in the hall and Gladys shrieking at something or other. She put on her light-blue suit with a white blouse and sprayed her favourite Chanel perfume liberally around her neck, with a dab on her wrists, before sitting at her dressing table to put on her make-up.

She looked in the mirror. Her hair was long and grey, but looked good coiled into a low bun. She thought she looked well for her years. In the two years since Reg had died, she had seen her face relax more, the laughter lines become more pronounced, the stress lines fading. Her eyes were bright, showing a contentment which had been lacking all those years.

When she heard Hannah on the stairs, she hurriedly patted on her powder and slicked her pink lipstick quickly across her lips.

'These two downstairs will be more of a hindrance than anything else; they actually suggested we start at Brown Thomas,' Hannah said as she came in the bedroom door to check on Lily.

Lily took a wad of notes tied up in an elastic band from her dressing table drawer. 'We had better get going, before Gladys decides to come upstairs.'

Cora whistled when she saw Lily.

'You look so good in that suit, you surely don't need to buy an outfit,' she said.

Gladys guffawed out loud.

'Don't tell me there's a woman on earth who doesn't want a beautiful new dress on her wedding day.'

Cora shook her head. 'I never had a wedding, so I wouldn't know.'

There was an awkward silence as the four women stood in the hallway.

'I feel I have created an upset, when I really didn't intend to do so. Forgive me,' Gladys mumbled.

Cora hugged Gladys tight on the shoulders. 'You weren't to know. Some day I will reveal all.'

'You can tell me first: will you take a commission for a view of our house from the park? We all know you are back painting.'

'In time, Gladys. At the moment, I'm painting for myself.'

Gladys stared at Cora. 'Tell us, what are you painting?'

When Cora didn't immediately answer, Gladys shook her head. 'I know, some day you will reveal all.'

Hannah clapped her hands. 'Less of the talk, there's a wedding outfit to be bought, we need to get going,' she said, ushering everybody out the door and on to the top step. Gladys was grumbling to herself that it sounded as if she had missed a great deal of gossip in the last while.

'This battle to save the park has taken over my life,' she said, not to anybody in particular, as they briskly set off towards Merrion Square and past Government Buildings. Gladys linked Cora's arm because she said Dublin was no longer as safe as it used to be.

'Between us we have four big handbags; it would be a very foolish thief who would try anything on us,' Hannah said.

'And we're the band of women who saved De Courcy Square Park. Sure the President should invite us to tea,' Gladys said and they all laughed. At Grafton Street, Lily wanted to try some smaller boutiques, but the others insisted on Brown Thomas.

'We should have booked an appointment with a personal shopper,' Hannah said.

'Are you mad, I know what I like,' Lily said, walking over to a rack with sequinned evening dresses.

'No dear, I have to warn you of the danger of mutton dressed as lamb,' Gladys said and Cora poked her in the ribs.

'What have I said wrong now? I'm only speaking the truth,' Gladys said, pulling a face because she was offended. Hannah took a blue dress with long sleeves from a rack.

'For God's sake, it's my wedding not my wake,' Lily laughed.

Lily tried on several dresses to humour the group, but she knew all along which she was going to buy.

'We need a break, and have you seen the prices?' Cora said, pulling at the tags of one designer dress.

'One has to pay for designer quality, though in this case it might have been more prudent to be more organised and plan a bridal wardrobe around the sales,' Gladys said.

Hannah was stretched out on a chaise longue, her feet up and her eyes closed. 'Mum, I think all these designers are way too young for you. Why don't I get my car and drive us to a nice bridal-type boutique? I saw a lovely one in Malahide the other day.'

'Right beside the retirement home you would still like me to view, I suspect,' Lily said, making Hannah open her eyes and sit up.

'That's not fair, you know it's not,' Hannah said.

'What's not fair?' Gladys asked as she looked between mother and daughter.

Lily shook her head. 'It was a poor attempt at a joke,' she said quietly.

'Well, you would want to brush up on those joke-telling skills,' Gladys said, more than a little annoyed that she had missed out yet again.

Lily slipped into the changing room to try on the first outfit she had put together, a long, flowing skirt covered in flowers. When she pulled up the zip, she felt young again. She added a silk cami top in light pink and a little white fitted jacket: with her hair swept up, a light pink rose pinned at one side, she knew she would be the beautiful bride she had always wanted to be. Slipping into the Gucci shoes she had seen the minute she walked into the section, she did a little twirl. The skirt, bordered with a band of cerise pink, fanned out in a kaleidoscope of tulips and roses, flowers both short and tall.

The others were chatting among themselves. When Lily stepped out from behind the curtain, Cora swung round first. 'You look amazing.'

'Bright and rather beautiful,' Gladys said.

'Mum, you look stunning,' Hannah said, extending her hand so Lily could complete a short twirl.

'This is probably the most unusual bridal outfit I have ever seen,' Cora said, pacing around Lily to take her in completely. 'So beautiful,' she said.

'Designer labels suit me,' Lily laughed.

Hannah tipped her mother on the elbow, taking her to one side. 'Mum, you look fantastic, but the price – it's all going to cost you nearly two thousand euros. The shoes alone are five hundred. You don't have money like that.'

'The one good thing about your dad is he left me very well provided for and in the last two years, I have barely dipped in. Now is the time.'

'Are you sure? Isn't it all a bit mad?'

Lily rubbed her hands together. 'Deliciously mad. Pass me my handbag. I have it in cash.'

'You haven't been walking around the streets of Dublin with thousands in cash in your bag?'

Lily didn't answer, but opened the clasp of her handbag, fished down to the bottom of the zip section and pulled out a a roll of money wrapped tightly in an elastic band.

'Mother, what if you were mugged, your bag was snatched?' Hannah said, sounding cross.

'But it wasn't, dear. I'm getting rid of most of the cash now and I will only be carrying a few hundred, which is more than enough for the flowers from Maisie at the top of the street and a very nice lunch for all of us.'

Hannah, when she saw the glow of happiness in her mother, couldn't stay cross for long.

'Well, come on, let's get this lot paid for, before you lose that cash,' she said, pretending to sound stern.

The others cheered, each volunteering to carry a bag, once the purchases were wrapped carefully in tissue.

As they walked out of Brown Thomas, Gladys turned to the rest. 'This wedding is turning into such a fancy do, I'm going to have to get a new hat,' she said.

# FORTY-FOUR

The late summer sunshine pushed into the front office, making the dust on the mahogany mantelpiece sparkle and the newspapers chucked in the corner go yellow and crisp. Cora's easel took up the bay window, a stool from the kitchen beside it for when her legs got tired, but she wanted to continue painting. The room was huge now, with the two desks gone along with the filing cabinets and all the rubbish on the shelves. Tom, Sam and Anthony Draper did the heavy lifting into the skip as she scooped files into refuse sacks. In the end, she sorted very little, firing files and loose documents into the bin bags. Sam persuaded her to keep the velvet couch and she was glad she had done so, pulling it into position by the fireplace. It felt more like her own home now, her completed paintings stacked against one wall, her painting paraphernalia along the shelves.

She surprised herself at how quickly she could clear away two lives. Notes Jack had jotted down in a rush of importance were faded, his ashtrays dirty with dried-on ash. Dust puffed up, hanging in the air as she gathered bundles of his stuff and threw it in the skip. She faltered when she came across a wrapper from a chocolate Twirl that Jack must have screwed into a ball before carelessly discarding it. She reached over and nudged it with her finger, flicking it with her nail, so it flew onto the floor. She had picked it up and was throwing it in the fireplace when she saw the courier arrive carrying two long rolls.

'Cora Gartland, special delivery,' the courier said, pushing the rolls towards her along with with an electronic pad and pen so she could sign for them. When he had left, she carried the rolls into the front room and placed them on a table.

This shipment from the US contained her life on Long Island, the last time when she had thought living was easy. Slowly, she unpicked the tape securing the rolls and managed to open one, pull out the contents, and then the next one. This was a glimpse of her life with Jack, a cherished happy time that was later so tainted. The first work she unrolled was 'The Manor House'. Her chest tightened to see the house, the flowers tall and scraggly, obliterating the path, the door ajar as if somebody had already gone in. She wanted it to have a prominent position because it represented the old Long Island. She pinned the painting to the easel. It deserved to be finished. She was sitting reacquainting herself with the drawing, remembering the day she sketched it, Jack sipping a gin and tonic, watching her, talking to whoever came along. Who would have thought life could change so utterly within a matter of weeks?

She saw Lily and waved. Lily pointed to the front door and Cora went to open it for her.

'Is it all right if I come in, Cora?'

'Sure, is something up?'

'I need to talk to you.'

'My God, you're not having second thoughts?'

Lily smiled. 'Nothing like that, but there's something I have to give you. I feel it's only right you should see it.'

'This sounds serious Lily, what is it?' Cora asked as she gently closed the front door. When Lily did not immediately answer, she added: 'Come sit on the couch Sam persuaded me to keep.'

Nervousness made Cora's voice sound falsely bright, as if she was desperately trying to defuse the anxiety rising inside her. Lily perched on the edge of the sofa. She took a letter from her pocket. 'I want you to understand I have not been hiding this from you. It arrived in the late post only yesterday.'

'What is it?'

Lily straightened her back. 'I'll come to that in a minute. Seemingly, Amelia asked the hotel to post it, where she and Jack had dinner that last night. The receptionist who took it slipped it in her pocket. As luck would have it, she was let go later that night. She only found the letter in her pocket this week, when she went to return her uniform. She posted it with a brief explanation and an apology.'

'Why would Amelia have posted you a letter?'

Lily sighed heavily.

'If you read it, I think it will answer all those questions. It's up to you, if you want to pass it on to Amelia's family. Maybe losing her is enough, without this on top.'

Cora nervously took the letter. 'Should I read it now?'

Lily stood up. 'Why don't I go and leave you in peace.'

Cora put a hand out to stop Lily. 'Please stay, I don't think I can do this on my own.'

Lily sat back down as Cora took the letter and examined it.

The envelope was creased; it looked as if there had been a poor attempt to iron out the paper wrinkles by hand. She lifted the gummed part of the envelope and took out the letter.

A solitary page, light blue in colour, which had been ripped from a fancy jotter. The writing was careful, as if the writer had time to think over every word. Scanning down the page, she tripped heavily over certain words: 'confession', 'death', 'love'. Scatters of sentences halted her abruptly, so she had to scan back and forth, as if her brain requested a retake. Flattening the letter out, she read it from the beginning to the end.

August, 2018

*My Dearest Lily,*

*You have been such a friend to me and now I ask you to do what no friend should have to do, take my last confession.*

*When you read this, you will have already heard the news and I apologise in advance for the pain this may have caused you.*

*I want you to know I loved Jack Gartland from the moment I met him, and it is my great sorrow that it has come to this.*

*I imagined a life in De Courcy Square with Jack and our children. I never imagined a different life, a life over which I have no control.*

*If I stay in this marriage, I will forever be looking over my shoulder, trying to double guess if he is with another woman or the woman in the photographs.*

*And that is not mentioning the pain of the deception, which has me doubled over in agony.*

*I am thinking straight, Lily. It frightens me I have come to this decision, but I know this:*

*I cannot live this life, where he loves me when he is here and loves another when he is not.*

*I cannot bring up a child in such a relationship.*

*I hear your voice saying, 'Walk away, walk away'. I am walking away. This is my way of walking away.*

*To this child growing inside me, I say we will all be together in death. It is the only way.*

*You may call it a coward's way, but it's my way.*

*I won't ask Jack to choose. I want him for myself.*

*Is it so bad to love somebody so completely? If he does not*

*want to live a life with me, to raise a family, then I am left with
no choice.*

*I ask that we be buried together and that everybody
remembers the good times.*

*Don't grieve, we can be a family in death. I am his wife
and I will continue to be, in death.*

*If they could bury us under a locust tree, I would ask that.*

*Love,*

*Amelia xx*

Cora folded the letter and put it back on the envelope. 'I
don't know what to say. Poor Amelia, and poor Jack.'

'Was I right to show it to you?'

'I'm glad I know. I'm not sure I could have coped with this
earlier.'

'Sam was in two minds whether I should show you the
letter.'

'Your Sam is a sweetheart; you're a lucky woman, Lily.'

'At our age, too. I know it.'

Cora handed the letter back to Lily.

Lily pushed her hand away.

'You keep it, it means more to you or to Tom.'

Cora jumped up. 'Shit, I forgot about Tom. How can he
read this letter?'

'It might help to know the truth, but I'll leave that decision
to you.'

Cora stood, her back to Lily. She looked out across at the
park.

'Lily, I wonder if none of this had happened and I had never
found out any of it, what would my life be like?' She picked up

a Long Island painting. 'This was my life and in a lot of ways, I miss it.'

'What are you saying, exactly?'

Cora flopped onto the couch. 'I'm not sure, but I think to show that letter to Tom Hooper could destroy him. It would also snuff out all the fond memories he has of his sister. I know what that's like and I am not prepared to do it to him.'

'I will go on your say. What will we do with the letter?'

Cora reached up to a shelf and took down a bottle of brandy and two glasses.

She poured out the brandy and handed a glass to Lily.

'Just wait,' she said, walking to the fireplace and throwing the letter and envelope into the grate. She grabbed a box of matches from beside the candle on the mantelpiece. Striking a match, she held the flame to one corner of the envelope.

'To the future, whatever it holds,' she said, raising her glass to Lily. They clinked loudly as the envelope smoked and blackened until a flame took hold, reducing Amelia's words to ashes. Cora downed her brandy in one go.

'I see you have picked up a few good habits,' Lily said. Cora asked Lily to wait, she had something for her upstairs. When she came back down, she was carrying a small package tied with a mauve ribbon. 'I wanted to give you something of Amelia's. I feel I know her well enough now to believe she would have approved.'

Lily took the gift.

'Please don't open it until the morning of your wedding; you will understand why then.'

'This is all very mysterious. Thank you, Cora, you may have come into our lives as a result of this terrible tragedy, but I'm glad you're here.'

'Thanks, Lily, and for keeping my secret.'

'It's one of my great pleasures that Gladys still thinks you're Jack's sister,' Lily said as she made her way to the front door.

Cora checked the grate: nothing there, only a small hill of ash. She wasn't surprised at Amelia's actions, though it saddened her greatly. She sat down at her easel, wanting to get lost in this world of watercolours, rather than dwell on Jack's terror as Amelia deliberately drove off the road.

# FORTY-FIVE

Cora took the blue silk dress from Amelia's wardrobe.

A simple shirt dress with mother-of-pearl buttons, it had been on the hanger with a long cardigan of the same colour and a silk scarf which complemented the hues of the dress.

Cora brought the outfit to her room and slipped it on. She wanted to dress up for Lily, to celebrate the love she had found.

She had meant to go and buy a dress the day before, but time had run away with her as she sat in front of her easel until the light went.

Stepping into her new high shoes, she carefully picked the framed watercolour. She noticed Gladys was already directing operations in the park as the preparations for the wedding continued.

She knocked once on the door of No. 22. Hannah opened the door.

'I know this is very unconventional, but I wanted to give Lily and Sam their wedding present.

'The service is in half an hour,' Hannah said, but she stood back and invited Cora in.

She called up the stairs to Lily, who came out onto the landing in a white dressing gown.

Cora felt suddenly nervous.

'I have a present here for you both, a painting,' she said.

Lily called Sam, who was in his suit trousers and shirt. They came down the stairs hand in hand.

'I apologise if I'm intruding, it's just I thought you might like to see it before your day takes off.'

'Cora, this is so special; you are never intruding,' Sam said.

She swivelled the watercolour around. Lily gasped at the two figures stooped over the sweet peas in the back garden, their heads touching. In the background the lilac tree stood guard; to the side the table was set for tea and cake.

Tears swelled in Lily's eyes. Sam shook his head in wonderment. 'You have captured every aspect of us, I can almost hear us chatting,' he said.

Hannah picked up the painting and examined it closely. 'This is so beautiful, the attention to detail exceptional. You are a very fine artist.'

Embarrassed by the praise, Cora made to leave but Lily stepped forward and wrapped her arms around her and gave her a tight hug.

'This painting will get pride of place in our home. You are the best friend,' she said, the tears beginning to flow.

'Mother, you will ruin your make-up,' Hannah scolded.

Sam stepped forward and kissed Cora on the cheek. 'The best present ever, a million thanks.'

Cora nodded shyly and quickly made her way out.

Across the street Lily and Sam's friends, along with his daughter Rosa, were beginning to gather in the park. She smiled as they created a wall between the little patch of grass where the ceremony was to take place and the surprise which awaited Lily and Sam.

Gladys, a wide-brimmed hat in her hands, gesticulated at

the house as if to tell Cora to hurry on. Cora waved back, showing five fingers to say she would be there in a few minutes.

Tom Hooper, pulling on a cigarette as he stood a little apart from the rest of the group, ambled across to Cora.

'You look well. Amelia's favourite dress suits you.'

Cora, nervous, pulled at the fabric.

'I meant it, no point wasting good clothes.'

'Thanks.'

'Is it hard on you, attending a wedding?'

'Not this one I don't think; I'm so happy for them.'

'You still love Jack then?'

'A part of me will always love him, be tied to him,' she said, walking across the street to the park, to join the others waiting for Lily and Sam to emerge from No. 22.

Cora leaned towards Tom.

'I know what Amelia would like on the headstone: a locust tree.'

'How do you know that?' he asked.

'Just something I came across,' she said, staring straight ahead and concentrating on the door of No. 22 to get the first glimpse of Sam and Lily in their finery.

Lily stood in front of the long mirror. She was ready. The package Cora had given her the other day was on the dressing table. She knew it was something belonging to Amelia. She opened it. Inside was a jewellery box. Tentatively, she pulled up the lid. She gasped when she saw the gold earrings with inlaid mother-of-pearl hanging from a French wire. Amelia only ever wore them on her wedding day.

Tears bubbled up to think of lovely Amelia and Cora, who knew exactly what memento to pick from No. 23. Her hands shaking, Lily put on the earrings.

'You look so beautiful,' Sam said.

'You know you shouldn't see me before the ceremony, it's bad luck.'

He laughed out loud. 'Nonsense, between the two of us, we have stored up enough bad luck already for both our lifetimes and then some. Bad luck is banished from now on.'

He stood beside her and she straightened his tie, while he flattened down his hair with his hands. Slipping on his suit jacket, he closed the buttons. Reaching on top of the wardrobe, he pulled down a box. 'An orchid corsage, to show you how much I love and adore you.'

Lily ran her fingers along the creamy white softness of the cattleya orchids. 'I have always wanted to wear an orchid corsage.'

She pinned it carefully on her jacket.

'My love, fairer than any flower,' Sam said, offering his arm to Lily. She giggled, a happy tinkle that swirled through the house as she linked his arm to walk downstairs. In the hall, they stopped as Lily took a deep pink rose and tucked it in the buttonhole of Sam's jacket.

'My love,' she said, kissing him softly on the lips.

When they stepped out the front door, the group huddled inside the park gate clapped and cheered.

Hannah, waiting at the bottom of the steps, offered her mother a bouquet of light pink roses intertwined with rosemary. Hand in hand, Lily and Sam walked across to the park, where Gladys and Anthony Draper had arranged an arch interwoven with pink and white roses.

As they stood for the ceremony, Gladys shed a few tears. Anthony Draper slipped in late. Everybody applauded loudly at the end and threw rose petal confetti.

Lily whispered to Sam, she had one thing left to do. Hand in hand they strolled to the lilac tree, where she bent down to place her bouquet. Hannah stepped in beside her. 'We have a special wedding gift for you, Mum. For you both.'

She nodded to Gladys, who, using her two fingers, whistled loudly.

Two young men shuffled from around the corner, carrying a heavy park bench between them.

'Where do you want it, missus?'

Gladys looked at Lily.

'It's your bench, Lily, you pick.'

Perplexed, Lily pointed to the spot where the old seat had been before it was damaged by the JCB.

As it was carefully put in place, Lily saw the engraved brass plaque.

*In loving memory of Eamon Griffin,*
*who tended to these gardens until his untimely death.*
*Loved and never forgotten.*

Lily sat down and slowly traced the letters of Eamon's name. 'I thought you would not allow plaques on seats,' she said to Gladys.

'I don't. This is going to cause a huge headache; everybody is going to be wanting one,' Gladys huffed, making everyone laugh.

From: **GladysSpencer@gmail.com**
To: **all De Courcy Square Association members**

Dear residents, tenants and friends,

It is our absolute pleasure to congratulate Lily Walpole of No.

22 De Courcy Square and Mr Samuel Carpenter, who had their union blessed in our beautiful De Courcy Square Park.

You all know Lily by now. She has lived on the square all her life and was to the forefront of the campaign to save the park.

Sam may not be so well known in these parts, but it was his skill and expertise along with that of solicitor Hannah Walpole which steered us through the difficult negotiations and to a settlement we could accept. Huge congratulations to the happy couple, may they have many wonderful years together.

At this stage, I feel I should point out that the use of the park for civil weddings or blessings is only allowed on very rare occasions and strictly to those with with a long and permanent association with the park.

Gladys Spencer,
Chairperson

# FORTY-SIX

## SIX MONTHS LATER

You are invited to 23 De Courcy Square, Dublin
on January 29, 2019
for an exhibition by artist
Cora Manning
*An Ocean Between Us*
*Long Island to De Courcy Square, Dublin*
RSVP: 23 De Courcy Square

Cora slipped on the royal blue shift dress. The silk slithered over her body, the beads at the high round neck flashing as she straightened the dress. Propping Amelia's sketch against the Chanel perfume bottle on the dressing table, she coiled her hair into a bun, just as Amelia had intended the hair to be worn with the dress. She sat on the bed to put on the strappy silver sandals. Standing up, she checked in the long mirror, which had once belonged to Amelia.

Donna had done her make-up, the eyeshadow complementing the blue of the dress, the pink lipstick reflected in the colour of the beading.

'Honey, Lily and Sam are here with the nibbles,' Donna called up the stairs.

Cora took one last look in the mirror. This was Cora Manning, artist, of De Courcy Square, Dublin, and formerly of Long Island, New York. Excitement rose inside her and a terrible fear, after months of hard work, that nobody would bother to show up. She had asked for RSVPs and got two from some people in offices at the far end of the square, people she didn't even know. When after a week, sick with worry, she checked with Gladys if in fact she had got the email invite and wondered if she would come along, she was astounded at her answer.

'Gosh, it's marked in the calendar on the side of the fridge. Of course we're coming. Anthony has arranged for a makeshift ramp, so I can bring Tony. We wouldn't miss this for the world.'

'But you never replied to the invitation.'

'Sure didn't you know we were coming,' Gladys said, giving Cora a puzzled look.

Cora smiled, thinking how Lily and Sam laughed heartily when she told them the story.

'You will be waiting a long time for an Irish person to send an RSVP or to even tell you they're coming to the launch of the exhibition,' Sam said.

'Sure everybody is dying to have a gawk, you have been the topic of conversation for months,' Lily said.

Before she went downstairs, Cora checked the first-floor exhibition room. These walls she had painted teal; the windows were bare but for the white blinds. This was the Long Island room, where paintings of her other life were on display. Underneath each frame was a typed card with the name and information about each watercolour.

She stopped at the watercolour 'Home from Work'. Taking a little card with round red stickers out of her pocket, she placed one on the printed card. This watercolour she wanted to mark sold because she never wanted to let it go. Jack may have deceived her at the end, but there were times when she knew he loved her and she had to be content with that.

She left the room when Donna called up the stairs again.

'Honey, we need some help down here,' she said, walking up the first few steps of the stairs.

'I will be down in a sec,' she said, her stomach queasy, making her rush to the bathroom and hold her wrists under cold water to help her calm down.

Sam and Lily were busy in the kitchen, Donna was arranging a huge vase of white lilies on the hall table, when Cora made it downstairs.

'Darling, you look so beautiful,' Donna said.

'It's nearly time. We should open the front door, but first I must check the exhibition rooms on this floor.'

In the sitting room, she threw some more wood logs on the fire. This and the dining room which overlooked the back garden were the De Courcy Square rooms. The walls were a burgundy colour which set off the watercolours beautifully. She placed a red sticker on the painting above the fireplace and on Tom's painting of Amelia's studio. Lily, who was carrying a silver platter of tiny bite-size bruschetta and cocktail sausages, stopped in her tracks when she saw Cora.

'You look so beautiful, I'm glad you got Amelia's dress design made up. She would have loved it.'

'I hope so.'

'Sam has laid out the glasses and the drinks in the dining room, otherwise everybody will crowd around this room and block up the hall. We haven't gone overboard on the nibbles, we want them drinking and flashing the cash.'

'On that note, probably best not to expect too much from the square's residents, but Anthony intends to bring a few pals who are looking for artwork and he has asked another friend, a journalist with the *Irish Times*, to review the exhibition.'

Cora inhaled deeply, 'I can't thank you guys enough, and you too, Donna, flying in last week to make sure everything was going to plan.'

'Doll, these paintings would fly off the walls in Manhattan, think on that.'

'Small steps, let me take small steps,' Cora said as she walked to the front door and swung it open, angling the old mahogany hall chair so it stopped the door from swinging shut.

Lily tapped Cora on the shoulder.

'We'll go home. Hannah is calling in to us first, and the three of us will be along in a while; otherwise there will be those insulted they weren't asked to help.'

They had just gone in the door of No. 22 when Anthony Draper and another man came along and placed a specially built wooden ramp, covering half of the granite steps.

Tom Hooper and his family, his wife Frances carrying a bunch of roses, were the first in the front door.

'Congratulations. Tom told me about the dress, a beautiful idea,' Frances Hooper said.

Cora turned to Tom.

'I have something for you,' she said, reaching into the drawer of the hall table and taking out the rolled-up studio sketch. 'There's a painting in the dining room you may also like. There's a red sticker on it...'

'You've painted it?'

'Yes, for you.'

Tom's wife and daughter rushed to see the painting.

'Thank you so much,' he said, and he probably would have said more if Gladys had not at that moment called for assistance getting the wheelchair on the ramp.

Gladys, with the help of Tom and Anthony Draper, pushed Tony's wheelchair to the front door.

'A lot of work getting here, but I know it will be more than worth it. I have told all the ladies in my bridge club to come along and to be sure to bring their chequebooks,' she said as she kissed Cora and politely shook hands with Donna.

Turning the wheelchair into the front room, Gladys gasped. The walls were covered with drawings and paintings of the square – some street scenes and others of the park. Tony pointed to the watercolour over the fireplace, the view of a red-brick house through the trees. The net curtains on one of the windows were slightly drawn back as if somebody was watching the artist at work.

Gladys stood taking it in. She knew every brick in that house, the windows obscured with her net curtains, the front door with the paint flaking where the dog always grazed his lead against the door jamb. It was the perfect watercolour, the house mysterious behind the trees, she thought.

Cora stepped in beside Gladys.

'Looks good over the fireplace.'

Gladys nodded, but turned to Cora.

'It has a red sticker, has someone bought it?'

'Yes, it sold before I even opened up.'

Gladys's face puckered as she fought back the tears.

Tony took his wife's hand.

'Cora told me she was painting it. I saw her over a few days working on it from her spot in the park, looking from the easel to our house. The painting is ours, Gladys, Cora painted our house for us.'

Tears rolled down Gladys's cheeks.

'I don't believe it,' she whispered.

'Believe it, my darling,' he said.

Cora stood back as Gladys reached out to the painting almost as if she wanted to touch it.

'It's exactly as it was the first day I saw our house, when you brought me into the park and told me to look across at that side of the square.'

'And you said it was your dream home, but the first thing you would have to do was put nets on the windows.'

Gladys laughed.

'I did too, I wasn't going to have the whole world knowing my business. I'm not as modern as Cora here.'

She stepped closer to Cora.

'Are you sure about allowing all and sundry to walk through your house? There are people here I don't know.'

'It's an exhibition open to the public, Gladys.'

'Yes, and one I wholeheartedly support as something very special on the square.'

Lily pressed in between Cora and Gladys.

'Don't worry, I'm sure Cora's secrets are safe,' she said.

Gladys grabbed Cora in a huge hug, before she stepped out into the centre of the room.

'Most of you here will know me: Gladys Spencer of the De Courcy Square Association. Dig deep people, these are the finest paintings and this is an artist we are more than proud to call our own.'

The crowd already in No. 23 De Courcy Square clapped and others on the street outside rushed in to join the party.

# A LETTER FROM ANN

Dear reader,

I want to say a huge thank you for choosing to read *Her Husband's Secret*. If you did enjoy it and want to keep up to date with all my latest releases, just sign up at the following link. Your email address will never be shared and you can unsubscribe at any time.

*www.bookouture.com/ann-oloughlin*

I was very lucky writing this book because I had the opportunity to spend so long in the world of flowers and learn their secret language. I found the more I studied the symbolic language of flowers, the more specific and interesting my choices became for my own garden. Every year when my flowers bloom, I will fondly remember writing this novel. If this books prompts any of you to delve further into the centuries old language of flowers, I can guarantee you will be richly rewarded.

My hope now is that my readers derive as much pleasure from reading the story of Cora, Amelia, Lily and Gladys, as I did writing it.

I hope you loved *Her Husband's Secret*, and if you did, I would be very grateful if you could write a review. I'd love to hear what you think, and it makes such a difference helping new readers to discover one of my books for the first time. I love hearing from my readers – you can get in touch on my Facebook page, through Twitter, or Goodreads.

Thanks,

Ann

facebook.com/annoloughlinbooks
twitter.com/annoloughlinbooks
instagram.com/annoloughlinbooks

# ACKNOWLEDGEMENTS

I was very lucky writing this book because I had the opportunity to spend so long in the world of flowers and learn its secret language. I found the more I studied the symbolic language of flowers, the more specific and interesting my choices became for my own garden. Every year when my flowers bloom, I will fondly remember writing this novel. If this book prompts any of you to delve further into the centuries-old language of flowers, I can guarantee you will be richly rewarded.

My hope now is that my readers derive as much pleasure from reading the story of Cora, Amelia, Lily and Gladys as I did writing it.

To sit down every day and write the words, sentences, paragraphs and chapters that make up a novel requires a lot of author support, particularly from the home team.

I would not be able to do so without the constant and loving support of my husband John and my children, Roshan and Zia; and to them, I say the biggest thank you.

Agent Jenny Brown of Jenny Brown Associates has championed my writing from the off and for that, Jenny, I am so grateful.

The whole team at Bookouture has supported my writing, and I thank them for their good humour, patience and being such wonderful editors.

Ann

Printed in Great Britain
by Amazon